The Future City

The Future City

by
Alain le Drimeur

translated, annotated and introduced by
Brian Stableford

A Black Coat Press Book

ISBN 978-1-61227-114-9. First Printing. September 2012. Published by Black Coat Press, an imprint of Hollywood Comics.com, LLC, P.O. Box 17270, Encino, CA 91416. All rights reserved.
Printed in the United States of America.

Introduction

La Cité future signed "Alain le Drimeur" (a Frenchification of "Alan the Dreamer"), here translated as *The Future City*, was originally published in Paris by Albert Savine in 1890. The text reveals that the author wrote it in 1888, probably inspired by the publication in America of Edward Bellamy's best-selling *Looking Backward, 2000-1887*, which caused something of a sensation and rapidly became the best-selling book of its era. *La Cité future* is one of numerous texts produced in the wake of Bellamy's offering an alternative account of life in a socialist republic in the early years of the 21st century. Although it was nowhere near as successful commercially as Bellamy's book, or some of the other utopias inspired by *Looking Backward*—most notably William Morris's *News from Nowhere* (1890)—*La Cité future* is an equally profound and interesting text, and is one of the most significant contributions to the French futuristic fiction of its era.

Like Bellamy and Morris, the author of *La Cité future* uses a viewpoint tacitly displaced from his own era as a lens through which the hypothetical future can be viewed; the imaginative device he employs may be no more probable than suspended animation or visionary dreaming but is considerably more ingenious and more intriguing in its corollaries. "Le Drimeur" carefully sets up a thought-experiment in which the principal reactionary forces in late 19th century France emigrate *en masse* in 1891 to the island of La Réunion, where they establish a Roman Catholic kingdom that deliberately cuts itself off from the homeland for a century. Not until the early years of the 21st century is a mail service established between Marseilles and Saint-Denis, of which two young men from the island take advantage in order to discover what has been happening in France since it was abandoned to secularist Republicans. The resulting image is not a straightforward future projection so much as a kind of anticipatory alternative

5

history, featuring a world that could not have come to be if the reactionaries had stayed in France, as they did in our world.

The thought-experiment has an extra dimension of interest by virtue of the fact that "le Drimeur" uses two protagonists rather than one, one of whom remains immovably committed to the religious and political ideals of his insular home, while the other is evidently ripe for conversion. The author also insists, early in his text, that he is not writing a "purely sociological work" but a novel—"which is to say, a love story," as he puts it—and therefore takes care to provide each of his male protagonists with a potential female lover in the new France, so that the two women can function as temptresses as well as propagandizing informants. This aspect of the experiment also provides a certain welcome distraction from the fact that the book is mainly a conventional item of utopian fiction, consisting of a long series of conversations in which the politics, economics and educational system of the socialist state are explained to the protagonists by various pontificating interlocutors. The author would probably have liked to make the story even more reader-friendly, but he was obviously not an experienced novelist, and was not able to take full advantage of the ingenuity of his plan.

None of the standard sources offer any clue as to who "Alain le Drimeur" might have been, and the pseudonym was never used on any other text. The body of the text offers some vague indications as to where the author might have fitted into late 19th century French society, but the indirectness of the narrative makes it difficult to be certain of exactly what his views and interests were. It is not until the final phases of what has, until then, been an earnest and relatively impartial text, that the author finally slips into satirical mode and offers evidence via his suddenly-abundant sarcasm of the full spectrum of his antipathies. When the characters visit a sculpture park commemorating the "lustrum" (demi-decade) of the late 1880s, brief vitriolic comments are made about many of the leading politicians of the day, and numerous journalists—an order of priorities that probably does not indicate that "le

Drimeur" was a political journalist himself, but certainly indicates that he read a lot of newspapers and often had strong reactions to what he read.

This section of the text appears to place the author's sympathies very firmly on the radical left of the Republican movement, probably far enough along the spectrum to qualify as an anarchist; his most sympathetic remarks are reserved for thinkers of that stripe, although the generally sarcastic tone of the section casts a shadow even over his praise, which is sometimes suspiciously whimsical or faint. More significant than the inclusions in the relevant section of the sculpture park, however, are the omissions, which seem to reveal some odd limitations in the author's awareness of what was going on in the contemporary world.

From a technological viewpoint, the author's idea of likely developments in the 20th century is extremely blinkered, more-or-less restricted to the development of dirigible aerostats, and that myopia is further reflected in the fact that he can only think of three scientists to place in the sculpture park, one of whom, Michel Chevreul (the inventor of an early form of soap) was 102 years old when he died in 1889. Louis Pasteur, whose rabies vaccine was first used in 1885, and who received an exceptional accolade when the Institut Pasteur was founded in 1888, was an inevitable inclusion, but Pasteur was also getting old by then, and the significant triumphs of the third man commemorated, Marcellin Berthelot, were well behind him. We may safely conclude, I think, that "le Drimeur" was neither a scientist nor much interested in contemporary science. His knowledge of music seems to have been similarly primitive and equally outdated; the only composer represented in the park is Charles Gounod, who was also on his last legs in the period in question.

Although the author is able to quote the names of more writers than scientists or composers, he only cites a handful of prose writers, and one of those, Octave Feuillet, was another obvious has-been, in his dotage by the late 1880s. "Le Drimeur" is much more confident listing visual artists, but blithely reveals tastes that nowadays make him seem like a stick-in-the-mud; although he could hardly have been unaware of the contemporary revolution taking place in painting, he obvious prefers Academic art and will have no truck with Impressionism or any other kind of *avant garde*. All of this suggests that he was by no means a young man himself—if, indeed, "he" really was a man—and might well have been in the twilight of his life, perhaps an old follower of the radical Léon Gambetta (who is only mentioned *en passant* in the account of the sculpture park, although he did not die until 1888) who became disillusioned by the way the Third Republic was going as its progress was continually rocked by the residual forces of reaction. Although the author chose a pseudonym whose significance relies on an English pun, the text is rather narrowly concerned with France and the French, and its reference to the rest of the world are rather anemic; it seems likely, based on the internal evidence of the narrative, that the author hailed from Normandy, and that he was probably only acquainted with Paris as a visitor rather than a resident. Unless the records of the publisher, Albert Savine, still survive somewhere, however, the identity of the author seems likely to remain a mystery.

The anonymity of an author rarely helps a text's longevity, offering a deterrent to its reprinting and translating as well as to its study by scholars, so it is not surprising that *La Cité future* effectively dropped off the radar of twentieth-century utopian studies, but that oblivion is unjust. Although the relative unlikelihood of the story's premise might have made it seem less interesting to contemporary readers, especially once the year 1891 had elapsed, the quasi-experimental framework and the removal of the work to the category of alternative history add interest for the modern reader.

Although accounts of hypothetical socialist organization are commonplace, *La Cité future* does have some elements that are more unusual for a work of its time, especially its slightly peculiar but nevertheless strident feminism and its slightly understated but taken-for-granted atheism. The tentative nature of its technological extrapolations, which are less adventurous than those featured in some works produced half a century earlier[1] makes *La Cité future* less interesting as a work of proto-science fiction than one might wish, but the lack of specific description of the bird-like aerostats featured in the text is somewhat compensated by the detailed description of the abundant advertisements displayed within their cheaper cabins—another opportunity for the author to deploy his sarcastic wit.

All in all, therefore, it is arguable that the novel has become more interesting over time, for ordinary readers as well as scholars, and that it is certainly worthy of attention now that we have reached the era in which it is set, so that we can, in effect, read it from the vantage-point of a "parallel present." The addition of a further dimension to a viewpoint that is already carefully complicated ought to enhance rather than detract from the reading experience, even though the extra distance makes some of the jokes difficult to understand (at least without the aid of footnotes). This translation also further fleshes out a whole series of French 19th century images of the future—especially the future of Paris—that have featured abundantly in my recent translations for Black Coat Press, whose sum provides a fascinating broad picture.

This translation was taken from the version of the book published by Albert Savine in 1890 reproduced on the Bibliothèque Nationale's *gallica* website.

Brian Stableford

---

[1] Compare, for instance, Félix Bodin's *Le Roman de l'avenir* (1834; tr. as *The Novel of the Future*, Black Coat Press, ISBN 978-1-934543-44-3), Joseph Méry's "Ce qu'on verra" (c.1845; tr. as "What we Shall See" in the collection *The Tower of Destiny,* Black Coat Press, ISBN 978-1-61227-101-9) and Théophile Gauter's "Paris Futur" (1851; tr. as "Future Paris" in the anthology *Investigations of the Future*, Black Coat Press, ISBN 978-1-61227-106-4).

THE FUTURE CITY

What new Jerusalem
emerges from the depths of the desert…?[2]

(This book is presumed to have been written at the beginning
of the 21ˢᵗ century.)

I

As everyone knows, the celebrations held throughout France on the occasion of the first centenary of the Revolution of 1789 excited an extraordinary enthusiasm. In large cities and small towns, public manifestations took on a double character of patriotism and fraternity such as had not been seen since the previous century's celebration of the Federation.

It was evident, from that time on, that France had been definitely conquered by what are nowadays called "modern" ideas. All the inhabitants of the country, even the most blinkered, had a very clear perception of it, and it was a fact recognized by the whole world. Nevertheless, many people remained on the nation's soil who stood aside from the general current and were firmly decided to stay there permanently. They had been called, at various times, legitimists, aristocrats, reactionaries or clericalists. They were then known, if we are not mistaken, by the simple title of "dissidents."

They were, for the most part, people faithfully adherent to the former religion of the nation, who suffered with bitterness a social organization conceived outside their essential dogmas: the divinity of Christ and the certainty of a second

---

[2] The quotation is from Racine's Old Testament-based tragedy *Athalie* (1691).

life. These details had been conformed over the generations in their sentiments of opposition, thanks to the political liberties that had already begun to be manifest in France, at least at intervals, during the 19th century.

In addition to them, but in smaller numbers, a few other parties, similarly on the defensive, were still fond of privilege and superiority. They could not reconcile themselves to laws and mores whose primary purpose was to establish and maintain civic equality. To tell the truth, the dissidents had finished up by taking their stand almost exclusively on religious terrain, in the Catholic camp.

As enthusiasm and joy usually provoke sentiments of tolerant good will, the majority of French citizens could not help, in the midst of the solemnities by which they were celebrating their political emancipation, considering with a particular interest the class of their compatriots who thus remained aside, draped in a noble and respectable intransigence.

The latter, for their part, understood at that same moment that all hope of a Christian Restoration had gone. They wondered what would become of them, in the beloved land of France, if they and their children were condemned to live there as strangers.

What usually occurs when complications have arrived at their sharpest point happened then. The solution that had remained veiled thus far, scarcely glimpsed by a few far-seeing minds, appeared in all its clarity and became imposing.

The dissidents would emigrate. The government would facilitate their emigration.

That double idea first saw the light of day in the Republican press, and was soon accepted by the entire Conservative press.

The religious part recalled, as an example worthy to be followed, the heroic resolution of the Scottish puritans fleeing the intolerance of their compatriots with William Penn and going to found a new fatherland in America.

For several months the project agitated the country.

In the same era Parliament was occupied in extending the system of Protectorates on the island of Madagascar. It had appealed to the inhabitants of the neighboring island of La Réunion to colonize that immense territory, and the latter, enticed the considerable advantages conceded to them, and deserted their domicile en masse, to the extent that the former Île de Bourbon was effectively abandoned.

The government let it be known through official channels that it would not be averse to putting that old French possession at the exclusive disposal of the dissidents, and that it would even take responsibility for transporting them there in State vessels.

Immediately, lists of signatures were circulated throughout France by an action committee, composed of renowned prelates, a few parliamentarians of the far right and a certain number of journalists.

At the same time, means were put in place of liquidating, without undue losses, the fortunes of those who were thus expatriating themselves. On that point too the Nation showed generosity. The government, supported by a movement of popular opinion that left no room for uncertainty, offered to buy back at their real and prevent value, all the property, movable or immovable, that would be abandoned by the emigrants, in order to restore it to circulation at an opportune time, in such a manner as to avoid a crisis in the market.

In a few months, the preparations were made, and in 1891, at the opening of the annual session of Parliament, the lists of signatures were appended to a petition, by which several thousand major citizens requested, in their names and those of their families, that the nation's representatives sanction the promises made by the central administration.

The debate did not give rise to any difficulty. The ratification of the governmental advances was decided by acclamation, and for the second time, the "émigrés' billion" was inscribed in our budget.[3] The Frenchmen who were about to separate themselves forever from their native land were not enemy brothers. The divorce took place by mutual consent, on the grounds of a duly established incompatibility of beliefs and principles.

A short time afterwards, the first departure took place at Marseilles. A fleet fitted out in La Jolliette harbor took away, as a first step, the general staff of the emigration. The included a general proudly bearing a heroic name, a predicator of Notre-Dame, a considerable number of bishops bearing miters and crosiers, all the survivors of the pontifical zouaves, and monks and nuns of every order. In their midst was the heir of the Spanish Bourbons, a new Joas,[4] who was going out there to retrieve a crown. The pope had sent the voyagers his blessing.

They raised anchor while singing hymns and saluting the land of their ancestors with long farewells. The white flag floated at the top of every mainmast.

---

[3] There had, of course, been a mass emigration of aristocrats and Churchmen after the Revolution of 1789, initially facilitated by the new government, albeit on less generous terms than these—a fact that adds considerably to the plausibility of the author's fundamental narrative device.

[4] This reference is unclear; the King of Spain in the late 1880s was the exceedingly young Alfonso XIII (born in 1886), whose mother served as regent, so there was no heir apparent; the rival claimant to the throne was Carlos, Duke of Madrid. The subsequent revelation that the King of Bourbon's name is Jaime does not help to clarify the issue.

II

Among the emigrants who left with the second convoy was the Norman family of the Martinvasts.[5]

At the time of which we speak, that family, which had lived for more than a hundred years near Saint-Lo, consisted of a father, a mother and four young households. It was connected to the aristocracy as much as to the bourgeoisie by its relationships and alliances. Madame Martinvast, the mother, was one of the Val Saint-Jacques, one of the oldest stocks of the region of Valogne. The eldest daughter had married the Vicomte de Rimbert, a former cavalry officer domiciled in the vicinity.

Placed in the middle of verdant countryside, the Martinvast abode consisted of a modest and comfortable country house to which were attached a farm and a sugar-factory. Louis, the eldest son, was primarily occupied in agricultural endeavors. André, the second, was responsible for the industry.

The younger daughter lived in the town of Saint-Lo, where she had married a functionary from the ill-fated Broglie-Fortou ministry.[6] The functionary had been removed from office after a matter of months, but he had continued neverthe-

---

[5] Martinvast is a commune in Normandy not far from Cherbourg; in the mid-19th century the owner of the Château de Martinvast, the scientist Théodose du Moncel (1821-1884)—a pioneer of electrical lighting and telephony and anticipator of television—established a model farm there, but the château was sold in 1867 to a Prussian banker.

[6] A reactionary contingent took control of the Third Republic for some while in the 1870s, initially installing Duc Albert de Broglie as prime minister in 1873-74, and then Oscar Bardi de Fortou from 1874-78.

less to live in the neighborhood, precisely because of his attachments to the Martinvast family.

Everyone had decided, for various motives, to leave for the Île de Bourbon. Monsieur Martinvast père had once held an important political position in the département. At present, nothing of that remained to him—not even a shadow of influence. Instead of increasing, and in spite of his good administration, his fortune was diminishing. New taxes, on the one hand, and the mediocre returns of the land and the factory on the other, were threatening to create embarrassments.

His sons were working without courage or success, mingling their recriminations every day with those of their stepbrothers, whom idleness rendered bitter and morose.

The women attributed the responsibility for the difficulties that surrounded them on the prevailing irreligion. Harking back to the times of the Terror, they believed that they glimpsed before them the greatest dangers: persecution, confiscation and death. In their opinion, the only possible salvation was a general return to the practices of piety, the faith retaking the place in social direction that it had had in the finest epochs of our history.

A few years before, the head of the family had considered the possibility of adopting the new ideas; he had been pushed in that direction fairly strongly by his younger brother, Dr. Martinvast, a senator and leader of the Republican party in the département.

The latter had separated from his family in his youth and had taken a separate path. Driven by sincere convictions, he had taken, from the political and religious viewpoints, a direction opposite to the opinions of his relatives. How had that happened? How had the exceedingly Catholic family of Martinvasts found itself suddenly impregnated with incredulity and paganism? No one could say. Everyone, however, had respected a dissent developed solely by reason and the right of independence. Relations between the two brothers, although rare, had nevertheless remained imprinted with trust and affection.

At a certain time, therefore, the doctor took advantage, as we have just said, of that mutually sympathetic disposition to try to take his brother with him. He preached and sought by all means to convert him, making him see a future closed to him and his children if he persevered in his illusions. The head of the Martinvasts hesitated momentarily, as if out of deference, but eventually recoiled before the practical impossibility of such a change.

As soon as the project of departure had been decided, everyone around him had set courageously to work making the necessary preparations. It had, however, been difficult to take the decision. Many things would, in fact, be lost: the charms of the patrimonial dwelling, familiar horizons, friendly gazes, and the soft light of their native sun. And what would they find out there? It was not easy to reply to that question—but they did not linger long over these considerations. All of them, without distinction of sex or age, were going, as in the crusades, moved by a supernatural attraction, to the cry of "God wills it!" In search of what? A Christian atmosphere—. That atmosphere, to which they were accustomed, to which they were bound by all the fibers of their being, by which they had, so to speak, been formed, they could no longer breathe in France.

Well, they would go in search of it and reconstitute it elsewhere.

It was thus that the entire Norman family gathered on the first of October 1891 on the docks at Marseilles, surrounded by an enormous accumulation of boxes and objects of every kind, each of them clutching some particularly precious object or animal. The men had dogs on leads; each of the children—there were several in each household—carried a bird, a flower, a doll or some other plaything. It was a curious and heart-warming spectacle.

III

We shall not pause for long on the internal history of what was henceforth called the Kingdom of Bourbon. Old France was gradually transported there, very nearly as it was here at the beginning of the second half of the 19th century. Nevertheless, after a few years, a certain backward movement was produced in public opinion and institutions, such that one might have believed that a return to times anterior to 1789 was taking place, there being no railways and only very limited use of steam and electricity.

Society there did not take long to organize itself into very distinct but amicably related classes: around the king, the nobility, who owned the hand and held public positions; below them the middle class devoted to commerce and private professions; lower down, the laborers, clerks and domestic servants.

In reality, the nobility possessed all political power. The intermediary class only had a consultative voice in the kingdom's affairs. As for the populace, it allowed itself to be led—but, by way of compensation, as exempt from taxation. Besides which, passage from the third to the second class was relatively easy, and from the second to the first; that election, operated according to broad and equitable rules, prevented any dangerous fermentation.

In the accomplishment of its superior duties, the privileged class exercised a remarkable conscience and a neophytic zeal, and found in that sincere devotion to the public good the surest guarantee of its advantages. The society lived happily and peacefully, for happiness is not incompatible with any political system.

To facilitate that reorganization, the Bourbon government had decreed, as everyone knows, that the island would remain separated from the rest of the world for fifty years, and the other nations agreed benevolently to support that voluntary blockade—with the result that, for half a century, no foreign ship entered the ports of the principality and no letters, periodicals or books were imported. The maritime movement of the new nation was limited to a little coastal trade and fishing in the waters close to the sore.

That isolation continued even beyond the obligatory half-century. The Bourbonnais had got into the habit of living on their own resources and were in no hurry to modify their initial habits. The other nations had, at length, lost sight of the island. From north to south and east to west, they had ceased to think about it.

Furthermore, the clergy, which had the upper hand in the general administration and held royalty in respect, opposed by all the means at its disposal the idea of resuming relations with foreigners—which is to say, with infidels and gentiles. Thus, even when external communications had ceased to be a crime, they became a religious sin and a case of conscience. Its influence had become so powerful that one could, in effect, consider that, apart from a few brief landings by ships in distress, rogue traders or indiscreet geographers, the isolation of that petty France lasted more than a hundred years.

Among the families that occupied an important place within that Restoration of the past, it is necessary to cite that of the Martinvasts.

When the head of that family died, twenty years after his expatriation, he was laden with honors, titles and decorations. He had had considerable authority in the king's councils and he had succeeded in constituting a large estate to which he had given the name of Vertpré, the name of his former property near Saint-Lo.

The second Bourbon king, who had succeeded Don Jaime, had even raised that estate to the status of a comté. Oddly enough, however, on his father's death, Louis, the eldest son of the expatriated Martinvasts, had refused to wear the title of Comte; he had preferred to retain his former name, and it was André, the representative of the cadet branch, who became the second Comte de Vertpré. There still remained, it seemed, in the Norman family exported to the Indian Ocean, some residue of the democratic leaven that had developed in France in the person of Dr. Martinvast of Saint-Lo.

The two branches of the Martinvasts of Bourbon continued nevertheless to live on very good terms, occupying more-or-less important roles side by side in the aristocracy for several generations.

IV

In the year 2001, the date at which our story takes place, those two branches are represented by two cousins of almost the same age, who are linked together by sentiments of profound amity.

One of them, Philippe, aged 25, is the descendant of Louis, the eldest son of the head of the emigrant family, who, had, as we said just now, continued to wear the name of Martinvast. He is the heir of one of the small boys we saw embarking at Marseilles laden with their infantile baggage. He still wears his old bourgeois name proudly and, since his adolescence, a secret instinct has borne him toward his former fatherland. He is eager to take advantage of the international communications that are in the offing and will finally put an end to the reclusion of Bourbon, in order to travel to France, in particular to visit Normandy.

The second is Jacques de Vertpré. He belongs to the cadet branch, in which the tendencies and aptitudes of the maternal stock—which is to say the Val Saint-Jacques family of Valognes—is particularly infused. He is a little younger than Philippe, being only 23. No passion for travel torments him; nevertheless, in order to be agreeable to his cousin, he is ready and willing to accompany him. The prospect of making a filial pilgrimage to Saint-Lo and Valognes is attractive enough; at present he is occupied in compiling a family history. By returning to the cradle of the family, he will doubtless be able to find interesting documents, records, portraits and sepulchers, which will permit him to reunite the chain of his ancestry and make the acquaintance of the forebears of his beloved parents.

Both of them are bachelors, with no personal obligations. If the Bourbon kingdom mingles, as it is henceforth permissible to suppose, in the concert of the other nations of the globe, the two cousins are, by virtue of their knowledge and their individual qualities, designated to be among the first to form part of its diplomatic personnel. It is, in consequence, good that they are traveling and going to breathe the air of foreign lands.

The studies that they have made at the Ecclesiastical College of Saint-Denis have been very extensive. They know several languages and are up to date in the sciences, such as they were known at the end of the 19th century. Finally, they have completed some years of service in the royal army, in which they are ranking officers—with the result that nothing stands in the way of their departure. The Messageries Maritimes de Marseilles has just organized a regular service between their country and Europe. Our young cousins will depart on the first ship that appears in the island's waters under the tricolor flag and docks in Saint-Denis.

With them, it is the little France that is going to visit the great. The nineteenth and twenty-first centuries will find themselves in one another's presence. We shall see the last offspring of Christianity going to discover a land transformed by the more-than-centenary reign of an egalitarian system exclusively based on positive knowledge. Let us follow them and travel with them. It will be an opportunity for us to pass in review the transformations that have taken place in our social order, with a view to realizing, with an absolute perfection, the program of the French Monroe—which is to say, the ideal of democratic France.

In seeing the old civilization and the new face to face, we shall be able to compare them, and, by the same token, will be able to judge whether our forefathers were right to enter, as they did, the path that was once known as scientific socialism.

V

We ought to say right away, however, that the following chapters do not constitute a purely sociological work. We do not have any intention of confining ourselves within the domain that the serious men of the past gravely dubbed political economics. It is, above all, a novel that we have in view—which is to say, a love story. We shall see, as it is narrated, the place that the new mores have left to the foremost of sentiments and human motives. If, by chance, in the course of the story, some detail appears that our predecessors would have been able to obfuscate, with good cause, we shall impute it

to the change that time brings to moral conceptions, and shall continue our observation nevertheless, as spectators whose good intentions curiosity, however broad, cannot impede.

To begin with, we shall inform the reader that Philippe and Jacques were, at the time they departed, relative novices with regard to masculine passion. Perhaps Philippe had had a few minor adventures in garrison—for, as on may well imagine, the Devil had retained a minor role in Bourbon—but at the most, he had only felt a slight brush with love. Jacques, for his part, if we are not mistaken, had had one purely spiritual grand passion around the age of eighteen for a young cousin of sixteen, which had lasted for two months—an unfortunate passion, for the young cousin, according to what we have been told, remained indifferent to his tender dispositions. He had, as one can see, not advanced very far on the path of amour.

For both of them, the future had been quite simple, with regard to the fate reserved for their intimate sentiments. On returning from their voyage they would marry young women of their own class; then they would become fathers and invest their happiness in living until the third generation. Thus it had been in the time of the patriarchs, said the old books, and, without going back so far, it had generally been similar

23

enough in France at the time of the first centenary of the Revolution.

Thus they would both perpetuate their family by linking it to another family analogous in temperament and aptitude; their children would bear their name, and after their death, their marble statues would be seen in the funerary chapel of the Comté de Vertpré, each lying beside that of his unique and inseparable wife.

It was in these conditions of mind an experience that they went to confront the present-day world. Philippe was full of confidence and audacity. He had no prejudice against transformed France. The bitter discord that had given rise to the emigration a century before had left no trace in his mind. It is necessary to say, moreover, that with time, the resentment of the Bourbons in general had softened considerably.

That heir of the Martinvasts had, in fact, been raised in the loving contemplation of the land of his fathers. Everything had talked to him about it: books, pictures and family stories. When the conversation turned to that subject in his presence, it was always with a note of affection and regret. "O France!" he often aid to himself. "Dear, great France, whatever has become of you today, I shall always love you." And his thoughts, full of patriotic memories, flew from the Gaulish epochs to the sumptuous splendors of the final years of the monarchy.

From the Revolution onwards, history went awry in his eyes. Through the events of the 19th century, however, he strove to discover the traces of ancient historical traditions, and succeeded. He was proud of the role that his country had played in the world, and at the same time, confusedly, he regretted no longer being part of a great people. What had happened in the last century? What role did his former fatherland play now? He did not know, but presentiments gave him to think that the nation had not declined, and that, beneath the verbiage of new ideas, it had still furnished a brilliant career.

Philippe Martinvast was a proud and handsome fellow. Tall and well-built, with frank eyes, black hair and a rosy complexion, he was almost exactly reminiscent of the Frenchmen of the south-west whose type blossomed so well in Toulouse and Bordeaux, the country that is always that of good wine, warm gaiety and straight talking. His mother, in fact, belonged to a family that was originally from Béarn.

Jacques de Vertpré, on the other hand, was more typical of the northern races. That character was recognizable in his blue eyes, his chestnut-colored—almost blond—hair, and his fresh and delicate complexion. He was serious by nature, but excessively sensible. His mother, who had been widowed rather young, had kept him with her for a long time, for he was her only child, and as a result of that overly prolonged material education the son retained something feminine in his mannerisms, preferences and character. Nevertheless, that tenderness of moral complexion was habitually veiled beneath a virile exterior subsequently imprinted by association with his comrades. The habitual reserve of his attitude and his language also contributed to masking it. All in all, Jacques was, like his cousin, a perfect gentleman—as people used to say— of casual, simple and seductive distinction.

Strictly speaking, he too was devoid of any prejudice against the new world that he was about to discover, but he was unenthusiastic, and deep down, he could not entirely help feeling a certain tenacious resentment about all that had happened in France since the Revolution. In a word, on the subject of France, he had neither regrets nor aspirations. Happy on his island, if he left it, it was with the desire to return as soon as possible.

VI

Scarcely had they boarded the ship than the two cousins bumped into a succession of astonishments of every sort, which produced in their brains, for some time, an effect similar to that of dreaming.

Greeted by the passengers and the crew with evident signs of interest, they nevertheless found themselves somewhat embarrassed at first in the midst of that floating population whose members considered them curiously while smiling at them in a benevolent fashion.

The first thing that struck them was that the ship was powered by electricity. They no longer saw above the deck the enormous noisy and smoky funnels that characterized ancient steamships. The masts and sails had also vanished; long-haul mariners had lost the ancient maneuvering skills.

The farewell ceremony was prolonged as far as the end of the jetty. For some time after the departure Philippe and Jacques leaned on the rail, having waved affectionately to their relatives and friends. When they lost sight of land, their hearts, it must be said, lurched in a brief moment of anguish.

When they turned round, the ship was moving at top speed, and the deck had already taken on its customary aspect of a public square, silent and tedious. At that moment they found themselves face to face with the steward who had come, cap in hand, to discuss the conditions of their voyage and give them any information they might need.

"Where are you going, gentlemen?" asked the uniformed employee, in a curt but nevertheless polite tone.

"We're going to Marseilles," Jacques de Vertpré replied. "From there we're going to Normandy by sea, disembarking as close as possible to Saint-Lo."

"Very good, gentlemen; things couldn't be simpler. In three weeks, you'll be in the capital of Provence. Three days after that you'll be able to land in Granville; from there it's not far overland to Saint-Lo."

"Oh! Ships move very quickly now," said Philippe Martinvast. After a moment's reflection, he added: "Nevertheless, three days to go from Marseilles to Granville by sea seems to me to be a trifle short. Did I hear you correctly, Monsieur? You said three days?"

"Yes, three days."

In spite of this affirmation, the young men did not seem convinced, and remained quite perplexed. Then, the steward, realizing their ignorance of recent events said: "Yes, it's true. You obviously don't know. We now have the Inter-Sea Canal.

This was a further shock for our travelers. We shall make mention of it again in passing, but we warn our readers that, in future, we shall not pause to mention each of their tremors. At length, in any case, they were able to learn the most extraordinary things without raising an eyebrow.

"What!" the both cried. "That famous canal has been built!"

"Was it the great Ferdinand who created it?" added Jacques de Vertpré.

"Who is the great Ferdinand?"

"I mean Ferdinand de Lesseps."

"No, it was the Confederation."

"What Confederation?"

"Why, the French Confederation, of course."

The two friends were silent.[7] They were not quite sure what the French Confederation might be. Nevertheless, having

---

[7] The author inserts a footnote: "We feel that we ought to inform the reader at this point that this work, which is set in the future, was actually composed in the course of the year 1888, anterior to various events that have transpired in the last eighteen months, such as the Panama crisis, the establishment of the Republic of Brazil, the electric lighting of a quarter of Paris, etc. It has, however, only been necessary to make a few slight amendments while the book was in press."

scarcely embarked, they did not want to pester their interlocutor with too many questions.

The latter, having some suspicion of their state of mind, continued. "Well, so that you know, this is how we're organized over there at present. Over a number of years, the Republic brought us to a federal situation. We began with what was called State Socialism. The State did everything. It educated, manufactured, constructed, engaged in commerce, etc. That was the heyday of bureaucracy. But the regime didn't last. It was too complex. The leveling that it imposed upon all the specimens of the race and all the parcels of land was tyrannical and stifling.

"By reaction against that centralization, things crumbled. For the great unity of the State was substituted the small unity of the commune, and it was the commune, in its turn, that did everything. Instead of a unique national yoke, the French had to support a communal yoke, often vexatious and arbitrary. The communes themselves, however, found that omnipotence very awkward. The city municipalities oppressed the rural municipalities, and there were often conflicts between cities, either fiscal or even armed.

"Over time, we have arrived at a kind of compromise between the two systems. There has been no reason to oppose the predominance of cities over rural areas. Thanks to easy and rapid communications, the cities expanded and filled up. Paris, especially became colossal. Villages, on the other hand, emptied. There were still many associated with factories, either industrial or agricultural, but more truly sedentary agglomerations. It was also cities that became, in all things, the impulsive force, the watchword. As the intelligence and authority of an industrial enterprise, the constructions of which are sometimes vast, are often concentrated in a narrow office from which control is exercised and commands issued, and as, in each region, commercial, administrative and social life are accumulated and concretized in a natural hub, those urban hubs converged themselves toward a more important center. In a word, life thinned out at the periphery of the social body and became more intense in the organic centers.

"That incessantly-increasing movement brought to light inconveniences for which it was necessary to find a remedy. The majority of rural communes, because of the smallness of their territory and the restricted number of their inhabitants, no longer offered a sufficiently large field for an association desirous of prospering. On the other hand, the interests of one locality were almost always interlinked with those of neighboring localities. That complication was a fertile source of difficulties. It was resolved, in order to avoid those difficulties, to suppress communal autonomy, and the primary social unit, the first level of administrative hierarchy, became the canton. It was in the urban hub of the canton that the active agents of all public utility services—police, arbitration, education, armed force, welfare, taxation, highways administration, health services, cremation, etc.—were based.

"At the same time, the principle of equality was totally misunderstood by the ancient communes. It was understood that the principle in question, so dear to the inhabitants taken individually, could not be applied to local groups without dire consequences. One can easily understand, in fact, that a citizen who is part of an unimportant group is no longer on equal footing with a citizen belonging to a large, rich and influential group, There was, however, no possibility of establishing a permanent and mathematical equality between the cantons. Identity, which is the ideal of democracy, evidently cannot be realized absolutely, either for social bodies or individuals. As a general rule, the principle of equality can only have a restricted and relative application to the determination of a maximum. That is what happened with regard to cantons.

"A rather high maximum number of inhabitants was established—twenty-five thousand, if I'm not mistaken—beyond which a canton had to be divided into two. In addition, account was taken, in the new administrative map that was drawn up, of the relationship between the density of the population and the extent of the inhabited territory, and the legal maximum rose in proportion to the density, to the extent that in large cities, the cantonal maximum can, I believe, rise to fifty thousand inhabitants, and even higher."

The steward had reached that point in his explanations when a sailor came to tell him that someone wanted to speak to him in the ladies' saloon. He excused himself.

"Forgive me," he said to his listeners. "I know who's summoning me. It's Madame Fanny Listor, a Parisienne who came to Madagascar a few months ago in the company of a trader with whom she had contacted a conjugal engagement. Communal life having ceased to please her, she's repatriating herself with her two children, at the expense of her latest husband, and not a day goes past without her asking something of me." In saying that, the steward could not help smiling. *You know women*, he seemed to be saying. *One always has to attend to them...* "But I'll come back soon," he added, "and we'll continue our conversation."

"Gladly," Philippe replied, "for thus far, quite frankly, we still don't understand very well how the Confederation functions."

"Don't worry—we'll talk about it again," said the steward. Drawing the two young men with him in the direction of the stairway, he added: "Let it suffice for the moment to know that present-day France is, before anything else, a sheaf of cantons, an association formed between groups of inhabitants, whose authority is limited by the Constitution. On that note— see you later."

And he disappeared down the iron staircase that led to the saloon, leaving our two friends rather uncertain as to what judgment they ought to make of what they had just heard.

VII

Philippe and Jacques retraced their steps, heading for the ship's rail. As they leaned their elbows on it, their eyes met and their faces, momentarily contracted by reflection, expanded as one with an impulse of mischievous gaiety.

"Oh, I think we're going to see some funny things," said Philippe, beaming.

"In all colors," Jacques replied. "Did you notice what the commissioner said about the beautiful Madame Listor?"

"How do you know that she's beautiful?"

"I haven't the slightest doubt about it, judging by the steward's attitude. Tell me—I thought I gathered that the practice of free union is part of the new matrimonial mores. Did you notice that detail?"

"It wouldn't surprise me," Philippe replied. "As soon as divorce has been admitted—I mean easy divorce, not too complicated or expensive, and soon resulting from simple mutual consent—it means the end of marriage; by which I mean the indissolubility and unity of the matrimonial pact. The French, today as before, doubtless don't stop half way. When it's a matter of religion or the family, they always go to one extreme or the other. They're not the kind of people who, in matters of dogma, have ever been able to pause at a given point, like the comfortable way-station of Protestantism. They won't, I imagine, have been any more able to stop in the matter of conjugal association at the barrier of judiciary divorce. Complete faith or absolute incredulity; matrimonial indissolubility or total liberty—it's simple; as elementary as conception and reasoning. As a matter of logic, it's logical…but it remains to be seen how they've accommodated in practice to that more than reckless innovation."

"Come on, Philippe," Jacques replied. "Men aren't animals, after all, to accomplish their natural impulses at hazard like that, without pausing to think about their children. Created by God to become angels after their mortal life, redeemed by him of their original sin and endowed with an immortal soul, they couldn't abandon themselves to love without some intervention of the representatives of civil law and religion."

"Obviously," said Philippe, raising his voice, "I share your opinion..."

He did, indeed, share all his companion's convictions in that matter. And yet, secretly he could not help thinking that there definitely remained, in fact, some analogy between humans and animals, and that the analogy in question was noticeable in the tendencies and necessities of their life. Did love demand, imperiously, to be preceded or accompanied by legal or pious formalities? Did young people really only love one another with a view to procuring children? Had Philippe wanted to delve into the utmost depths of his conscience, perhaps he might have found a few doubts on those points.

The sea was quite beautiful. Our young cousins let themselves go for a while in contemplating the infinite azure. In the distance, flying fish appeared from time to time, skimming over the water. Large gray birds dipped their wings in the vessel's wake, accompanying their movements with plaintive cries. The breeze was scarcely sensible in spite of the ship's speed. Everywhere around them, an intense light and profound silence reigned.

After a while, they began walking back and forth along the deck. At each end of the ship there was a tent. The one in the bow housed the black population, in crowded conditions. That category of passengers had special quarters below decks for eating and sleeping. The external shelter only served for them to get some air. The two cousins were not surprised by the presence of those African natives, whose relatives formed a significant fraction of the population of Bourbon.

Beneath the other tent, at the stern, were a few white passengers. Jacques and Philippe soon went to sit down there. As chance would have it, the passengers gathered there were almost all French. The ship had raised anchor at Tamalave and had made no other port of call but Saint-Denis, so there was nothing astonishing about it.

At first glance, all the passengers appeared to belong to the stronger sex. Their costume consisted, indistinctly, of a long jacket, loose-fitting knee-breeches and a pair of leggings. On observing some of the faces that turned toward them, however, and taking more account of the attitudes and mannerisms of that audience, Philippe and Jacques did not take long to realize that it included a number of women. The latter wore clothes that were slightly more brightly colored, and their hairstyles were more complicated—at least among those who had long hair, for some seemed to wear it rather short, in the male fashion.

The subjects of the King of Bourbon could not help exchanging a smile as they made these observations. At the same time, to put on a polite face, they selected newspapers from those scattered on a table facing them.

"Canteen-workers, Cousin…that's all," said Philippe, in a low voice, leaning toward Jacques with his mouth hidden behind a paper.

"Neither men nor women," replied Jacques. "All Annamites."[8]

And they set about reading the news-sheets. Both of them were quite fond of journalism. Jacques was even the owner, in the district of Saint-André, where he had a residence, of a little weekly publication. In that paper, which was called *L'Étendard de Saint-André*, he ardently supported, in opposition to the first sinners of reborn liberalism, the principles of divine right and authoritarian monarchy.

The first papers that passed before their eyes were from Madagascar. Our young people understood straight away that the possession in question, having been governed for a long

---

[8] The Annamite mountains are a region in what was French Indo-China when the story was written, on the border of the modern Vietnam and Laos. Traditional male and female costumes in the region were very similar.

time as a conquered country, was on the point of arriving at that period of development at which colonies administer themselves, maintaining no other relationship with the metropolis than those resulting from racial affinity and common interests.

They hastened to reach the French papers. The first thing they noticed was their volume and extent. Our friends had no idea of the numerously-paged sections in the form of which the majority of our daily newspapers now offer themselves to the public. What struck them immediately was their low price. Per issue they cost almost nothing, and on subscription, even less.

Evidently, Jacques said to himself, *French journalists run no risk of failure; they live on their insertions and perhaps distribute their moist proofs free at street-corners; the news, gossip and commentaries doubtless serve no other purpose than to serve as a vehicle for expensive advertisements.*

While rummaging through these various papers, they both sought to lay their hands on one or other of the publications that had existed at the time of the emigration, about which their fathers had told them stories. They did not find any. They were all new titles, insignificant or bizarre, often printed on behalf of a profession or a locality.

Jacques was about to begin a methodical reading of the *Express*, a major Parisian newspaper, when, beneath a magazine with a bright red cover, which was none other than the old *Revue des Deux Mondes*, he spotted a simple bright yellow paper in a medium format, whose title began with an F.

He lifted up the magazine slightly, and the four letters F-i-g-a appeared to his curious gaze. There was no doubt about it; he had before his eyes the *Figaro*, so dear to the founders of the Bourbon colony, a few issues of which, slightly expurgated, had been deposited in the museum at Saint-Denis. He finally succeeded in displacing the imposing *Revue*. It was, indeed, the *Figaro*, but with a subtitle: *Figaro*, "the paper without advertising."

Ah! Jacques thought. *So there are two kinds of periodical; papers of mere publicity, undoubtedly, and informative*

papers...or are they instruments of propaganda and populari-
zation? Has the profession of journalism become purely com-
mercial? If so, how do the apostles of the right and left, sow-
ing the good word sincerely and disinterestedly, operate now?

The *Figaro* was now, therefore, a simple news bulletin. Very light and very short, it published three issues a day.

Aha! An article in large type. What's that about? Latest news of the crash of the balloon Zenith...

Jacques de Vertpré set was about to run though the various incidents of that catastrophe, of a kind entirely new to him, when a certain sensation suddenly materialized in the tent.

Our two friends were obliged to stop reading at the same time.

VIII

It was Madame Fanny Listor who came in, accompanied by the steward.

Madame Listor had come up from her cabin because it was nearly time for the evening meal. She had made a tour of the ship twice, beneath her umbrella, and now she was coming to mingle with shipboard society. Her children, accompanied by a governess, were following her, playing. When she appeared at the entrance of the tent, she was in conversation with the steward. She was speaking rather loudly, like a person indifferent to the presence of others, and was amusing herself with a black boy she had met on the way, making him chase flies. She had asked him whether he wanted to entire her service as a "groom" and the child, who did not understand her language very well, had only replied with an embarrassed and beaming smile.

"How funny they are, these pretty ebony children!" she said, ducking her head in order to come into the reading-room.

At the sound of her musical and sonorous voice, doubtless familiar to everyone present, most of the passengers stood up in order to go to her and shake her hand. Those who were not on intimate terms with the newcomer followed hr movements with their eyes. Involuntarily, Philippe and Jacques participated in the general attention.

In an instant, Madame Listor became the center of the improvised salon. There was no longer anyone but her in the tent. People enquired about her health and that of her children, and talked about various incidents of life aboard. She replied to everyone in a cheerful tone, with a charming ease, without the slightest banality.

The two cousins having risen to their feet in their turn, the steward came over to them in order to introduce them to the young woman.

"These, Madame," he said to her, "are the two passengers who embarked at Saint-Denis. They're the first inhabitants of the Île de Bourbon who have decided to cross the sea in order to visit their ancestors' fatherland."

"Very good, Messieurs," said Madame Listor, after a rapid glance of inspection. "I'm charmed to make your acquaintance. You're our compatriots. The France of today is doubtless very different from the one you have founded out here, but have no fear—you'll get a warm welcome there."

While she was speaking, Philippe and Jacques felt as if they were enveloped by the charm that her person emitted. Her soft and luminous gaze went straight to their eyes, without affectation or reserve, and she gave evidence of her sympathy by means of a very cordial handshake.

Madame Listor was not wearing the costume we described jut now—a costume common to both sexes; she was clad, like mothers, in a dress tailored in the antique fashion and tightened at the waist by a belt. Her ivory neck extended from the gap of her corsage like a spring stem forged by sunlight and dew. She was not wearing any jewelry, only two bouquets formed by red berries picked in Madagascar, one between her breasts and the other on the broad-brimmed fathered hat that shaded her black hair.

She went to sit down on a divan beside an old man with a long white beard, who was none other than the ship's doctor, Dr. Priot.

In his turn, the captain made his entrance. Evidently, dinner time was imminent. The head-waiter had a habit of watching out for the ship's master before ringing the summoning bell. The latter began to ring incontinently at maximum volume, hurling its cheerful note into the silent immensity.

While the procession from the tent to the dining room began, Jacques and Philippe went to pay their respects to the captain.

"Ah, there you are!" the latter said, as soon as he saw them coming toward him. "Just the men I was looking for. My grandfather often told me that a great-uncle had taken part in the religious emigration of 1891. That great-uncle was an abbé in the vicinity of Marseilles, principally occupied in organizing pilgrimages to the Holy Land. There wasn't yet a railway station in Jerusalem in those days, and the voyage to Palestine was complicated—but he liked that. He was an adventurer, in his way. So, when the question came up of going to live in the Île de Bourbon, he was the first person in Marseilles to put his name down. He was called Père Benedict. Have you heard mention of him?"

"Of course!" Jacques replied. "Père Benedict left a popular name on the island. He founded an order of missionaries, and on the highest of the Sous-le-Vent province's volcanic peaks he erected a colossal statue to Notre-Dame de la Garde, which is now the object of frequent pilgrimage."

"Ah—I recognize him in that," the captain replied. "He must have died content, the brave Abbé Benedict."

IX

Captain Tropez was no sea-dog. He was a learned officer, a very good navigator, who, once descended from his bridge, was the most amiable and sociable of men. His vessel was, in his eyes, like a family drawing room, in which there ought to be a bond of union, and we must say that he acquitted that mission with a great deal of tact and intelligence, putting as much good will as precision into his explanations of marine matters, and, on the other hand interesting himself sincerely in his passengers' stories and observations.

The meals at which he presided, therefore, were ordinarily pleasant in their frank cordiality. Everyone joined in the conversations, and by the end, it was not rare to see a cheerful gaiety reigning there, which might have made one think that the guests were old friends.

That day, the conversation was principally devoted to the present condition of the different countries of Europe. Everyone wanted to help bring the two Bourbonnais up to date with what had happened in the last century, and thus prepare them for the spectacles that they would soon have before their eyes. The latter did not ask many questions, but welcomed with a great deal of curiosity and gratitude what was said to them as the others anticipated their interrogations.

The captain had graciously seated them beside him, so that they would not miss a word of what he said. Facing the captain was the steward, with Madame Listor to his right and another lady to his left, who was dressed in the masculine fashion. She had a dark complexion, a very intelligent and mobile gaze, and a slightly anxious expression.

The meal was very well served by black men.

"You mustn't be astonished," the captain said, if you find a great many Africans and Chinese in France. Presently, almost all domestic employment and drudge-work is done by them. You'll see them on the docks in ports, on the platforms of railway stations, in the corridors of hotels, in private dwellings and coal mines—everywhere there is an ingrate task to be done, unworthy of a voting citizen.

"Emigration societies have been formed that bring us in sufficient numbers from Africa and Asia the servant personnel that we need. The black people that you have noticed in the bow of the ship are merely a company of servants bound for an employment bureau in Lyon.

"The State controls and subsidizes these societies. It controls them in the interests of humanitarian principles, in order that the personnel are not subjected to ill-treatment. It subsidizes them because it has found in their traffic a guarantee of internal peace. Its subsidy takes the form that you will discover in all enterprises functioning with the collaboration of the State. It guarantees a certain revenue and takes a share of the profits, when there are any.

"The coolies—that's the general name by which we designate these foreigners, today, Chinese and others—owe the price of their return journey to their transporter. Once acquitted of that debt they can dispose freely of their person and their pay. They can never become French citizens, though, and in case of necessity—which is to say, if they behave badly or become too numerous—they can be forcibly repatriated."

Jacques and Philippe listened with a great deal of interest to the words emerging from the captain's mouth.

"I can understand," said Jacques, "why these foreigners are refused the title of French citizens, for a nation, in order to be homogeneous, must be composed, as far as possible, of individuals of the same race and the same physical constitution—and, you will doubtless add captain, the same mental capacity. Between a Sudanese and a Poictevin, for instance, there is an abyss that several generations of Sudanese living in France is insufficient to bridge. But suppose, by chance, that a highly educated African or a exceptionally literate Chinese were to settle in the heart of France and ask to be admitted to its nationality, would you refuse him?"

The short woman dressed as a man who was to the steward's left wanted to reply to that, but the captain, forestalling her with a rapid gesture, explained that in such a case, naturalization was not refused.

"All foreigners," he continued, "who come to France at their own expense can request and obtain nationality. Nevertheless, I ought to say that the conditions imposed upon them differ according to their origin. There is a scale for naturalization, as for many other things. The greater the racial affinity is between the French and the candidate's nation, the easier naturalization is. In addition, there are cases of exceptional naturalization, based on the individual merit of the foreigner requesting to be French."

"Very good," said Jacques, "but speaking only with regard to immigrants of the black and yellow races, what do you do with the children they have during their residence in France?"

"We do what we can in order that these foreigners can have children, and their descendants follow the course that they determine themselves. To that end, the immigration societies must bring nearly as many women as men. Once in France, the coolies find meeting places organized specifically for them: maternities, crèches, schools and hospitals reserved for them.

"In fact, my dear Messieurs, there are very few mixed-race individuals, mores being entirely contrary to the mixture of blood. Those born in that condition are, as it were, the bastards of the new civilization. They're French, but they enjoy only a limited consideration. Thus far, fortunately, they only represent an insignificant element in the population, and one can say that they count for nothing in terms of influence.

"It is possible that, in time, we shall see the questions like the ones that divide the American republics arise among us—I mean questions of color, questions even more arduous than the conflicts to which political parties are exposed—but we haven't got there yet."

Jacques resumed speaking then. "I'll admit," he observed, "that this intrusion of black and yellow people into the beautiful land of Gaul spoils my view slightly in advance, I see it as a new invasion of barbarians, carried out by means of railways and steamboats, with the complicity of the invaded. And I wonder what the memory of Vercingetorix or Jeanne d'Arc will be worth, in the long run, to these newcomers and their descendants—not to mention the architectural legend of our old cathedrals and palaces, the glory of our scholars, saints and heroes."

The captain remarked with satisfaction that his interlocutor, while having these reservations, nevertheless considered France as his own land, and that he had not in any way repudiated that part of his heritage in the common patrimony of traditions registered by history.

"It's certain," he replied, "that in that respect our country has changed a great deal. We are no longer in the times when Parisians knew no other Africans than that of the Faubourg Saint-Denis, and when Colonel Tchenkitong amazed our compatriots by demonstrating to them that a Chinese man could have intelligence.[9] There has been a veritable exchange between peoples since then—and we, believe me, have become travelers, colonists, polyglots..."

The two cousins' eyes grew wide; they could hardly believe their ears. Their astonishment was so obvious that the captain paused momentarily.

"And why not?" he continued. "That was a new habit to acquire, a fashion to take root. It was quickly done I assure you, thanks to the momentum given by the State, the University, the cities and the associations... Today we're not far behind England in the importance of our foreign trade, and we have several millions of nationals outside the metropolis.

---

[9] The Chinese diplomat whose name would nowadays be rendered Chen Jitong (1851-1907) wrote several books in French, signing then Tcheng Ki-tong

42

"The employment we have made of foreigners in our in-ferior services has been one of the consequences of the great impetus given to international communications. We have found it, as I said, a guarantee of social improvement. In free-ing citizens from the accomplishment of painful or humiliating professions, we have raised the level of the electorate—which is to say, the nation—and diminished the inevitable margin of separation between the most elevated and the most humble of us. The latter already have to reason for discontent. Thos whom fatality causes accidentally to fall, do not fall as far nowadays. Peace, cordiality and a sentiment of solidarity thus holds more securely in the legal land."

Smiling, the captain added: "Which is not to say that the members of democracy have all become gentlemen like you, Messieurs Bourbonnais; they are nevertheless all well-disciplined, and, on the other hand, one can affirm that, all things considered, they have every reason to be satisfied with their lot. The best reason of all is that everyone, as a general rule, is employed according to his natural aptitudes, and works according to his taste."

"Oh, really? What about the military service that you compel?"

"Military service! Conscription! It's a long time since those Medieval customs ceased to exist, my dear Monsieur. No one today is a sailor or a soldier against his wishes. But it would take too long to tell you about that, wouldn't it, Mad-ame Myrtil?"

As he concluded, the captain turned toward the short la-dy who had already attempted to intervene in the conversation. The young woman had been following the discussion with interest, but she was now beginning to adopt a bored expres-sion that had not escaped the captain's notice.

It was as well, for her and doubtless also for the other guests, to have a change. That was why the captain abruptly threw the ball to the steward's left hand neighbor.

X

Rosa Myrtil might have been 22 or 24. She belonged to a lyric troupe that had been putting on performances in Tananarive. Her engagement having ended, she had made a voyage around Madagascar in a yacht, in the company of a young creole; now she was returning alone to France, heading for Paris.

For some time already, as we have seen, she had been trying to take part in the conversation between the captain and our two cousins. Thus, she was quick to seize the opportunity that had been offered to her.

"We would do better, in fact," she said to begin with, "to bring these Messieurs up to date with matters of art, theater and the status of women; that would be more amusing, it seems to me, and we could all say something."

"That's my opinion too," said Madame Listor. "That would truly render a service to our amiable companions."

Jacques de Verpré observed, with a smile, that he and his cousin desired nothing more than to have a few preliminary notions with regard to those various subjects.

"Already," he added, "we believe that marriage is no longer a feature of mores. Isn't that so?"

"Not any longer," replied Madame Myrtil, raising her voice. "Marriage, such as it was once understood, no longer has any legal existence. It had been imagined primarily, it is necessary to say, in the interests of children. Today, the lot of children is separately regulated; it is completely assured outside the family.

"On the other hand, ancient marriage was associated with a system of succession that has similarly ceased to exist. The Messieurs at your sides can tell you about the changes that have been made to property rights and their transmission. What it is essential to know is that no one any longer receives anything from another than by donation or testament.

"To get back to marriage, or rather, to what has replaced marriage, this is what has happened: conjugal relations are absolutely free—absolutely, you understand—and the matrimonial contract is a convention like any other. When a woman expects a child she makes a declaration to the municipal officer, and is then subject to medical supervision. If she is absent from her domicile she must return to it as soon as possible, and there, she finds herself at her disposal a comfortable and tranquil Maternity. From that time on she abandons the near-masculine costume that we who have not had the honor of being mothers wear, and resumes traditional feminine dress for a variable length of time. She does not leave the Maternity until a year after the birth of the child. The mother then resumes her entire liberty and the child, for whom the superstitious formalities of ancient baptism—always painful and often dangerous—have been avoided, passes successfully through the crèche, school and college, brought up communally throughout, with other children of the same age, at the canton's expense."

Jacques de Vertpré did not hear this explanation of a system worthy of Lacedaemon,[10] imprinted in his eyes with a veritable cruelty, without profound displeasure. *How*, he wondered, *have people allowed themselves to be drawn to such a monstrous extremity? To remove a child from its mother...that's much more serious than the attack on the liberty of the father which was once so extensively discussed.*

He continued, however to eat and drink without saying a word, keeping his reflections to himself.

Philippe, for his part, did not seem too disorientated. He asked whether all women were constrained to this general regime, and whether there were not some among them who, aided by sufficient personal resources, were able to stay at home in such circumstances, so as to keep their children with them and their husbands.

---

[10] Lacedaemon, allegedly a son of Zeus, was the mythical king who supposedly founded the city of Sparta.

"There are a few," said Madame Listor, "and I am an example of that. I have no husband, for the moment, but I have kept my children nevertheless."

"It's true," Madame Myrtil continued, "that the regime I've described is not obligatory. It is, however, followed by the majority of our fellow citizenesses. Very few people are in a position to do what Madame Listor has done. On the other hand, the Maternities are organized in such a way as to satisfy women of above-average delicacy. What is the point of procuring by onerous sacrifice that which is freely offered? In any case, Madame Listor will permit me to say that, in consequence of mores, between children raised by their parents and those who have been formed in public establishments, a moral separation his established that is not always to the advantage of the former."

"Oh, that's arguable, my dear lady," Madame Listor put in. "but let's pass on..."

"Yes, let's pass on," replied Madame Myrtil.

Jacques was struck by the easy assurance with which the young artiste explained everything. "In sum, Madame," he said, "I see that the family has ceased to exist. It seems to me that in France, there are now only couples."

"There are now only couples—that's right!" exclaimed Madame Myrtil, laughing. And she began to sing: "Life is a journey/that is best made in pairs."

"But still, these couples," Philippe went on, in his turn, in a slightly humorous tone, "while being entirely free, as you said just now, are at least formed in the presence of the Mayor?"

At that, the entire audience burst out laughing, and Philippe found himself drawn into the general hilarity.

"Yes, one still sees some formed like that," replied Madame Myrtil, tipped back in her chair and scarcely able to contain herself, "but only in the theater. In your time—no, I'm mistaken, in your parents' time—in the theater, it was always the notary or a scrivener who made marriages; in reality, it was the mayor of a parish priest. Well, the fashion has reversed. Today it's to the notary, not the mayor, that it is necessary to address oneself in practice, if we don't have the skills required to draw up contracts ourselves—which is to say that a few prudent women stipulate certain personal advantages in writing, or some indemnity in case of anticipated or ill-timed abandonment. To tell the truth, though, almost all our engagements of love are made orally."

At this point Madame Myrtil became serious again; she regained possession of herself, as if in order to complete her explanations in a dignified manner.

"These engagements," she added, "last as long as love itself lasts—sometimes for a few days, sometimes for a lifetime."

The serious side of the matrimonial question had thus been broached. If they continued to talk in that fashion, it was to be feared that they might fall into considerable annoyance, or might end up in untoward argument. Philippe, a trifle anxious, turned from time to time to look at his cousin, who had ceased taking part in the conversation. He took account of the significance of his silence, and feared seeing him burst forth explosively. What should he do? He could not, however, let silence follow Madame Myrtil's last words. So, abruptly, without transition, he set about changing the subject of conversation.

"These new mores," he observed, "have not, I imagine, been without repercussions in the theatrical arts?"

"Indeed, Monsieur," Madame Myrtil replied. "The basis of comedies and dramas is no longer the same. Adultery, that inexhaustible source of interest for the honest people of the last century, no longer exists. On the other hand, the notion of honor has been modified, and decency has vanished. The extent of patriotism is now considered relatively narrow. In a word, everything has changed in scenic conventions—and yet, the public taste for plays is still the same. Comedy, in particular, continues to be well-treated in Molière's house, in spite of the abrogation, already long ago, of the Moscow decree.[11] I merely warn you that it has become very sincere. The genre has broken absolutely with the residue of prudery that was still predominant in the last century. We have gone back to Aristophanes. You have been warned."

The meal was reaching its end.

The captain asked the young artiste if she might consent, in order to provide a specimen, of contemporary musical art, to sing one of the pieces in her repertoire.

"All the passengers," he added, "would be grateful to you."

"Gladly," Rosa Myrtil replied. "And why not? I will even say. Captain, that I'm grateful for your suggestion. Song is a need for me. Since I embarked, I've suffered from not being able to use my voice. I feel that it's being kept prisoner, here in my throat. It's true! I have a crazy desire to set the silent mass of aerial waves that surrounds us, superimposed on the incommensurable mass of liquid waves, a-quiver. But for that, it's better to be on deck."

"Yes, on deck!" cried the audience, in unison. "Let's go up on deck."

Everyone got up. There was harmonium in the corner of the saloon that was easily portable.

"Carry that upstairs for me," said the steward to two of the waiters at the captain's table.

In a few moments, the whole company was reinstalled not far from the tent we mentioned before.

It was already getting late, but dusk had hardly begun to mark the sky. A few ruddy waves extending from the horizon marked the place where the sun had just been eclipsed. The calling of birds had ceased. The sea, gently stirred by a light

---

[11] "Molière's house" is the Comédie Française; numerous French heads of state took an interest in it, as a kind of national theater, and moved to protect it in various ways; Napoléon I even took the trouble to do so while deep in trouble in the heart of Russia in the decree of October 15, 1812.

westerly wind, took on rocking movements beneath the rapid and indifferent ship. At the same time, it swelled beneath the prow, as if to retain it with long pleats charged with foam, and which, on breaking, filled their air with a bitter freshness.

The steward placed his hands on the keyboard, and a veritable concert began.

XI

Light harmonious sounds emerging from the instrument rose insensibly above the silence, bringing to attentive ears the insinuating and concentrated sensation of commencing sensuality. First there were vague and discreet vibrations, similar to the sounds of the moving ship, the plaint of the wind, the flight of birds and the muted seething that the sun provokes in its course.

The instrument put itself in counterpoint to the ambient environment.

Gradually, the tonality increased; melodies succeeded long chords, and human music began to resonate frankly in the imposing solitude, taking possession, as it were, of the empty immensity.

Then Rosa Myrtil began to sing.

In a warm and emotional voice, she intoned the great chant, so familiar today, in which the charm and cost of life are exalted.

"...What is a human being? A speck of animate matter, an organism set in motion for a few days by a pendulum. For as long as the sustaining breath lasts, and the pendulum swings, a human lives and exists, thinking, feeling and acting. Nature, to obtain what it desires therefrom, supports such beings, drawing them alternately from suffering to pleasure.

"Whence comes life? Why is there life? A mystery. Humans receive it, transmit it and love it. They love instinctively, young or old. It is their sole and unique wealth. They attach themselves to it, even unhappily, for suffering is still living.

"What, then, is the mission of human beings? To live. Their ideal? To live long, to live abundantly. Their law? To live sagely."

Rose Myrtil had one of those communicative voices that goes directly to the sensibility of listeners and the mere sound of which melts hearts. It was like the vibration of her entire being. Just as the intimate contexture of a musical instrument reveals itself in its resonance, the young artiste, by means of her passionate and troubling tones, gave an intuition of her true nature, with her character, her temperament and her physical constitution.

Jacques de Vertpré was not the least impressed among those who were listening. He was beginning to find that the young doctrinarian, whose speech had displeased him so much a little while before, did not lack a certain flame, and that there was even a great deal of sentiment in her song.

Rosa Myrtil continued. She listed the joys of life.

"For a woman, where is happiness? In maternity. For a man? In love. For all, to a lesser degree, it is in health, in mental tranquility, in communion with nature, in work and in success. Work is not a punishment, it is a diversion that relieves ennui, the reef of civilization. It is an exercise that maintains our strength...

"There are necessary joys, common to all humans, and accidental or superfluous joys. Only the former are real joys. They consist in the satisfaction of our legitimate instincts. Those joys are simple. The first, the keenest, is obtained at the price of a kiss. In all well-regulated societies they are within the range of everyone...

"Happiness is equal for all; everyone has a share in it. Sometimes, it extends equally throughout an existence. Sometimes, it is condensed into an hour of felicity. The shepherd on his mountain has nothing to envy the powerful or the rich, for he has no enemy who comes to poison his days with hatred. The chagrin, envy, dread, remorse and spleen that set torment in the bosom of the most brilliant positions are unknown to him...

"It does no good to seek happiness. It almost always hides from those who pursue it, while it comes to those who do not give it a thought. Let humans avoid suffering, and the simple contentment of living will suffice. Happy are the unconscious; they neither suffer nor enjoy; they possess the true life."

These stanzas, magisterially recited by the young artiste, gave our young friends an exact idea of the general disposition of our minds at the present time.

Jacques listened, seduced by the charm of the music. An intimate rebellion, however, rose up within his being, and the words "pagan" and "paganism" emerged mutedly from his mouth. The word "pagan" seemed, in his mind, to contain an irremediable condemnation of everything he heard. In Bourbon, if such theories had been emitted in his presence, he would certainly have raised a violent protest—but he was not at home, and understood that he must restrain himself.

As for Philippe, he was less conflicted. He surrendered himself without constraint to the pleasure of hearing a beautiful voice deployed in an absolutely free air.

In whatever manner one understands life, he thought, *the objective of leaders of people is nearly always the same, and the results obtained don't differ essentially from one civilization to another, at the same terrestrial latitude. Nevertheless, there's a great distance between these vague and relaxed theories and our ancient beliefs, so beautiful and clear.*

The third and final stanza enumerated the different forms of life; the singer celebrated the beauties of vegetable life, and the grandeur of sidereal life. She specified how those two organisms were combined in the animal organism and how a single motion animates everything that exists.

"Nothing is stable in nature. It never stops. It is renewed by incessant change. Human beings vary according to the weather, their age, the season, their attitude, the time of day, heat and cold. The earth too is modified. The heavenly bodies drawn through space change their orbits every day.

"And humans remain anxious before this continuous palingenesis, in the bosom of that infinite agitation. They are like little children then, on the threshold of their ignorance, and, applying the ideas of the human brain to the immensity of space and time they ask: at what time were these luminous or obscure globes fashioned? What hand set the in circulation? What purpose do they have? How long will they endure? And what is my own origin? Did I emerge from humus, ether or water? Did I begin as a seed? Am I the product of a fortuitous fermentation? Or did I first appear as an adult under heaven? Insane are they who cannot stop before the abyss of the unknowable. Everything that is said and everything that is thought on that subject can never be anything but error.

"The earth is the seat of human life, but it is also our prison. We are riveted to it like plants, and our minds cannot, under pain of vertigo, surpass its horizon. Let us beware. If we were to pierce the mystery of life, its charm would be broken. For humans, it is a joy not to know the future, as it is to forget the past."

The ship continued its progress. Darkness had fallen. Through the blue of the atmosphere, the planets now appeared like golden nails. The coppery orb of the moon standing out in all its clarity, seemed suspended only a few cables away from the vessel. The entire audience, including the crewmen and the Africans, were listening in the profoundest silence. Their gazes, like rays of starlight, all converged on the singer.

The latter concluded her recitation in a slow and deep voice. Her eyes plunged into infinity, her arms extended in a grave and ample gesture, she resembled some priestess of sibylline evocation. In the blue-tinted penumbra, her form was profiled in its entirety. One might have thought her the genius of the impenetrable.

A brief moment of silence succeeded the incantation.

Then, changing the theme, Rosa Myrtil successively intoned other pieces from her theatrical repertoire.

In his turn, Jacques de Vertpré, solicited by the audience, performed a few songs from the Kingdom of Bourbon. By means of one descriptive song of a very original turn he presented to the imagination of the audience the deep harbors of the island, its volcanic peaks, its towns built in amphitheaters surrounded by coconut palms, its terrible storms, and its thickets of bamboo, which rendered sounds similar to those of a lyre under the caress of the wind.

Then he intoned his country's national hymn:

"The shadow of error has descended over our great fatherland; we have fled, carrying the torch of faith...

"The Master of the World who fashioned us in his image bears the name of God. He is a personal being...he has created humans in order to be inhabitants of Heaven. This life is merely an ordeal. The true life is in the beyond, happy or unhappy. That life is eternal. Humans arrive there such as they were on the last day of their terrestrial life.

"God has formulated moral law himself. He specified its rules in a definitive fashion when he came, twenty centuries ago, to spend thirty years on earth. The bishops inspired by him are his ministers.

"The primary sacrament is the Order that makes priests; the second is the Coronation that makes kings.

"A king crowned by a bishop is inviolable. He is the absolute master of everything outside Religion.

"Catholics alone can make their salvation. It was in order to guarantee, to them and their children, the faculty of achieving a happy eternity that our fathers took the road of exile.

"Good is good; he condescends to the wishes of those who pray. A day will come when he will render light to his chosen people, and Israel will return to the cradle of its ancestors..."

It was already late. After a few mutual felicitations on the good employment of the beautiful evening, everyone went down to their cabins.

After a few moments, nothing could any longer be heard in the silence of the night but the monotonous lapping of the waves and, from time to time, the curt instructions of the officer of the watch to the helmsman.

XII

The following morning, quite early, Philippe Martinvast was on deck, pacing back and forth, while his young cousin stayed in the saloon to write a letter to his mother. He was nonchalantly smoking a cigar when he saw the steward coming toward him.

"I beg your pardon, my dear Monsieur," the latter said. "I regret having to restrict your liberty, but smoking is not permitted on board. The ship is a floating house, and the prohibition of tobacco is a house rule."

"Oh! Forgive me—I haven't seen any mention off that prohibition anywhere."

"There is indeed no notice to that effect, but the prohibition is so generally known that there is no need for one. It is, in any case, one of the conditions of the national grant that we receive."

"The Society Against Tobacco Abuse must have become very powerful to have such provisions inserted in your schedule of conditions."

"There is no Society Against Tobacco Abuse any longer, Monsieur Martinvast. Today, it's the legislature that makes war against that deadly narcotic, in the hygienic interests of the race. Tobacco has been driven out of schools, the army, workshops and railways—everywhere that regulation can take effect. At present, the battle is won; people hardly smoke at all. To do so it's necessary to isolate oneself, to hide. Smoking has become a vice, almost a shameful vice."

The steward could not help finishing his sentence with an expression of total disgust.

"How terrible!" exclaimed Philippe, smiling—and he threw his cigar into the sea. "No matter," he added. "France has lost a good source of taxation. By cleverly taxing tobacco, alcohol and gambling, a State can generally satisfy its general needs. What have you done with regard to alcohol, then?"

"Alcohol has almost suffered the same fate as tobacco. Once, it was found everywhere, and it was moderately expensive. Today it's sold for its weight in gold, and can only be procured by means of numerous formalities. It has, so to speak, ceased to fulfill any alimentary function."

"And is it to the temperance societies that you owe that good result?"

"No. Here again, it's the legislature that acted and, without mounting an attack on individual liberty, has succeeded in changing education and custom. It understood that the primary interest of a country is the vigor of its inhabitants and did not want the public budget to have an interest any longer in the development of habits prejudicial to health."

"Do you at least export it"

"It's no more appropriate for us to poison foreigners than our own people."

"But what have you done with the industry, then? What has become of the flourishing manufacture that extracted alcohol from cereals, vegetables, tubers, wood, rags—everything—inundating France and neighboring countries with its produce and measuring its profits in millions?"

The steward did not reply immediately. He was confused by the profound discord that can arise between two minds by virtue of the different environments in which they have been formed.

"Industry," he replied, after that pause, "seems to us to be made, not to enrich the industrialist no matter what the cost, but to furnish useful products. If it is supported by an artificial and harmful need, we refuse it any encouragement; and, far from opening outlets for it, make every effort to redirect its effort toward other objects. Industry is shaped for the benefit of the consumer, not the consumer for the benefit of the industry. Such is our system today."

"But they still have to find these other objects of manufacture you mention. And civilization, as you must know better than I do, consists in the main of artificial needs. I can easily believe that you've discovered new superfluities, which are healthy, or at least inoffensive, but permit me to tell you that you seem to have become very austere in your modern France. What have you done with gambling? Doubtless you've pursued all its manifestations with the death penalty."

"Oh no! Don't worry, Monsieur Martinvast—the death penalty is reserved for true criminals. Perhaps you'll think us inconsistent, but we haven't judged the passion for gambling as redoubtable as the ones we were discussing just now, which lead to alcoholism or stupidity. It can't have any great extension today, in any case, for individual fortunes are very restricted. Without encouraging it or applauding it, we consider gambling as licit, and the debts contracted thereby are obligatory. It's a good lesson, it appears, for a gambler who has lost but does not want to pay to be forced to cough up."

"I say once again that you've deprived yourselves of a excellent source of taxation."

The steward could not help smiling. He nodded his head, in the manner of someone who has a surprising revelation in store for his interlocutor. "Well," he said, after a brief pause, "I can see that you still have feudalistic and bourgeois ideas. Be assured that I'm not accusing you of any crime, but the world has moved on quite rapidly in the last century. If you imagine that we still maintain on our land and sea borders, on our roads and in our smallest villagers, that army of customs officers and tax collectors who once covered the nation, you're strangely mistaken. No, we're no longer in the times when half the French were occupied in shaving and skinning the other half and one could not carry out any action of civil life without paying, when everything was ransomed: consumption, circulation, even the death of individuals, and the money thus raised was dispensed in welfare and unnecessary subsidies. We no longer have any indirect taxation. International trade is free, and only unhealthy things are prohibited."

Philippe's eye opened wide, as he sketched an incredulous smile. The steward added: "The State provides for its needs by means of its land revenues and, if there is a need, contributions agreed by the provinces. A province, in its turn, maintains itself by contributions agreed by the cantons, a canton by contributions agreed by the citizens..."

"Ah!" cried Philippe, interrupting him. "There we are, all the same. For me, indirect and direct taxation amount to the same thing."

"Wait, wait—for this is the most remarkable innovation. I shall doubtless surprise you. Listen: the contribution is the same for all the citizens of the same canton. Ah! You didn't expect that, I'm sure. The maximum and the minimum are determined for the entire country by State legislation; this year it's seventy francs in the locality to which I'm attached. The province and the canton contribute according to the number of their inhabitants."

"It's certainly a very simple method," Philippe observed, who was utterly astonished but sought nevertheless to remain calm, "but I confess that I don't understand a uniform contribution for all the inhabitants of a locality. How can the rich and the poor be subject to the same charge?"

"Your reflection would be just, Monsieur Martinvast, "if pecuniary inequality still reigned among us as it did in the past, but differences of condition have been significantly ameliorated, and what had to happen has arrived; political equality has, at length, given rise to contributory equality. What is contribution? It is, in principle, the counterpart of political power. Well, since political power is the same for all citizens, is it not just that contribution should also be the same?"

"Very good, Monsieur—that's one new items that will certainly make a deep impression on my compatriot when I return to Saint-Denis and tell them about it. I shiver at the thought of what Monsieur Adolphe Say,[12] the hereditary chief

---

[12] The Says were an important family in the history of French economics, being descended from Jean-Baptiste Say (1787-1832), a famous champion of free trade. Jean-Baptiste's brother Louis-Auguste was as fierce an opponent of Adam Smith as Jean-Baptiste was a supporter, and his descendants might well have taken a different view of the Third Republic,

of our economic sect, will say about it. We assumed, dare I say, that you were submissive to progressive taxation, with all its corollaries of inquisition, denunciation, harassment, corruption and so on. We imagined that your fiscal system had no other aim but to prevent the excessive accumulation of savings. But no, I see that you have wanted...how shall I put it?...to keep things simple."

"I'm not saying that we've always had a situation as simple as it is today," the steward remarked. "In this matter, as in so many others, we've undertaken experiments, some of which have been painful. Then again, we had an arduous task to fulfill. It was necessary for us, as you have doubtless suspected, to pay the debts of five or six generations. Oh, I don't want to speak ill of our 19th century ancestors—the century that we call today "the century of borrowing." We honor the memory of our forebears and we know that they were at grips with exceptional difficulties. It's no less true that we found ourselves in the situation of the son of a family of old, discovering only debts and mortgages in what appeared to be a brilliant succession. It was necessary for us to make many sacrifices, believe me, and a great deal of effort and discipline was required to liquidate that past completely.

"Today, fortunately, our burden is much less great. And in addition to the official social contribution we have, thanks to destiny, the purely voluntary contribution, on which we are fortunately able to count. If a locality has an exceptional expense to bear it appeals to the generosity of its inhabitants; if necessary, it organizes a lottery, and always gets out of difficulty.

---

but the entire family was Protestant, so it is difficult to imagine any of them following the clergy. Léon Say was a member of the government of the Third Republic in the 1870s and 1880s, but the text refers to him subsequently in a way that implies that he would not have joined the emigration, so this reference remains puzzling.

"By leaving a certain margin for individual enrichment, we have maintained one of the spurs of labor, and, in fact, have served the community well. The rich don't like to pour abundant funds into a public purse anonymously, but they willingly give of their own accord. Isn't giving, in fact, the greatest of joys and luxuries?

"Thus, by the influence of mores, proportionality, as it was once conceived, has been established in participation in general expenses. It is produced without constraint and conflict; it is not mathematical, but, without having the title, it is broadly progressive, believe me. The rich always pay more than others, and their whims are increasingly appreciated.

"In the cities you will see our gardens, our hospitals, our museums and our schools. Almost all these establishments are due to private liberality. The suppression of familial organization and the old regime of inheritance have given that current of generosity an extremely lively impulsion."

"I can believe it," said Philippe, who was uncertain whether to applaud or criticize. "What strikes me about all of this is that you seem, in certain respects, to have returned to antiquity. Thus, this voluntary contribution, this public offering, seems very primitive to me."

"I don't deny that, my dear Monsieur, but humankind does not march straight ahead, you know; its path is spiral. Our century, which differs so profoundly from the nineteenth, is closer to anterior ages. The only true progress consists of multiplying the number of people content with their lot. Well, that progress we have attained, believe me.

"The simple and the indifferent we have guaranteed against poverty. To the ambitious, the aristocrats and the ameliorators we have opened all careers. What can I say? Societies function naturally in the interests of those who rule them. Once, it was to the profit of a few individuals; today it is to the benefit of all the electors. I have no need to tell you that they are quite numerous."

"Ah!" exclaimed Philippe, as if the word "elector" had just reanimated the fire of the conversation. "Are there still as many voters as in the pat?"

"In fact," the steward replied, "there are many more, because the population has increased and because women have the right of suffrage. Proportionately, however, there are fewer, for the age of majority has been advanced to twenty-five, and there is some discussion of fixing it at thirty.

"Furthermore, those who do not make their contribution have been eliminated from the electorate, everyone admitting today that, in order to participate in authority, it is necessary to cooperate in communal charges. Contribution is, as I have told you, presently considered as the price of power. There are a certain number of French men and women who, in consequence of imprudence or debauchery, reach the point of no longer being able to pay. There are others who, out of indifference or avarice, take advantage of the opportunity that everyone has to refuse. All of those are deprived on the title of citizen or citizeness as well as the numerous and precious advantages attached to it. They have no political or civil capacity, and are denied the right to work as civil servants or to employ others.

"One of the major concerns of the general direction of the nation is that systems of education and contribution should be organized in such a way that young French people, having reached the age of majority, can easily acquit their debt to society. It is careful to ensure that the numeric force of neuters never surpasses that of citizens who pay their subscription.

"In sum, you see, the contribution is equal and voluntary, but only those who pay it in full are part of political society."

"Very good, Monsieur; you'll permit me nevertheless to remain bewildered by so much new information. It's too much for me—I can't assimilate such systems immediately. I can understand the equality of the contribution, but the facultative nature of the contribution...that's such a radical inversion, such a..."

"But that's the easiest thing to understand."

"How?"

"Hasn't indirect taxation always been facultative? Haven't the representatives of the people always been free to accept or refuse the budget? They've always voted it, you'll tell me, under pain of falling into impotence or barbarity. In the same way, we're careful today not to do that. Except that once, when the majority—which is to say, the greatest number—said: 'it's necessary to pay,' everyone was obliged to do so. Today, every individual remains free. Anyone who wants to refuse the contribution has only to give a year's notice.

"Ah, I see your difficulty! 'How is it that there are still people who pay the contribution?' you're going to ask. To that I only have one answer. The advantages attached to the title of citizen are always superior in attraction to the cost of their attainment. Do you see? That's the key."

Philippe remained silent momentarily. Then, his face cleared in a soft and sympathetic smile.

"Confess, at least, Monsieur," he said, "that it can still be useful sometimes to smoke. If I hadn't lit up just my last ever cigar now, you wouldn't have given me all this interesting information, for which I'm grateful."

With these words the two interlocutors separated, with a cordial handshake, and Philippe went to look for his cousin.

XIII

Jacques de Vertpré had thought that he would be able to take advantage of the morning to write a long letter to his mother. To that effect, he had installed himself in a corner of the reading room, hoping that the other passengers, when they left their cabins, would go straight up on deck and leave him in peace on his divan.

He had already written several pages when the door opened. It was Rosa Myrtil who came in, carrying a manuscript. The young woman was also in search of isolation, in order to learn a part. To say that she was acutely displeased to see Jacques would perhaps not be entirely accurate. But she had genuinely not expected to find him there.

She went straight toward him, while he stood up in order to bow to her. The conversation and concert in which they had both taken part had put them on the path to familiarity.

"Bonjour, Monsieur de Vertpré," she said, cheerfully, in an amiable fashion. "How are you today?"

As on the previous day, she was in masculine costume, but on a whim, she had let her beautiful chestnut-colored hair down to fall upon her shoulders. A discreet and delicious perfume, a kind of henna absolutely unknown to the young Bourbonnais, emanated from her entire person.

"Too bad—you've taken my place," she added, smiling. "Since my departure from Madagascar I've adopted the corner where you're sitting to learn my roles. What shall I do now? One can't breathe freely enough in the cabins; on deck one often breathes too freely and is not tranquil."

"But that can't be, Madame," said Jacques, swiftly. "I'll go and write somewhere else. I'll return your place to you—it's yours." He had already gathered up his pens and paper and made as if to leave."

"No, no," Rosa Myrtil said. "Let it not be said that I evicted you in that fashion. Stay…look, I'll sit down beside you. If I don't get much work done today, I'll catch up another day. What are you doing? Writing? Why not use one of the little boxes there?—it's much quicker, and always legible."

Jacques had, in fact, noticed as he came in a few boxes lined up on the table, like minuscule sewing machines. They were writing machines, but he had only looked at them vaguely and had not immediately taken account of their purpose.

"Those machines..." he said. "I think I'd prefer, even if I were able to use one, to make use of my hand. My letter is much more personal then. Isn't handwriting, like style, a reflection of ourselves?"

"As you wish...but permit me...are all these sheets one single letter? I understand...at sea, one begins to scribble. We have no telephone at our disposal here, and it's necessary to fill in the time. Even so, how can you compose such epistles? It surpasses all measure. No, truly, it's incredible. You still make use, then, in your epistolary correspondence, of those interminable phrases by which our ancestors made up for the penury of words, and remain hieratically submissive to the crazy rules of that old instruction manual known as orthography? How distant we are from one another! We write very simply; we only have one style for correspondence: the telegraphic style. Poor French language! It was once poorly furnished with expressions, and it's a miracle that people were able to create masterpieces with it in olden times that are still readable today. Scholars—particularly physicians—had horrible disfigured it with their pseudo-Greek bombast and their twenty-syllable words. It was only with difficulty that, from time to time, a worker or a child could introduce a short, picturesque and earthy word into the lexicon. What a change there has been in the last century! We've simplified the written and spoken language, and also condensed it, and, without the Académie getting involved, we've finally given a baptism—a French baptism, or at least modern baptism—to thousands of ideas that previously had no proper appellation. But my dear Monsieur, during the time it takes for you to write such a letter, one could type a whole volume."

"All right," said Jacques. "That's possible—but, excuse me, I don't like to live too rapidly. If one goes flat out at everything, one end up with nothing to do three-quarters of the time. Then one yawns, gets bored, and does unnecessary or stupid things. If I'm addressing myself to someone of whom I'm fond, I have the satisfaction of remaining in intellectual communication with her for longer."

"That's a different matter. If Monsieur is writing love letters, I have nothing more to say. Go on, tell your Bourbonnaise how nasty we are."

"Not at all. You're mistaken—I'm writing to my mother."

"Oh, it's to your mother..."

Madame Myrtil met Jacques' gaze momentarily, then looked down at the script that she had just opened on the table in front of her, and started leafing through it.

Their conversation, animated until then, was temporarily interrupted.

Jacques was about to resume writing when, turning to his neighbor, he said in a soft and hesitant voice: "Don't Frenchmen of today write to their mothers any longer?"

"Yes—children still love their mothers; and I don't need to tell you that mothers still love their children. All in all, though, the relationship is no longer the same as it once was."

"No longer the same, you say..."

"No, you heard correctly."

Rosa Myrtil did not seem particularly pleased to have to explain this point. However, as Jacques appeared to be waiting for a response, she continued.

"Firstly, as you know, children don't usually live with their parents; they only see them at intervals, on holidays or when they are visited. That's already a significant innovation. Then, as women often change spouses, family relations are doubly difficult to maintain. Finally, there is no longer the community of affection between brothers and sisters that once formed one of the principal attractions of the domestic hearth.

Full brothers and sisters—which is to say, children born of the same father and others—are rather rare nowadays."

At these words, Jacques started, and made an instinctive movement of revulsion.

"What do you expect," Madame Myrtil continued, "now that marriage no longer exists? And frankly, your marriage left much to be desired."

As she pronounced those last words she raised her head again and looked directly at her interlocutor. Her initial explanations had been embarrassed, but now she seemed disposed to speak more resolutely.

"What do you mean," said Jacques, resuming his original expression, "by my marriage?"

"I mean marriage as it was practiced in the 19th century, and as it is doubtless still practiced in your country. Let's see: marriage was invented, was it not, to favor the birth and education of children. Well, in the epoch of which I speak, marriage was virtually sterile—which is to say that men and women formed associations, not to follow the paths of nature, but to regulate them according to their whim, or, rather, to avoid them. Marriage was vitiated, for nature does not intend that human seed should be wasted.

"When, exceptionally, spouses faithful to one another abstained from mingling love with calculation and fraud, other evil features of the institution appeared. It wasn't rare for a woman to pay with premature death for the accomplishment of what she considered to be a duty. A first wife having been exhausted by the uninterrupted ordeals of maternity, the husband took a second, sometimes a third, who succumbed in their turn to the same duty. Tell me how that was human and reasonable! Other husbands, informed by sad experience of their inaptitude to furnish healthy offspring, were drawn in spite of themselves to engender more; matrimonial union made it a kind of necessity. The procreation feared by some was considered obligatory by others; and those fecund parents were sometimes infirm, or sick individuals afflicted with indelible infections, whose children could only be consecrated to vice or misery. Far from forbidding them to reproduce, the conjugal law engaged them to do so, almost forced them...

"However, if the couple remained deprived of offspring, in spite of their good will, it was not permitted for them to separate with a view to seeking an alliance more appropriate to their respective temperaments...

"Truly, there was no reason to be proud of that form of association. What do you expect? One does not associate indissolubly things of unequal duration without abuses of one sort of another resulting therefrom—but virility lasts longer than nubility.

"People ended up finding that regime a trifle barbaric, no longer answering to social necessity. Children had no need, as in incomplete civilizations, of remaining in the care and protection of those who gave birth to them. Once separated from their mother's breast, they found means at their disposal, in conditions of absolute security, entirely appropriate to favor their development and education.

"On the other hand, marriage was difficult to reconcile with the current of equality that was drawing us onwards. Children remaining in the care of their parents found inequality imposed upon them, for the number of births varied between households, either by the effect of will or that of chance. Now, on pay-day, the worker, clerk or functionary received the same wage, whether he was a bachelor or had five children for whom to provide. Who were the victims of that equality of salary, combined with the inequality of pecuniary burdens? Fathers in general, and, in particular, those who contributed most children to the nation. That lasted for nearly a century after the Revolution of 1789. Throughout that time, the country was submissive to those two contradictory rules; salary was calculated by the needs of a bachelor. Children, at least up to the number of six, remained the responsibility of the father, if he was married.

"How can one be astonished, in view of that, that the French race was in danger of extinction? Once the plurality of children was no longer a cause of fortune but a danger of ruin, it had to be the case. Oh, I know that there were still plenty of births in the poorer classes, where people were accustomed to misery and where it was permissible to extend a helping hand. But how can you expect a race to improve if its inferior products are the only ones to reproduce, and the elite is condemned to atrophy? By the elite I mean the group of those who have succeeded by virtue of their personal qualities—their intelligence, their hard work—in overtaking others. They are the ones who ought to have been engendering and raising the level of the race. But no—they had neither the inclination, nor the means, nor the courage.

"But the worst thing of all was the indissolubility of marriage, the absolute prohibition of changing anything in the contract that regulated its conditions. Why, I ask you, did the Revolution, the great Revolution, only prohibit lifelong commitments to the unmarried? Can you tell me? Why enchain oneself thus, when one has nothing in view but pleasure? The birds of the air only come together for a season, and do not do so with a view to a sterile coupling.

"Oh, how could anyone ever conceive of a world in which men and women, in order to live honestly, form pains in their youth on the basis of the most mobile of passions an association obligatory in perpetuity? Oh, how obvious it is that marriage had been regulated by priests, doubtless with a view to avenging their compulsory continence! Spouses weren't merely united; they were garroted, riveted to their chain. Today, that's the inexhaustible subject of our farces. When we need to laugh, that's what we talk about."

Suddenly changing her tone and expression, she added: "Oh, the wives, the wives!" Rosa Myrtil became suddenly animated, raised her voice and thumped the table. "How could our predecessors allow themselves to be reduced to such a role? They were no longer anything but wives, lovers, mothers. It was..."

She stopped.

She as beautiful thus, and stirring, while she deplored the fate to which, in her opinion, the old civilization had condemned her sex. Jacques, who had only endured her explanations with great difficulty, so shocking were they to his beliefs and habits, remained confused in confrontation with that sincerity and vehemence.

"Well, yes, Monsieur de Vertpré," she added, as she calmed down. "That's why your marriage, invented in the interest of the progress of the human species, was abolished by us, in the interests of the progress of the French race. In any case, it could not have long survived the emancipation of women, for whom it had been, for many centuries, nothing but disguised slavery."

"Madame," said Jacques, in his turn, "I don't want to wound your convictions in any way, but you will permit me to conserve, with regard to marriage, an appreciation other than yours. Nevertheless, like you, I have a firmly fixed opinion on the subject. We are not seeking to indoctrinate one another, are we, Madame? Otherwise, I would reply to you with arguments well known to all Bourbonnais, which are irrefutable. You're trying to justify your social innovations; that's fine; you're playing your role. As for me, I have only one thing to do: to preserve my way of seeing. Besides, I repeat, I am not married; you ought not, therefore, to have anything against me, and your critique cannot have any personal element."

"Oh, I don't have anything against you," Madame Myrtil replied, smiling.

At that moment, the head of Philippe Martinvast appeared, as he went past the gap in the doorway. He was evidently looking for someone or something,

"Ah! There you are, Monsieur Martinvast," Madame Myrtil shouted to him.

He came in.

"What about you—are you married?" she asked him, point-blank.

"Me? Why?" Philippe found himself suddenly nonplussed. It seemed to him that he had stepped on a piece of orange peel—but the unsteadiness did not last. Since setting foot on the boat he had come to expect surprises, and had become very circumspect. So, without further comment, he contented himself with relying, coolly and slowly: "No, Madame, I'm not married. I..."

"Then long live liberty!" Rosa Myrtil cried, petulantly, cutting him off.

With that she stood up, folded up her manuscript, and headed for the door.

As the young men tried to retain her she said: "No, no, let me be. I can't waste my time chatting like this. Goodbye, Messieurs Bachelors." And she disappeared, leaving our friends to themselves, each ready to make reflections that were not entirely obliging.

XIV

A few days went by, during which the journey continued without incident. When they crossed the equator, there were a few special celebrations reminiscent of hazing, especially among the crew-members, but nothing of importance.

The ship was approaching Aden. Other vessels appeared at intervals, coming from the Red Sea or preparing to enter it.

The captain had authorized our young travelers to go up on to the poop-deck with him, and they took advantage of his permission. They searched the horizon with telescopes, and followed the ship's trajectory on charts—and when the captain talked to them about the progress of science, new customs and recent international treaties, they hung upon his lips.

It had not taken them long to find out, once embarked, that Alsace and Lorraine had long since come under French jurisdiction, and that the Rhine, all the way to its mouth, served as a barrier to the German nation. They were, as one might imagine, profoundly glad to hear that, and had resolved to interrogate the captain with regard to the circumstances that had led to that fortunate event.

One day, when they were with him in his cabin during calm weather, with the ship placidly following its route over a smooth sea, they resumed conversation on that subject.

"It was doubtless at the cost of a frightful war," said Philippe Martinvast, "that the French recovered the lost provinces."

"No, no," said the captain. "The restitution was achieved peacefully, by means of a treaty based on the will of the populations, thanks to the moral ascendancy taken by our country, and also the effect of a new spirit animating the nations."

"Really?" said Jacques de Vertpré, astonished.

"My word, yes. You're doubtless wondering how the French were able to absorb the impact of their defeat in 1870 and renounce any revenge. That's one of the more astonishing facts of our recent history. It's difficult to explain the great patience that was required, but, at the present time, everyone deems that the generations that have elapsed between the terrible year and the epoch of the treaty of territorial reconstitution have thoroughly deserved posterity.

"In admitting that a war of revenge would have given us complete satisfaction, it would have been necessary to expect a German attempt at revenge, and thus from one revenge to the next, there would always have been war on the horizon, with its insane ferocity during hostilities and its slavery and ruinous expense in times of peace.

"When we were armed to the teeth in order to avenge ourselves, no one could any longer be found to raise the battle cry. Our fellow citizens in the annexed provinces did not want to be ravaged yet again by torrents of armies. The German were beginning to criticize the work of their great Bismarck; they found that their famous Emperor Wilhelm had been rather badly inspired in going to found a new German province on the left bank of the Rhine, and were not inclined to risk their federal system, their economic progress, their wealth and their acquired reputation for the conservation of a region hostile to German assimilation, which threatened to become a Poland or an Ireland—which is to say, a source of troubles, futile sacrifices and social disintegration.

"In France, commercial interests and family affections rebelled at the idea of a conflagration. People wondered whether the Republic was really responsible for the last errors and misfortunes of the monarchy, and easily found it possible to answer: No. Should they expose themselves to being taken for cowards by remaining thus armed? The world had been edified with regard to French bravery long ago, and recent generations surely did not cede anything to earlier ones. Was it not admitted by everyone that the reverse of 1870 was due of faulty organization, not a diminution of our worth? Was it, therefore, for the sake of mutual murder that the nations had made progress, had emancipated themselves? What was the purpose of all our scientific discoveries? Ought they to serve merely to perfect human slaughter? What about railways and telephones? Was it the case that they had only been invented to render instantaneous mobilization possible?

"People therefore remained in that state of mind for some years, everyone saying; 'It would be veritable folly to fight.' Meanwhile, public charges were accumulating: all the country's money and intelligence was converging on the army, and evaporating there in vain expense—which is to say, in pure waste. 'If we aren't going to fight,' someone said, one day, 'why squander all the nation's resources like this? Why allow ourselves to be stifled indefinitely by the yoke of excessive militarism? Are we going to continue to allow the youth of France to vegetate in the guardrooms and stables of barracks until we're completely exhausted?' Even the officers, on land and sea, were saying to one another: 'If, by the force of events, we're reduced to a purely gymnastic role as trainers of men, and if our rifles and our cannon only ever fire into empty space, what's the point of all our glorious braid, why our pensions, our medals, our privileges, our swords?'

"In the meantime, the democratic idea continued its progress. People administering their own affairs felt that they were being dragged into the broad path of large international federations, assembled under common laws of solidarity and arbitration. In reality, war no longer had any object. Why make war? Are there any royal patrimonies to increase? No. Are there people rebellious against civilization that it is necessary to put down? None. Do you want to reduce to slavery the inhabitants of a neighboring country, or do you fear being treated as serfs yourselves? But it has been a long time since war had that character. Between the victors and the vanquished, there is no difference once the peace treaty has been signed. War, let us admit, had become a matter of money. Now, is it appropriate for enlightened and honest people to enrich themselves by methods reminiscent of armed robbery?

"Everything went so well, therefore, that in time, Germany took advantage of the first diplomatic opportunity to give Alsace and Lorraine their independence. The compensations they demanded from France, for form's sake, were insignificant. Today, those provinces are part of the French Confederation."

While the captain spoke thus, Philippe and Jacques manifested their inner joy in their facial expressions: *How glad we are! And what joy there will be in the Île de Bourbon when we report this news.*

"But tell us, captain," Philippe added, "exactly what you mean by the French Confederation. It has been mentioned to us, but in a very summary fashion. What does this Confederation do? What are its attributes?"

"It does very little, my dear Monsieur. "You doubtless know what the present role is of cantonal circumscription?"

"We know that."

"Well, above the canon there is the province. That encloses in its bosom all the cantons of a region."

"Understood."

"Now, once, in the times of social pantheism, when the State provided everything, the provinces, or parts of provinces that were called départements, were all indistinctly submissive to the same regime. Today, the provinces are autonomous. Flemings and Provençals are no longer gripped in the same vice."

"Forgive me for interrupting, captain," said Philippe again, "but I imagine that, in consequence of the incessant displacements resulting from the ease of communications, there has been absolute fusion between the various elements of the French race, and that the division into provinces has lost its reason for being."

"You're mistaken; on the contrary, linkage to one's domicile has become very tenacious, and very important. Every Frenchman is required, by very reason of the furtive instability of residences, to have a well-established point of legal attachment somewhere. Then again, you already know, or must at least have deduced, that we no longer have any universal or obligatory military service, which displaced our fellow citizens far more than railways. Besides which, even if our nationals were drawn into perpetual motion, it would still be necessary to allow Provence, for example, and Flanders, the ability to regulate themselves differently, one does not think and act in the same way when one lives in Marseilles and when one is in Lille. Humans are, in fact, passive beings, as you know; they're like liquids that take on the shape of the vessels in which they're contained.

"The greatest liberty is thus granted to our provinces, as they grant it to our cantons. The regulatory authority of cantons goes as far as possible; beyond that, that of the provinces extends as far as it can. The Confederation assumes the rest—which is to say, concern for interests common to the entire country. It has, in order to be able to do that, a representative in the urban hub of every provincial and cantonal circumscription, alongside governors and mayors elected by their respective councils.

"The State watches over the frontiers, negotiates diplomatic treaties and occupies itself with international matters. Internally, it is in charge of everything concerning general circulation. Thus, it became the proprietor of all the railways. It does not exploit them but it creates them, maintains them and polices them. It guarantees throughout the land the principles of 1789—which is to say, the rules contained in the Declaration of Human Rights. It is also the sole custodian of armed force.

"It is also charged with guaranteeing individual security, and by that token, must ensure the repression of crimes. It arbitrates conflicts between the provinces, as the provinces arbitrate conflicts between cantons. It has at its disposal the means necessary to prevent the oppression of citizens by one another. By means of grants and rewards, it encourages and stimulates individuals, cantons and provinces in the paths that seem the best. Finally, it disposes of freely recruited legions made up of professional soldiers, in order to be able, if necessary, to pacify rebel or turbulent provinces and reinforce the troops of the Latin League when a significant conflagration takes place therein."

At that moment, the attention of our two young men was stung once again. "What is the Latin League?" they asked, at the same time.

"The Latin League," the captain replied, "ought to have been in question already, it seems to me, when your grandparents' exodus took place, for even in that epoch, people were talking about a United States of Europe. It forms a kind of first tier of international association.

"Pay close attention. You can discover in the classification of peoples something analogous to the gradation that goes from the canton to the State via the province.

"The Latin League, reconstituting, so to speak, the old Roman Empire, has united in a single bundle all the countries of Southern and Central Europe which have a racial and linguistic affinity. Its action extends today all around the Mediterranean and as far as the mouths of the Rhine and the Danube. It supervises the interests common to all those countries, arbitrating their difficulties and pacifying their conflicts.

"For some years, the movement of concentration and mutual trust that initially brought together the older civilizations has been further propagated, and we shall see before long, above the Latin League and the other similar associations of the old world a new tier in the hierarchy, which will be called the European Union. After that will come the Continental Union.

"Thus, thanks to the progress of education, communications and trade, it is now permissible for us to glimpse and even more complete progress. The continents will unite with one another; earth and humankind will be administered and protected by a supreme authority, in which all the great human families will be represented."

The captain had got to his feet; Jacques and Philippe had followed his example. All three were now standing on the bridge, looking out into the silent immensity.

Our young Bourbonnais did not know whether not to believe everything that the officer said, so implausible did his assertions seem to them. *Perhaps*, they thought, privately, *we're dealing with an enthusiast, eager to syndicate the planets and the stars.* Their skepticism and mistrust showed in their entire attitude. For a few moments, the three interlocutors strolled without saying a word, the captain taking account of the embarrassment of his two passengers, but doing nothing to help them out of it. He was content to observe them from the corner of his eye.

Jacques de Vertpré, making an effort to collect himself, finally broke the silence and resumed the conversation.

"Well captain, considerable changes must have taken place in ideas, and astonishing reactions. So the idea of the Fatherland..."

"Ah!" said the captain, swiftly, interrupting him. "I expected that. Well, if you care to reflect upon it, you'll see that the idea of the Fatherland that is rightly so dear to you, which consoled our ancestors for a while for vanished supernatural beliefs, has not disappeared but has merely been enlarged.

"What is the Fatherland, in fact? It's the limit of our customary horizon, the frontier where our interests stop, beyond which there is no longer anything for us but indifference, hostility or the unknown. In the early days of our history, when comtés and provinces were incessantly at war with one another, the Fatherland was a territory of three or four thousand square kilometers. Later, the ancient rivals of feudal Gaul came together and formed alliances, either against the English or the Germans. The Fatherland was then already more extensive—and on the other hand, war was less frequent. That double movement has continued ever since, peace making progress as the idea of Fatherland was enlarged. The ideal, as I said, is Fatherland Earth."

"Do you think, then, captain, that if we ever arrive at that distant goal, there will be no more fighting at all?"

"Oh, no—that's not what I think at all. I believe that there'll still be fighting, that there'll always be fighting. There will be times when these associations of peoples that I'm mentioned will be temporarily dislocated, and that within each people there will be sudden uprisings, and unexpected bouts of madness. There will still be riots, rebellions and civil wars, like the Sonderbund war in Switzerland and the War of Secession in the United States.[13] It's necessary to resign oneself to the occasional reappearance of anarchy in the world, with its great ugly head. But war will become an exceptional occurrence, a historical catastrophe. It will no longer be an endemic state, as in the times of barbarism and the Middle Ages. It will no longer even be a chronic state, always threatening and, so to speak, periodic, as in the recent centuries of our history.

"Within the limits of the Latin League, this is what has happened. Peace is as secure as it was within France a hundred years ago. For that, we have a Latin army, which is responsible for maintaining international order. That army is strictly subordinate to the representative power, and the administrative head of the League can command it in person. That, you know, is one of the surest guarantees of liberty and peace. When the army is not fighting, it is employed in works of general interest. Later, perhaps, we shall have a European army. Then, who knows, that of the old continent, and, as you say, that of the Earth: the Police Force of Humankind..."

On hearing these words, Philippe and Jacques could not help bursting into laughter. In their eyes, that was to push the field of hypotheses beyond all imaginable plausibility. Immediately correcting that involuntary and perhaps irreverent impulse with words, however, they said: "Of course, of course. All that is rigorously possible, and it would incontestably be a very fine thing."

"You understand," the captain went on, definitely getting slightly carried away, "that when a several generations have gone by in a land like Europe, without people trying to kill one another, the danger of war is significantly reduced.

---

[13] The Sonderbund War of November 1847 was caused by the desire of seven Catholic cantons to isolate themselves from their Protestant neighbors (Sonderbund means "separate alliance), but their attempt was rapidly crushed by armed force.

"You also understand that as soon as a League id formed, or even a union of Leagues, as it must have at its service not merely an army but an administration, a Parliament, it forms, by the same token, a more or less considerable group of people who isolate themselves from their local interests and become citizens of the League. They constitute the nucleus of a new Fatherland. They are the primary guarantors of order in all the states in the coalition. That is how the growth of the Fatherland leads to the prolongation of peace, and vice versa."

"We do understand," said Philippe, in his turn, "that the future, and even the present, belong to large international organizations, to Zollvereins founded on a commonalty of interests.[14] It is still the locomotive and the telegraph wire that are the principal causes of these changes, are they not? But many objections present themselves to my mind when I envisage the movement of concentration that will suppress among the people what doubtless no longer exists among the people submissive to the egalitarian regime—by which I mean individualism.

"There are some of the objections to which can glimpse something akin to a solution. Thus, in your League, I imagine that there have been certain compromises between the confederated states, that one will provide the central service with its language, another with its monetary regime or its system of weights and measures, another its military uniform...but there are several details, captain, which remain obscure to me. For example, are the treaties of association that link States together perpetual or temporary? Do nations, in associating thus, abdicate to the profit of the Union their rights of sovereignty and property? Those are the questions I ask myself, and do not know how to solve."

---

[14] The Zollverein, or Customs Union, was founded in 1818 and expanded to take in most of the German states, becoming an important element of the unification of Germany as a nation state.

While listening to these observations, the captain nodded his head by way of assent. He saw with pleasure that Philippe, while raising question, was taking account of the phases through which human evolution had passed.

"Very good, very good, Monsieur Martinvast," he said. "I see what you're trying to say. No, we no longer possess our absolute national sovereignty, that's obvious. As soon as a nation emerges from its isolation and associates with another, it can no longer be completely independent. Its sovereignty passes to the Union—just as a savage ceases to be his own sovereign when he enters into community with others; which is to say that he becomes civilized.

"With regard to the treaties, we began by making, on a temporary basis, common and reciprocal laws for the inhabitants of frontiers, others concerning fisheries and pasturage, and yet others regarding industrial and literary property, the extradition of criminals, the international application of civil judgments. We applied local laws, not only to goods, but to persons, even strangers, on the pretext that all laws are laws of policing. Then, after some lapse of time, we perceived that in the domain of general interests, no significant differences remained between ourselves and our neighbors and that the barriers placed between our territories no longer served any purpose. Then we abolished the barriers; political fusion occurred and treaties of solidarity were made, formally renewable at first, then tacitly—a situation that ended up continuous and now seems unbreakable. Until now, every nation has striven to preserve its own property rights. But in time, the Unions will take them over and no one will contest it."

"In fact, then, you're linked together permanently."

"Permanently. Do you remember what France was a century ago? If in those days, a département had wanted to reclaim its independence or an ancient province had wanted to reconquer its sovereignty, they would simply have been retained, by armed force, in the French association—isn't that so? Or one would have said to their inhabitants: 'Go on, then, if it pleases you, but your territory is ours.' Well, States have become, or will become, in time, similar to those départements and provinces with respect to great patriotic personalities already created or yet to be created."

"But what will become of kings in the midst of this movement of concentration?"

"Only a handful of kings remain, retained by the traditional affection of their subjects. The majority have been expropriated."

"What! Expropriated..."

"Yes, expropriated for reasons of public utility, in exchange for a just and preliminary indemnity accorded to them and their family."

"Pardon me, captain—just one more question," Philippe put in, "for my head is turning in the midst of this reordering, this new gravitation for which the narrow horizons of the Île de Bourbon has not prepared me. To speak only of the Latin League, is it universal suffrage that appoints the members of the supreme assembly, Diet or Congress?"

"Ah, you fear, I imagine, Monsieur Martinvast, that electors have still to choose, as they once did, between candidates whom they do not and cannot know. No, no, reassure yourself. The electoral system has been greatly simplified. The members of the Congress are elected by the Parliaments of each nation. Those—I don't know whether you know this—are elected by the Provincial Councils, and so on; which is to say that the members of the Provincial Councils are themselves elected be the Cantonal Councilors. Only they are the product of direct universal suffrage."

"Good, good," said Philippe. "That gives me great pleasure. Can you imagine that I still thought you were prey to the electoral system of a hundred years ago—a puerile and barbaric system full of ambushes and frauds, as we can now agree between ourselves."

"Oh, it's been a long time, Monsieur, since we emerges from our swaddling-clothes. Before arriving at the very simple system in place today, however, we took some false steps, I can assure you. Thus, to cite only one of our attempts, we

81

funded at one time, full of hope a mechanism that we called the capacitory regime. All the citizens were passed through a sieve, taking account firstly of their intellectual aptitude and secondly of their physical strength. They were divided into three categories, corresponding approximately to primary education, secondary education and higher education. Those who came, by virtue of their intellectual aptitude, into the first and second classes were lowered by a class of their physical aptitude left something to desire. Thus, we were to have three electoral colleges, the primary college for local elections, the secondary college for regional elections and the superior college for national elections.

"It was all very fine in theory. Selection was operated on the basis of personal value, seriously established. The superiority rested on real factors, intelligence and strength, which ought to march hand-in-hand to constitute an elite. What good is mind if the body is impotent? What good is strength if it is in the service of ignorance? Well, it didn't succeed. The triage was carried out at the age of majority—which is to say, at twenty-five. But there were belated intelligences that only reached their perfect development at a later date, then baring electors of an inferior rank to important situations. There were doctors whose development was already almost extinct at the same age. The system failed, therefore in several respects. For that reason and others that it would take too long to list, the trial failed. It was quickly thrown on the scrap-heap of parliamentary old moons.

"But I believe that I'm forgetting myself in educating you, young Telemachus," the captain went on, smiling. "There's the port of Aden appearing in the distance. Ships are becoming more numerous. Do you see that line out there on the horizon? That's the ancient land of Egypt. It's time I had a word with the engineer and the helmsman. I'll leave you, until later."

82

XV

Philippe and Jacques would have liked to continue their conversation with the captain. They remained preoccupied with the fate that events might have brought to navigation of the Red Sea and the isthmus of Suez. Given the very cordial farewell that he bid them, however, they could not insist.

"If we were to go to see the steward," Philippe said, "he could doubtless bring us up to date with what has become of the work of Ferdinand de Lesseps. I remember that at one time, England wanted to take possession of it, and all the maritime nations, in order to avoid that usurpation, dreamed of seizing a parcel of land somewhere along the strait in order to establish a fortress; which would have given each of them a 'right of veto' on the circulation of ships. Who knows? Perhaps all the countries given to navigation have a pass key; which would, in parentheses, make that link between the Occident and the Orient a very precarious one. Perhaps, on the contrary, it ended with a veritable neutralization. The steward will be able to tell us about that."

"Let's go and try," said Jacques.

They went down to the deck. The steward was not there. They looked for him everywhere, in the offices and in the vicinity of Madame Listor. They did not find him. Eventually, they discovered him in the dining room, in conference with the head waiter, whose accounts he seemed to be checking.

"Well, Monsieur," said Philippe, heading toward him, "We're approaching the Red Sea, it seems—so we're going to see the land of the Pharaohs and traverse the whole length of that sea fertile in miracles."

The steward smiled, realizing that they wanted to talk to him. "Indeed, Monsieur Martinvast," he said. "In a few hours we'll be calling in at Aden. As you can see, I was just giving instructions to the majordomo, who will go ashore there." Turning back to the latter he gesture permission to withdraw.

"You're about to arrive," he continued, "in the promised land of cosmopolitanism. From Aden to Suez there's a kind of great gallery, in which all kinds of people rub shoulders and all languages echo. A universal Capernaum and Sea of Babel! It's no less true that it's there, in the crucible hollowed out between the torrid plains, that the nations of our hemisphere have commence to fuse. It's the cradle of the Federation of the Ancient Continent.

"There, where the great entrepreneur de Lesseps only saw a canal—a material task in the tradition of the labors of Hercules—and which might have been a cause of permanent international jealousies and armed conflicts, there is now a common base of alliance for all the nations east of the Atlantic. All peoples, white, black and yellow, have appeared on this shore, either in the hope of having total or partial domination over it or extracting a tribute from it. They have seen that the place cannot be taken by one alone, and that there would be no point in several occupying it, and have held out their hands. For the first time, a pact was drawn up linking all the nations of the Old World, having for its objective the conservation of a great terrestrial amelioration, its maintenance and use. It's there, as I said, in the location of primitive civilizations, that the first foundation-stone of true and final civilization has been laid."

"We were looking for you, Monsieur," Philippe interjected, "precisely in order ask what has happened in this region in the last century."

"I'm very happy, Monsieur Martinvast, to have anticipated your desires. The Red Sea, from Aden to Suez, is an absolutely free channel of communication, administrated in the region of the de Lesseps canal by a cosmopolitan company. The privilege conceded to the illustrious founder has been renewed, but the toll imposed on ships had diminished considerably; its purpose is to remunerate the company for the expenses of maintenance and improvement. The company, in which many individuals and many interests are grouped, has become something akin to a small Republic, reminiscent of the old East India Company. If, one day, the continental Union of the Old World is completely realized, it's doubtless there that it will have its seat. Egypt, in the meantime, lives in part on the produce of its concession. By the way, you presumably know that the Sultan reigns in Cairo today..."

"No, we didn't know that," said Philippe, with a surprised expression.

"Yes, the Commander of the Believers has taken refuge in the Nile Valley. Russia, which sought for a long time to warm its feet in the sun, has taken Constantinople. Stamboul has become the southern pendant of Moscow, the old city of the North. To get back to the canal, it was decided, with a view to guaranteeing liberty of passage, that no warship, or even commercial vessel, should anchor on the edge of the Red Sea within a radius of fifty miles."

"And what about Panama?" asked Jacques de Vertpré, abruptly.

"Panama! The Panama Canal, after giving rise to embarrassments no less considerable, has produced an international effect even more considerable. Not only has it aided the Federative movement considerably in both parts of the New World, but it has opened the way to worldwide ecumenical association. All peoples, in fact, make use of it and profit from it.

"It's the sea that has long given rise to attempts to make contracts between nations. While the habitable land was divided as property between the peoples, the sea didn't belong to anyone. It was the great road, the public highway of humankind. Now, in a civilized world it's necessary that free circulation be assured. In order that a bold hand might be extended over the Oceans, modifying communications and relationships, there needed to be consultation between peoples and compromise. Fortunately, that is what has happened, and a kind of revision of the seas has taken place. Anywhere that one nation inhibited circulation, it has been persuaded to withdraw. Thus, Gibraltar has been expropriated and neutralized in its turn.

"That regulation has not, however, suppressed the privilege that each nation possesses by right over the liquid strip bordering its coasts. There are still so-called territorial waters, just as there is now territorial air..."

As he pronounced these final words, slowly, the steward looked into the eyes of his two interlocutors. He expected to see some emotion produced in their expressions, and wanted to enjoy the effect.

They, having pricked up their ears, had indeed fallen into bewilderment.

"What is territorial air?" asked Philippe Martinvast. "What do you mean, Monsieur?"

"It's quite simple. We mariners are no longer the only navigators. For some fifty years, aerial navigation has been practical and we have colleagues on high above our heads. The air has therefore become a means of communication, like the sea. It has been agreed between the nations that each country should have a right of sovereignty and policing up to five hundred meters above its territory."

"Really?" Philippe exclaimed, enraptured. "Balloons—I mean what our forefathers called balloons—are now steerable, like boats, against winds and cyclones! My God, what a feat, what a marvel—what a revolution that discovery must have brought about! After that of horseless carriages and correspondence by iron wire, that of boats without water! It's scarcely possible, that being realized, that social organization can resist upheaval."

"You're right, Monsieur Martinvast, nothing as important has been produced since the great emigration—which is to say, since the voluntary exile of your forefathers. The consequences have been multiple and immeasurable. Now that the invention is familiar and exploited, nothing seems simpler and it's astonishing that humankind had to search for so long for the solution. You'll see that. As a boat resembles a fish, an aerostat is modeled on a bird. It's reminiscent of a gigantic eagle carrying a certain number of superimposed gondolas in its claws. It's powered by electricity. And there aren't only balloons; there are also flying men, and aerial cyclists. The moon, my dear Monsieur, our satellite, our future colony, is awaiting its Christopher Columbus. But I don't want to spoil your surprises and admirations. I repeat; you'll see that, and you won't fail, I'm sure, to be interested by it."

"Certainly!" exclaimed Jacques de Vertpré in his turn. "But how is it that we haven't yet seen any aerial vessel?"

"Like birds, my dear Monsieur, aerostats are made for flying over land. They can't, without exposing themselves to particular dangers, fly over great liquid plains like those we are traversing. They do—there are some that go from France to America—but it's exceptional. Thus far, the competition they provide to maritime navigators like us is not redoubtable, especially in the regions south of Aden, where there are no mooring towers for them."

At these words, with a single movement, the two young men raised their heads interrogatively. The steward continued.

"Yes, I need to tell you that, since you've drawn me that far—although I would have preferred, I repeat—to leave you the pleasure of the discovery. Just as a ship, once launched, remains in the water for as long as it lasts, an aerostat, once in suspension, remains constantly in the air. At its point of departure and at aerial stations it finds mooring towers, which serve for the ascent and descent of both goods and passengers. The first French aerial convoy departed from the Eiffel Tower. How many towers have been constructed since then is incalculable, and almost all the old bell-towers of churches are still used. At the top of those edifices, great aerostatic scaffolds are replacing the old telegraph aerials. All the tall buildings you will soon see, bristling on the surface of civilized lands, are like vertical stations. They're immense elevators surmounted by powerful hooks.

"That's amazing—extraordinary," repeated Philippe Martinvast, in a hushed tone.

Jacques de Vertpré's enthusiasm, by contrast, had suddenly cooled at the thought that the ancient bell-towers constructed by Christianity had become part of the equipment of transport companies.

"But that's enough unveiling of what you'll soon see with your own eyes," the steward added. "Permit me not to tell you any more today."

"Thank you," said Philippe, shaking both his hands. "Thank you for the good things you've said to us. What a fine voyage we're going to have, in going to encounter all this progress!"

"We're truly very grateful," said Jacques de Vertpré in his turn, a trifle awkwardly, not succeeding in concealing his new irritation. "Yes, very grateful... Until next time..." As he spoke he bowed to the other.

XVI

From Aden to Suez the sea was constantly rough and the heat unbearable. Jacques de Vertpré, suddenly gripped by fever, spent in the entire journey in his bunk. Dr. Priot came to see him.

Dr. Priot was an excellent man and a very good physician. He immediately recognized that the younger cousin's illness was not serious, and contented himself with prescribing a few simple measures.

As he was about to leave, Jacques retained him.

"Perhaps I was mistaken, Doctor," he said, "to undertake this long voyage." His voice was plaintive. With his eyes fixed on the ceiling of his cabin, he seemed to be prey to some somber presentiment.

Philippe, who was sitting beside him, got to his feet. "Come on, Jacques," he said, amicably. "Are you going to let a temporary indisposition disturb you? You're suffering slightly from a change of air and diet, that's all. All of us are liable to our debt to fatigue in this fashion, aren't we, Doctor?"

"Indeed," replied Monsieur Priot. "Your malaise, my dear Monsieur, is nothing extraordinary or abnormal, and you have no reason, it seems to me, to regret your departure."

Jacques did not reply immediately. After a few moments, in the same tone, he said: "You're kind, Doctor, and I appreciate that. But you don't know what's happening within me…in my mind." Again he stopped and passed his hand over his forehead. A tear slid down his cheek. Then, bursting into sobs, his breast heaving, he exclaimed: "Doctor, the world I've glimpsed is producing an effect of repugnance."

"Why is that?" asked Monsieur Priot, gently.

"Because it's a world without God." Immediately, Jacques allowed himself to burst into abundant tears.

It was a touching and singular spectacle that our travelers' cabin offered just then: a tall young man crying like a little child in a fit of nostalgia provoked by fever; a physician astonished by the religious preoccupation that had appeared in the midst of the crisis, that kind of preoccupation not having been manifest in invalids for a long time; and Philippe, very embarrassed and a trifle confused by his cousin's weakness, and anxious about the responsibility he had taken in bringing the latter with him.

In reality, Jacques, impressionable and sensitive, was paying is debt not merely to fatigue, but also to all the surprises that he had already experienced and all the novelties he was anticipating. From all that he had learned and foresaw, there resulted for him an impression of emptiness and despair. His mind, dominated by religious ideas—especially the belief that mortal life is merely a preparation for an ulterior life—felt painfully tormented, troubled and chagrined by the thought that a great nation, his own, was going blindfold along the path of science and labor to...where, alas? To the eternal abyss, perhaps followed and accompanied, to complete the misfortune, but the great majority of peoples.

Philippe drew the physician to one side and explained to him that his cousin had already occasionally experienced, in Bourbon, similar fits of unhealthy emotion. In his opinion, there was no cause for alarm.

That was also the doctor's opinion.

They both came closer and Monsieur Priot, shaking his patient's hand, said: "Come on, my dear Monsieur, don't abandon yourself to dark thoughts. You're weak and emotional. You need to rest, sleep if possible. Keep calm; tomorrow you'll be in the pink again—or rather the blue, if the sea finally consents to calm down and resume its azure hue."

"The doctor's right," said Philippe, for his part, shaking his cousin's hand in his turn. "Try to fight it. Damn it, the Bourbonnais couldn't remain blockaded in their island until the end of the world. Perhaps France is in error in certain respects—that's possible—but doubtless in good faith. Then again, do you think that the good Lord, our Lord, will not be indulgent toward her?"

Jacques remained silent. A smile of resignation slid over his lips while he replied with a feeble squeeze to the hands that shook his, and when that moment passed, he was not displeased to find himself alone. The sea, which had begun to calm down, was nevertheless splashing noisily against the ship at every pitching movement.

The young traveler allowed himself to be lulled by that virile rocking, looking through the small porthole facing him at the green-tinted and foam-flecked waves that were racing after one another without ever catching up.

He was drowsy when a discreet hand knocked on his door.

"Come in!" he called, with a start—and he saw Rosa Myrtil appear.

The latter explained that she had been informed of his indisposition, and had come to serve as his nurse.

"You're really too kind, Madame," Jacques said to her, slightly embarrassed. "The doctor has just promised me that I'll be better tomorrow. Besides which, I have my cousin, on whose assistance I can count. I'm all the more grateful for your interest because I have no need of it. In truth, I'd hate to be an occasion of fatigue and annoyance for you."

"Ta ta ta," retorted the newcomer, laughing. "All that is words, old politeness, absolutely obsolete. We're going to subject you to our customs and mores." She expressed herself with playful gravity, as if she were talking to a child, accompanying her last words with solemn gestures, which were already bringing a hint of cheerfulness back to Jacques' face.

All this is very singular, he thought, unable to suppress a smile—albeit a slightly sardonic smile, pierced by intrigue and anxiety.

"This, my dear friend," added Rosa Myrtil, "is what is usual today. Men praise us, respect us, honor us; they desire to render us happy, and one might say that we are the unique object of their adoration. On the other hand, though, we are required to care for them in their maladies and indispositions. That is, in our view, one of our social missions. We put the

91

same devotion into it that the daughters of Saint Vincent de Paul once did. We're all Sisters of Charity now. You'll see."

So saying, leaning over the bed, she adjusted the sheets and the pillow. She cast an eye over the infusions and other remedies placed on the shelf on the bed-head. Then she picked up a folding chair and turned back to Jacques.

"Relax, then, handsome young Bourbonnais. Stay calm; I'll move back a little way. There! Pay no attention. I'll look over my roles. Sleep, if you can—and if you need anything, call me. Later, when it gets dark. I'll sleep in this cabin—over here, do you see?" And she went to touch the bed opposite his. "Unless," she added, returning and leaning close to the invalid's ear, "you'd prefer me to sleep beside you..."

At these words, the sick man shivered, and for a moment his eyes became wild. The young woman noticed that and realized that she had gone too far, too quickly—that she had been wrong to treat a novice traveler molded by the Île de Bourbon as a Frenchman of our day.

At the same time, through the vapors of the fever, Jacques perceived that it was not his mental curiosity alone that was going to make discoveries—that his affective qualities, his individual inexperience and his youth were going to be simultaneously put to the proof. He felt awkward, in an uncomfortable position, but he began smiling again.

Rosa Myrtil, confused by his bewilderment, was now looking straight into his eyes.

He gazed at her for a few seconds, timidly and obliquely. Eventually, he turned his head and buried himself in his bedclothes, contenting himself with stammering a few embarrassed thanks. He was eclipsed; only the top of his head could be seen.

Suppose we let him rest, dear reader—or try, or to pretend to rest—and go to see what is happening on deck.

XVII

The sea has become calm again; the atmosphere is gradually clearing, and the sky is resuming its brightness. Almost all the passengers are coming and going on deck, breathing the air delightedly and congratulating one another on the improvement in the weather. The ship's officers are passing among them, smiling and confident. In the bow, the black people are taking advantage of the calm to shake off their torpor and tidy themselves up.

Philippe Martinvast is accosted continually, and asked for news of his cousin. Madame Listor having insisted on being taken to see the invalid, they go together, and when they return they strike up a conversation.

"All in all, my cousin doesn't have much to complain about," Philippe said. "If he's suffering a little, at least, as you've seen, it's in pleasant company."

"It's the least that can be done for him," Fanny Listor replied. "Madame Myrtil is only doing her duty. If she hadn't got there first, it would have been me or someone else—any other female—who would have taken her place."

"After all," Philippe continued, "His illness isn't serious. From now on, it's not his health for which one might fear, but for…for…"

As he spoke he smiled ironically, but he could not find the word he needed, and Madame Listor, looking him in the eye, added to his embarrassment.

"What, then?" she said. "Of what are you afraid, Monsieur Martinvast?"

The brave Philippe had, perhaps a trifle hastily, desired to give the conversation a new tone. His cousin was not there and the circumstance had emboldened him. Nevertheless, he was beginning to bite his lip. The right note was not easy to strike. The foundation and form of conversations had changed so much in a hundred years, especially between men and women. He had not succeeded in extricating himself from the verbiage of our ancestors.

"I'm more afraid for his heart," he said, finally.

"Ah! I understand!" said Madame Listor. "What tenderness of expression, my dear Monsieur! His heart! But are you sure that the heart plays an important role in that?"

"For his virtue, if you wish."

"His virtue! What do you call virtue, then, where you come from?" And Madame Listor burst out laughing. "Of what does virtue consist, for a man? Tell me. In not becoming intoxicated, no doubt—by wine or by women? But is quenching a thirst getting drunk? Perhaps, too, that is only a negative virtue of the second order. What name do you give to honesty, courage and generosity?"

Philippe felt decidedly off-balance. Again he tried to reestablish his position.

"You understand, Madame, that when I tell you that I'm afraid for my cousin, it's just a manner of speaking. It was only in jest that I indicated to you the danger of losing...his virginity...there..."

"What, really?" exclaimed Madame Listor, turning sharply back to Philippe. Then she collected herself. "Yes—in fact, that must be; it conforms with your beliefs and your rules. But still, after all, it's very good. I admire that, personally—that one remains for a long time in novelty and bud...from the viewpoint of the improvement of the race, it's excellent...provided that one doesn't wait indefinitely.

"In France today we make every effort to keep our young adolescents and undersized twenty-year-olds on the bridle—the jury of virility often emancipates them too quickly—but we have difficulty doing so. The producers and the products suffer a great deal from the overly hasty cessation of that special state you call...virginity. Ugh! Leave that word, I beg you, to the fair sex...that state, I mean, which is your cousin's..." After a pause, she added: "And also yours..."

"Oh! I didn't say that," Philippe put in.

"What?"

"I didn't say that. Don't put words into my mouth."

"But you're from the same country, the same family, the same civil and religious legislation—the same era, so to speak."

"Possibly...but...enough; I'd rather not explain myself on that point. Let's talk about something else, if you please."

"I'd like that. It wasn't me, in any case, who raised the subject."

They remained silent for a few moments.

"So," Madame Listor resumed, after that lapse of time, "one isn't obliged to be entirely logical in Bourbon?"

"It is the same in Bourbon as elsewhere, Madame. Coherence is much appreciated there, but, in fact, inconsequence plays a rather considerable role. Should one complain about that? Is what we take for inconsequence really inconsequence? Is it not appropriate to follow one's instinct as well as one's reason. Some people claim, I'm told, that humankind as a whole only obeys its instinctive intuition, and that reasoning has no purchase upon it. Certainly, my cousin is a better man than I am; he's more serious, more sincere, wiser, and I hold him in particularly high esteem; but perhaps, I sometimes think, if he were in my skin, he'd act like me; and reciprocally, if I were in his, I'd doubtless do as he does. In religious matters I consider myself as orthodox, as faithful and as fervent as Jacques. Nevertheless, I'm led to believe that, on the present subject, the Church, our guide, asks too much of us to be sure of obtaining it sufficiently. That puts me sufficiently at ease, as you can imagine. I know, on the other hand, that it has indulgences ready for youth...maternal indulgence. All in all, you put it well: logic in a fine thing, but not to excess..."

Madame Listor smiled.

"Charming," she said. "Charming. Perhaps you're right, Monsieur Martinvast. You remind me of the Frenchmen of the *ancient régime*, as history depicts them for us. They were utterly charming, like you, it's said. What a misfortune to have lost that casual manner and that grace, that consummate artistry of life, which permitted the association of the most dissimi-

lar things, in order that they might be enjoyed simultaneously."

Philippe was not sure whether she was speaking sincerely or joking.

They went to sit down on a bench, as if to rest from their
strolling, and there, they watched the comings and goings mechanically.

"What are you doing, my dear Monsieur Martinvast?"
Madame Listor said, suddenly. "One might think that you
were dreaming."

"Me! Not at all. I'm observing, learning. The sight of
these people, these costumes, isn't yet familiar to me. I was
just making a reflection that might seem bizarre to you. It
seems to me, judging by the portraits of our ancestors, that
French physiognomy has been modified somewhat. There too,
it seems to me, uniformity will have made progress, and the
democratic mean must have imposed itself. I imagine that the
French men and women of today all resemble one another like
brothers and sisters. Is that true, Madame, or am I mistaken?"

"You're mistaken, my dear Monsieur. It's possible that
facial differences between the provinces have diminished. The
mean—the famous mean of which you speak—has been established, I believe, to some degree, while nevertheless raising its
former level with regard to height and strength. We have no
lack of individual eccentricity, though, and we possess in all
the provinces, you may be sure, very distinguished and very
varied specimens to our race, since we have taken the trouble
to cultivate it. You presumably don't know, yet, about our
competitions for the improvement of the human species. Well,
I, who am speaking to you, have placed first twice, once as a
young girl in a beauty contest, and then as a mother, after my
second child, in a maternity contest."

As Philippe bowed ceremoniously, she continued: "Yes,
Monsieur, and my entire preoccupation, I can tell you, the goal
of my life, is to have beautiful children. That's the chosen
basis of my glory."

Philippe nodded in approval, thus inviting Madame Listor to take her confidences further.

"I'm not dissatisfied with Fatma or Sadi—those are the names of my two children, who are traveling with me—but I hope for even greater success in future. Until now, I've proceeded by selection in the choice of my spouses; henceforth I'll try for the increase of the race. At present, I'm searching, making enquiries…when I get back to France that will be my primary concern, for I want to utilize my best years."

"You didn't find anyone satisfactory in Madagascar?" Philippe observed, softly, trying to abandon himself to the flow again.

"No; I left my last husband there, when his health deteriorated. He was no longer in shape."

"Oh, really…really…and aboard the ship, you haven't noticed anyone who might be suitable?"

"Nor here. For some time, I thought about the steward, and wondered if I should leave him aboard…that's why I employed him, from time to time, in rendering me small services. He's tall, it's true, and well-built, more thin than stout, and good-humored…unfortunately, he has a defect, a fault of construction—a limp."

"What!" said Philippe. "I hadn't noticed. What about the captain?"

"Oh, the captain's blond…for me, that's a deal-breaking vice. Besides, he has a wife in Marseilles, to whom he's engaged for some time to come."

At that moment, the steward passed by. He came down from the bridge, and was heading for the stairway to the saloons. He seemed to be in a great hurry. Philippe stood up nevertheless as he went past as if to shake his hand.

"Excuse me," said the officer. "I'm expected below and I'm late. How is your cousin?"

"Well enough."

The steward hurried off, but not without having bowed respectfully to Madame Listor. Scarcely had he gone than she

97

said: "You see. His left leg is a little shorter than the other, and one of his hips rises when he walks."

"Yes, perhaps," Philippe replied. "I hadn't noticed it until now."

"But you're not a woman," said Madame Listor, getting up in her turn and closing her fan. "Come on, it's time that you went back to your cousin. Excuse me for having kept you for so long.

They parted. Philippe watched his beautiful companion draw away, her gait proud and supple. At the same moment, a kind of flash passed before his eyes.

"Damn it!" he murmured. "The man who leads that woman to glory, the object of her desires, will be a very happy fellow, I swear."

With that he twisted his moustache, and, with who knows what ideas passing through his mind, headed for his cousin's cabin.

XVII

When one enters the Mediterranean from the Red Sea, it seems that one is arriving in a new world. The air is lighter and the sea's movements are gentler. One breathes a civilized atmosphere. From that moment on, a European feels at home and enjoys the ease of having returned to his natural environment.

It was at dawn on a mid-April day when the ship emerged from the strait of Port Said.

The blue of the sea was still partly veiled by mist, but in the distance, through the violet tints of the horizon, the sun was just visible, spreading its golden fingers and fiery coruscations on a warm spring day. Higher up, almost in the clouds, at the western extremity of the gorge, the statue of de Lesseps stood out sharply on its tower of pink granite, serene and silver-haloed.

All the passengers were outside early, congratulating one another on seeing the great sea again, considering with interest the friendly waves that extend from the land of the Crusades to the fortunate soil of France, bathing enchanted islands in the course of their journey.

The captain had announced, at the passengers' request, that on the day when they entered the Mediterranean there would be an on-board dance. There was, therefore, throughout that day, an activity of a special character. The ship was decorated with great care. Everyone took part in it—the crew, the passengers and the blacks.

When, in the evening, the fires of the sun began to die away, the ship—already a long way from the coast—was gliding over an admirable sea, entirely decked out with bunting. Its multicolored flags were flapping in a gentle breeze blowing from the isle of Cyprus. The orchestra, composed of a few musicians recruited from among the travelers, launched a few timid chords into the air, immediately restrained.

At about five o'clock, the dancing began.

At first there was a general round-dance, designed to get the entire audience animated and in movement. Even the children joined in, bringing their petulance and naïve gaiety to the diversion.

Sometimes, the chain swayed rhythmically, to the sound of antique refrains, repeated in chorus. Sometimes it hurtled from one end of the ship to the other, deploying its spiral in multiple folds.

The spectacle was very pleasant. The helmsman, left alone on the bridge with sole responsibility for the direction of the ship, could not help darting an oblique glance at it from time to time. The heads of the engineers appeared, curious and smiling, through the portholes of the engine-room. The Africans, crowded in the bow, all standing, leapt about, clapping their hands, seemingly desirous of mingling their voices with those of the dancers.

That round-dance was followed by several others, and the first sequence of the program lasted until nightfall.

At that time, the children retired, and the officers also went their separate ways. The lanterns were lit. On the illuminated ship, it was time for quadrilles.

Dr. Priot, who had just sat down on a bench, seemed disposed to play the role of spectator from then on. Half-suffocated by the heat, his upper body leaning back, he was fanning himself with his handkerchief.

Jacques de Vertpré, who was completely recovered from his indisposition, came to sit beside him, and was soon joined by his cousin Philippe. Our voyagers were no more disposed to continue dancing, being ignorant of its new manifestations.

"Well then, Monsieur de Vertpré," said the doctor, "dancing's a good remedy for fever. Why wasn't it offered to you a little sooner, eh?"

Jacques smiled and shook his head. "Dancing, you say, Doctor? It might yet play its part. My cousin and I had no fear of risking ourselves just now in the farandole, but with respect to the quadrille, we're doubtless barbarians."

"Perhaps so," the doctor went on. "Well then, do as I do and watch...let's watch together. I don't know whether you'll find great differences between our dances and old French dances—for I suppose that in Bourbon, you've conserved the dances of the century before last. Fundamentally, you know, dancing is still dancing..."

"Evidently," Philippe put inn, having sat down on the other side of the doctor. He was in the process of wondering whether, all things considered, he had been right to follow his cousin's example and retire from the fray so quickly. In the meantime, he had no objection to make to Monsieur Priot's aphorism.

The latter continued: "I mean that dancing is agitation, men and women letting themselves go. Why? To get into a good mood and invite one another to love. People agitate in much the same fashion everywhere, and always have. The black people we see over there doubtless put more savage ardor into it when they do it, while we bring more grace and temperament to it, that's all.

"I'd add nevertheless, going back to what one I said about our mothers and fathers, that we play the game more naturally and more simply than in the 19th century. Then, as now, ladies went to a ball more-or-less uncovered, but it was understood that it was not to charm the male sex; they were following the fashion and nothing more. The cavaliers put on airs, but it was not to be seductive; it was simply being a man of the world. There was no sincerity in a ball, except for the poor young women to be married off. No one was unaware of the fact that it was necessary to take them in order to...how shall I put it?...exhibit them.

"Today, people are more conscious of what they're doing, and don't hide it from one another. Furthermore, our dance parties—as you'll realize, especially when you get to France—are better organized, at least in my opinions. Once, balls were a medley of swayings, inflections and various rotations, alternating at hazard, with no plan or order. Today, they're regulated according to a gradation, a crescendo, which makes the mingling of gymnastics with passion into a very rational exercise."

"Pooh!" said Jacques, who did not hide his sentiments with regard to his indulgent physician "Do you, by chance, have the obligatory minuet? Or have you returned to dancing its ancient character of liturgical ceremony?"

"No, no, not at all, my dear Monsieur. But in the same way that there is in banquets, for the order of the courses, an order imposed by custom, there is a quasi-compulsory ordinance for balls. You'll soon see, and you'll be able to judge for yourselves."

The quadrilles, in themselves, did not interest the cousins overmuch. In fact, they resembled those in Bourbon. The costumes, gestures and attitudes attracted their attention more. Oh, in that respect, they were a long way from the island's customs. There was a great deal of liberty, and even, in their eyes, let us say, a certain amount of license. At the same time, they were obliged to recognize nevertheless that there was not overmuch poor taste.

This doesn't resemble one of our domestic balls, they thought, *but a public and carnivalesque ball exempt from both inconvenience and restraint. It's a harmonious and graceful excitation, in which, after all, we only see well-educated, polite people taking part, doubtless accustomed to the easy satisfaction of their desires, who are all able easily to mix intelligence and enjoyment in amorous and social relationships— plus a free-and-easy insouciance, thanks to which any danger of excess, conflict or explosion is removed.*

For both sexes, the costumes were naturally more adventurous than in everyday life. At the same time as they ensured a greater freedom of movement, they made bodily forms more evident, and left a greater surface area bare.

We don't wish to imply that Jacques de Vertpré was not, at any moment, shocked by what was happening before his eyes. As for Philippe, it was easy to see by the expression on his face that he was following the spectacle with a frank, almost naïve curiosity.

After the quadrilles came the fandango.

"At this point," said the doctor, "people dance communally, whether it be the minuet or a Spanish dance. Here on board, when there's a ball, we choose the latter for preference, for it isn't uncommon for us to have travelers from Spain with us. The character of the third act of the ball is that people dance, so to speak, in isolation, neither in groups not in couples. In the following act, it's the waltz. Oh, then there's enlacement...at present, as you can see, the man and the woman dance facing one another; they turn, go back and forth, deploying their graces in beautiful attitudes, putting into their faces everything they possess of tender allurement. They seek one another out, retreat from one another and fascinate one another mutually. For the spectator, it's much the most interesting part."

Combining words and gestures, the doctor continued to become more animated. He thought it best to restrain himself.

"I'm speaking," he said, lowering his voice slightly, "of a spectator like me, exclusively fond of pure beauty and disengaged by age from any suggestion of intimate alliance. As for you young people, beware—I fear that you might feel itchy legs and a muted desire to leap up and join the general whirl."

The music had changed its rhythm. The orchestra was now playing joyful Andalusian tunes, vibrant and cadenced. From time to time the castanets made their wooden rattle heard, like the call of a quail.

The new dance was in full swing when Madame Listor suddenly appeared, without anyone having seen her coming, in close proximity to our spectators. She seemed to be drawing her dancing partner, an Italian with a black moustache and a slender figure, toward her by means of voluptuous gestures; he too was putting a great deal of passion into his pantomime.

When the orchestra struck a particular chord they both stopped momentarily, face to face, in similar poses. Madame Listor, leaning slightly backwards, rounded her beautiful ivory arm over her head. Her half-closed eyes spread their soft light over her body, and her upper lip, shaded with a light down, sketched the most engaging of smiles.

For a few seconds she remained there, like a statue, scarcely touching the floor with the tips of her feet. Draped in the pleats of an almost-diaphanous dress, she displayed her irreproachable beauty like a flower in the sun, spreading around her person an aureole of delight. Only the breath in her bosom revealed the movement of life within her.

On a further orchestral chord, she collected herself, flexed her limbs, pivoted on her axis and disappeared, still accompanied by her cavalier.

"Well, young men," said the doctor, enthusiastically, "did you catch that vision? Did you share the dream?"

They were still trying to follow with their eyes, as far as possible, the superb alma that had just been eclipsed, so neither of them replied immediately to Monsieur Priot's question.

"You've just seen woman in her full splendor," the doctor added, "with all her seductive power. How perfect she is, that Madame Listor! She's divine…that's what we adore, we men of today, what we exalt, what we pursue…and it's certainly well worthy of our adoration, that magical beauty. It's true, isn't it? Take the richest and most glorious among us; to dispose of such a marvel, wouldn't he abandon, if he had to, all of his popularity and all of his fortune?"

"Well, Doctor," said Jacques, "it seems to me that you aren't yet the entirely disinterested and cool-headed spectator that you mentioned to us a little while ago."

"Oh, you think so? Well, so much the better. It's a sign of vitality, after all."

"I believe, in fact," observed Philippe, in his turn, "that women wouldn't explain themselves with such warmth with regard to the impression that the sight of Madame Listor might cause. It's evident, Monsieur Priot, that a certain masculine sap still remains; it hasn't all melted away within you, by any means. There's still ore in the mine."

While expressing himself thus, Philippe slapped his shoulder in a familiar manner.

"There's still ore in the mine," the doctor repeated, smiling, as if he were talking to himself. "Perhaps..." Then, slowly, with intermittent pauses, he added; "My youth still sings, you say...did you hear my life resonate?"

He became thoughtful.

Philippe, getting to his feet, called attention back to himself. He was, he said, going to circulate a little. In reality, he was going to try to see Madame Listor again.

Jacques and the doctor, left together, continued watching.

Every time the hazard of the dance brought Rosa Myrtil toward them, she looked at them amicably. Sometimes, she said something to them or addressed a smile to them.

"Your nurse is very gracious too," said the doctor.

Indeed, she was dancing charmingly. The simplicity of her costume showed off the supple agility of her movements. A velvet dolman tightened below her bosom; loose trousers of the same material gathered beneath the knee: that was her entire costume. Her hair was loose and her calves were bare. At her corsage was a beautiful yellow rose, such as only the far south can produce: a rose picked in Port Said, with the ball in mind. Around her waist she wore a golden scarf.

She was clicking castanets and, from time to time, back-to-back with her partner, she extended her lips languorously, as if for a kiss. When they were about to touch she pirouetted, bent down and came up again face-to-face with her partner.

"See how sprightly she is," said Monsieur Priot. Then he added: "She's an enthusiastic apostle of new mores and ideas—you know that, don't you? Intelligence and passion—her entire being is summarized in those two words. Her senses count for almost nothing in the flame that devours her. She must only have, I think, amours of the mind and the imagination. Oh, such women are seductive, like all the rest...but at the end of the day, they lack something, don't you think? They lack nature...blood...what do I know? It's a shame...amours of the mind produce poetry, oh, yes—as much poetry as one could wish, but rarely…very rarely…do they give rise to prizes for *élevage*."[15]

Jacques de Vertpré was unable to explain himself with regard to Madame Myrtil. To be sure, she was perhaps a trifle…a trifle impulsive…as witness her cajolery the other day, as soon forgotten as committed. At the same time, though, he found her so helpful, so devoted. He let Monsieur Priot speak, therefore—until the word *élevage* sparked a response.

"Do you have such vile words in your present language, my dear doctor?"

"What vile words? You mean *élevage*? But it's an old world. Don't you speak in Bourbon of *élever* children, of *éleves*? *Élevage* comes from that. In what, tell me, does *élevage* differ from education. Don't allow yourself to become obsessed by words, or rather by the usual reference of words. Has our language not been formed, in large part, from chance appellations, slang expressions and ancient neologisms that started out by being shocking before finding their place on more refined lips? That reminds me of the old quarrel of the century before last, with regard to civil or religious obsequies. The word *enfouissement* was outrageous, was it not, whereas the word *enterrement* was noble and appropriate? Well, I ask you, now, what is the difference between them? Are there any synonyms more equivalent?[16]

The doctor started laughing.

"I don't say," Jacques continued, "that it's wrong to pay attention to the improvement of the race, and to the maintenance of public health. I would rather, however, that people were not more careful of the physical than the moral."

---

[15] I have left this word in French because the etymological discussion that follows would otherwise be untranslatable. The word *élevage* is almost exclusively used with reference to livestock-breeding, which is why Jacques takes exception to it, although it derives from an innocuous verb: *élever* refers to bringing up children and an *élève* is a pupil.

[16] Both words mean "burial."

"Ah! Permit me, my dear Monsieur, to tell you that that is a distinction we no longer make. Nowadays, we only know the physical. 'Let us make healthy Frenchmen,' we say, 'and the rest will be gives as a bonus.' The rest is strength, concord, wisdom and prosperity. The physical precedes the moral; it is its pedestal, its base. That's why we pay particular attention to it. Have you ever seen a soul without a body in Bourbon? Now, we believe, ourselves, that the body gives what you call the soul its form, its character, its essence—in a word, that the moral is a product of the physical, a resultant, a vestment. Look, in our view, it's like a sound, and we pay attention first and foremost to the instrument that produces it."

"All right," said Jacques. "I'll admit that thesis momentarily, although it isn't mine, for the sake of argument. But that wouldn't be a reason to give, for example, every encouragement to utilitarian arts and none to the liberal arts."

"What!" said the Doctor, sharply, while shifting from right to left on the bench. "What are you saying? Utilitarian works, liberal arts? Are you still Gallo-Roman on your island? For us, mark me well, there no more liberal arts, nor non-liberal arts. We simply have art, which we consider as a useful thing."

"Ah," Jacques observed. "I thought, because of the slightly disdainful manner in which you talked about poetry a little while ago, that art, its sibling, would at most be tolerated in your Republic."

In spite of his forbearance, the doctor was allowing himself to manifest signs of impatience, as people do who are making vain efforts to make themselves understood. "For us," he said, "art is an industry. It is the ultimate product of human activity. What characterizes it is that it consists of making something out of nothing, or at least nothing sensible. Thus, the painter creates his picture, the sculptor his statue, the musician his symphony, the litterateur his written or spoken drama. The raw material is the idea. The tool is a certain turn of hand or mind, which nature still only distributes with a certain degree of parsimony. The products of that art are objects of value, of exchange, and in that name we favor their production and their sale. At the same time, though, we take care to give a higher priority to necessary industries—industries that ensure life—than to that merely useful industry.

"Useful—yes, it's incontestably that; it recreates, nourishes and equips our minds. It even renders us precious services from day to day. In the environment of a dense population, in which all the roles associated with the primordial industries are occupied, it opens a supplementary outlet to public activity. In an era when the hours of leisure are, for everyone without discrimination, more numerous than the hours of labor, and in which one might say that half the population is employed in amusing the other half, it is an important resources for filling in free time. Thus, the State considers it a good thing, and without according it any privilege, it envisages it benevolently, seeking in a certain measure by means of its purchases, commissions and rewards, to support good taste—which is to say, a taste for healthy, noble and comforting things.

"As for poetry, I'll admit that I might have been wrong just now to speak of it as I did. Still, it's necessary to agree on what we mean by it. Are you talking about rhymed works? Oh, those are, properly speaking, works of art, a variant of musical art. We have nothing more to say about them. Have you in mind the taste for beauty that causes you to seek and discover the harmonious and pleasant aspects of people and objects? But that's a pure sentiment. It can add charm to existence, but it does not produce anything concrete or positive. Poetry—oh, I know, it's everywhere..."

The doctor paused, then continued: "Everywhere, and nowhere; for it's in the eyes that beholds more than in the object beheld. It's in the nervous system that thinks and feels, as light and colors are in the sun. It's what forms the basis of eloquence, I know—and what a particular power it assumes then. It's also that which ignites and maintains passion. And what a flame! What a firebrand!

"But where poetry degenerates, where it is permissible to be disdainful in its regard, is when it only engenders unhealthy or noxious products—as was once frequently the case, it's said. That's why, I admit, we have a certain prejudice against poetry and poets. Plato had the same prejudice; it was even deeper in him than in us, since he excluded them from his Republic."

While our two interlocutors were letting themselves be drawn in this fashion far away from their initial subject, the fandango had finished, giving way to the waltz. The night was getting darker and the ship's illuminations seemed more flamboyant. Perfumed incense-burners were now swinging amid the lanterns, mingling their fugitive blue flames with the general clarity.

Jacques de Vertpré and the doctor returned their briefly-distracted attention to the ball.

The orchestra became less sonorous, softly swaying the couples to the sound of a dreamy, contemplative music composed of two or three incessantly-repeated strophes The male and female dancers, pressed against one another, whirled in silence, the seemingly semi-conscious women abandoning themselves to the arms supporting them.

Jacques had not forgotten what Monsieur Priot had said to him a little while before about "amours of the mind," and he began to make vague comparisons between the different impulses that the ancient languages confused in the single word "love."

"Tell me, Doctor—you mentioned Plato just now, but you no longer appreciate Platonic love, I assume."

"Oh, not at all. Platonic love is merely an illusion. It attaches itself to a shadow instead of seizing the prey. It stops at the blandishments with which nature sows the path to true love, instead of going determinedly to the goal. No, truly, for myself, I prefer love for the stars. Love, you see, has only one objective: the transmission of life. Since nature makes of us what it pleases, and as, on the other hand the subtle collaboration that it gives us is not without recompense, why not lend ourselves benevolently in all simplicity to the execution of its designs?"

Jacques did not reply immediately. His eyes filled up with a kind of vertigo, and he had the sensation that he too was spinning and waltzing. In that state of mind, strange and implausible ideas came to him, ready to sketch themselves on his lips before even being clearly defined.

"Is life, Doctor," he replied, abruptly, "the life that we transmit, the purified essence of our being or merely a base product of our nutrition?"

At that question, slowly posed, the doctor seemed struck by a veritable amazement, and his gaze was momentarily alarmed.

"Oh, as to that," he replied, "I don't know what to tell, you. Nature, I believe doesn't make such distinctions. From that viewpoint, it's all the same. The fermentations by which molecules and atoms are renewed or transformed remain mysterious endeavors to us. I'm not one of those, however, who see nothing in life but a flower blooming on a dung-heap; no more do I consider that love is an inversion of disgust. Life appears to me to be a supreme alloy, and admirable conformation, a magical flash between two distinct magnetisms. A man has the vital force, the impulse; he is the flame; a woman has the seed and the form; she is the torch. Why two factors instead of one? No one knows. Some claim that the role of the man is secondary in the great work of the human race; that nature interest him in procreation rather than associating him with it, having nothing in view but providing in his person a protector and purveyor for the mother—the superior being—and her progeny…but is that appreciation well-founded? What is certain is that the two factors seek one another out or avoid one another, following the laws of instinctive sympathy. That's what love is…and it's also what dancing is."

The waltzes had finished. There was a momentary pause, and Philippe, who had made a tour of the ball, returned to take his place beside the doctor. Our young people thought that the fête was over, but the musicians did not leave their seats. Between the ladies and the cavaliers there were precipitate comings and goings, furtive signs, words whispered in ears. Evidently, there was still something to come.

Indeed, the orchestra struck up again. First, there was a long sonorous introduction, during which male and female dancers gathered at opposite ends of the deck, men on one side and women on the other. Then, when the two groups had formed, looking at one another, a suddenly and irresistible gallop broke out. The two phalanges launched themselves upon one another, divided, mingled, and then immediately reconstituted into couples who were carried away by the stampede. Shortly thereafter, the orchestra intoned a solemn march, a truly triumphant hymn, and our spectators saw all the dancers passing in front of them, in a rhythmic procession, two by two, radiant with grace and smiling affection.

Our two cousins were all eyes, wondering with a keen emotion what was going to happen. And as the head of the procession seemed to be about to descend the stairway, Philippe exclaimed: "But where are they going, arm in arm like that?"

The doctor turned round abruptly.

"Where are they going? They're going to their rooms, of course."

And, shaking their hands, he went away himself.

Philippe and Jacques remained pensive. They were not laughing, nor were they thinking of crying scandal. They both felt, this time, that they were in the presence of a social and moral conception utterly different from the one they knew. There was nothing else for them to do but observe it.

Philippe, nevertheless, in thinking about Madame Listor, also felt a vague sentiment of irritation and resentment.

XIX

Marseilles! That is French soil appearing on the horizon.

At that sight, all the inhabitants of the ship are gripped by impression, from the captain to the most impassive African. For many passengers, it is their native land; for all of them it is the end of a long voyage. It is the ground on which they will be able to stand and walk.

Between the ship and the coast several black dots are perceptible, which seem to be getting nearer to the new arrivals. Already, there is a launch hooking on to the side of the ship; one might think that it had emerged from the hollow of the nearest wave. A man in uniform stands up in the middle of the oarsmen; his face is fresh and rosy. He is the representative of the sanitary authority, come to inspect the vessel.

The ship continues to make progress. Instead of black dots, one can now make out launches, which use the force of oars or move under full electrical power in order to accost the ship sooner.

Now the news reporters are aboard. They are enquiring about the incidents of the voyage, the cargo, and passengers of note who have made the journey. Our two Bourbonnais are of particular interest to them. News of their departure from Saint-Denis has been received a long time ago. While four reporters subject them to a routine interrogation, a photographer takes an instantaneous portrait of them without anyone noticing. Meanwhile, an artist makes a sketch of them, with a general view of the ship.

Another launch. It's a group with a banner, undoubtedly a deputation. The whole crew looks on curiously.

A venerable old man introduces himself, escorted by five or six men with placid faces. One of them, distinguished by the youthful levity of his face, still beardless and chubby, holds a standard in both hands, on which is embroidered a flower surmounted by a host and a bleeding heart, from the middle of which emerges a cross.

While our cousins, in their common surprise, show these symbols of their religion to one another, the group, already informed, heads toward them, and the old man, uncovering his white-haired head, bids them welcome.

"We are, Messieurs, the representatives of the Catholic parish of Marseilles. We wanted to be the first too greet the descendants of those who left France more than a century ago, referring to go into exile rather than witness the temporary decadence of our dear religion. Honor to you and your fathers and grandfathers, who have been able to found and organize a nation following the ancient laws of the Church. We, whom various necessities have retained on out native soil, would be very honored if, during your passage through Marseilles, you would care to receive the hospitality of our houses and visit out temple."

Jacques and Philippe shook the hands of their coreligionists effusively, expressing the joy they experienced in discovering thus, at the moment of their arrival in the motherland, Christians of their faith.

"We are all the happier," Jacques de Vertpré said, "because we had reason to dread that Catholicism might be absolutely extinct among you."

"Reassure yourselves; the tradition has been piously preserved, not only in Marseilles but in a few other cities as well. Catholicism is indestructible and imperishable—do we not have divine assurance of that? Where it is uprooted, it is reborn, like those plants which, for centuries, reproduce themselves from season to season in the same soil, abandoning to the earth their seed and stems, growing and forming the vegetal layer that sustains and nourishes them by themselves."

"And the plant has not degenerated too much?" asked Philippe Martinvast.

"No…we are content, for we are free. We are free because we do not bear umbrage to anyone. Our situation is modest, but it is sufficient for us. We meet when we wish, and

113

practice our ceremonies with no more hindrance than other religions. A small subscription suffices for our communal expenses. The incumbents are selected and remunerated b the parish." The old man bowed and added: "It is me, Messieurs, who has the honor of being the officiant of the parish of Sainte-Marie-Madeleine in Marseilles."

Our two cousins bowed respectfully.

"It is true, alas," the old man continued, "that our holy religion no longer has the rank and the authority that it might claim. It is confined in the conscience, in the circle of private and domestic functions. It has been necessary for us, simple believers, to be content with a place that you, the heroes, justly found too small. What can you expect? We have our sacraments, we hear the echo of the divine word in reading our holy books. Is that not the main thing? Like our ancestors the Jews, we have fallen in our turn; but, like them, we remember and we hope. We leave the State tranquil, and there is an agreement of sorts between the various religious professions that each remains on its terrain without criticizing neighboring religions and without issuing propaganda."

"That's very good, very good," repeated Philippe, who was beginning nevertheless to have doubts about the perfect orthodoxy of the religious delegation. He found a certain suggestion of its kinship with the protestant societies described in certain books, and that discovery diminished his enthusiasm.

The conversation could not be prolonged, for the captain had only authorized the presence of the envoys for a matter of minutes. They were about to file away, and their banner was already raised when Jacques thought it appropriate to say a few words about the pious symbols that had initially attracted his attention.

"The Holy Eucharist," he observed, "is still, I see, the primary object of your religion."

"Certainly, Messieurs, the corporeal presence of God in the host is still the foundation of our religion."

That response reassured the two cousins slightly. *At least*, they said to themselves, *they have, as they say, kept the essential.*

They shook hands again, thanking the others for their urgency. They would not be staying long in Marseilles, but at least they would find a mean of visiting their church.

While the delegates moved away, each one bowing in turn, the old man had placed himself beside the banner, as if to be the last to leave.

On lifting their heads in the intervals between the bows they were making, our young men's eyes had been attracted and held several times by the similarity of the physiognomies of the old man and the young standard-bearer. Their facial expressions were remarkably similar, in spite of the age-difference, doubtless due to the identity of profession and belief. Our travelers made the same observation, purely automatically, without having the slightest intention of asking for an explanation.

When it was his turn to leave, the priest, who seemed to have become anxious and embarrassed, took a step forward and resumed speaking, with a certain awkwardness.

"This is my son," he said, indicating the young standard-bearer. "I have the honor of introducing him to you. He will, I hope, replace me in my priesthood."

The young man remained mute, smiling in an innocent and child-like manner.

Philippe and Jacques shuddered simultaneously under the impact of an internal shock. They bowed, however, without saying anything. They did so even more profoundly than for the other delegates, trying to dissimulate as much as possible the impression that the final introduction might have produced on their faces.

When they found themselves alone again, Jacques de Vertpré shook his head in a discouraged fashion and said to his cousin: "Alas, it appears that our Catholicism has also been changed."

While expressing himself thus, he thought of the proud motto brought from Rome and inscribed on the fronton of the Cathedral of Saint-Denis: *Christus regnat, Christus imperut.* It is Christ who reigns, Christ who commands. And he felt humiliated and degraded by the thought that Christianity was obliged to make itself so humble and small in order to be tolerated. *So, alas*, he thought, *the true religion has been reduced to the status of an inconsequential tradition among the descendants of the eldest daughter of the Church.* At the same time, though, he tried to react against that first impression. *Perhaps*, he added, *we shall find more authentic Catholics elsewhere. I'd like to hope so.*

Philippe did not know what to think. He was not driven to recrimination to the same extent as his cousin, but the incident had had the effect of a disappointment and a bad omen, and he sought distraction from it.

"Practices do indeed," he murmured in reply, "appear to have changed...but as long as the dogma has been preserved—Transubstantiation, the Incarnation, the Redemption, the Trinity..."

He did not continue the list because a surprising spectacle had suddenly attracted his attention, and Jacques' too.

An aerial vessel had just descended on the port side, very close to the ship. Suspended at the level of the deck, it was moving parallel to the ship, matching its speed. It was evidently an aerostat of luxury and whimsy; it had the form of an immense swan. To simulate harness, false reins extended from the bird's beak in golden tresses to the banquette on which the young and elegant couple who were steering it were seated.

The couple were in conversation with the captain, standing on the bridge. The visitor explained how, having been on the point of making his daily flight northwards with his wife, he had recognized the ship that was approaching the port, and wanting to come to meet it, had immediately descended toward it. Now that he had good news of his friend the captain he was about to fly off in the direction of Aix.

And indeed, as he set his hand on a delicate machine of polished brass, the bird surged ahead, flapping its huge wings, swiftly maneuvering its tail, and thus gained a great height in a matter of seconds. One might have thought it one of the gods of Olympus rising into the empyrean after some terrestrial adventure.

The port was now very close. The entire city was displayed in its amphitheater. On the docks, apparatus of every sort designed for loading and unloading ships appeared at intervals.

The disembarkation took place about midday, close to the location where the railway station and aerostat station were combined. Sets of carriages were waiting there, on rails bordering the harbor. Directly opposite, a vertical chain of seven or eight gondolas was suspended from a high tower, on the terrace of which several large telescopes were perceptible.

A broad corridor formed by high railings was designed to protect the travelers from the crowd of cab drivers, curiosity-seekers, etc. On setting foot on land, however, a great emotion overwhelmed our young Bourbonnais, and they felt a disturbance in their entire being. The particular curiosity of which they were the object on the part of the crowd added to their embarrassment.

How did they find themselves, after a quarter of a hour, in the Grand Hôtel des Phocéens on the Cannebière? It would have been difficult for them to say, exactly.

XX

The Hôtel des Phocéens is very close to the disembarkation point. It possesses the principal clientele of travelers coming from the Orient and serves as a sort of terminus hotel for the Compagnie des Messageries Maritimes, which owns it.

That evening, almost all the passengers who were stopping over in Marseilles found themselves gathered there, in a large hall, for the occasion of a banquet offered by them to the captain and the other officers. The meal was very cheerful, as celebrations of that sort usually are; everyone rejoiced in a successful journey; the notable incidents of the crossing were recalled in their turn, and—a detail of particular interest to us—our two cousins were once again, by virtue of the particular circumstances of their voyage, the object of genuinely cordial attention, kind thoughts and good wishes.

As soon as the meal was over, the diners dispersed. The officers went back to their ship and the travelers went to make their preparations to continue their journeys. The majority of the latter—those, at least, who had not much luggage—were to take off in the first aerostat early the next morning.

Only a few guests went into the lounge, Philippe and Jacques among them, escorting Madame Listor and Madame Myrtil, who had been seated next to them at the table. The young Bourbonnais were due, as we know, to spend a few days in Marseilles, and had no obligations for that evening. As for the ladies, although they had no prejudice against aerial navigation, they still preferred the ancient diligence—the locomotive, that is—and their departure would not take place until quite late the following morning.

There was no more doubt about it; Philippe and Jacques had become their faithful cavaliers. How had that happened? For Jacques, of course, there had been the devoted assistance of the nurse. But for Philippe? Well, for Philippe, it was the effect of a still indeterminate, conflicted, embarrassed but nevertheless real attraction, having its source in a certain analogy of nature, instinctively felt, in some inchoate mirage of the future.

The fact was rather bizarre to observe: on the one hand, two young foreigners, gauche, unpolished, ignorant, utterly at a loss and out of place; on the other, two women of consummate culture and extreme refinement. Jacques and Philippe were very much aware of all the elements of that singularity; they were astonished by it, and when they thought about the conversations they had heard, the spectacles they had seen, especially at the recent ball, they were very close to finding themselves at fault. However, they wanted to demonstrate their amiability until the end, and since life aboard ship had produced the hazard, they intended to lend themselves to it with a good grace until the separation.

While Rosa Myrtil and Jacques de Vertpré were sitting in the glazed bay of a large window projecting over the Cannebière, Madame Listor and Philippe walked back and forth in a wide corridor communication with the lounge.

Philippe explained the plan of the future journey he had decided to make with his cousin. Modifying his original plans somewhat, he would go by boat through the Canal des Deux-Mers only as far as Bordeaux; then they would travel by rail to Saint-Lo, where they would doubtless stay for a fortnight, and would then arrive in Paris.

"Then I shall see you again before very long," observed Madame Listor, "for I hope you'll do me the honor of visiting me."

"Certainly," said Philippe. "It would be a great pleasure for me and I wouldn't want to miss it. And what are you going to do, Madame?"

Madame Listor explained her intentions in her turn. Once back in Paris, she would make arrangements for the education of her children. It was high time. Perhaps she would abandon them entirely to the establishments of public education. That would be hard for her, but to have them always in her possession was, in practice, almost impossible. Perhaps it would be better to do as everyone did, On the other hand, she was thinking of becoming a mother again. For that, it was preferable for her to be alone. She would prefer not to wait for very long. At the moment, she was well disposed...perhaps she would not be for much longer...

Philippe had refrained from interrupting. The last subject of conversation was not yet familiar to him, even though it was being raised for the second time. He was tempted to smile, but he knew that what he was hearing was very serious.

"In sum, I shall see," Madame Listor added. "Once in Paris, I shall consult my friends."

She stopped speaking then, as if to let her interlocutor speak. It was the appropriate moment for Philippe to attempt to express his opinion on the subject.

"It would certainly like to be able to offer some advice regarding what you've said," he observed, "but in my present state of intelligence with regard to the mores of today, it's very difficult for me. There is one detail that strikes me, however, in what you've just said, which I could identify to you, but I dare not."

"Speak, speak."

"You want to establish, you say, in some circumstance or other, a new maternity more comfortable and more glorious than the others. That's all very well...but are you sure that you're not already on the way to that new triumph?"

At these words Madame Listor froze, looking at her young companion in a fashion that was almost incensed. Philippe trembled from head to toe. What price would he pay for the indiscretion into which his avid curiosity had recklessly dawn him? He had not supposed that his companion's grace could take on such a grim expression.

Fortunately, by means of a sudden readjustment, the expression became calmer, amicable and mocking indulgence coming to take the place of the anger that had taken possession of the face.

"Oh, Monsieur Martinvast, what are you saying? Are you being indiscreet, or have you taken it into your head to be jealous? I see what's vexing you—it's the ball the other day...the last figure. How young you are, and easily deceived! For one thing, I had no sooner reached the foot of the staircase than I had already detached myself from the procession...Madame Myrtil did the same. Ha ha! You thought..."

On that she began laughing.

"No, it's true," she continued. "You're not yet able to understand us. Certainly, women are far more accommodating than in the past. They don't put so much ceremony and procrastination into their methods. When a well-educated man, of a suitable age and appearance, presents himself to them as seriously smitten, they generally do not reject him; it's even understood that their duty is to cede to that indirect injunction of nature. And their spouses, when they are engaged, do not usually demand the prerogative of an absolutely exclusive right...but when, like me, one is dedicated to increasingly beautiful creations, when one has the right to be ambitious for the greatest of honors, oh, then it is permissible to preserve oneself, to observe. Yes, Monsieur Martinvast, one preserves oneself, one exercises discrimination."

As they continued walking back and forth, Philippe could not help covering his beautiful companion with his gaze. Once again, he admired the charm of her gait, the absolute perfection of her entire person. From time to time, he let her go ahead in order to get a better view of her, then rejoined her at the moment when she turned to wait for him.

She too, at intervals considered interestedly, and covertly, the bearing and appearance of her young companion. Her eye, in enveloping him from head to toe, seemed to express admiration, perhaps even a keener sentiment. From time to time, the corner of her lip tightened, and her siren body stiffened visibly.

In the same way that water placed on the hearth, when it is about to reach boiling point, begins to murmur, Madame Listor's soul was beginning to stir; a mysterious prelude began, announcing within her the intermittent awakening of the most profound of desires.

For his part, Philippe was racked by an evolution that was taking over his entire being. Have you ever observed the quest of an ardent bloodhound? It runs freely, at hazard, but as soon as it happens upon a trail, it stops; then it resumes its progress, retraces its steps, and then goes forward again. An invincible power has taken possession of it, and is guiding it. Suddenly, its voice, until then contained and mute, gives rise to a dull growling in its throat. Look out! It's going hunting. Philippe, likewise, was ready to launch forth, the brave lad!

While talking about their plans, and thus delivering one another to their mutual influence, Rosa Myrtil and Jacques de Vertpré were both watching what was happening in the street, following with their eyes the animation of the crowd coming and going in the lunar light of the electric beacon.

They too had made one another party to their respective dispositions. They too had agreed that they would meet again in Paris.

From time to time Madame Myrtil stopped directing her eyes outside and, leaning back in her rocking-chair, contemplated her neighbor pensively. She feared that Jacques might take away a bad impression of her. Why did she attribute so much importance to his esteem? How could she, a great artiste, a convinced adherent of modern philosophy, attach any value to the opinion of an unknown tourist, imbued with ridiculous beliefs, who even made his stupidity a point of honor?

She did not understand that at all, and was surprised by it. At the same time, she remembered what the history of the 19th century had taught her. Catholicism and its morality was already, in that epoch, only sincerely professed by a tiny minority, and yet that minority had imposed it on everyone. People were afraid of its judgments and its anathemas. The majority, which was already devoted, as today, to free and rational life, dissimulated and blushed before those last representatives of the Christian religion.

Was there still in her mind a final vestige of that subordination born of habit? Or had she yielded, without perceiving it, to the charm that he inspired by virtue of his attachment to the tradition of his ancestors: an incontestable charm; the only thing had sustained the old conservatism for such a long time?

Yes, that chivalrous fidelity pleased her imagination. She believed that she saw a reflection of it in Jacques' serene forehead, his beautiful bright eyes and his youthfulness.

Where, she thought, *do that gentleness and virile innocence, which our young people no longer have, come from? Is it attributable to the prolonged influence of their mothers? Or is it the naivety of their reason that is transparent in their physiognomy? At any rate, he's a complete man, physically perfect—and as for thought, perhaps he still believes in little Jesus in swaddling-clothes, Satan's horns, the apple and the earthly paradise, the fires of Hell, supernatural apparitions and all the stories, somewhat indecent in conception, with or without sin, for the examination of which all which all the mitered heads in the world once convened...but he's intelligent nevertheless. What a lacuna, alas...what a lacuna!*

Then, her gaze insensibly took on an attitude of protection and solicitude. She would have liked to indoctrinate that amiable subject, to relieve him of his unpardonable illusion. She would gladly have devoted herself to it, by virtue of her nobility, her preoccupation with duty, and her firm good will.

Jacques was doubtless not completely devoid of suspicion as to what was passing through his companion's mind, but he was not overly preoccupied by it. *Curiosity*, he thought, *must be playing the largest part in the interest she's bringing to bear.* For himself, he did not feel any danger of being carried away. His heart was well protected, on the one hand by respect for religious law, and on the other by the exclusive worship of Christian womanhood. However, he took advantage of all the opportunities for reaction that decorum left open. What harm is there in indulgence in gallantry, as long as one in not disposed to go where it might lead?

"Well, Monsieur de Vertpré," Rosa Myrtil said, suddenly, stopping the movement of her armchair, "would you be kind enough to tell me, before we part, what your general impression is of everything you have seen and heard thus far, and everything you have discovered about our world."

"Oh, Madame, I beg you, spare me that labor. At the present moment, confusion reigns in my mind. If it were necessary to extract a summary judgment therefrom, I would, I swear to you, be extremely embarrassed. And if the judgment were unfavorable, you would doubtless find my criticisms unwelcome.

"There is, however one point to which I would like to return, with your permission. That would be to tell you, quite frankly, that what you have put in place of the family and marriage, offends and shocks me as much as that is possible..."

"Oh! Really?"

"Yes; I find that practice of commonality—or, rather, anarchy—in love utterly revolting. Thus, the sight of that ball the other night, its conclusion...what damnable license! When I add to that all that you have told me yourself, it seems to me that shame rises to my face..."

"And yet you too," Madame Myrtil replied, "have your balls, your festivals, your indulgences, which must have almost the same purpose as our dances. Why look at it so short-sightedly? Can one really do things better? We add music, grace, finery...and openness...what more do you want? Oh, I know, these pleasures don't lead to eternal marriage; but on that, as I've already told you, it's necessary to take one's stand. Love is no longer enchained in our world; its wings are no longer clipped.

"Does that displease you? But think about the advantages it brings. One, the history of love was a veritable martyrology. In the annals of criminality, one finds it in every line as a motive for misdeeds, and everyone took a malign pleasure in poisoning its cup. Today, it is entirely disengaged from its bitterness and formalism; above all, it is rid of that absurd character of forbidden fruit that religion and mores had maintained since Adam and Eve. That our remotest ancestors should have had that superstition is understandable. They didn't know what they were doing, and one day, perceiving that they were caught in a trap, they were ashamed of it. Eve, in particular, in the times that followed, had particular reasons for believing that she had been the victim of a curse. But after millions of years and generations, surprise and dead are really no longer permissible.

"Neither do you have any need, believe me, to see love as a vice in order to be driven by it. No…for us, on the contrary, it's a sacred thing. Whatever appearances striker you, my dear Monsieur, you can see that our national temperament has gained in wisdom and the spirit of virtue. That suffocates you, doesn't it? Well, believe it or not, men are honest today, even in love. Don't laugh; I assure you of it. They no longer have any ready excuse for one of them who deceives a friend of a benefactor in that fashion. I'll say no more. They put into it, as far as is possible, a certain dignity. Thus, they no longer feel bound to yield to the first appeal of a coquette; they no longer make Joseph—the first of the Biblical Josephs—a butt of jokes, as the good Christians of old once did in their youth.

"What is the result of all that? It is that love has become a plaid and courteous game. No more drama; no more bloodshed. When, in the darkness, we hear the cries of red deer tearing one another apart in the depths of the woods before the eyes of impassive hinds, we can say: 'That's bestial' without any fear that the expression will rebound on us."

Jacques allowed Madame Myrtil to talk. What was the point in arguing? They were too far apart in thought ever to reach an understanding.

"Look," she continued, "you exaggerate everything, in that order of ideas. Truly, is it such a serious business?" She paused momentarily, her eye fixed on her interlocutors; then she resumed: "No, it's not amour that is precious, that is sweet. One abandons oneself to it from time to time because that's the law of nature. To be sure, the other day, at the ball, I could have done what everyone else was doing, if I had not agreed in advance with my partner that nothing would happen…"

"Oh!" said Jacques, swiftly, interrupting her, as if he wanted to catch that detail of the conversation on the wing. "For some, then, that final departure was a simulacrum?"

"Of course. No, wait, that which is good, what one reserves with care, is the sympathy of intelligences, the union of minds. Yes, that's what is truly delectable...loving amity, the love between souls."

On hearing Madame Myrtil express herself thus, Jacques de Vertpré, very surprised, remembered what Dr. Priot had said to him a few days before about 'amours of the mind'— but at the same time, the word *soul*, pronounced with feeling, was gentle in his ear. It had, therefore, not been entirely banished from the French language, since it still strayed over women's lips.

He was finally about to speak in his turn when Madame Listor and Philippe appeared, seemingly disposed to retire from the lounge. On seeing them approach, they too rose to their feet. It was time to part.

They shook hands effusively, and after a few minutes employed in all of them pronouncing words of farewell simultaneously, they went back to their rooms.

XXI

The next day the primary sentiment of our young people was that of the isolation to which they found themselves reduced by the abandonment of the relationships they had formed at sea. Their journey, however, had scarcely begun. France, the object of their aspirations, had only just begun to open its doors to them. It was now that was necessary to march forward.

They went down to the ground floor of the hotel, to the information room.

"First, it's necessary to set a course," said Philippe Martinvast, reasonably, still impregnated with maritime terminology.

The room was full of notice boards, placards, newspapers and various items of apparatus for ringing, writing, telephoning, etc. Here and there were outlets for water, heat or electricity. Higher up, at ceiling level, there was a transmission-belt revealing the presence in the house of a domestic power-source.

"Ah!" said Philippe, stopping before a yellow notice. "First, let's see what the weather is likely to be." So saying, he retained his cousin amicably by the arm.

In a bulletin that appeared to be renewed several times a day, they saw all possible indications—barometric, thermometric, hygrometric, etc.—gathered together, with various ingenious diagrams. The weather was set to remain fine until the day of the new moon, when there would be a storm in the Mediterranean accompanied by rain and a south-south-easterly wind.

"Good," said Philippe. "We'll have to try to be in Bordeaux before the anticipated change. But when is the new moon? Ah—here's a calendar with the day marked in bold type."

127

Jacques followed the indication with his eyes, and saw that *Tuesday 18 April* was indeed marked on a special display in large letters. The observation seemed particularly agreeable to him.

"Tuesday the eighteenth of April," he murmured, very softly. "That's lucky. I confess, my dear Philippe, that I feared for our old French almanac. I had a secret dread of the decad, Sainte-Carotte and those names like Nivose and Pluviose that once told Americans that the French were under snow when they were bringing in their own harvest. I'm glad to see that it hasn't happened.[17]

They drew closer to the notice. In smaller letters there were a certain number of ephemeridae, items of astronomical information, tide-tables and indications for working the land, etc.

"I'm searching," said Jacques de Vertpré, still in a low voice, "but I don't see any saints of any species. Here's a name, but it must doubtless be one of recent fame; it means nothing to me...a glory of the world, perhaps, who has given his name to a day as one might give it to a street..." As he continued looking through the series of days, however, he exclaimed: "Oh! Look, here's Saint-Georges...Sainte-Clotilde.[18]

---

[17] The Revolutionary calendar introduced in 1792 gave new names to the months and abolished the week, substituting ten-day periods [decads]. The Saints' days were, of course, abolished too, but one notorious version of the calendar, presumably a parody drawn up in jest, but which attracted a great deal of attention and ire, substituted "Sainte-Carotte" [the Holy Carrot] for the name of St. Louis (King Louis IX).

[18] It is not obvious why St. Clotilde would be retained in the calendar that Jacques is looking at, although she was the wife of a Frankish king, credited with his conversion to Christianity. It is understandable that Jacques eyes should be drawn to the name, however, as Sainte-Clotilde is one of the major quarters of his home town of Saint-Denis in what we know as La Réunion. The Saint-Georges commemorated might con-

God...but what? Sully, Jeanne d'Arc...Denis Papin, Jenner, Lamarck, Saint-Simon... Frédéric Passy...what a hotchpotch! All the epochs of France, from primitive times to the present day, mixed up! Inventors, lay apostles of peace, lifeboatmen of every sort mingled with the elect of God!"

"Hold on," said Philippe, for his part. "Nowadays, it seems, they only count the years of the century. Look." There was, indeed, a number in the corner of the placard that could only be the number of the year. "What does that mean?" he continued. "I thought we were in the second year of the 21st century—which is to say, the year 2001."[19]

Our young people did not understand. The number of the year was 23. Later they would learn that, with respect to the numeration of the centuries themselves, universal chronology had taken for its base the most ancient era scientifically established. When they were told that it was from China that the element of calculation had been borrowed, they burst out laughing. It is necessary to say that in their eyes, the Chinese were cretins.

Suddenly, the clock chimed. Philippe and Jacques turned their heads and saw a rather complicated clock-face with large and small pointers, shiny or mat, some of which were moving at various speeds while others seemed to be fixed.

"That's even worse," Philippe murmured. "It's a sphinx rather than a clock."

"My God! How complicated everything is now," Jacques replied.

They took the chronometers they had bought in Saint-Denis from their pockets, but as they alternated their gazes between the watches and the clock, the room's attendant, suspecting their embarrassment, came over to them.

---

ceivably be one of several individuals with that surname rather than the saint, but that argument is not applicable to Sainte-Clotilde.

[19] 2001 was actually the first year of the 21st century, but Philippe's mistake was still common among the innumerate.

"You have before you, Messieurs," he said, "universal time and Marseilles time. The latter is the old time that was counted in dozens like the months, each hour being divided, initially into two, then four, and then sixty. Many people still make use of it, in spite of its complication. Universal time is regulated by the decimal system. They day, composed of ten hours, begins when the sun reaches the most populous meridian of the earth, which is in Asia…with the result that for Marseilles, according to the old system, it's now nine o'clock in the morning. That's doubtless the only indication that you can make on your dial. For the entire world, for administration, postal services, electrical communications, science, the press, etc., it's one fifty-two."

"Very well," said Philippe. "It's a matter of a new habit to form."

The attendant was about to leave them when he changed his mind and said: "I am, Messieurs, I assure you, entirely at your disposal to give you any information you might desire. Would you like a guide? Do you need money? Ask me, without hesitation, anything that might be useful to you."

"A guide…what do you think, Philippe?" Jacques asked, turning to his cousin.

"My word, that's a good idea. We'd find that useful."

"Well, I'll send you Matteo," said the attendant. "He's a courier, a native of the city, in whom you can have every confidence and who is very knowledgeable."

"It's also necessary to settle the question of money," Philippe observed.

"How much do you need, Messieurs?"

"How much?" Philippe repeated. "I don't really know. Our crossing was extremely expensive, and I don't know what things cost. Look, I'll tell you frankly what we've brought. We left with the intention of traveling in France for two or three months and we brought twenty thousand francs with us, in gold."

The attendant initially pulled a face that seemed to say: "That's not very much, but there might be a way out of it."

Aloud, he said: "If you don't have enough money, you could always get more. Today, Messieurs, it's as well you know, twenty thousand francs doesn't constitute a very large sum. It's not that there are great many expenses to make in order to live in our country; necessities are very cheap here—but the purchase price of luxury objects has risen steeply. Luxury and the superfluous are very onerous here, and monetary value has diminished considerably."

Jacques and Philippe looked at one another, somewhat perplexed.

"Are foreigners taxed, perchance?" Jacques asked.

"Not anymore, but they have to pay for everything, whereas we get many things free."

"Will we lose much on our louis?" asked Philippe, in his turn.

"No, Messieurs. I'll exchange them, if you wish, for twenty-franc livres and fifty- and a hundred-franc coins, which are our present currency. In addition to that there is paper—notes and bills...oh, there's a great deal of paper. I can tell you that gold and silver have hardly any value in themselves—we've discovered so much of them. The world's population has increased considerably, wealth has spread, the mines have inundated us. There was talk at one point of basing the currency on a new metal, very rare and very precious, or on an equally rare and beautiful gemstone, but fashion, the regulator of affairs, never took it up. Coinage, at the present moment, has become very similar to paper money—a conventional symbol; it's little more than a token. The pricing standard for international relations is the quintal of wheat. For the Latin League it's a day's labor."

"Good, good," said the travelers, wondering how they were going to cope in the midst of all this new information.

After a few moments, Philippe raised his head. "We definitely need a guide. Would you be so kind, Monsieur, to send Monsieur Matteo to us right away."

The attendant rang a bell. A man appeared, still young, with black hair and a bronzed complexion. He was the guide they had requested.

After a few minutes' discussion, intended to acquaint him with what was expected of him, the two Bourbonnais, escorted by the two employees, were going to the strong-box in order to exchange their money when the sound of a bell, louder and more prolonged than all the rest, filed the room. Immediately, everyone there picked up a funnel from those arranged around the room and put it to his ear, listening attentively.

"What's happening now?" exclaimed Philippe and Jacques, turning round.

By way of reply, Matteo gave them each an earpiece.

"Shh!" said the attendant. "Listen—it's a communication from the *Semaphore*."

"The fire that broke out last night in the Rue Mirès," said a distant voice, "was extinguished in a few minutes by means of the Berthelot extinguisher fluid.

"Two young men from the Cannebière chloroformed themselves at sunrise. They had made it known that they could no longer bear the monotony of life.

"Two others, whose names we gave yesterday, fought a duel with swords on the field maintained by Major Bartholo. The battle was fierce. They then shared an excellent bouillabaisse in the restaurant attached to the establishment."

Then came indications of financial matters, the schedules of steamships, announcements of sales and sports news.

"...Today, at midday, an ovation to the centenarian Marc Lignousse. The public will gather in the Allées de Meilhan...

"The South American Congress, in order to bring the rebellion in the State of Patagonia to an end, as authorized the employment be the Federal Police of explosives of the first category."

Philippe and Jacques heard other news items, the majority of which were incomprehensible to them.

Matteo, wanting to commence his role as their cicerone immediately, explained to them as soon as the communication had finished, that the *Semaphore*, the oldest newspaper in Marseilles, released all its news in this manner, at hourly intervals.

"Would you like to hear the previous bulletin? It's recorded one the phonograph over there, next to the telephonic plaque."

He steered them toward a black urn, on which he pressed a button.

"The States of North Africa"—it was now a cavernous voice that was speaking—"are still in negotiation with the Sultan with regard to forming a syndicate with him. The Sultan has announced that he will make his decision known within a month...

"The Superior Council of Hygiene is pressing the Minister of Health for the Spartan Law to be urgently put into effect...

"The judges at Aix have found Sieur Argeles guilty of raping a woman on the highways between Toulon and Cannes. The accused's passion could not be justified. Argeles has been sentenced to pay compensation of a quarter of his wealth. He will be submitted to a medical examination for the selection of the sanitarium where he will be treated...

"The Institut, in its annual general session, is protesting for the fiftieth time against the socialization of its temporal domain, nationally attributed to the Ministry of Public Education."

Mateo stopped the phonograph's report.

"That's very curious," said our two cousins, speaking in loud voices.

The people in the room smiled on seeing them wonderstruck by such simple things.

Heading for the door, Jacques de Vertpré, who had the attendant beside him, resumed speaking in a quieter tone: "I heard mention of a crime punished by judges. Do you, by chance, no longer have juries?"

"Pardon me, but today, juries and judges are almost the same thing. Both are elected, not for a few days only, like the worthy jurors of old, utterly bewildered about being transported into the assize court, but for a long period. They no longer meet in dozens—that was too many—but there are still several of them, in order to avoid any personal responsibility..."

"What? To avoid any responsibility..."

"Certainly—isn't it the same where you come from? It's impossible for judges, however good they are, not to be mistaken from time to time. It's necessary, however, that no one should be able to say: 'On that day, in that case, that judge or that jury made a mistake.' It's not in the interests of society, or of the individual judge."

"Another thing, Monsieur Matteo...you still have duels?"

"Still. People have protested in vain that it's absurd...since it's in the blood of the most intelligent people in the world! We prefer the duel to the vendetta—what do you expect? That way, a matter of honor is liquidated in a few hours. Then again, it leads directly to reconciliation, while other procedures..."

"And suicide, Monsieur Matteo, like that of the two young people from the Cannebière—that's doubtless a scourge that is cruelly prevalent."

"Not as much as you seem to think. There are still a few cases, it's true. For one thing, it's a recognized right nowadays to kills oneself, if one so desires. We won't seek to prevent someone condemned to death, for example, from anticipating the fatal operation of the machine. Then again, the procedure has been put within range of everyone; people can now kill themselves painlessly, without any difficulty, in the most correct fashion. The public don't pay much attention to it. It's a manner of leaving society, in the English fashion, that is sufficiently appreciated in a population where positions are threatening to become rare.

"In spite of that, the event remains uncommon. Life is now so sweet, so easy...here and there, however, unquiet minds are still to be found, formed in the antique mold, which dream of a feverish, combative, egotistical existence—a disorder eventually stifled by spleen. It's an inevitable effect of atavism, but which the passage of time is attenuating day by day."

While Jacques posed these questions in haste, Philippe leaned close to Matteo's ear, to ask him what the phonograph meant by the Spartan Law.

"The Spartan Law…that's quite a story," he said. "It arises from the fact that people are beginning to get anxious about the enormous increase in the number of human beings. The disappearance of all the Malthusian institutions of the old regime—I mean the family, monastic celibacy, military celibacy, the blind decimation of poor nurslings; in brief, the cessation of all the restrictions imagined by the instinctive foresight of our predecessors—has given population growth an utterly unexpected momentum. On the other hand, the extent of habitable land is threatening to be restricted by the increasing cooling of the poles. The Eskimos are descending into the still-temperate regions that feed the world. Even Africa, having become habitable again, is beginning to fill up. People have been led to ask how the number of a adult's productive years can be limited. They've begun to discuss means of sterilizing at a given moment, without recourse to surgery, persons of one or other sex—females especially—which would be quite simple. Thus far, they haven't got very far on that path. What the Council of Hygiene wants is for the nation to rid itself of deformed children, as was done in Sparta, not brutally but by scientific and merciful methods of elimination. There would be a special jury for that. The mass of the public in resisting though. 'As soon as human beings begin to breathe,' they say, 'they have a right to life. France is, in any case, rich enough not to think twice about ameliorating and prolonging the life of its infirm citizens. War having entirely disappeared, we no longer need to think exclusively about making soldiers, and thanks to human ingenuity, there is still a place in the sun for everyone.' That's the crowd's view. Other people take a middle course, requesting measures for the physically-unsound at least to be prevented from reproducing."

Having said this, Matteo, who had continued walking, opened the door to the hotel's strong-room Philippe went in ahead of him, a trifle confused by all the novelties that had simultaneously dazzled his eyes.

Jacques de Vertpré was already occupied in changing his money, for it was he although he was the younger, who held the communal purse of the voyage.

"Hey," said Philippe, tapping him on the shoulder, "you'll give me a little pocket money, won't you?"

"Here you are," Jacques replied, turning round and giving him both a small wad of minuscule bills, a handful of gold coins and twenty silver one-franc coins. This—which is to say, the money—is small change, you understand?"

"All right," said Philippe. "What about the copper?"

"Copper coins no longer exist."

"There aren't any?"

"No."

Philippe said nothing more. *That's not surprising*, his gesture seemed to say. *You'd need billions*.

Then, buttoning his overcoat and adjusting his hat, he took a step toward the street. "We might as well go out now," he said to his cousin and Matteo.

"Let's go," they replied. And all three set out to visit the city.

XXII

What our two voyagers noticed first of all was the uniformity in the costume, bearing and even in the faces of the passers-by. Everyone who was walking, crossing paths and agitating was properly dressed, behaved politely and showed every evidence of an easy, rational, contented discipline.

Even the houses, the streets and the monuments gave an impression of symmetry, or regimental order.

After walking a short distance, Philippe could not help remarking: "Do you know what I think, Cousin? It's as if I'd been transported into a vast infantry district."

"Personally," said Jacques, "I was thinking vaguely of an immense convent."

Nevertheless, on closer inspection, they did not take long to observe that the passers-by wore differentiating badges on their collars, in their hair or on their sleeves, not obvious at first glance, but very varied. There were numbers, insignia, plaques and stripes of various colors, and the outlined shapes of arrows, pomegranates, tools and so on.

There, they thought, *is an entire figurative language, to which it's necessary to have the key*.

At the same time, in the buttonholes of men and women, they recognized the little knotted ribbon that, in the Île de Bourbon as in ancient France, constituted a decoration. They were of all colors, knotted in every fashion, and almost all on the breast, much in evidence, often repeated three times in the superimposed lapels of the waistcoat the jacket and the overcoat.

This last observation made Philippe smile, and he took it as a pretext for striking up a conversation with Matteo, who was looking straight ahead as he marched, saying nothing, waiting for his clients to open communication.

"Monsieur Matteo," he said, slightly sarcastically, "it seems to me that you have a great many decorated individuals."

"Yes, Monsieur Martinvast. I can say that in Marseilles, almost all of us are. Marseilles is in the process of becoming the model city of the Confederation.

"Ah!" said Philippe, adjusting his tone. Contrary to his assumption, the guide seemed to be treating his remark seriously. It was therefore necessary to fall into step. "But in that case," he went on, "I imagine that decoration has little value."

"I beg your pardon—the hierarchy of distinctions is infinite. They are of every kind; each of them has several degrees. The series differ according to the provinces and the cantons. But there is always—take note of that always—a certain merit in obtaining them; that's their guarantee of value. The ribbon, you see, constitutes an inexhaustible means of action for social improvement when general mores have fashioned it as we have over centuries. Consider the results obtained thereby. Once, it was a glory to be decorated, but nothing forced you to be. Today, it's virtually a humiliation not to bear one or two badges of merit. What a motive force! What a lever!"

In saying these words, Matteo raised his arms to the heavens, his eyes lighting up in their enlarged orbits; his demonstrative and inflammatory nature was beginning to reveal itself.

"It's necessary, as much as possible, is it not," he went on, "for people to have goals ahead of them, imminently? Without a goal, what can you do? Without a goal, a Frenchman would not know why he was alive. For him, the goal is like a beacon that attracts him, a point of support that sustains him, a spur that directs him. Well, the decorative system provides that necessity in large measure. Scarcely have you obtained one cross than it shows you another to be won, and until the age of retirement, it keeps you constantly breathless. All that at scant expense…scant expense, you understand?"

Philippe and Jacques had understood all that perfectly by themselves, but they let Matteo talk, taking pleasure in his

138

convinced and ingenuously declamatory tone. At the same time, by means of the gestures and signs they made to one another, they seemed to be saying, not without irony: *Oh, fortunate people! Fortunate government!*

"Time," the cicerone continued, "is thus passed in jumping from one stage to the next. Fortunately, we have enough stages for the longest and most favored lives. Our distinctions, in any case, are not always platonic; prizes often follow their accession—which is to say that a material and pecuniary advantage sometimes accompanies a ribbon. Then again—and it's here that the great merit of the system appears—when we need to punish someone, the decoration system serves us again. The withdrawal of decorative insignia is our primary punishment. The fear of losing a rosette or slipping down the scale of honors spares us a large quantity of social failings. Frankly, Messieurs, where could one find punishments more moralistic, more economical and more human?"

Matteo had paused on that final question, and turning to face his two clients, he folded his arms proudly. Then he resumed walking, his head slightly tilted to the right, rubbing his hands with the air of a man satisfied with himself.

Jacques de Vertpré tapped him on the shoulder. "There's a woman wearing a chevron. What does that signify?"

Matteo turned round immediately.

A woman had indeed just walked past them who was wearing six golden chevrons on her arm. Still young, slender and supple, she was dressed in maternal costume. Her long hair, gathered beneath the nape, descended in shiny waves to her waist.

Jacques and Philippe, having turned to follow her with their gaze, perceived that the crowd stood aside to let her pass. At one point, when she wanted to cross the street, carriages stopped to give her a clear passage.

"Who is she?" Philippe asked. "The wife of a general?"

"Not at all," Matteo replied. "She's a mother who has six children approved by the medical college, that's all." As his interlocutors looked at him without saying anything, he added:

"I see that you're not informed either about our legislation or our customs in that regard. Our law, Messieurs, is formulated in such a way that a woman has an interest in having children, and having beautiful ones. Honors, grants, sumptuary privileges—we make use of all means to give maternity the prestige it merits.

"Mothers have places reserved for them in popular gatherings. People make way for them everywhere and they never have to wait. The municipality takes care of their needs and ensures them allocations, which increase progressively as children are born, and furnishes them in the case of the legitimate cessation of salaried employment with an indemnity equal to the salary. Only mothers can wear their hair long in public. Certain precious fabric and certain jewels are reserved for them by sumptuary laws. Finally, they're the only women who can own uncovered carriages harnessed to four horses. Furthermore—the supreme honor!—it's they who give their name to their children. Filiation is organized according to matrilineal descent.

"Oh, really!" said Jacques de Vertpré, brusquely, evidently unable to tolerate modern ideas on that point. "You'll never make me believe, Monsieur Matteo, that one can inspire a keen desire for maternity, given the habit you have of tearing away their children once they are weaned, in order to fill I don't know what crèches, boarding-schools or asylums."

"Forgive me, Monsieur de Vertpré, but we don't tear children away from mothers. It is the mothers who discreetly leave the establishment of the Nativity when their presence is no longer necessary." In saying that, Matteo struck an oddly challenging pose, placing his two index fingers in a cross beneath his nose. Then, raising his voice, he continued: "It's necessary that the separation should take place some day. Would it be better to do it, as in the past, when communal life has been prolonged for ten or twenty years? Don't you find that it's much more painful in those conditions? Then again, today's separation, apart from not being obligatory, is also not absolute. Mother and child continue, as you're not unaware, to

140

see one another, to visit one another and to stay with one another at intervals, if it pleases them. Education alone belongs to the community, to the canton; that's the important point. The mother who has completed bringing one individual into the world can, in that way, without hindrance or concern, seek another if it suits her..."

"If it suits her," Jacques interjected. "But how can you expect that, outside a family constitution, a woman will confront the pains, the privations, the dangers and physical disgraces that are the inevitable corollary of her noble function?"

"Have no fear," said Matteo, interrupting in his turn. "Our women are not brought up to dead maternity. They are valorous. They have, in proportions that were once rather rare, the specific qualities of their sex. Their months of pregnancy are, in any case, embellished and made pleasant according to their personal tastes, by the most ingenious anticipation. Their delivery, thanks to the discoveries of science, is most often carried out without a whimper, painlessly, in a vague, insensible semi-consciousness, to which the newborn gives a happy awakening. And afterwards, similarly, for as long as breast-feeding lasts, the mildest and most relaxed life is led under the watchful eyes of medical personnel.

"There is one disgrace, it's true, that we have not been able to ward off—I mean the considerable alteration of form. Oh, the unfortunate ransom of amour! How dearly nature makes women pay for the services they render her! The price that they pay may seem unjust, for it is women alone who are its victims, and they are afflicted in the beauty that is their attraction. That painful ordeal naturally demands compensation. Well, our mores, I can affirm, furnish it as broadly as possible. What is the reason for the countless liberties, privileges and attentions with which we heap women? That is it. It is truly a duty for men, the unconscious authors of such damage; it is a duty, as I say, to make up for it.

"That inconvenience notwithstanding, have no fear that they ever remain distant from their mission. No, have no fear.

141

When we recently carried out trials of artificial fecundation and incubation, they were the first to protest."

"Nevertheless," Jacques replied, obstinate in his criticism, "what interest do you expect men to have in those they have engendered, when you have removed all the attributes of paternity from them? How can you expect that they will not recoil, especially from the idea of having daughters, whose destiny will be to enter, like everyone else, into the circulation of free love? Fathers! But, according to what I hear aid, they no longer exist. What is the stronger sex today? A herd of nameless males, devoid of authority, devoid of responsibility, throwing the life of which they are the dispensers to the wind, like a handful of grain, and no longer having to sustain them, in endeavor and in honor, the idea of one day transmitting their name and their patrimony to their descendants."

"Don't worry, Monsieur de Vertpré, don't worry; men will always love women. That's sufficient—and as for the rest, what is the objective to be attained? It's that the race should multiply abundantly and strongly, isn't it? That's all; nature has no other aim. Well, you'll judge for yourself the impetus that the great French family has gained, the unprecedented progress that it has realized physically since the ancient family, the petty family, corresponding to the semi-savage condition, has disappeared.

"Are you quite sure, Messieurs, that children were generally well brought-up when their education depended on their legal mother and father? Did fathers always provide good examples? Were mothers never too weak? Were hygiene, discipline and tenderness the rule in every household? Believe me, it's not such a simple matter to fashion human products. The educators responsible for it today are carefully prepared for the task. They are, in addition, first-class people. Along with physicians, they're the foremost functionaries in the Confederation.

"Look, I who am speaking to you"—Matteo extended his lips in a placid smile while relaxing his voice—"am neither the first nor the last with regard to the attributes appropriate to our sex. How many descendants have I had, do you think? Impossible to know exactly—but I can guarantee that, to my knowledge, there are a good thirty for whom I can take certain credit…almost certainly, for there is a resemblance. Well, I wouldn't want to be responsible for their education. Not ever. I feel that it wouldn't suit me. And I'm not the only one in that situation, I beg you to believe. I don't say that I won't take an interest in some of the heirs of my blood one day—a few boys, perhaps—if I have the means, or that I won't leave them some souvenir in my testament; but that will be all. In good faith, what more do you expect me to do?

"And then, finally, with the old system, how could you ever arrive at equality, at sacred equality?" On that word, Matteo, raising his eyes to the heavens, took off his hat respectfully. Then he continued: "With the narrow, authoritarian family of ancient Rome and the Middle Ages, there were as many educations as households. We, Monsieur, who want to ensure equality, attempt to establish it in the cradle, at the mother's breast. Do you understand?"

Now Matteo leaned forward, setting his eyes against Jacques', so to speak. *Can you understand the depth of the design?* He seemed to be saying. Finally, he smiled and, breaking off the conversation, they both hastened their steps in order to catch up with Philippe, who had been walking along the street alone for a few minutes, not having found overmuch charm in the cicerone's explanations.

143

XXIII

The conversation lapsed. The general aspect of uniformity that reigned everywhere began to weary our voyagers. After a certain time, the monotony invaded them completely, importing into their minds a painful sensation of emptiness, taking them by the muscles of throat and giving them a vague desire to yawn, to stretch their arms and accelerate their pace.

Matteo had told them in vain that they would get used to it in a matter of days; that they would soon be ecstatic in the face of the perfect order; that the prevalent resemblance between the passers-by did not exclude a certain relative individualism or a great and healthy cheerfulness; that they would see it for themselves, etc. Gradually, the two cousins became increasingly indifferent.

What have our compatriots come to? they thought. *Even the pebbles on the shore, rolled against one another as they have been for centuries, have not yet attained this equality of standardization. The general type is certainly handsome— straight nose, curt forehead, discreet jaw, fresh complexion, slender joints; it recalls the ancient Greek type, with a few more muscles. But how does one now distinguish Peter from Paul? Alas, it's evident that everything has softened and leveled out. Furthermore, the distinction there was between men and women has diminished sensibly. Where, then, are those reliefs, those curves, that intelligent calisthenics took so much trouble to produce under the continuous and progressive action of the corset? Where now can one find the characteristic face of an intelligent man or the original physiognomy of a fashionable woman? Fortunately, men have kept the beard...unless that too in extirpated some day!*

Jacques and Philippe shook their heads while making these reflections.

At a street corner, by chance, something reawakened their attention. It was a nuance, a modification seized by their instinct, which their inexperience did not allow them to grasp immediately.

The population was the same; the buildings were still similar; but there was a certain something revealing a different milieu.

"It seems to me," said Philippe, not without hesitation, "that we're in a different quarter."

"Indeed," Matteo replied, "you're not mistaken; we're now in the third canton, which is called Borély. It's the canton of citizens who work in wood: carpenters, joiners, cabinet-makers, wheelwrights. Just now, we were among the citizens occupied with finance and private administration—office-workers and clerks. In agglomerations like Marseilles, the cantons almost all correspond to a specialty; that's inevitable..."

"How do they correspond to a specialty?" asked Philippe. "This, you say, is a canton in which people dedicate themselves to wood-working. Are there nothing but work-shops in the quarter, then? Are there no butchers, no tailors? Is there no school, no doctor?"

"I beg your pardon," Matteo replied. "The canton is complete, all given to a particular kind of work. You doubtless know what a canton is?"

His interlocutors nodded their heads.

"You also know what was once meant, in the infancy of the social art, by cooperative societies?"

Another affirmative nod.

"Well, our cantons are like cooperative societies, based on election, linked by contracts with the province and the nation, free to make treaties between one another that might be useful to them. There are cantons that devote themselves exclusively to a particular kind of work. That happens in big cities. There are others that are subdivided into sections in order to exploit several branches of professions.

"Each of them, however, has to have certain essential organs: a communal house, educational facilities and emergency services, baths, a gymnasium, courts, food and clothing stores, meeting places for meals, conversations, reading and pleasure, with all the necessary administrative personnel. The profits realized by the produce of the work serve, first of all, to pay the general expenses. The excess is divided between the members of the organization."

"Per head?" Philippe asked.

"No, not entirely, but very nearly. That depends to some extent on the cantons. Here again, the maximum plays a certain role in limiting the inequalities that might be produced. Thus, there's certainly a premium given to activity, to merit, but it's minimal—quite minimal. You may believe, however, that, no matter how minimal it might be, it still stimulates astonishing competition, like that which animates jockeys as they approach the winning-post, when they're disputing half a length. It's astonishing how little it takes to infuse people with competitiveness and make it go to their heads. A trifle suffices, an illusion or an appearance.

"The only important innovation we've introduced into that kind of association is that, in general, the director or overseer doesn't receive a greater part of the profit that a simple manual worker."

"Oh! That's a bit much!" Philippe exclaimed, stopping abruptly. "What about the providers of capital—how are they remunerated? And how are the responsibility and the particular competence of the directors appreciated?"

Matteo, who thought that what he had said was quite simple, was a little put out by Philippe's exclamation and attitude.

"That's how it is, though," he replied, softening his tone. "The remuneration of capital is part of the general expenses; it's trivial, however, credit being easily available everywhere. As for the assimilation of the overseer and the worker, it comes from the idea that one kind of work is worth as much as another, that it's a product of equally estimable effort in all cases. The supervisory work is generally restricted to veterans, in whom experience and regularity compensate for the diminution of activity. It's not considered that the application of mature or old men is more precious than that of young men. Besides, overseers today don't have much more responsibility than simple associates."

Philippe was no longer listening, unable to understand. These theories, new to him, might be sound, but for the moment, they were tedious and irritating. Mechanically, he struck the ground with his cane, and, his thoughts having taken wing, he dreamed that he was in Paris, that he had seen Madame Listor again, and that he had found, instead of this mechanical existence in which he was caught up, something of the brilliant, diversified life of the French of old.

He resumed marching alongside the imperturbable alignments, considering the immense buildings extending as far as the eye could see, with their infinite series of identically-sized openings, similar balconies, chimneys opening at the same height and smoking in the same direction.

But these cities, he thought, *aren't cities any longer. They're beehives with shelves and cells, compartments in which each individuals must doubtless find, in order to breathe, the regulation cubic capacity of air. Alas, it's the cellular system in all its horror. Oh, it's true, the ensemble doesn't lack comfort. I can see electricity, water and heat circulating everywhere. But isn't the comfort itself aggravating if it's always the same? Then again, I don't see any beggars or sickly individuals. Where are the clarinet-players, the blind, those admirable vagabonds with long beards in large faded and threadbare cloaks, who once gave in France, it's said, and still give in Saint-Denis, such a picturesque quality to the life of streets and bridges?*

While letting this train of thought carry him away, Philippe Martinvast, could not avoid the impression of grandeur and wealth that the sight of public monuments inspired. The further he walked, the more important structures he saw at the ends of streets, in squares and in the middle of gardens, evidently intended for public use. Unlike the private dwellings, these were very varied; they had a marked artistic char-

147

acter, and also an aspect of veritable opulence. Gold, marble and color were lavishly displayed there.

Then, gradually modifying his mental disposition, he said to himself: *No, evidently, it's not into those huts, those boxes, we noticed at first that the life of the French people of today has passed. It's there, in these studios, galleries and amphitheaters, that they spend their time. I can see that they live in public, in the open air, as much as possible, enjoying the broad advantages that the cantonal system ensures them. On the one hand, the instinct of sociability is developed, and on the other, wealth is distributed in a different fashion than at home. Yes, that's it. Personality is effaced, but groups prosper.*

In fact, a certain labor of transformation was beginning to take place in Philippe Martinvast's mind, which he could scarcely measure, and about which he was secretly anxious. To what contagion was he falling victim? What would become of him? He had tried to resist it, but it seemed to him that a subtle philter was beginning to invade him, troubling him. He passed his hand over his eyes, saying to himself: *Let's see, I'm still Philippe Martinvast; I'm awake; I'm not dreaming; I'm in Marseilles, traveling, on the way to Paris, where I've arranged to meet Madame Listor...* He had no difficulty recognizing himself.

After all, he continued, *perhaps the old society was really just a juxtaposition of different individuals, jealous of one another. Perhaps the strong could, to some extent, oppress the weak there. It wasn't the reign of cordiality and justice. Alongside private existences overflowing with striking luxury and gaudy superfluity, history tells us that one saw general interests of the first order left in miserable neglect...*

Truly, destiny is bizarre. And to what singular results it leads! My cousin Jacques had good reason to say so. One might think that one were in convent here, of monks and nuns living together. Who would ever have believed that our good monks, so scorned and mocked, would become the models of a new existence? Those worthy cenobites had, therefore, while they were organizing themselves in view of a second life to be earned, realized at the same stroke something close to the ideal of earthly life! How far away we are from individual or family life! Nothing remains but to institute public dormitories...is a box not sufficient for the happiness of the individual?

Suddenly, Philippe stopped again. Another thought, quite different from the ones that were agitating him, had just occurred to him.

"Soldiers, Monsieur Matteo—I don't see any. Where's the uniform?"

At the same time, he turned around, searching to discover whether he might not see a pompom or a bayonet somewhere, and pricking up his ears to catch the beat of a drum.

"Oh, there!" he exclaimed, raising himself up on tiptoe and pointing at a man in an amaranthine helmet standing at a street corner, correctly buttoned and belted. "Yes, there..."

Matteo, making himself as tall as he could, looked in the direction indicated to him.

"Ah! Over there, I can see...well, no, it's simply a policeman, not a man-at-arms. The police are responsible for seeing that the rules are followed, maintaining the streets, putting out fires, preventing disorder and misdemeanors, but its agents only have defensive weapons—which vary, it's true, according to the canton, from truncheons to revolvers. As for the public force belonging exclusively to the nation, it only reveals itself and intervenes when the need arises. There are guard-posts at intervals ready to empty at the first telephonic signal. When they're left tranquil, they devote themselves to useful occupations. In cases of flagrant crime, the public force is everyone."

"Then it's lynch law that reigns here?" Philippe put in.

"Not t all. There is no lynch law in a well-ordered nation. The crowd, which is a blind and dangerous animal, cannot improvise justice. I mean that in the face of an obvious and present breach of the law, every citizen, although unable to

149

punish, may take any urgent conservatory and reparatory measures that the circumstances require.

"Since we're talking about police, I ought to tell you that the senior officer is no longer Harlequin's favorite laughing-stock, as in the Classical era. Nor are the agents any longer called thugs. They're our special guardians, or watchmen, and instead of playing tricks on them, we honor them and assist them when the occasion arises."

"Permit me not to believe that," Philippe interjected. "That the French have ceased to joke and tease, that they have developed a serious respect for the law, I can't easily imagine. It would, in any case, be to the detriment of their distinctive qualities."

"Nevertheless, it's the case."

"All right…so, soldiers—since that's what we're talking about—are very rarely seen?"

"No, hardly ever."

"Since when?"

"Since when? Since we took stock, Monsieur Martinvast, of what the regime of military conscription had delivered and cost over the course of a century—by setting aside the colonies acquired, almost all of the onerously, and the départements annexed, sometimes troublesomely, and on the other, the billions spent and the two woeful names that marked the conclusions of the only two wars in which the national territory was at stake: Waterloo and Sedan."

Philippe lowered his head and reflected briefly. Then he said: "Then there are no longer garrisons in France. My God, what is a provincial town without a garrison?"

Matteo resumed his sly and indulgent smile. "Oh yes—it seems that garrisons were once the soul of towns, if one might put it thus. We're told that people never wearied of watching the beautiful soldiers marched past by their officers. When they went on exercises, when they showed their boots to the sergeant, when hay was given to their horses, the entire town knew it—it had to know it. It's still like that in Saint-Denis, Saint-Paul, Saint-Jean and all your localities, isn't it?

"Well, here, all that has changed. The old citadel-barracks—the last Bastille—has been demolished. The old military traditions by which it remained haunted, on contact with which our young citizens were exposed to losing, without equivalent compensation, the best of their innate virtues, have disappeared with it, forever. By a natural sentiment of distributive justice, the poor, the ignorant, and the warriors themselves, demanded that the rich, the literate and the pacifists should be thrown therein like them, and the overfilled walls burst. The apprehension of the life of the quarter ceased at the same time to be counted by the number of caprices of the officer class.

"Our legions, composed of professionals, are better equipped and better armed; that's all we need. They exercise and are maintained in rural areas. They serve as instructors in the maneuvers we carry out from time in order to educate us in the theories of combat we begin to learn as children. Finally, they watch over our arsenals, for the nation is the sole depository of all the murderous engines that increase the strength of a combatant to such a high degree. That's all. The military no longer absorbs us, and the uniform has lost its deceptive glamour."

"Ah! One question!" said Jacques de Vertpré suddenly, having taken no part in the conversation for some time. "To how many unarmed civilians is one combatant equivalent today?"

Matteo scratched his ear. "Oh, I don't really know—I'm not very good with numbers like that, and it's always so problematic. I imagine though, that with the terrible progress of destructive science, it requires relatively few men to reckon with civilians.

"The important point at present, is not to have a great many soldiers, but to watch over, as I said just now, the military equipment, and not to leave it within range of large agglomerations, where trouble might always break out. That equipment is the country's safeguard. Fortunately, no example has so far been produced in which it has been surrendered by

151

treason. It's true that all the members of the militia are bound by a solemn engagement and that the foremost of our social virtues is fidelity to one's word. Our codes have extremely severe penalties for those who fail in that first principle of honor."

Matteo stopped at that point, but continued after further reflection; "Well, to get back to your question, which is rather important from the viewpoint of the internal administration, I don't say that one combatant is worth a thousand civilians, but I believe that, in the French Confederation, we have one armed man for every thousand inhabitants. Isn't that good—provided that we're well armed?

Matteo was glad to have found another opportunity to prevail.

"It's not many, in fact," Philippe observed. "We have nearly as many troops in Bourbon."

"That doesn't surprise me, Monsieur Martinvast. Out there, you still maintain the traditions of the Middle Ages: the Crown, with its two natural supports, the army and the clergy; brutal force and persuasive force. Oh, you're still warriors and heroes..."

In saying that, Matteo assumed, out of courtesy, and admiring attitude. Then, with a hint of malice, he added: "On an island, though? No matter. Oh, the game of war occupied humankind for many centuries, I know. Perhaps they were good times...for the commandants, at least. In those days, the government was the army, wasn't it? What did the army do? It made war, it maneuvered. And what did the people do? They worked to maintain the army. Today, it's no longer like that. We're already far away from the Age of Steel of the Quaternary Epoch. The noble game of arms is prohibited. We leave to inevitable scourges and cataclysms the task of periodically pruning humankind. International brigandage had been virtually suppressed. When one country takes territory or precious objects from another, that is called theft, as between individuals. Oh, people are prosaic today. They're disciplined, industrious peaceful. Glory is no longer measured by the number of skulls scalped, nor the commemorative medals of large-scale slaughter; it's only accorded to benefactors of humanity. Our greatest men are those who prolong or ameliorate human life; they're the inventors of the locomotive and the magnetic coil, the two great agents of the recent evolution of society. Honor no longer resides in simple individual bravery, but in science and charity. There you are, Monsieur Martinvast. Do you understand, Monsieur de Vertpré?"

The tirade was too beautiful, and Matteo had managed his effect too well, for the two cousins to hesitate before applauding him. So, all smiles, they saluted his final words with a profound and laudatory bow.

XXIV

It was time that Matteo stopped speech-making, for the traffic was beginning to become troublesome. In a short time, the crowd had increased considerably and was moving with astonishing speed. The passers-by now seemed to be in their best clothes, and almost everyone was heading in the same direction.

Our strollers had not paid any heed to this movement at first, but it was impossible not to notice it now. Music could now be heard from all directions. Choirs were moving by, singing. In the avenues, the streets and the alleyways, flags and streamers were beginning to float from windows—and on all sides banners were advancing, surrounded by various groups. Bells and bagpipes were resonating in the atmosphere, and the voice of cannon was thundering in the distance.

Matteo, no less than the others, was momentarily intrigued by the manifestation that was in preparation. *Is it a choral competition?* he wondered. *Is there some prize to hand out? Is the city forming a procession ahead of some glorious and benevolent Marseillais?* Suddenly, he slapped his forehead. "Oh, of course! It's the centenarian!" And he reminded Jacques and Philippe about the *Semaphore*'s communication announcing the apotheosis of Marc Lignousse, a new centenarian, for midday. The celebration, it will be remembered, was to take place in the Allées de Meilhan.

It was toward that park, in fact, that the current of the crowd was flowing, and our strollers could already see the tall trees, covered in the tender verdure of spring.

At that moment, in the midst of the quincunxes, an immense chord rose up; it was all the fanfares combined setting out to play a solemn hymn together. At the same time, above the crowd, seated on a platform, a man with a long white beard appeared. That was Marc Lignousse, whom others were carrying in triumph.

Matteo broke into a run, drawing his companions after him.

In a matter of moments, all three found themselves in the midst of the celebrations, close enough to the old man to be able to make out his features and take account of the expression of grateful joy on his face.

Although he was a trifle frail and stooped, the venerable Lignousse was still very presentable. Carefully dressed, with his beard and hair lustrous, it was obvious that he had been the object of particular care for the sake of this supreme procession. His eyes moist with emotion, he leaned over to the right and the left, replying to an amicable sign from one person, shaking hands with another. And while he advanced in his papal chair, flowers laden with perfume rained down all around him.

Now it was a choir several hundred strong that was filling the air with its chords. From the bosom of those harmonious clamors, a few words, in fragmentary phrases, reached the ears of our voyagers.

"Longevity is worth more than wealth; more even than glory..."

"Happy are the old, for they know the pure charm of life; they savor it drop by drop..."

"Every new day is for them a day gained, a day of celebration..."

Philippe and Jacques understood that it was again a matter of the joy of living, as in Rosa Myrtil's cantata.

Behind the procession, eddies formed. Our companions were forced to stop momentarily, lifted up as they were by the popular wave. Matteo, however, did not want to stop fulfilling his function.

"You can see around us," he said "almost all the elements of the population. Look, there are the mariners; over there, the horticulturalists. Can you see the distinctive symbols in their collars?

"Among the women, there's an accountant, and there's a typographer—and there's a clockmaker, a businesswoman, an

155

engraver, a photographer...for all of the fair sex work, keeping an equal distance from overexertion and dangerous idleness. All the professions compatible with their physical aptitude are open to them, except for that of public functionary...

"Further away, you can see an elected representative of the people, the administrator of the canton of La Corniche and a delegate to the Junta of Marseilles. He's chatting with the representative of the Confederation, accredited with regard to Provence...

"That other group of women, coming forward, are free or available women. You'll notice that they don't have gilded collars like the engaged women. Ah! There's another centenarian—a woman, this time. Look at her. Isn't she as gracious as she is respectable? What a fine, placid, relaxed attitude!"

As the female centenarian passed close to the travelers, Matteo bowed profoundly. She was leaning on the arm of a handsome adolescent. "That woman," he observed, "will have wanted to watch the enthronement of her new colleague. All the centenarians who are still fit will have done the same, and we'll doubtless see more of them, for Marseilles has a considerable number. The rule in this matter is that citizens and citizenesses who reach a century of existence become the pensioners—I might almost say the spoiled children—of the canton. On the other hand, they're put out of the frame from the political viewpoint, and they have to surrender their private properties. It's not to penalize them that the law decided that, but in order to remove any kind of care from their final days. Every year, independently of solemnities like today's, there's a holiday celebration at the communal house for all the centenarians in the canton."

"The young man accompanying the old woman," said Jacques, "is presumably one of her grandchildren."

"Yes, probably," Matteo replied. "He is, I imagine, a great-grandson descended from one of her daughters. You can see that the color of his jacket differs from that of his sleeves."

"That's true."

"That means that the child is an adolescent who hasn't yet reached full puberty. That garment protects boys until the end of childhood—which is to say, about twelve years of age—until the medical jury deems them fit for the work of life. Woe betide any woman who draws that young man into a premature liaison; she'd be liable to the most rigorous punishment."

"Do young women enjoy the same protection, Monsieur Matteo?"

"Absolutely. Look over there; that's a virgin; you can recognize her by her blue scarf. Until nobility she is strictly guarded and preserved, primarily in the interests of the race, and also in the interests of her own health.

At that moment, in fact, in the shade of the trees, a young woman appeared, not far away from our voyagers; they rested their gazes on her momentarily. Her stride was graceful and her fresh face radiant. Then, wanting to resume the conversation, Philippe turned to his guide and said: "You mentioned rigorous punishments, my dear Monsieur. Is your penal system severe, then—draconian?"

"Truthfully," said Matteo, shaking his head and pulling a face, "our system is severe, and it isn't. We settle most matters with the measures I've already mentioned to you: the withdrawal of decorations, criticism, reprimand, restriction of civil rights..." He paused, and then continued: "Well, listen carefully: our punishments are divided into three categories, according to whether the crime harms the delinquent himself, several individuals, or the public in general. It's the last cases that are the most serious. In each category there are a large number of punishments between which the judges may choose, according to the individual with whom they have to deal, for a particular punishment might be a reprimand for one but not for another. Sometimes, a small sanction applied to a particular point produces more effect than a heavier repression. As far as possible, the guilty are punished in the place where they have done wrong, and in their domicile. Those are our principal guidelines.

"Let's suppose to take an example, that a man is deprived of work for eight days; he must remain seated for that length of time on a special bench on the external wall of the communal house. Let's take another, deprived for a month of the right of amour—that's a special action reserved for men between 25 and 40. He'll be forbidden to leave the city and subjected for the duration of his punishment to individual surveillance. A man on whom a twenty-four hour fast is inflicted, or an exclusive diet of bred for three days, is subject to analogous control.

"I told you that we're severe without being... In fact, for damages caused to individuals, you'll doubtless find us indulgent. On the other hand, you might judge us pitiless and terrible, as in martial law, for damages caused to the public interest. That category, I suppose, include culprits who have recklessly caused explosions, misappropriated weapons from our arsenals, committed fraud in writing or orally, adulterated food, money or goods, or even spread an infection by scorning regulations—for those faults are not only the most calamitous but they're also, for the most part, the easiest to commit.

"Don't imagine, however, that we have inscribed, in the number of means of redress or terrorization, the whip, the collar or other instruments of torture. No, there has sometimes been a question of returning to those methods, but thus far we've refrained. Our punishments are negative and operate by deprivation. That's the accepted principle. When it's necessary to have recourse to fines we hold firm to it, I won't hide that from you, and always in proportion to wealth. By way of compensation, we no longer have prisons."

"What, no more prisons!" cried Jacques and Philippe, in unison. "That's quite extraordinary."

"Well, no, we no longer have those sinister gehennas with dark walls, where the condemned spent month after month at the State's expense, acclimating to that tomb-like life to the point of returning there fatally and repeatedly, contracting an indelible diathesis that rendered them permanently inert and vicious...no. When we deprive a man of his liberty to come and go, it's only for a few days, and we confine him to his home, either on his word of honor or under police guard.

"Deportation, on the other hand, we employ rather broadly, especially with respect to recidivists. Our islands of exile, which each correspond to a category of delinquents, are not at the antipodes but a short distance from our coasts. The most important establishment is on Belle-Île. As for the death penalty, we rarely apply it, although it's available for many cases."

"Ah!" said Jacques and Philippe, simultaneously, their faces immediately taking on an expression mingling surprise and dread.

"Yes, Matteo continued, "it's one of the necessities of the Republic to be rigorous and comminatory, without mercy. The dread that the ancients considered as the commencement of wisdom is today regarded as the last word in the art of government; it's the key to the vault of the definitive social state. In order to punish as little as possible, one must sow as much fear as one can.

"Once, societies had artificial barriers that were almost sufficient to guarantee them against derelictions; there was the innate belief in the intervention of a supreme being, fashioned and imagined as a social guarantee; there was the prestige of royalty and the Church; theirs was faith in Hell and Paradise. Today, when eyes are descaled, we only have one real barrier; the threat of the law, and, if necessary, of the irremediable punishment.

"What do you expect? In a society whose objet is the happiness of life, in which the sole and unique good is life, it's hardly astonishing that the deprivation of life should be envisaged as the ultimate punishment, the final, indispensable and fatal word.

"Then again, in ancient times, there was also a hierarchy of classes, which simplified government. With equality, administration has become infinitely more difficult. Our republics, having no other basis henceforth than democratic law, have an absolute need, in order to survive, of being very

159

strongly disciplined. That's why the death penalty remains suspended above our heads. It almost never strikes us, I repeat, but it's always there; it's the ultimate reserve of social authority."

The two cousins looked at one another from time to time. Their gaze testified to both a impression of terror and a sentiment of compassion.

"What you say," Philippe observed, "is perhaps fundamentally justified. I admit, however, that I was expecting to find the scaffold permanently suppressed."

"Oh, yes, certainly!" replied Matteo. "The scaffold, the guillotine, torture—all the barbaric practices that once accompanied capital punishment—has been abolished. When it's decided that a man must cease to live, the man is immediately delivered to an apparatus that cuts short his days painlessly, only leaving in his place, after a few seconds, a pinch of ash. He is fulgurated and cremated. No public exhibition; no appeal for mercy, nothing that..."

"No mercy, you say?" Philippe put in.

"No, since there has been no king, there has been no more right to mercy."

"What! But our history tells us that the presidents of the Third Republic used that prerogative extensively. Isn't that true?"

"It's possible, Monsieur Martinvast, but those presidents were pseudo-kings: civil list, palace, military guard, hunting preserves, irresponsibility—they had almost all the regal attributes, and they naturally employed a practice whose original purpose had always been to add prestige to royalty. But all that has changed. There is no longer a president-king; there is no longer a unique judge, able to overrule all the criminal procedures of the Confederation on appeal, merely by examining the files. The law and the judiciary mechanism no longer risk being irritated by the pleasure of a sovereign surrounded by quasi-divinity. Besides, since the indescribable abuses of the regime of imprisonment have ceased, recourse to mercy is much less useful. We have left to the entire country—which is to say, to the law—the faculty of relieving someone of the effect of another law. The legislature rarely uses that faculty. It does sometimes grant a more or less general amnesty, but it's very exceptional that it extends mercy to a single individual."

This was too much for Jacques, who could no longer contain himself. "But your society is like the Inferno!" he eventually cried. "Go forth, poor Frenchmen, abandon all hope..."

"If it's an Inferno, Monsieur de Vertpré, it's a very mild Inferno, I can assure you. Did the ancient code of military justice, which death featured in every stanza, prevent soldiers from singing and sailors from dancing? How many of them per year, in time of peace, were shot for doing so? Here, it's the same. One almost never hears mention of serious condemnation. Oh, I know, that apparent rigor marks a complete turnabout with respect to certain tendencies of the century before last, but that's how the world is made; everything passes and returns.

"It's true that in that era, when one looked so closely at the existence of a malefactor, one sometimes saw thousands of men kill one another in military action over a pigtail, and strong minds treated those who spoke in favor of international arbitration as tender hearts and naïve dreamers. On the other hand, if an individual infected with a contagious disease communicated it freely to someone else, who died, there was no redress; it was not even involuntary homicide. Oh, they were strange times."

In saying that, Matteo began to laugh, in his hearty Provençal fashion, loud and mocking, and he repeated: "Yes, it was a strange time, when horned beasts were surrounded with more solicitude that humans."

Philippe cut that fit of hilarity short. A further reflection had just crossed his mind.

"How, then, are contagions prevented?"

"How is it done? What was done once for animals. There is an obligatory declaration of the disease, surveillance by the health authorities, and—almost invariably—isolation in a public sanitarium."

"That's it," said Jacques in his turn. "*Le Lépreux de la cité d'Aoste.*[20] The immured! And on the other hand, you no longer dare say 'hospital.' You prefer sanitarium...one truly doesn't know whether to laugh or become angry."

"Laugh, laugh, Monsieur de Vertpré," Matteo riposted, softly. "Never become angry."

"In fact," Philippe observed, again, "prophylactic measures can be a good thing, as with regard to prostitution."

"Prostitution!" exclaimed Matteo. "What's that? What do you mean by that?"

"What?" said Philippe. "You don't know the word?"

"No," said Matteo. "Do you mean that amour is a medium of exchange? At all times, women have traded it, either for amour itself, for the hope of maternity, for honors, protection or wealth. Do you mean lasciviousness? But that's a simple malady."

"It's not surprising that the meanings of words are no longer familiar," said Jacques, intervening again. "The French of today no longer have adultery, or abortion..."

"Indeed not," said Matteo.

"Nor infanticide."

"Nor that," said Matteo again.

"No longer having any vice or crime, it's only natural that they no longer make any distinction between conjugal conventions, whatever they are. As morality no longer exists, there are no longer sins against mortality...really, it's entirely edifying..."

Jacques could not help laughing, but his laughter was bitter.

"By the way," he continued, "have you at least admitted incest, in imitation of what happens in other animals species?"

---

[20] *Le Lépreux de la cité d'Aoste* is an 1811 novel by Xavier de Maistre, in which the imprisoned leper (based on a real historical individual) recounts his woes to a sympathetic soldier.

At these words, Matteo had great difficulty containing himself; Jacques' sarcasm caused the blood to rise momentarily to his face. He remained calm, however.

"No, Monsieur," he replied, "there is no more incest than before, in the time of bastards without a family and without a name."

The conversation paused there. For a few moments, all three directed their gazes at the crowd surrounding them—but their eyes perceived nothing at first, because their minds remained preoccupied by what they had just said. The thoughts of the two cousins were seeking distraction when Matteo, wanting to venture another word in response to Jacques' last observations, said in a conciliatory tone:

"The book of *Genesis*, my dear Messieurs, was right, you know when it deplored the fact that our mother Eve had picked the fruit of the knowledge of good and evil. The misfortune procured since the beginning of humankind under the pretext of good and evil is immeasurable. What is good? What is evil? Races have exterminated on another over that question. By means of a gradual effort, we have returned to a state close to that which is presumed to have preceded the original sin. We no longer philosophize about what is called moral good and evil. We simply seek that which, being compatible with sociability, is in conformity with our instinct; on the other hand, of course, we avoid that which is contrary to our present interest…and also that which is contrary to the interests of the future, for we no longer say: 'Après nous le déluge.' We intend to transmit to our successors, improved and increased, the common heritage of those who have preceded us."

Philippe was beginning to yawn; as we know, he did not like long conversations, and, on the other hand, he was still preoccupied with the labor that he felt taking place in his mind. Finding that he had gone deeply enough into the matter, he intervened, saying: "It's understood, Monsieur Matteo, that you have rediscovered pure innocence. Eden has reopened its gates. The pigeons are your emblem."

The celebrations were still going on.

163

It is still noisy, still crowded; there is joy, health, beauty and laughter everywhere. Another centenarian—oh, this one is considerable ravaged by time. Poor old chap! He can barely drag himself along on his crutches; his head is oscillating, and his nose remained red with cold beneath the hot sun. Large round spectacles and an acoustic trumpet hang from his belt, substituting with difficulty for the weakness of his senses.

At that wretched sight, Jacques, unthinkingly, ran forward, picked up the trumpet and said to the old man: "My poor friend, what charm can life still retain for you?"

"What charm?" the centenarian replied, his eyes widening in astonishment. "But I'm alive, my dear Monsieur, and that's sufficient for my happiness."

"How much better you would be in Paradise," said Jacques then, moved by pity, forgetting momentarily that he was in a public square in Marseilles.

"Yes," said the old man, increasingly surprised, and with an indefinable smile. "Yes, I remember—I heard talk in my youth of those beautiful dreams of eternity." After a pause, he added: "But if you only knew how much I prefer a single spring morning!"

So saying, he went on his way.

Ah! Here comes another woman, to whom people are giving way and bowing without looking at her. This one is not yet a mother, but will not be long in becoming one. Childhood is also broadly represented. Here are babies whose mothers hold them up in the air, agitating and turning them at arm's length; there are schoolchildren wearing the uniforms of nursery schools, whose entire lives are spent in play.

Meanwhile, people are beginning to leave the Allées de Meilhan. Groups are forming in order to depart. Here's a musical society passing by, filling the air with its rousing tunes and exciting emotion as it goes.

"Do you hear, Messieurs?" said Matteo, excitedly. "It's the *Marseillaise*. You doubtless recognize our national anthem. It's still the same tune but we play it a little more slowly, more solemnly, have you noticed? And we've changed the words. Today, the *Marseillaise* is a hymn of peace.

"Ah!" said Jacques—who, needless to say, did not like either the old tune or the old words.

"Yes," Matteo went on. "Moreover, it was for peace that the tune was composed, since it's an ancient hymn."

"What!" Philippe exclaimed. "That's what you make of Rouget de Lisle's inspiration? What about history?"

"History!" replied Matteo, suddenly becoming sarcastic. "There's a whole heap of histories...it's never been anything but an accumulation of legends." At the same time he raised his right shoulder and made a half-turn, as if to say: "Go on, then, you who are still in it..."[21]

"Really, you're exaggerating," Jacques observed, mildly.

"History!" repeated the cicerone, again. "A conjectural science; a mine of anecdotes. Yes, I swear. Everyone arranges it according to his whim. Historians are merely story-tellers. Ten years after an event, go back to it. Don't try to narrate it— you'll lie." Then, returning to the question: "Rouget de Lisle might have made up the words, it's true, but the tune isn't his. That legend has been demolished several times over—but it's continually reborn, it seems; believers don't like to be disturbed.

The two cousins wondered what Matteo might have against history. Had it committed some injustice in his regard? Or, as was more likely, had that science really fallen, in contemporary regard, to the rank of mere chronology?

"For exactitude, you see," Matteo added, "absolute and complete exactitude, outside of what is mathematical or tangible, it's a waste of time searching. Pure truth is forever enchained at the bottom of its unfathomable well."

---

[21] Matteo might be right about history in general, but there does not seem to be any plausible evidence that the tune of the *Marseillaise* was composed by anyone other than Rouget de Lisle.

When the band passed close to them, they were literally deafened. At the same moment, by virtue of an impulse that they could not explain, they began to march, following the current. One, two…right, left…

Drawn away by the torrent of the crowd, away they go, all three of them marching in step, behind the musicians. Look at them! Philippe, in particular, is radiant. How amusing humans are!

XXV

We shall not recount in detail the other excursions that Jacques and Philippe made in Marseilles and its environs. We shall also pass over in silence the special visit they made during their stay to the Catholic assembly, in accordance with the promise they had made. Our readers are familiar with present-day geography; on the other hand, they have no particular need to be edified on their own account by the various aspects of the new social conditions.

What is more likely to be of interest is the impression that can be produced on minds left outside its movement, and distanced by more than a century therefrom, by abrupt unveiling of the spectacle of the modern world, in a seemingly-fantastic setting, established from day to day according to the hazards of the voyage, without partiality or profoundly-examined controversy.

On that subject we are glad to be able to quote here from a letter written by Jacques de Vertpré to his mother aboard the ship that transported him from Marseilles to Bordeaux. There we shall see his sentiments described by himself. We shall only eliminate the intimate and purely affectionate sections.

"...At every step, my dear mother, we make new discoveries. Sometimes they are odd, sometimes—and more often—they are heart-rending. Philippe is beginning to sympathize with them. I even dread, although I scarcely dare to say it, that he is acquiring a taste for them. It's true that, thus far, things have almost always been presented to us in their best aspect, relatively speaking. One might think that our informers had been given an instruction to keep the other side of the coin hidden.

"As for me, I don't allow myself to be taken in, and I still consider myself to be on a mission in the midst of infidels, on morally-diseased ground; I'm resigned to it and am alert. Eve-

167

rything I see makes me love and adore our dear Île de Bourbon all the more. How very glad I shall be to return!

"...The Canal des Deux-Mers, on which we are sailing, is very well-established. All the ships that used to pass through the Pillars of Hercules under the guns of Gibraltar have adopted this route, and it's a major source of revenue for the national treasury and the province of Gascony. One finds oneself in the midst of merchant vessels and a few warships—I ought rather to say police-ships, for it seems that there is no longer any war, properly speaking. These ships carry functionaries and agents of the public force. The sailors aboard them are volunteers hired at an average salary. I also see huge ferry-boats that go to the shore to pick up passenger- and goods-trains on their floating rails and transport them without derangement to the other bank. In spite of the breadth of the channel, there are a certain number of aerial bridges of the Eiffel genre, which outline their black teeth against the sky at intervals.

"...We were in the vicinity of the old Languedoc canal, and Philippe and I were trying to see whether we might be able to make out Toulouse on the horizon, when we were approached very politely by a passenger in a red fez who had embarked at Narbonne, and whom we had noticed nearby on several occasions, seemingly prowling around us. The passenger had curly black hair and a swarthy complexion, and a soft moustache extended beneath his fleshy nose. When he heard us mention Toulouse, he hastened to give us information us about that city, which was indeed nearby: its present population, its industry, everything we could desire. Then he added:

"'Pardon me, Messieurs, but I'd like to ask you a question in my turn. Are there any Jews in Bourbon?' He, it seemed, was Jewish. I had had little doubt about that, judging by what I knew about his race, but I had not given it any thought and I did not even know whether or not there were any Jews in France.

"I told him that we have no Israelites in Bourbon.

"'Do you think, at least, that they would be admitted there? Would there be some place for them in commerce or banking?'

"I frowned, and did not hide my suspicion that it might be imprudent to attempt the adventure. My God! It's not that we are ready on our island to detest that race...I know that with regard to them, our views are akin to those of Protestants with regard to Catholics. We might hold it against them that they consider our Christ as a mere Luther, but no, we have no prejudice against them, or jealousy. If there had been no Jews, there would be no Christians. Except that we only want to have a single religion in our nation. When religion serves as the basis of a society, that is indispensable.

"After the response I made, he was about to withdraw, for he evidently had the information that he had wanted to obtain for some time, but we, stung by his question, retained him and continued to converse with him. It was good that we did, for we learned many interesting things in consequence.

"...Thus, it appears that Jews are fairly widespread in France, and that their ethnic character has resisted all social change. It's still the same people, indifferent to political power, aggregating as much as possible in finance and business, economically and prolifically. Before marriage ceased to exist, they had already obtained a considerable numerical advance relative to the other inhabitants by virtue of the fecundity of their families. Since marriage has ceased to exist they are, remarkably, numbered among those whose conjugal arrangements have more fixity—which can still be seen—and if there are still a few households that keep their children with them, it's mostly among those that they are found. They continue to profess, as in the past, the dogma-less religion that they have received faithfully from their ancestors, and that serves them as both a bond and a password.

"...I asked my interlocutor whether freemasonry was still as prevalent among Jews as it had been in certain epochs of the 19th century. 'No, Monsieur,' he replied. 'That bizarre establishment has been carried away by the whirlwind of intellectual oxygen that swept the world at the end of the 19th century, some time after the exodus of your forefathers. French common sense awoke forcefully, and took a broad revenge in that era on all occult and public affectations of whatever sort; obsolete lumber vanished in its blast and it was necessary to renounce the game of playing conspirator for form's sake, alas.' He added, in jest: 'Two venerable brothers—two, no more—are still in the asylum in Oléron, where they are being studied as a biological curiosity.'

"Here the Israelite burst out laughing. 'They're two lunatics who cry out incessantly at the top of their voice: *Down with the clergy, death to the priests!*—for it's well-known that the last French freemasons had scarcely any other refrain. A great peril fills their unhinged brains with terror. They're frightful to behold. It's sufficient to set before their eyes a priestly hat or a doll costumed as a Jesuit to make them fall into a catalepsy. A scientist, curious about matters of atavism, tried to reconstitute their genealogy. One of them—the more fanatical—had an ancestor, he thought, who was a porter in a Catholic seminary. The other descended from an old priest of the religious decadence, who had abandoned the soutane in order to marry a serving-woman. According to the scientist, French freemasonry, in its final state, was nothing but religious mania in reverse.'

"...You mustn't think, my dear mother, on the basis of what I just said about the island of Oléron that all the insane are relegated to islands. The Israelite in the red fez explained to us that only the most dangerous and incurable lunatics are thus isolated. There are, in any case, far fewer lunatics than in the past. That is due, we are told, to the fact that life is simpler, and more uniform. Oh, yes, it's more uniform. Then too, it's claimed that sobriety is much more extensive. In the same way, they add that no one is any longer driven made by affairs of the heart, since freedom in love has been decreed, just as no one despairs by virtue of reversals of fortune, since inequality in wealth has been drastically reduced. The fear of Hell is no longer there to produce its particular terror. Finally, honors having lost their prestige, the delirium of pride is no more to be feared. Perfect, perfect…you recognize the same old song, don't you, mother dear?

"…Oh, what a strange country! I never cease repeating it to myself. It seems to me that people have adopted the rule of envisaging everything as it was done before, and then doing the opposite. What a criterion—and how flattering for our common ancestors! The worst thing of all is that our continental compatriots are quite unconscious of their aberrations.

"…The Jew who is traveling with us is a commercial agent, so he's well-informed on the commercial condition of the region through which we're traveling. According to him, the Midi has suffered less than the North from the freedom of trade. I mean that it has been less subject to necessary transformation. That's understandable; the industry of the Midi is its own industry, which depends on its soil and its sunlight, while labor in the North, primarily mechanical labor, operating by means of assemblies of workers, is an occupation of choice and circumstance, able at any moment to be replaced by something else.

"Viticulture, however, has been much improved. It has had to struggle not merely against certain scourges but also against a gradual tendency of the wine-growing zone to decline. 'It's true,' said the Israelite, 'that everything changes: the currents of the sea, the dispositions of the atmosphere, the division of land and sea; it's not astonishing that the temperature, the seasons, and the productions of the soil are imperceptibly modified from day to day.' Whatever the reason, even on a reduced scale, the exploitation of the vine still plays a large role in national toil.

"…There is not even any silk culture. It's from the Far East that all the cocoons now come, and also there that they're unwound. That was the reason the Japanese were created, they say. The weavers are also installed in the Far East; only the clothes are made up in European cities, where the legal entitlements to the invention's modernization remain. Thus, the mulberry-growers keep their leaves and the soil of the Midi does very well, I'm assured, beneath that shade, to which they have a right. Olives are still extensively cultivated.

"…It's the same with the preparation of perfumes, which requires, as you know, a great deal of care and dexterity. I forgot to tell you that during our stay in Marseilles we were enabled to breathed odors we had never encountered before. Truly, absolutely new and quite astonishing discoveries have been made in this area. You'll judge for yourself, for I've set aside a few unknown phials for you, which are veritable olfactory revelations, capable of making our young Bourbonnaises swoon. I might be mistaken, but it seems to me that these scientific and refined people attach a great deal of importance to odor. Indeed, the Neo-French seem to only to begin perceiving when nature leads the by the nose.

"…People are not content to run the gamut of pleasant odors; they also create execrable emanations, intolerable gases that suffocate and threaten death. Use of them was made, I'm assured, in the last military operations. A simple *cordon insanitaire* renders a city or a camp absolutely unapproachable. On the other hand, infective bombs and shells full of harmful microbes are dropped from balloons.

"…I would never finish if I recounted in detail everything that I have seen and everything I've been told. Have I told you already that many French people are now exclusively vegetarian? Well, that has extended so far that on ships, as in hotels, there are two dining rooms one for vegetarians and the other for—how shall I put it?—carnivores. Philippe and I know nothing about it, and, the beginning of the voyage, we were taken in. For two days we went to the wrong room and found ourselves subjected to the strictest fast. Philippe complained, and only then did we discover the cause of our error.

"Vegetarians imagine that by abstaining from meat they'll live longer, that they'll be less brutal, less aggressive, they they'll have few illnesses…what do I know? Always the preoccupation with terrestrial life.

"…To sum up, the same reflection constantly comes to mind the further I go on my journey. These people have made a great deal of scientific progress; they're full of good will; they even practice certain very commendable human virtues—but what a shame that they have lost the moral sense and are obstinate in seeing nothing beyond our vale of exile! How can they imagine that they have founded a just and durable society when they have specifically excluded from its institutions and customs all the true principles that are the foundation of societies worthy of the name?

"...Ding dong...there's the bell ringing. We're within sight of the quay at Bordeaux. Forgive me, my dear mother, for ending this letter abruptly. I put into it, for you, my most tender respects and my religious affection."

XXVI

We are glad to be able to inform the reader that we possess, relative to the next stage of our young cousins' journey—this time by railway—from Bordeaux to Saint-Lo, a document as interesting as the preceding chapter's letter. We have been able to make a copy of the notes which Philippe Martinvast made in his travel journal during the journey. Again, therefore, we shall allow the travelers to speak for themselves.

"...Immense fields; more separation between the parcels of land. The countryside offers a strange appearance. It isn't, as in Bourbon, a checkerboard of multicolored squares. It's like a succession of large monochrome carpets. Around a few village, one still sees, disposed in a fan, strips of land serving as private gardens, but most of them only contains flowers. On the horizon there are groups of male or female laborers working against the green or gray background. There are drivers of steam-ploughs, groups with hoes, workers guiding mechanical weeders. As in the mowing season, the machines have to do the hard work over the great undulating plains. Here and there, a factory in which the products of the earth are transformed.

"...One can see endless orchards for cider-apples, pasturage occupied by numerous flocks of sheep—oh, in countless profusion. One can only say that there are sheep everywhere. The democratic cutlet is doubtless in fashion. They must have decided that ovine flesh offers less inconvenience for alimentation than beef and veal.

"...The meadows are admirably maintained. Some are vast in extent. At the same time, it seems to me that there are many more woodlands than I was led to expect. That might explain the abundance of running water and the calming coolness of the climate. I notice many horses in the fields. Evidently, equine breeding is in a state of prosperity.

"...That's strange. Many woods, but no—or not many—cereals. Where are the wheat, barley and oats grown, then? I ask a traveler about that. He replies that cultivation is only applied to products destined to be used when fresh, whether it's a matter of nourishing people and animals or industrial materials. Everything that, without being too burdensome with regard to its intrinsic value, can be employed in the dry state comes from abroad. Thus France, the granary of the Occident, the blonde daughter of Ceres, is no longer a land of wheat. I no longer recognize the land of my ancestors.

"…Remained thoughtful for some time. The train runs, or rather glides with a rapidity and smoothness that delights me. I'm gently rocked, as on a calm sea, while the rails murmur their long steely resonance. At every station, I can hear the music of bees in the distance.

"…Game seems to be extremely abundant. Numerous rabbits watch the train pass, scarcely disturbed by the noise of the locomotive. They take a few steps, as if to show off the whiteness of their tails, but don't return to their holes. In the fields, squadrons of hares carry out large-scale maneuvers, running as if pursued by a pack of greyhounds. It's superb. At least democracy hasn't suppressed hunting! There's every kind of large game, furred or feathered. I've already seen pairs of roe deer standing like sentinels at crossroads or on the edge of woods at least ten times. Where's my rifle? I have to say something to all those animals.

"Hunting, we're told, has become very important. They do it in every fashion, with guns, falcons, arrows and hounds. All the men are fond of it, and many women. It's also the object of extremely detailed regulation. There are associations of every sort organized for its usage. The old hunts are funded by shares; never have they been as popular or as brilliant. There are no taxes on hunting. Hunters supervise the conservation and reproduction of the game themselves, as they have the primary interest in maintaining it.

"Extraordinarily, the woods only have serious value by virtue of the hunting they provide. They bring in more thereby than cultivated land. It's said that this is an era in which landowners are letting their farms go, and that reforestation has commenced. Will France, then, become as leafy as in the old-en times of Gaul?

"Al this is very surprising. I did not imagine the French peasant nourishing himself on partridges and pheasants. It's better than chicken casserole, I admit. Game evidently plays a large role in alimentation today. I asked whether it was the same for fishing. 'Absolutely,' was the reply I received.

"'But I thought there were no more fish; that river-beds served as sewers.'

"'Make no mistake, the rivers are clarified when necessary. Excreta go into the sea, where possible, on to the land, when it is fertilized, and on to the fire when they're no longer good for anything.'

"So sport is a popular pleasure! The French citizen enjoys the ancient aristocratic privileges without contest. They have leisure time, in any case, and it's necessary for them to employ it. I imagine, nevertheless, that the individual ration in such matters must be rather meager. Oh well, who says democracy says moderation. A democrat is like a sage, he is content with little. As long as his share is not inferior to his neighbor's, he is satisfied.

"What is also worth noting is that hunting and fishing are now classed among the number of major social interests. The wheel of civilization has rotated and brought back, in a new form, the time of Red Indian hunters.

"...One circumstance that has struck me forcefully, throughout our journey, is that the countryside is denuded of inhabitants and that the cities are overflowing with them. What would we, who sometimes complain, rather naively, about the depopulation of the fields, say to this? The cities have immense suburbs, and their attraction is felt from a great distance. Outside them, nothing...a void...silence...it's like the sea.

"At intervals, however, one sees a railway station, with large shops, a small house for the guardian of this or that, an inn, a stables, a barn, a pubic shelter, and ancient bell-tower that serves as a mooring for aerostats, a factory surrounded by a camp of absolutely identical habitations—but all of that extremely sparse. The locomotive has drained the agrarian population; it has reduced it to the strictly necessary. As the citizen, in any case, takes no more time to travel forty or fifty kilometers that it once took him to go to the city gate—when cities still had gates—one imagines that he can exploit the fields without needing to live there.

"In a word, there is no longer any but a sparse rural population. The peasant is becoming extinct…is extinct. Perhaps that is one of the great effects of the evolution that has brought men closer together and unified them. The French congratulate themselves for it. They claim that the isolated life, infinitely less well-distributed with regard to the facilities and pleasures of existence, also favors superstitious credulities, the oppression of the weak by the strong, eccentricity—what do I know? They no longer know any but communal life, the reciprocal friction that engenders, they claim the egalitarian and positive instinct.

"…Impossible to list all the novelties in the matter of railways and telegraphy. Road locomotives, individual trains, wide tracks, narrow tracks, monorails—they have everything. The land is striped with steel. I've even seen a highway entirely armored in iron, doubtless for the circulation of electrified vehicles. A thousand ingenious means for the avoidance of accidents. There are no more barriers at level crossings, though. A simple lifting arm that the locomotive itself activates before crossing the road warns passers-by that they must beware. Along the trains there is a platform on which watchmen come and go, to prevent criminal assaults. Telegraphic wires are no longer suspended in the air like a musical stave; they're at ground level. I can't imagine what one experiences in those tangles, in the bosom of that complication, of which the instantaneous character is the mark. It's diabolical, to lose one's head there. Sometimes I confess, I'm afraid—of what? I don't know: of being killed, of being melted. A human life is such a small thing in that frightful mechanism.

"...My God, I understand, up to a point, why, in the bosom of this mechanized existence, the modern French are scarcely able to attach themselves to the charming speculations that delighted our forefathers and still serve in Bourbon as a theme for refined dissertations. I'd like to talk to them about the immortality of the soul, the beauties of spirituality, the knowledge of God and oneself, the eternal primacy of right over might, but they wouldn't listen; they'd take me for a charlatan, or smile pityingly at the obvious deterioration of my reason.

"...I can hardly take my eyes off the fields; they remain gladly fixed on the good old national soil. The land, I've already said, is no longer exploited in the name of individuals for the benefit of individuals. The rights of the old landowners have been transformed into shares, and, according to circumstances, it's either the canton itself or an agricultural society that exploits and administers it. They claim, in this fashion, to have all the advantages of large land-holdings without the inconveniences.

"At the beginning of the last land revolution, the inhabitants of villages tried to form exploitation societies, but they didn't succeed. They were peasants, used to living their own lives exclusively, often divided by family resentments or interested jealousies; they were resistant to the association and lacked the necessary technical knowledge and administrative personnel. The initiative in cooperative agriculture thus rested with share-issuing societies; with financial societies that became owners of immovable property by means of non-refundable mortgage loans; and then with exploitation societies that originated in what were initially called 'agricultural societies.'

"These societies were not only cultivators but manufacturers; the produce that they took from the ground they processed, transforming it to a greater or lesser degree. It was with them, in the main, that the State made contracts when it became the owner of the land. A few of them have been absorbed by cities and transformed, as I said just now, into cantonal services. Others have remained autonomous. As for the fate of employees, the latter distinction hardly matters, for in particular enterprises, work is regulated. Employees cannot be deprived of their right of control and participation in profits; they have the same guarantees in all cases.

"…That, then, is progress. A return to tribal organization. France exploited like virgin territory newly conquered from nature. What is the life of the world, then? A cycle of seasons.

"…It remains to be noted that the surface area of arable land has diminished noticeably. The soil is less tormented. It is doubtless time for it to rest and reconstitute itself. It is now distant lands that are opened every year by the impact of the plough. Not only have forests absorbed a portion of the fields, but there are also more roads, and since the most modest towns now grant themselves parks as far as the eye can see, parks where people play a host of games unknown to us, where they stroll, go out in boats, on horseback or in carriages, and where there are varied and charming panoramas.

"…The system is always the same; the individual has almost nothing of his own, but the associations are opulent. It seems that all the ancient châteaux, country houses, villas and mansions scattered through the countryside have been collected, along with their old trees, their beautiful pathways, their lush lawns, to blend in with the edges of towns, for the common enjoyment of all the men and women of France. Once, property meant individual enjoyment; today, the word doubtless signifies communal enjoyment. But then, if property is no longer private, one might as well say that it no longer exists, that there is no more property. Well, that saddens me—but what can it matter to me, after all?"

At this point in Philippe's journal there is a sketch that we regret not being able to reproduce.

On one side one sees, in the midst of a cheerful landscape, a building of monumental and picturesque appearance, and then, beside it, is a drawing of a man with a blissful expression, dressed in a theatrical uniform. Underneath, the following notes can be read:

"Abbaye de Fontevrault. This establishment, after having been, successively, a nunnery and a prison, is occupied today by a circle of men of letters. The establishment is very well-organized, it's said, for study, work and recreation. The above portrait depicts the physiognomy of one of these monks (I can't think of any other name to give to its inhabitants). One can judge the fine appearance that the release from individual cares continues to procure. As manual labor, the worthy brothers have chosen the printing that brings them in very healthy profits. Their costumes are inspired by artistic fantasy.

"...It appears that there are a great many circles or communities of this sort, for men, for women or for both sexes, with or without provision for children. People in these phalansteries devote themselves to various occupations: agriculture, industry, the manufacture of beverages, conserves, medicaments, etc. Almost invariably, a manual trade, a source of pecuniary profit, is combined with the preferred occupation that serves as the attraction sand rallying-point of the association. The preferred occupation itself is sometimes music or painting, sometimes hunting or fishing, sometimes speculative or scientific study. Sometimes the association has no other goal but repose and recollection. Thus there are familisteries and beguinages that guarantee their associates an isolation as complete as that which Charterhouses once provided.

"The greatest liberty is afforded to all these congregations. All that is required is that they do no harm to the interests of the race and that they respect individual independence. Thus, engagements of continence are prohibited, at least until a certain age or in case of infirmity. Nor can any serious hindrance form an obstacle to leaving the society. One understands, therefore, that communal life, in reality, leaves the individual free, as soon as supernatural ideas are banished— and there cannot even be any question today of vows, properly speaking.

"This kind of association gives no privilege to the associates, nor any release, either from contribution or personal obligation. The communities it produces are on the same footing as ordinary societies exclusively devoted to working the land or manufacturing. Like all associations, they must submit to inspection by the regulatory or financial officers of the province or the nation. Thus is convent life reborn, with at least an idea of the divine, solely for the happiness of this life. What new Middle Ages will it produce?"

The reflections on the famous abbey concluded here. Afterwards, the following can be read:

"I traveled a little beyond Nantes, with a notary—I ought to say, with a business agent, a private adviser, for there are no more ministerial officers buying the right to exploit some monopoly or other. They have been replaced in their legal attributions by ordinary functionaries submissive to hierarchical control. This man of law brought me up to date with the current regime of succession.

"First of all, there is no more succession *ab intestat*—which is to say, the transmission of wealth operating directly by virtue of the law. In other words, the donations by virtue of death are no longer presumed, as at home, according to the usual rules of affectionate attachment. On the other hand, it is no longer assumed that a child ought to be considered as a continuation of the persons of the father and the mother. 'Where is the mother,' it is said, 'or the father who can say, pointing at their offspring: that child is similar in all respects to me; he is me...' The child, it is added, is neither the exclusive reproduction of the father nor the absolute image of the other. He or she is a new combination, a third person. From that, it is induced that property does not necessarily give rise to the right of hereditary transmission.

"'What about nobility?' I asked, incidentally. 'Does it still exist? Does it remain transmissible in the same way, as incorporeal wealth?' The reply was no. The nobility of the old regime no longer exists. It was, in any case, essentially hereditary. Its last vestiges were stifled by a veritable glut of personal and life-limited titles. Those proliferate today as much as decorations. There are an incalculable number of barons, reverends, honorables, and chevaliers awarding themselves, liberally or by virtue of some affiliation, the particules de, von or Mac, or any other heraldic symbol of their choice.

"To get back to the rules of transmission of fortunes, everyone may dispose of his movable goods, crops and constructions as he pleases, in the form of a donation or a testament. Nevertheless legacies made to the profit of a mortmain establishment are void after a hundred years—which is to say that after that date, the profit reverts to the state. It is considered that a testator cannot have any idea of what might happen a century after his death, and that for ulterior time, his liberality is vitiated as no longer being made in knowledge of the cause. On the other hand, so-called rights of mutation have been abolished. Because wealth passes from one hand to another, it is said, that is no reason for the treasury to eat into it.

"...One rather odd thing is that movable fortune, which is, in large measure the only fortune nowadays, is mostly in the hands of mothers. Men have voluntarily laid their wealth at their feet. It's one of the most characteristic results of the new legislation and the new mores.

"...Land, in its entirety, the lawyer told me, has been returned to the nation, in exchange for compensation paid by the State in the form of annuities or perpetual rents. It is the same with the subsoil, roads and watercourses. Today, it is the State that makes indefinite concessions to cities for their placement; it is the State that cedes to exploitation societies, for various durations, the right of cultivating a certain terrain. The State administers its wealth as it all governments did without contest at the origin of nations, where they were governments of conquest or governments of exploration. It disposes of that wealth and draws one of its most significant income from it. In those conditions, it is understandable that there can never be any question of property in land in testamentary or other distributions.

"…I feel light dawning in my mind. It seems to me that I'm beginning to grasp the functioning of this strange social organization, the engagement of its gears.

"…Let's see then, where would I find my place in this order of things if I were part of it? Would I install myself in an ordinary municipal association? Would I ask to be admitted to an independent society? Or would I go to present myself at the door of one of those elective communities in which the same affinity brings together all the participants? In truth, I don't know. Fundamentally, the organization is the same everywhere. Do I see myself as a director or a simple employee? It doesn't really matter, since the person who gives orders has few advantages over those who take them. What would I do to win my neighbor's money and make my fortune? Oh, that's the big question…but no, since lucre is no longer the goal of work and life in the new mores.

"It's true that there has been a fundamental transformation in that respect. In olden times, to gain one's compatriot's money—which is to say, to make it pass from his pocket into yours—was everyone's ambition; it was the most noble employment to which human faculties could be put. In an intermediary epoch, people changed their minds. 'Between members of the same nation,' they said, 'it's scarcely appropriate that one spends one's time robbing one another competitively. With foreigners, all right. Between them and ourselves, let's see who's the stronger and more cunning.' But today, there are no longer any foreigners, properly speaking. As soon as there is talk of humankind and universality, when the love of the planet replaces the love of the fatherland, what good is there in wasting one's efforts speculating on the distress of one, the malady of another, the caprice, vice or ignorance of a third, in order to elevate one's wealth above that of other people? What am I saying? What good? It would, it seems to me, be a sin. There can no longer be a question, throughout the world, as in the bosom of the same family, of anything but a courteous and limited competition, incapable of

183

putting universal equality seriously in peril. Were, then, would I go? What would I do?

"What are the French seeking now, if money, authority and honors are no longer sufficient to tempt them? What do they need? The satisfaction of their conscience? The joy of duty accomplished? Hmm! That's very austere. In sum, what is their objective, their ideal? Do they know themselves? It will be necessary for me to press them hard on that last question for me finally to discover the key to their conduct.

"Oh, I know what they'll say to me. They've already repeated it many times over. I can already hear them: 'The progress that consists of increasing, for the greatest possible number, the enjoyment of life.' Always the same formula, always; human society organized for the happiness of all. They never get past that sentimental theory.

"...We've been in Normandy for an hour. I wouldn't have been alerted to that by the names of the stations, but my eyes, my heart, my old Norman nature have revealed it to me. Yes, there are the undulating fields, the shady manors, the rich pasturelands, the charming woods, and that air of ease, of facile living, that are familiar to me even though I only know them by hearsay. Oh, the personality of the provinces, how marked it still is in spite of the progress of similarity! That's the true basis of administrative subdivisions, for it rests on the territory's own nature. It seems to me that I'm seeing my native land again, and I'm buoyed up by joy. Jacques shares in that intimate delight. We go back and forth within the carriage, trying to see the country in all its aspects. Old family ballads come back to memory and we sing: 'I'm going to see my Normandy again; it's the land that gave me birth.'[22]

"How many times did the aspirations of our fathers and mothers reach out toward that privileged land? We're the first to be able to see it again. How lucky we are!

"Here's Saint-Lo."

---

[22] The first lines of a popular song composed in 1836 by Frédéric Borat.

XXVII

When they have descended from the carriage, Philippe and Jacques open their eyes wide, watching the comings and goings curiously, sometimes stopping and looking behind and around them. It seems to them that they are about to recognize someone, or even be recognized themselves, amicably sought out and welcomed with open arms—but no; the crowd through which they are moving is indifferent; no hand is extended toward them, no accolade is offered to them.

They feel vaguely disappointed. What! Have they forgotten, then, that the Martinvasts had left Saint-Lo a hundred years ago and that in every country in the world, a few months suffice to commit the most glorious names to oblivion. They are not in a port like Marseilles, where every arrival is anticipated. Nor is there anything in their costume that might attract attention; they are now dressed in the latest fashion.

They understand immediately that if they want to obtain information about their family there is only one thing to do—to inquire at the municipal offices. They therefore go to the town hall.

The latter is installed in the principal church of Saint-Lo: a former Jesuit church with a wide fronton, with no tower or steeple. A few of the canton's administrative services have been located in the former sacristies and other appendages. The church itself—which is to say, the triple nave, serves as a communal hall for the inhabitants. The judiciary court can be seen on one side, and the location serving for the deliberations of the cantonal council on the other. In the middle of the transept is the stage reserved for the authorities who preside over meetings, and not far from that stage the former pulpit now fulfils the functions of the podium. All around, on the walls, against the columns are pictures, commemorative plaques and a few statues. In the corner next to the entrance, posters, among them a large pink placard giving the program for a

185

celebration to take place the following Sunday, which is called "Red Fruit Festival."

Philippe and Jacques, who had initially taken off their hats on the threshold of the edifice, put them back on, and, standing immobile under the porch, they contemplated the interior of the former temple with a melancholy gaze.

It's here, they thought, *that our forefathers prayed; it's here that they were brought at birth and on their death. These vaults have resonated nuptial hymns for them. God was resident here then. Today, God is no longer here. With him have departed the compassionate Christ, the Madonna with the modest smile, and the martyrs and saints who personified ancient virtue. The angels have flapped their wings and returned to Heaven.*

After a few moments, Jacques, moved by his own reflections, could not help exclaiming: "Oh, the profanation!"

There, was however, no trace of violent destruction around them, nothing that revealed a hostility to the former purpose of the edifice. It simply seemed to have been transformed, gradually and peacefully, as if to prepare it one step at a time for various local needs. Everything in the ancient church that had had an artistic character or historical interest had been piously preserved. Thus, one could still see the funerary monuments of ancient bishops, a few sacred vases, several banners and a few pious paintings. Even the bells would have been able to continue their former office, for the long stout ropes were still there, hanging to one side of the travelers.

They did not have the courage to study that singular town hall for the moment. They headed for the archives—but scarcely had they taken a few steps than they found themselves in the presence of a telegraph office. They stopped.

"You know, Jacques," Philippe observed, "I have a desire to talk to someone. I'd like to get out of myself a little, away from these surroundings."

"Truthfully, perhaps you're right."

"Who shall we call?"

"That's true—who? Matteo, do you think? No…Madame Listor…if you were to ask her for news..."

No suggestion could have suited Philippe better. The same idea had sprung to his mind.

They asked for a connection. The voice replied that Madame Listor was very busy seeking new lodgings since she had deposited her children at the University, and was not at home at present.

"Bad luck," Philippe exclaimed, making a gesture of regret. "Well, let's try Madame Myrtil, shall we?"

"Alright; go on then—speak."

After a few seconds, a dialogue was established.

"We've arrived in Saint-Lo, my dear Madame, and we hastened to recall your amiable memory. We'd be very happy to hear you say that your health is good and that you're satisfied with what you've found in Paris."

"Health very good. Nothing to do for the moment in Paris. Very bored. Touched by your concern. Will you be arriving soon?"

As the plaque vibrated, Philippe repeated what he heard, turning toward Jacques. The latter was of the opinion that their sojourn in Normandy might well last a week.

"Can't leave immediately," Philippe continued, returning to the telephone. "Have much to do here. Large celebration tomorrow."

"What celebration?"

"Summer festival, Pentecost—don't know exactly…cherries."

"You mean Red Fruit Festival. Will there be a concert?"

"Yes, undoubtedly."

"Will be there directly, then. Retain room at your hotel. Send luggage by tube. Arrive by aerostat in two hours."

"Oh, good!" Philippe exclaimed, moving his head away from the apparatus momentarily. "My opinion, my dear cousin, is that your affairs are going rather well. Did you hear?"

"Yes, yes," said Jacques, who had had his ear close to Philippe's for some time. "Let her come—I have no objection, if the journey is of any interest to her."

"Delighted, delighted," Philippe repeated, once again addressing himself to his correspondent in Paris. "We'll await you with impatience."

This new prospect appeared to reanimate our two voyagers slightly. Within an instant, their mood had changed. They went to enquire after their family with a new will. First of all, though, what was this tube by which Madame Myrtil was sending her luggage? They asked the telephone attendant. He told them that there was a network of pneumatic tubes that served to transport letters, newspapers and small parcels throughout the country.

"Oh, really!" exclaimed Philippe, with admiring astonishment. As he had become cheerful again, he added: "But passengers don't travel by tube as yet?"

"No, Monsieur, not yet," the clerk replied, smiling.

Then they went to the archives.

The curator did indeed have information about the Martinvasts—a good deal of it, in fact, from before and after the suppression of family laws. Thus, without searching for very long, he discovered the death certificate of Dr. Martinvast, the brother of the Martinvast who had emigrated. The doctor, whom we mentioned at the beginning of our story, had died at the age of eighty-three, having been mayor of Saint-Lo, and had left three children. His grave could be seen in the old cemetery. On the other hand, he knew that several new Martinvast lines had propagated since the time when descendancy had been established via women, but it would take quite a long time to collect the documents concerning them. He therefore suggested to the voyagers that he should draw up and give to them in a few days a complete genealogical chart of all the people bearing their name, from the exodus to the present dat.

"In the meantime," he added, "you might like to visit the old cemetery and your former estate at Vertpré, if that enters into your plans."

Philippe and Jacques were entirely in agreement with that. They therefore hastened to make that double visit before the arrival of Madame Myrtil.

XXVIII

As they crossed the threshold of the old cemetery, our two cousins felt overcome by the particular sentiment of compunction that grips visitors at the entrance to ancient refuges of the dead. At the same time, they were struck by a very painful impression on observing the neglect into which the old field of rest had fallen. The paths were disappearing under parasitic grass; in every direction, the tombstones, laden with moss, cracked and crumbling, were losing their purchase. Tree branches hung negligently down to the ground, mingling with brambles. At intervals, however, a vigorous yellow flower pierced the undergrowth; it was a half-wild camellia or rose that was losing its note of gaiety in the midst of the mournful foliage, as if to announce a return to life.

The cemetery was no longer in use; that was obvious. In any case, the presence at one of its extremities of a funerary temple surmounted by a tower characteristic of crematoria would have been sufficient to inform even ill-informed travelers of the fact.

Guided by the indications they had brought from Bourbon, Philippe and Jacques did not take long to discover the tomb of their last French ancestor, whose eldest son had emigrated.

"Look here, Philippe," said Jacques, tearing the ivy away from a large slab of white marvel. "This is one of the ends of the broken chain of Martinvasts; the other end is in our mortuary chapel in Bourbon." So saying, he knelt down.

Philippe, his head bowed and uncovered, associated himself with his brother's pious thoughts. Together, they then collected, to the right and the left, a whole set of souvenirs dedicated to members of their family: periwinkles that had grown around the tomb, ivy leaves, a marble shard, a sprig of cypress.

The monuments relating to Dr. Martinvast's branch of the family were not on the same side of the cemetery. Separated in life, the progressivist Martinvasts and the traditionalist Martinvasts were still separated in death. The two cousins did not take long to find them, however, for the doctor's tomb was designed to attract the eye; it was certainly the most grandiose in the whole necropolis. The epitaph, very long and eulogistic, reported that the mausoleum had been erected at the expense of the town and the département, Dr. Martinvast having ended his career as Prefect after having been Mayor, and had even been the first regional Prefect elected by the general council.

Considering that glorious and proud tomb, still radiant with prestige in the midst of all those old relics of the past, Philippe and Jacques could not help making a comparison with the modest grave, doubly buried by earth and brambles, that they had just visited. *To those who are faithful*, they thought, *oblivion; and for their children, exile, life restricted to the horizon of an island. To those who denied paternal beliefs and examples, illustriousness, power and wealth.*

Jacques extrapolated the argument in order to admire the martyrs to filial respect all the more. *We're the pure ones, the irreproachable ones*, he said to himself. *We alone have the right to be proud...and to all the baubles of glory. Where is honor? Where is duty? In the conservation of the spirit of the family; in the unfailing attachment to ancient principles.*

Philippe, without issuing recriminations against his own antecedents, was not far away from feeling flattered at the sight of the glorious development that the other part of the family had achieved; once again he felt himself drawn sideways. While walking, he murmured vague words. "Immobility," he said to himself, "is a respectable thing—noble, even—but as soon as one is in a minority in observing it, it's the surest means of being distanced and reduced to impotence. It's a virtue, to be sure, but a negative virtue. What am I saying—a virtue? Immobility doesn't exist. The Earth seems motionless with regard to a boat that is moving, traveling upstream; but the Earth itself is moving around the sun, which is gravitating around another mobile star. It's the same in the immaterial world. There's no fixed point. Should one expect to find that fixity in the human brain? Poor brain! What is there, then, beneath the vault of the skull. A diamond-encrusted rock, an infusible metal, a ray of eternal light? Alas! Nothing but a soft pulp, nourished by plants and meat; a will-o'-the-wisp whose flame goes out at the slightest breath. When the wind blowing across the fields makes the wheat undulate, is there an ear that resists and says: 'Me, I won't budge'? All obey, all incline— and people do the same. Anyone who sets out to resist a current goes with it. There are, in truth, neither progressivists nor traditionalists. So-called progressivists are those who abandon themselves without protest to the unexpected fluctuations of the human movement. Self-styled traditionalists are those who curse the impulses that push them. But all are carried, tossed to and fro, at the same time by the great inevitable and inexplicable force."

Decidedly, Philippe was in the process of going astray. His mind was changing tack. He was entering at full sail into the crisis of mental emancipation. There was nothing he could do about it. The more he shook his head, the more he was agitated by temptation.

"What is the line," he said to himself, again, "that separates reasonable obstinacy from stubbornness? We're faithful to our ancestors—but were they faithful to theirs? Why were they so firmly attached to certain rules? Was it not by mere habit? Was it because the rules were just, or because they obtained a profit from them? Someone once said—on of our prelates, I think—that one often finds a sin at the commencement of a great fortune. Is that possible? Besides, is what one calls a sin always an evil act? Sins are judged according to systems of education, but are those systems not multiple, variable, contradictory to one another, conventional and continent? Whatever its source might be, that great fortune, after a few years everyone honors it. Is virtue then, merely the means of being nothing, doing nothing? An unnatural enjoyment, made of bitterness and renunciation? Good advice to give to someone else, but to avoid for oneself?"

"Look," said Jacques, all of a sudden. "Here are our great-uncle's children."

That appeal interrupted Philippe's reflections.

Indeed, the entire descendancy of the cadet branch of the Martinvasts was displayed there, in a succession of tombstones, until the doctor's second generation; after that, nothing more. The sequence stopped. Afterwards, no doubt, cremation must have replaced inhumation.

Our two cousins did not take long to be convinced on this point, for they were only two strides from the crematorium, and at the gate they perceived the caretaker, armed with his keys, who seemed to be expecting their visit.

"We would like," they said, as they introduced themselves, "to look at your…establishment."

"Very well," said the caretaker. "At your service."

"We ought to warn you that we've never seen a similar factory…we come from a very distant country. We're in Saint-Lo because our family originated here."

"May one know which family?"

"The Martinvasts."

"Ah, yes, of course! We've burned many people with that name here. Not long ago, there was Jean Martinvast-Soeuf, a militia instructor. Before him, there was Pierre Martinvast-le-Hudic, a superb young man. He was in his prime at twenty and entitled to the most beautiful women in the canton. He died in a collision between two aerostats in the fog over Lisieux. The passengers fell on to the roofs of the town. What a frightful catastrophe! Have you not heard mention of it?"

"No."

"Before that, I remember a Lady Marvinvast-Louvent, who belonged to the medical corps and rendered great service to the country. In fact, there was something of a tradition at one time among the Martinvasts to practice medicine. You must have seen the monument to that famous doctor of that name, who cared for the sick for a long time before devoting himself to administration..."

"I beg your pardon," Jacques interjected. "You've just listed a certain number of dead Martinvasts. In your account, they all bore a second name."

"Of course."

"Well, what is that second name?"

"But it's the name of the father. It is, at least, the name indicated by the mother as being that of the father." The caretaker did not understand why he was being asked such questions, and his embarrassed attitude testified to his surprise. Without further explanation, however, slowly and silently, he set about escorting his visitors into the first room of the crematorium.

"This," he said, "is the depository. The bodies are brought here the night after their decease. The faces are veiled, as you can see, but respiration would be manifest, if it were to resume. All the bodies remain in communication with extremely sensitive electrical apparatus, which would sound the alarm in case of the cessation of lethargy. After fifty or sixty hours, they're taken to the furnace that I shall have the honor of showing you."

The caretaker was already turning as if to head for another room when Philippe stopped him.

"No more coffin, then; no more bier?"

"No, Monsieur, no more box. We put the deceased, wrapped in a mortuary sheet, on a purpose-designed wickerwork couchette and bring it here in a special carriage.

"Always by night?"

"Always."

"Then the relatives and friends don't keep vigil over the body, nor form a procession?"

"No. When a man is dead, one clings to his memory incontinently, but one avoids seeing or exposing oneself to his remains. That's a principle here. We avoid all circumstances that might provoke a man to disgust and shame with regard to his fellow. That's today's modesty. On the other hand, cadaveric idolatry now seems to us to be a barbarity worthy of savages. As for ordinary condolences, they're offered between the surviving friends, either at the home of the deceased or the seat of a society of which he was part...around his portrait, when there is one...but no more lugubrious processions, no more funeral strolls through the streets in broad daylight, following the miserable human debris...and no one, apart from the service operatives, witnesses the cremation."

"There is, at least, I suppose, an official confirmation of the death at the domicile."

"Yes and no. In the case of a death outside the hospital is exceptional; it hardly ever crops up apart from sudden or accidental deaths. There is a special verification then, of course—but more often, as the death occurs in a treatment house, the confirmation is automatic."

"In cases of illness, then, people are not cared for at home."

"It's very rare. There's more chance of a cure in the treatment houses than anywhere else. They're so well-organized. Oh, it's no longer the large communal room of yore. Every invalid had his own room, strictly isolated and separated from the others. And when his final hour comes, soft, consoling, nostalgic music, instead of the lamentable apparatus of old, lulls the dying man to sleep amid the flowers strewn on his bed. Since we no longer spend our money on playing soldiers with the sons of laborers and workers, we can care for our suffering compatriots decently. Finally, the habit has caught on; the ancient prejudice against the hospital has been erased. Everyone goes into those houses of health, as all the officers in the army once had themselves taken to the Val-de-Grâce. For certain maladies, it's even obligatory."

"And it's long time since these...new habits...were acquired?"

"A very long time. It goes back to the end of the 19th century, to the period known as 'the Terror of the rich.' Foreigners though you are, you can't be unaware that in that era, universal suffrage led in our country—as was inevitable—to

195

an organized campaign against those whose fortune was above the mean. For them, everything was sold at the highest price, and in mediocre conditions. To the masses, on the other hand, everything was given free and in conditions of achieved perfection. The proletariat thus had its revenge. It was a misfortune to be rich, as it had previously been to belong to the class of 'petty employees.'

"What happened? In a few years, there were no more rich people, properly speaking, or very nearly, and everyone was subject to the same regime, in sickness and in health."

Philippe did not reply immediately. That perspective opened on modern society troubled him. As he still had one more thing to say about incineration, however, he continued: "What happens, then, Monsieur, in this system, in the case of a suspicious death that might be attributable to a crime?"

"Well, there's a delay. The corpse stays here. It's embalmed, if necessary."

"What if the criminal presumption only arises after the cremation?"

"Then," said the caretaker, spreading his arms wide and lowering his head, "it's too late." Straightening up again, he continued: "A truly great misfortune! Would the discovery of the murderer bring the victim back to life? Oh, I know what was once alleged. What about society, they said, and public condemnation, and the utility of deterrents, what about them?" Oh, the fine evidence that country doctors once used to find in the earth after several months of fermentation and putrefaction, eh? That's what it's necessary to talk about. There was, it's true, in the beginning, based on the consideration you've raised, a certain opposition to the system of cremation—but the multiple and considerable advantages attached to it soon tipped the balance in its favor. There were, at that time, so many deeds qualified as crimes that remained unsolved or unpunished that people said: 'one more or less hardly matters.' To preserve two or three problematic pursuits per year, it wasn't worth the trouble of continuing to put into practice throughout France the putrid system of human warping and remaining forever servile to the obsolete rites of ancient funerals."

"I might be mistaken, Monsieur, but you seem to be saying that autopsy is now prohibited?"

"No, no—on the contrary. Today, doctors have much better facilities than before for their post-mortem investigations. Every inanimate body can, if there is reason, serve their studies, unless the deceased had made a formal disposition to the contrary—and take my word for it, very few people express that reservation. What medical science has gained from these new practices is inestimable. That is incontestably one of the principal causes of the prolongation achieved in the average lifespan."

Philippe listened to all this with a veritable constriction of the heart. His physiognomy had already taken on an altogether unaccustomed expression, and on his blanched cheeks a kind of constraint was legible, like that which precedes tears. Jacques blood was half-chilled. He was astonished that the caretaker could talk so casually in that lugubrious room—which, for his own count, he was in a hurry to make his exit.

"Here, Messieurs," said the caretaker, a little further on, "is the crematory furnace, Siemens system.[23] A body is burned in here in an hour, without smoke or odor. Would you like to see it in action?"

"No thank you!" the two cousins exclaimed, in chorus.

"Were in a sight hurry," added Jacques. "And then..."

"Nevertheless," said Philippe, pulling himself together, "tell me: what do you do with the ashes?"

"Oh, there are so few! They're thrown to the wind or scattered on the ground. There are some people, however, who take in into their heads to reclaim the meager remains of their relatives. Look, here are the urns that we put at their disposal.

---

[23] The electrical engineer Alexander Siemens (1847-1928) began building furnaces and crematoria after being released from the Prussian army following the Franco-Prussian War, and his model became the standard one employed in France.

They're shaped like antique urns, for this isn't the first time, you know, that the dead have been burned. We sell the urns very dear, because they're considered as a luxury, but I repeat, very few people ask for them. What do you expect them to do with them?"

The man really was speaking with the insensitivity of ancient ossuary attendants.

"What!" said Jacques, disgustedly. "But even in the antiquity of which you speak, these precious relics were religiously preserved."

"Yes, that's possible," said the caretaker, adjusting is attitude slightly. "I told you, there are a few people who make collections of them—corporations, for example. There are also women, mothers who keep them at home in family chapels. But all in all, that's rare and exceptional. What do you expect me to say to you?"

While conversing thus, they had returned to the entrance gate, and Philippe searched for an amicable word with which to terminate the conversation.

"We need, you see, Monsieur," he said, trying to smile, "a little time to familiarize ourselves with all these notions, which are diabolically…diabolically…refrigerant."

"Oh yes, undoubtedly," the employee replied, allowing himself to laugh. At the same time, he took off his hat and looked at the visitors significantly. Philippe understood, and made a sign to Jacques. The latter immediately slipped a coin into the hand extended toward him, and took his leave.

When the gate had closed, Philippe, who wanted to relax his muscles, jumped down the three or four steps that his cousin had already descended with his feet together, in a childlike fashion. Falling upon the other's shoulders, he exclaimed in his ear: "Heaven and earth will pass, my dear Jacques, but there is one thing that will never pass—no, never—in the democratic nation of France, and that's tipping."

At the same time, he turned round to make sure that the caretaker had not heard.

And they went quietly on their way.

XXIX

Vertpré, the ancient dwelling of the elder branch of the Martinvasts, as we recall, was situated on the outskirts of Saint-Lo. A few years before it had become the town's "laboratorium"—in other words, the municipal workhouse; which is to say that unemployed inhabitants, whose maintenance was the responsibility of the canton, were sent there.

Philippe and Jacques had not taken long to find out about the change of purpose to which their old family property had been subjected. However, a perfectly natural curiosity drew them to see, even in its present state, the old dwelling that had served as a model for their patrimonial residence in the Île de Bourbon, and from which Jacques derived his name.

They were received with considerable respect by the director, who briefly brought them up to date with the various phases through which the property of Vertpré had passed and then offered to show them the house and explain its functioning to them. That functioning was itself an object of particular curiosity on the part of the voyagers.

Philippe wondered how the new civilization had resolved the problem of the right to work and the other social difficulty of what to do with useless mouths. Jacques de Vertpré said to himself: *Aha! I'll finally find the weak point on modern society. Yes, it's here, in our old domicile, that we'll witness the evident demonstration of the practical impossibilities into which atheistic social conceptions are bound to run*. And that prospect gave his attitude, normally placid and modest, an almost conceited confidence, mingled with an expression of challenge. He was convinced that he was in reach of a certain and keenly-desired triumph.

"Our house," the director told them, "is like a hospital in which those who are out of work come to recover.

"Suppose that a workman is the victim of an accidental unemployment; we give him a daily aliment for his activity.

199

To the extent that we can, we maintain him in his particular profession, and he remains our guest until he finds a normal job...

"Other individuals, male or female, might be idle for the simple reason that they're lazy, or because they have an inert nature, or because they lack indiscipline and incapable of working without strong supervision. Those people we consider almost as invalids in the true sense, and we attempt to inspire them, or simply to give them an appetite for application and regularity. It's a new form of social training that we're undertaking; we're bringing the subjects up to scratch. After a variable length of time we decide their fate. If they've recovered their appetite for labor, they go back to ordinary life; if they demonstrate that their inertia is fundamental and a kind of impotence, we put them into an asylum. If, finally, we recognize that they are vicious, mulish and incapable of reform, we exile them to an island. These questions are settled administratively, with al desirable guarantees.

"What is interesting about the house is the variety of means that we employ in order to reactivate the springs of productive activity that have failed in the individual. The number of occupations that we can try is incalculable, and it's very rare that we don't find one among them that pleases or unfortunate idlers. For that is our first principle: find the work that pleases and suits the worker.

"Our second rule consists of giving our guests the greatest possible latitude. We don't force them to do anything; and that is as well, for inaptitude for work often has no other source than an immoderate love of liberty. Now, if one tries to compel these reinforced liberals, they baulk; if, on the contrary, they are abandoned to their own independence, they soon feel empty and useless. Then they come to solicit a chain—an obligation of some sort. You will, moreover, be able to judge what I have just told you for yourselves."

So saying, the director commenced the two cousins' tour of the establishment.

"But everyone seems to be busy, Monsieur," said Philippe, after a few moments. "One would not believe that this is a municipal workhouse."

Indeed, in the section they were passing through at that moment, everything was redolent of order and well-regulated activity, but the director told them that it was not like that everywhere. "Look at that courtyard over there, and the adjacent locales," he added.

As he spoke it he went to a window, from which one could see a long sequence of galleries, courtyards and large halls, with fountains and trees. In the middle of the space, which seemed to occupy the center of the establishment, there was a considerable population, swarming and slovenly, of men and women of all ages.

The visitors paused momentarily. *That*, thought Jacques, *is exactly what I expected. We're about to put our finger on the sore.*

"You can see there," said the director, "all at once, the people who have just arrived in the house for the first time, those whose treatment has been ineffective and are awaiting removal either to an asylum or to an island refuge, and finally, the particular clientele of poor devils of both sexes who are neither genuinely infirm, genuinely vicious nor utterly lazy, but who, for one reason or another, have not yet got out of difficulty, and who come here from time to time either to have a meal or to spend the night."

The spectacle was poignant. That mass of living misery, moving confusedly, impressed the two cousins vividly. Philippe wondered how, from a society apparently so well-organized, so much pitiful refuse could emerge. As for Jacques, after a few moments of mute contemplation, he turned to the director and said:

"Confess, Monsieur, that you have a heavy burden in your arms there, and that with this system of organized insurance against all human ills, you have come close to suppressing initiative and personal responsibility. It's so comfortable for people devoid of ambition to live for free, warming them-

201

selves in the sun. That might become common practice, and even pass, in the end, for the last word in human wisdom. Aren't people afraid of seeing the generous activity of those who produce exploited in this fashion to the point of abuse? Don't they see a terrible danger in what, I imagine, must be the continual increase of the dregs of the population, the scum of society…?"

At these words, a sudden change was produced in the physiognomy of the director, who turned abruptly to face Jacques. The latter was stuck by it, and immediately broke off. After a brief pause, it was the director who resumed.

"Why, my dear Monsieur, employ those expressions, which sound as bad in the mouth of a Christian as that of a democrat? The scum of society! The first apostles of your religion would not have spoken scornfully about the dregs of the population, for in the soul of the most wretched of human beings they recognized a divine spark. What we cherish is a profound sentiment of human equality, with which we are increasingly imbued.. On seeing an unfortunate man, we say: 'He's our fellow. Why has he fallen into difficulty, and not us?' No, we don't feel that we have the right to be haughty, or severe, for, more widely experienced, we're conscious of our own weakness; and, without have calculated exactly the part that hazard might play in anyone's destiny, we've observed that it's dominant. I say hazard; I ought to say: the unknown component of natural and fatal laws."

Here there was another pause, after which the director hastened to resume the conversation at the point where he had left it. "To get back to what you said just now—which is to say, about the inconveniences presented by the gratuitous maintenance of the needy unemployed, I don't deny it absolutely; but it's necessary not to exaggerate them.

"Initiative, you say, will disappear. Are you sure of that? Humans will always egotistical; that's their nature. They don't want to be equal to their superiors so much as to be superior to their equals. You could, I think base your argument on that, with regard to the fate of the initiative of which you seem to be so fond.

"So far as we're concerned, we don't raise altars to the old economic stimulant that was called competition. No, we no longer to push people to fight, in any fashion, and we are perfectly content with friendly rivalry, for our ideal is peace and reciprocal good will.

"You also say: why keep in society its useless members, drones who drink the honey made by others? To that I reply: they are in our society, these drones, without having asked to be there; they are here because of their parents, who had the right to procreate. We cannot take away their lives unless they have committed some capital crime. That useless and onerous life, we have to give them. Now that they have it, we respect it.

"Inconveniences are everywhere; all societies have some burdens; but what can you expect? Ours are the consequence of a rule that we cannot repeal."

"What rule is that?" asked Philippe. "What principle, exactly?"

"That our society guarantees all its members, no matter what, the satisfaction of their needs. It has no other reason for existence."

"And what are the officially-recognized needs, Monsieur?"

"To eat, to drink, to vitalize, to rest when necessary and to avoid suffering."

"To vitalize, you say—what do you mean by that?"

"It's a new word, which refers to the work of life. The word 'love' was too general, and not sufficiently precise. I warn you, though, that in this matter, words are used up rapidly; it's often necessary to change them."

A slight smile brushed the lips of the three interlocutors. The Jacques said: "At least, Monsieur, I suppose that you don't give all these unfortunates a soft bed and food of the best quality?"

"No, obviously. The lot that we provided for them is, in general, inferior to that of the public; but the minimum that we assure them is nevertheless comfortable. Take note that our objective isn't merely to prevent them from dying. We want our regime to enable them to become strong, happy and fit. When they have the good fortune to arrive in that condition, they almost always decamp; we don't see them again."

"Truly, it's the promised land of the leisure class; idlers must grow as densely here as ears in a field of wheat."

"Yes, there are many here, I won't deny it...that doesn't worry us though, for we're richly endowed by the welfare system, and we have other advantages. On the one hand, the production of the things we need is extremely rapid, and on the other, our consumption is simplified. Thus, the minority of the population—which is to say, the category of workers— enjoys considerable leisure, while providing for the needs of children, old people, sick people, prisoners and also the poor. There's even a danger that work might become too rare and that it will be necessary to ration it.

"Well, that's a law of human organizations. They're always imperfect in some respect. Progress merely consists in continually restricting the imperfections. It's like river-boats; no matter how well-constructed they are, their pumps nevertheless have to obviate the inevitable leaks that each of them suffers. In the same way, no matter how tightly closed the lock-gates are through which they pass, there's always a trickle of water that gets through.

"In any case, it's a burden," Jacques repeated again, "and then...look, I can understand that to the poor, properly speaking, one lends assistance of a temporary kind—a few nights' hospitality—but to support poverty constantly is, in truth, to maintain it, to render it irremediable."

"That's the way it is, though, my dear Monsieur. We don't make such distinctions. When, after three days, a poor man is still poor, we continue to help him."

"At least you could take your help to their homes, in order to spare the poor from shame."

"Shame? The poor are no longer ashamed. Why would they be? We're no longer scornful of poverty, and wealth is no longer the basis of respectability. Why should we scorn poverty? All of us, whoever we are, have either passed through it, or might pass through it someday."

"That's no reason not to give individuals the right to help one another."

"No, no," replied the director, insistently, "the poor are our concern. We don't want to abandon them to the inequalities of individual generosity. If individuals render private services, and make donations to endeavors that please them, that's their business. They have a useful role to play: to add a little superfluity and luxury to social support...but as for welfare itself, the provision of necessities, that's what we do, and we alone. But let's continue our visit, Messieurs, I beg you. Let's not pause here longer than is reasonable."

On these words, all three resumed walking.

To list everything they saw would take too long; we shall only cite certain details that were of particular interest to our travelers.

Firstly, there was an immense kitchen garden presenting the latest developments in horticulture. In early summer, it was a veritable enchantment for the eyes. The director explained that the gardeners were almost all former clients of the hospital wards, who, having been gradually reanimated, had joined the staff of the house because they had not wanted to leave it.

There was work there for everyone; frail old men could be seen there who had no other mission than conscientiously treading the large plots of land in order to make the soil more compact; others who were removing weeds, and others who were planting peas. There was even one whose role was purely passive, who was taking the place of a scarecrow in the middle of a newly-sown plot.

"But you must cause considerable damage to private industry," said Philippe suddenly.

"Private industry!" the director replied. "Do you think that there are individuals who still have the idea of devoting themselves t small-scale growing for profit? What difference is there, anyway, between private industry and ours? Tell me, what do you mean by private industry? Is it exclusively that of the isolated individual? But we don't give any privilege to isolation. What kind of rivalry do you have in mind, then? Is not everyone, no matter who we are—individuals, societies, cantons, provinces—part of a whole, and do we not have, in order to maintain our instinctive syndication, the great law of shared benefits? When an individual or a society reaches a certain future in respect of profits, the excess is shared with the canton. In the same way, when a canton acquires an excess of resources, it shares with the province, and so on. How can there be any hostility between the work of one and the work of another? In France, there are only shared interests."

"Oh, I didn't realize," Philippe replied. "I didn't know...yes, it's true. But then, tell me, are all these accounts subject to official verification?"

"Of course."

"Even individuals and non-commercial entities that aren't required to keep books?"

"It's the same for everyone without distinction. There's no longer any difference between commercial and non-commercial enterprises. Everyone is obliged to keep accounts. The authorities have to be able, at a given moment, to discover the financial situation of a province, a city, an association or a citizen."

"Then there's no more liberty!" exclaimed Jacques, vehemently.

"What do you mean, no more liberty?"

"But there isn't!"

The director did not know how to respond to Jacques' exclamation. The latter, having made the claim, perceived that he would have had difficulty justifying it. The two of them stood there, looking at one another, astonished to find themselves disconcerted.

Fortunately, Philippe came to their aid. "Liberty," he said, "liberty…as soon as one is in a society, one's liberty is limited to some extent, I agree. And the denser society is, the less free one is. There is, therefore, less liberty in a big city than a small town. Today, you've taken it upon yourselves to diminish the special obligations of traders—or, more accurately, you regard everyone as a trader—about which there's nothing monstrous, and I can't see too much of which to complain…but it's property for which I'm concerned, Monsieur."

Property rights were dear to Philippe's heart, as we have already observed. Since the opportunity has come up, he tried to explain himself, and continued: "You spoke just now about sharing profits. However, the profits I make are my property. If I'm obliged, above a certain figure, to share them with the community of which I'm a pat, they're no longer my property. In which case, I can no longer see anything but a progressive tax. However, I've always heard it said that property is the indispensable foundation, the very basis of society."

"Don't be alarmed," replied the director, seemingly desirous of appeasing Philippe. "Don't be alarmed on behalf of property, and always beware of the refraction of words. Words seen through the lenses of prejudice almost always give a false idea of things. Property, no matter what anyone says, has never been anything but a more or less extended right of enjoyment, not an appropriation, strictly speaking. We are really only the proprietors of one thing, Monsieur Martinvast—do you know what that is? That which we incorporate, that which we eat and drink. Outside of that, we only have rights that are more or less precarious, more or less modifiable, more or less subject to reduction, under various labels, by taxes, servitudes, duties, or the requirement to share that I mentioned just now.

"Look at what happens in your country, in Bourbon. You imagine that you are the proprietor of your house, your fields and your livestock. If a few regiments come to carry out exercises in your neighborhood, your house will be invaded, your animals requisitioned, your crops ravaged. Is that a property? Do you want to build a house? If you're in a city, you have to submit to rules for the alignment, the ratification of the plan, the choice of materials, the employment of workers, etc. When the house is built it will be necessary to refrain, will it not, from making too much noise. You have some land..."

Here the director interrupted himself and raised his arms to the heavens.

"How can a man ever say that he 'has some land'—but let's admit it. Will you at least have the right to let it lie fallow, if you want to? Not at all. If thistles grow there, your neighbors will hasten to take legal action against you and demand compensation. And what about the expropriation that threatens you...and the estate duties that will abridge your right of transmission...? No, you see, there has never been any absolute, sovereign property, and there cannot be any. Between people and things, only contingent and limited relationships can exist.

"Well, our individual enjoyment with regard to wealth is considerably less than in the past. Why? You know that already. It's because we've changed our concept of society and our social tactics. A reduction of the exclusive privilege of the individual, and an extension of communal advantages: that's our formula; that's our theme. Now, to reach our objectives, we need rules, like that of the sharing of profits, for example. Property still exists; it's differently regulated, that's all..."

The conversation did not go any further, and our three interlocutors placidly continued their tour.

They soon arrived on the edge of a beautiful meadow traversed by a stream. There again they had before their eyes a numerous personnel occupied in the most various occupations: guarding livestock, training colts, fishing, etc. The scene captured the attention of Philippe and Jacques.

Not far away, amid the verdure of the trees, well-ventilated workshops were visible with distant views over the countryside. There were shoemakers there, carpenters, weavers and painters. The nearby sound of a fanfare informed the visitors that music had a place in that conservatory of labor.

Our young cousins ended up finding a real charm in their inspection. Even Jacques was disarmed. The concessions that the director had made to him were sufficient.

Later, when they went back to the town, they told themselves that, all things considered, it was a fine destiny for the habitation of their forefathers, to have become the general headquarters of social assistance in their canton of origin. They were even led to consider, both of them, that establishments like that at Vertpré were at least as worthy as the poorhouses and local prisons of Bourbon.

XXX

The next day, as we have already said, was to be a feast-day in Saint-Lo.

Since early morning, in fact, joyful bells had sown gaiety through the town. Rosa Myrtil, who had arrived punctually the previous evening, was up early, and was now walking through the streets with Philippe and Jacques, pausing and looking around, very inquisitive about the preparations for the solemnity.

At about ten o'clock they went to an assembly in the old church. The audience was considerable, as was commonplace since Sunday had once again become a general day of rest, the great day of recreation, adornment and socializing. A powerful organ filled the nave with its sonority. Everyone there was singing.

Our trio listened attentively.

The choir's stanzas were celebrating the beautiful summer season, the pleasure and produce that it would procure. There was a mutual felicitation with regard to the long days that the June sun would bring, and a hopeful anticipation of the success of the crop.

After the first hymn, another was sung, after an indication given by one of three people sitting on the central stage: "Humanity is a great family in which everyone ought to contribute to the conservation of the peace." Such was its approximate meaning.

Afterwards, there was a pause, during which Rosa Myrtil replied in a low voice to the questions of her companions, explaining to them what they were seeing.

"On the platform," she said, that's the mayor, with the head schoolteacher to his right and the physician to his left. All three, as you see, are wearing colored capes, one white, one blue and one red. That's a distinctive sign, which they only put on here, in order that they might be recognized at a distance as easily as at close range, even when they're seated.

"In the stalls to the right and left there are various notables: the representative of the province, the representative of the State, the elected functionaries, a few ladies who are at the head of certain services. In general, you'll observe, the men and women are separated; there are special places for babies, adolescents and old people. In the church, that's necessary; it's a place of meditation, where people occupy themselves with the conduct of life—individual life as well as the communal life of the entire canton. There's no argument here—political, electoral and technical debates are confined to the public hall installed in a neighboring annex—and no excitation of the senses. Illusion, spectacle and laughter are reserved for the theater. But listen—here's the mayor at the podium. He's going to make the usual communications to the audience.

The mayor was a middle-aged man with an open and tranquil face Seated in the pulpit, he riffled through a few pieces of paper and got ready to speak.

"My dear friends," he said...

Then, very simply, in a paternal and casual tone, he began to make a few recommendations concerning the procession that was to constitute, in the afternoon, the principal part of the festival. He invited all the parishioners to decorate the streets and supervise the good order of the procession, urging them to bring moderation and decency to their joyous manifestations.

As today was the anniversary of a fire that had destroyed a part of the town a few years earlier, he recalled the names of two courageous citizens who had given their lives in the catastrophe in order to save a woman and a child. He took advantage of that to say that life is precious, but that it is nevertheless necessary to be ready to sacrifice it in a good cause "It is in civic bravery," he added, "that true human nobility resides. Those who dedicate themselves to honor, charity and science are marked with the seal of glory. There lineage remains illustrious and their names are written in the national annals, in the golden book of models of humanity."

He then made a few comments regarding matters of common interest: the condition of the crops, the progress of commerce, and news of the cities of Caen and Paris. Then he made a few announcements related to the coming week, asking those present at the meeting to pass them on to people who had not been able to come.

Finally, after mentioning new births, giving the names and personal status of citizens who had come from elsewhere to be enrolled in the canton of Saint-Lo and listed the compatriots who had been obliged to abandon their domicile, he passed in review those inhabitants who had died in the previous week, pronouncing a few consoling words with regard to each of them.

While listening to this communication, Philippe Martinvast had a smile on his lips. *One might believe that one were in a Catholic church*, he thought, *with the difference of a few prayers and a few signs that we impose for reasons of piety. The counterfeit is complete. They've taken from us everything that his human and tangible in religion, everything that might cement the alliance between the inhabitants of a locality, everything that might temper passions.*

After the mayor, it was the head schoolteacher who spoke about the progress of the children, the results obtained in adult courses and the new books acquired by the municipal library. He ended his speech with a few comments related to agriculture and meteorology.

The physician took the podium in his turn. With regard to an epidemic that had recently broken out in Saint-Lo he had to give a few more items of hygienic advice. At the same time he mentioned a new remedy that had just been sent to the municipal dispensary, indicating the circumstances in which it could be claimed.

The ceremony ended as it had begun, with songs, the last of which was the cantonal hymn of Saint-Lo. Our readers know that every canton now has its rallying song, in which

212

whatever is remarkable and characteristic about the town and its surroundings is celebrated.

Immediately after noon there was, in spite of the festival, a weekly meeting in the public hall. Philippe and Jacques, who did not want to miss any aspect of the provincial Sunday, went to it, escorting, as in the morning, the curious and sprightly Madame Myrtil.

There was not to be any argumentative debate, but a lecturer—or a troubadour, as one says nowadays—was due to tell the story of the last American succession. When we say America, we mean, of course, North America, the former South America now being occupied by the United States of Brazil. The reader ought to be warned, however, that it was not a matter of the War of Secession that had occurred in the 19th century, but a more recent event little known to the public.

Everyone knows that America has retained the advance over the people of Europe that it obtained over them in times immemorial, taking the lead in the human caravan. When Europe wants to know where it will be in fifty years time, it has only to look across the Atlantic. America clears, scouts, explores and maps out the route. From time to time it makes a mistake and has to take a step back, but it soon makes up the lost time. The rest of the world comes after it, profiting from the experience acquired and perfecting the scientific and social inventions it has sketched out.

It was America that first granted the right of suffrage to women, which we have imitated, estimating that social propulsion would then be wiser and more prudent. It did not stop there, however; in granting the vote to the better half of the nation, we have sagely decided that persons of the female sex should be electors, but not candidates. In America, things have been done differently, precisely because of the latest secession.

One day, as a result of a secret conspiracy extended throughout the States, women rebelled against the Constitution and claimed eligibility. "If anyone can claim to be the object of a choice, an election," they said, "it's us."

213

The men were obstinate in their casuistic distinction. "No," they replied, "that's impossible; there's no precedent."

"You don't want it? Well, we'll go on strike." And they were as good as their word.

That is what has been called the Great Secession. No American woman would allow an American man to come within three meters of her.

The minstrel lecturer went into rather length detail about the various phases of that singular war, which he had been able to witness. The Union's troops had been powerless to repress it, for, extinguished in one place, it immediately burst forth somewhere else. Finally, the men had been obliged to capitulate, and the new national representation currently consists of more citizenesses than citizens.

"It will not be astonishing," said the narrator, in conclusion, "if, in a short time, hegemony belongs to women in all the states of America. The further one travels over the human planet, from south to north-west, the later women develop, but at the same time, the more improved they are. In France, we're close to the median, and males are still dominant, but in the future, the equilibrium might one day be reversed. Who knows? Perhaps American men will be struck in their turn by civic incapacity as the revenge of their women."

On these words the story ended. A salvo of applause saluted the orator and the assembly immediately began to disperse.

"A mixed parliament!" said our two young men as they got to their feet. "That would be very curious."

"It's true," Philippe continued, "that in everyday life one sees mixed meetings of men and women proceeding quite comfortably, but they're restricted, fortuitous and intimate meetings." He addressed himself to Madame Myrtil. "My God! I know full well, when on thinks about it, that men and women are very similar in bodily form, and I recognize that the normal functioning of the feminine organism cannot, in a strong race constitute an obstacle to political activity in itself. However, it's necessary to admit that men are always more powerful physically and mentally than women, even in America, no doubt. Why not recognize their power of domination, then? Oh, I know what you're going to say: the difference in strength comes from the vices of education, centuries-old abuses that women have had to suffer, and which a better-inspired upbringing might eventually remedy. So be it—I admit that too. And yet, if women have always been victims, isn't precisely because, in the beginning, they were weaker? Let's admit the observation nevertheless—but there's still something else. I'm not unaware of the fact your mores have brought the sexes significantly closer together, and their relationships have become less inflammatory, but even so, to make them debate together, to expose them mutually to the intoxicating atmosphere that takes possession of an assembly as soon as human speech is inflamed by the fire of passion, that seems hazardous to me, and with regard the affairs of State, that seems to me..."

"Yes, yes," Madame Myrtil interjected. "Don't forget, my dear Monsieur, that we're talking about America. What that pilgrim said scarcely affects French women... Let's go see the procession. We can discuss it later. In Bourbon, at any rate, you have nothing to fear. Bourbon's a hot country, where women mature early, and in those conditions, your predominance, Messieurs, is not in peril. Let's go."

It was, in fact, time to go, for the procession was already on the move.

The Red Fruit Festival in Saint-Lo, as elsewhere, is entirely devoted to putting in evidence two or three classes of young women, those who are closest to nubility. As a complement, it has the Festival of the Fields, which takes place two weeks later and in which adolescent boys soon to enter virility are paraded before the eyes of the crowd.

Nothing more charming can be imagined than the interpretation given to the ceremony that year by the population. Cherries, strawberries, redcurrants and raspberries, all those flirtatious hors-d'oeuvres of summer, even sweet-brier berries, were represented there with an artistic grace well worthy of exciting admiration..

To the sound of delightful music, in bright sunlight, here are the young women going by, crowned with flowers and ornamented with the fruits of the day, like jewels; some hold bouquets in their hands, others garlands mixed with foliage. Between the groups, banners flutter in the breeze. Beneath the feet of these maidens the ground is strewn with fresh herbs and leafless roses. To the right and the left, carpeted with branches or hung with draperies, from all the widows, balconies and roofs, a joyful crowd cheers and smiles.

The procession is terminated by a group of schoolmistresses. Very proud of their pupils, they receive abundant compliments and felicitations from the crowd watching the review.

All this is very pretty, thought Jacques, *but it's still pagan, alas.*

We know already that everything that was not consecrated by the intervention of God was disqualified in his eyes.

As for Philippe he observed a new imprint left by Christianity. Even processions had been borrowed from religion, along with what was artistic and popular.

They've stolen everything from us, he thought, *and left us nothing. It's true that we too, it's said, obtained our rites from ancient races. In fact, humankind has no lack of means at its disposal for edifying and remaking itself.*

XXXI

After the procession, the population split up and moved off in several directions. While the children and adolescents went into the gardens to play various games, some of the adults headed for the park consecrated to dancing, others for the theater.

The theater in Saint-Lo, like the majority of modern theaters, is designed primarily to put on performances in daylight. For a long time now, thanks to destiny, we no longer have to wait, in order to devote ourselves to the delights of spectacle, for night to spread its darkness. Our leisure time permits us to enjoy our recreation in the sunlight, in the open air, without exposing ourselves to the fatigue of late nights or the dangers of fire.

It was also in that direction that Rosa Myrtil headed, followed by her two acolytes. It is necessary to say that as soon as her presence in Saint-Lo was known, she had been asked by the local authorities to adorn the theatrical performance with a song from her repertoire. She had agreed, and three places had been reserved in the front row for her and her friends.

The program was very full, as often happens in large cantonal festivals. After a very effective drama, an item from the ancient repertoire, the jig, was performed; then there was a sequence of short compositions, more or less mingled with songs, related to the modern conditions of life and certain purely local incidents.

Philippe and Jacques only understood that third part of the performance imperfectly. They thought that they were able nevertheless to notice that the theatrical art had moved, on the one hand toward the choral chant and on the other toward the lewd joke; that it had ceased to revolve exclusively around amour; and, finally, that it was less inclined than in Bourbon to aim to terrify the audience or move its members to tears.

What struck them most of all was the crudity of the language. They did not hide that from Madame Myrtil.

"What excess!" murmured Jacques. "What license! It's scandalous!"

"It is, in fact, a bit stiff," observed Philippe, for his part, tugging at his moustache. "How can you hear all that without flinching, Madame?"

"How? Out of habit. Then again, is there really anything improper or obscene in what you just heard? Well, we call a spade a spade now, that's all. What harm is there in that? It's true that we no longer have those fallacious euphemisms that doubtless make you say, as our ancestors did, on looking at a woman, for instance: 'What a fine figure! What a graceful neck!' as if a figure—which is to say, stature—could be said to be fine, or as if a pharynx were ever graceful. We put the word first.

"Isn't the theater, in any case, made for frank language? If we didn't have the theater, Messieurs, or books, where would we hear, and how would be able to read, that which people think every day without ever wanting to say it aloud?

"In Bourbon, frustrated as you are in matter of love, the theater serves as a distraction for your imagination, so you translate there, as we once did ourselves, eroticism in all its forms. On the stage, however, the prejudice of false language still constrains you, so you continue to play, as in the past, the game of double meanings, implication, allusion and reticence—all things that seem to us to be inconvenient, out of place and libidinous—whereas we practice frank liberty in a straightforward manner.

"Notice that the audience is entirely made up of adults, entry to the theater being strictly forbidden to those who have not yet reached the age of majority. Given that, why hold back? Why should we dabble in puerile mystification?

"You've given me an idea, though. A little while ago I was asked whether I'd sing. I was hesitating between an ode to amity and a cantata on sincerity; now I've firmly decided on the latter."

218

From time to time, the attention of the voyagers wandered from the stage to the auditorium. The theater is, in fact, an excellent place, at least in smaller towns, to appreciate the type, the character and the hierarchical disposition of a population.

Anticipating their questions, Rosa Myrtil hastened to satisfy their curiosity.

"There, on the privileged balcony," she said, "are the mothers of the first rank. That central box you can see above is reserved for the administrators of the canton—which is to say, the authorities. You won't be astonished that public functions are always avidly sought here; they always have been in France; people make fun of that, but they're wrong. Public office, it can't be denied, confers a sort of nobility. Furthermore, its holders obtain a relative pecuniary advantage over simple individuals.

"At present, private individuals obtain fewer benefits than a man who is part of a particular society. The latter is less favored than a canton employee, and so on. The more considerable the number of people to whom a person is useful, the greater the advantage he receives. The functionary of the state is the highest-paid of all citizens. That emolument serves to some degree as a regulator of salaries, and simultaneously constitutes a maximum that individuals may not exceed. The laws are made in consequence, and, leaving aside certain exceptional individuals rendering signal services to the country—I mean inventors or great creative artists of unusual illustriousness—one can say that the most lucrative as well as the most honored position is that of national functionary.

"It's by means of these dispositions that one can be almost certain of seeing public affairs confided to the nation's elite."

On hearing the explanation of this admirable regulation, Philippe and Jacques nodded their heads, as a sign of understanding if not of assent.

Their interlocutor continued. "Here, in front of us, that forestage box is the lodge of honor, for any of the inhabitants who, for a various length of time, has deserved some recompense. The enjoyment of that lodge is extremely sought after. The names of people called upon to take their lace there are attached to a notice-board in the Town hall and published in the announcements."

Rosa Myrtil had reached that point in her explanations when someone came to tell her that her turn had come to go on.

As soon as she appeared on the stage, a profound silence fell. The public knew her as the recognized interpreter of the particular kind of music that, in the form of recitation, lends itself to serious thought, and prepared to listen to it deferentially.

"What is the virtue," she said, "that elevates and ennobles human beings? It is sincerity. It is especially appropriate to the sons and daughters of France. Sincerity is probity itself.

"Sincerity, combined with honesty of intention, makes exemplar citizens. Look at the face of a sincere man; his forehead is pure, his eyes have the clarity of crystal. The grip of his hand is cordial. You can put your trust in him...

"Lying is a betrayal. Let those who love truth avoid it, as much as possible, even to the extent of the everyday, conventional and transparent duplicities with which conversations are too often enameled.

"Sincerity is not the same as cynicism. Indecency is as hateful and degrading as sincerity is praiseworthy; it is antisocial, for it distances people from one another.

"Nor is sincerity that intemperance of the tongue that causes echoes to repeat the ideas that pass through the mind. On the contrary; let the tongue be always bridled. It is often good to be silent. One should only speak to say things that are useful and true..."

The cantata concluded with a vehement exhortation, developing to an entirely lyrical rhythm.

"Let the French remain sincere, simple and clear, and they will always be the most sympathetic branch of the great human family."

A thunder of applause covered Rosa Myrtil's final chords, and a rain of flowers fell at her feet.

While she was returning to her hotel, between her two companions, she said to them: "I sang about sincerity because of certain reflections you made. I would have preferred, however, to render my song about amity. It's very beautiful, and better suited to my voice."

"Oh?" Jacques said. "How does it go, then?"

"I can't reproduce the tone in a low voice."

"But the words?"

"Oh, the words. Give me a moment to remember them. This is the meaning, more or less...

"Let is congratulate ourselves; amity is in flower again upon the earth. Since antiquity, it has been unknown. What, however, could be more beautiful than the absolute union of two beings, putting their entire confidence in one another, helping one another, consoling one another, congratulating one another mutually? Amity doubles the strength of everyone; it is made to fill and embellish life.

"Why did it disappear? It was marriage, indissoluble monogamy, that stifled it. Men and women were so tightly welded to one another that they could not maintain a true friendship outside the household. On the other hand, amity cannot cohabit with amour, and for the spouses of old, it could only appear as the consequence of long association, in the evening of life, when time had, so to speak, suppressed any difference of nature between them.

"Now, amity is most useful at the age of adulthood and in maturity. The charm and services that veritable amity provides are familiar to us now; we could not live without them.

"Amity only establishes its bonds between persons of the same sex. Between the sexes, it is amour that forges bonds. Amour is dominating but intermittent, variable and fugitive sentiment. Amity, on the contrary, is a durable sentiment, a stranger to the somersaults of passion, almost independent of dispositions of the body. One can sagely base and consolidate one's life thereon.

221

"Let us congratulate ourselves; amity is in flower again."

By way of conclusion, Madame Myrtil added: "That's it, approximately."

Our young men made no immediate reply. The indirect attack launched once again in that circumstance against marriage, damaged the effect of the piece in their minds. Driven by a secret desire to make a riposte on that subject, however, Jacques soon spoke up, saying: "Ancient virtues and practices doubtless had some good in them, Madame. Nevertheless, one might think that if they disappeared, it was because better ones had been found. Amity, in particular, if I'm correctly informed, was not without producing a few abuses. Between men, as between women, did it not sometimes lead its adherents outside the laws of nature?"

"Oh, Monsieur," exclaimed Madame Myrtil, sharply, "you're speaking about aberrations that have nothing to do with true amity, and which still existed in the time when the sacrosanct institution of marriage was in favor. Our present mores no longer permit them. We have, moreover, decreed rigorous punishments in case they reappear—which the ancient codes did not, I believe, or only incompletely."

XXXII

On going back into the hotel, our voyagers found a letter from Madame Listor and a card from the mayor of Saint-Lo.

Madame Listor expressed her regrets at not having been able to answer the telephone herself. She had put her children in school and had been obliged to change lodgings. All that had taken up a great deal of time. There were still many things she needed to do, including making a few short journeys, before everything was entirely settled, but she hoped to have finished soon. She signed herself imply *Fanny Listor*, without any form of salutation.

At first glance, that conclusion of the letter seemed a trifle curt to the Bourbonnais, used to the most distinguished sentiments and most entire devotion of their usual correspondents. Rosa Myrtil told them, however, that there was no induction to be drawn from the circumstance, and that the pruning of useless phrases had been generally adopted in all written correspondence.

The mayor's card was a invitation. "The mayor would be happy to receive, along with the other people contributing to the festival, Rosa Myrtil and the two voyagers brought to Saint-Lo by patriotic sentiment."

"Is it for dinner?" asked Philippe Martinvast, swiftly.

"Not exactly," Rosa replied, who was holding the note. "We have dinner at midday like everyone else. It's for supper this evening."

"What time?"

"Eight o'clock—here, read the card: 'Gathering at eight o'clock; a carriage will be sent.'"

"Very good," said Philippe.

While all three went slowly upstairs, to make their preparations, Jacques de Vertpré said: "People no longer dine in the evening, then?"

"No," Madame Myrtil replied. "People commonly eat their main meal at midday—that's the hour of hunger. The evening meal is a whimsical one, which is accommodated to various purposes: banquets, meeting of friends, ceremonial gatherings, intimate suppers, etc."

"And how should we dress? Doubtless you'll bare your shoulders, Madame?"

"Me, no. Women don't undress is such circumstances."

"Oh! I thought…in Bourbon…"

"No, at meals, décolletage is only admitted for voluptuous occasions, organized with a view to amorous pleasures. Outside of that, we refrain from needlessly inflaming our sensitive neighbors."

Jacques made no reply. He was no enemy of sincerity, but on hearing such…frank words emerging from a woman's mouth he felt a trifle disconcerted.

"As for you, Messieurs," Rosa Myrtil continued, "formal dress is *de rigueur*."

"Fortunately," Philippe observed, "we brought our dinner-jackets from Saint-Denis."

"What are dinner-jackets?"

"Why, our black jackets with long tails. We also have our black trousers, our black waistcoats and our white cravats to knot around our white collars."

"What an abomination!" cried Madame Myrtil. "Do you still wear that frightful garment, which makes such a somber stain in the history of French costume, in Saint-Denis? Oh, how horrible! How were our grandmothers able to love our grandfathers in that mortuary uniform? What!—on days of celebration as on days of mourning, you still put on that vulgar finery, and appear with it in the midst of bright feminine costumes? No, truly, it's incredible! You go even further—you cherish that sinister get-up; yes, you cherish it, don't deny it, as our ancestors cherished it and venerated it. When they weren't wearing it themselves, they put it on the shoulders of a domestic, didn't they, or those of their relatives, in order to be able to contemplate its back and its sacred tails until they were completely worn out. No, I implore you, don't exhibit that cramped outfit, that suit of armor, here; the entire town of Saint-Lo would burst out laughing, and you'd cover me with confusion. If you don't have contemporary formal dress, well, stay as you are; the fact that you're travelers will excuse you."

"What is that dress, then?"

"A red, blue, or yellow jacket—it doesn't matter—knee-breeches of the same color; silk stockings or soft boots according to circumstance."

"Alas, we don't posses anything of that sort. But in order to repair the omission, we can go to a clothing-merchant."

That was, in fact, the best thing to do. A supplier was summoned—and an hour later, Madame Myrtil came down-stairs, accompanied by two cavaliers in red cots, which really did cut quite a dash.

The advertised carriage was waiting for them. During the journey, our young people observed the interior of the vehicle with a certain curiosity, as well as the horses—for they were both horsemen—and the harness. The carriage was quite sim-ple, but comfortable and tidy. The horses were speedy, well-trained and well-conduced.

The driver had nothing characteristic about his costume, nor a large cylindrical hat with a cockade, as in Saint-Denis, nor buttons bearing his master's badge.

"Perhaps coachmen no longer wear livery today," Philippe observed, circumspectly.

"For a long time, in fact, there has been no question of it," Madame Myrtil replied. "That old relic of slavery has been completely forgotten. Those who guide horses have garments adapted to the conditions of their work, but there is nothing in those garments to evoke the idea of the possession of one man by another. Today, my dear Monsieur, a man can no longer be an object of luxury for his fellow. Household employees, no matter what their role, are, so to speak, associates, whose pay is proportionate to their employer's means. Inside a house, the particular symbols that distinguish the servants have no other purpose than allowing them to be recognized among the people present. Those symbols may be a removable collar, a belt, a sash or an armband, according to circumstance."

"And footmen are no longer placed beside coachmen?" said Philippe.

"Shh!" riposted Rosa Myrtil, putting a finger over her lips. "That's a word that sounds bad nowadays, and which it is forbidden to pronounce. There are no more valets of any sort. Another obsolete word. We're now in a chapter in which it's necessary to renew expressions quite frequently. Nor do we any longer have any domestics, properly speaking, but employees, orderlies, clerks and attendants; and staff is very limited. The number of auxiliaries attached to personal services is minimal. Besides, that kind of employment is rather poorly paid."

"Truly, you astonish me. I thought, on the contrary..."

"No, and that feeble remuneration reflects the fact that the work in question is usually not very hard."

"Then you make salaries proportional to difficulty?"

"Yes, of course. Isn't that fair?"

Philippe and Jacques did not reply. There were so many things that seemed fair, and simultaneously impracticable.

"Come on, isn't that fair?" Madame Myrtil repeated. "Thus, Messieurs, what is most highly rewarded today is drudgery. It has, apparently caused our administers much difficulty. You understand what I mean by that? Work that is tiring, dirty, dangerous; work that no one wants to do, which is impossible to carry out as a matter of taste or preference, but which is nevertheless fundamentally necessary, even if it's only infirmary service. Well, we impose some of that drudgery on foreign workers; some of it is carried out by way of disciplinary punishment or in conformity with a kind of lottery—social roulette—to which we all submit; as for the rest, in order to get it done, high wages are required. It's by means of drudgery that the bankrupt recover their position and misers amass gold."

At that moment the carriage stopped. To their great surprise, the young men—who had anticipated entering a private house—found themselves in an establishment seemingly devoted to public alimentation. The Mayor of Saint-Lo was receiving guests in a restaurant.

"That's strange," murmured Jacques, as he got down. "So the Mayor doesn't entertain at home. I thought that in the provinces, at least..."

"No—the Mayor no more than anyone else," said Madame Myrtil rapidly. His domicile is, in any case, a furnished house."

"And this carriage," Philippe added, as he closed the vehicle's door, "isn't the Mayor's carriage."

"No, of course not; it must be hired...unless it's the municipal rig."

The Mayor was waiting for them on the threshold of a large apartment already filled with people. He welcomed them with a marked urgency and introduced them to the other guests.

A few moments later, our voyagers were lost, as if drowned in the brilliant waves of the illuminated rooms.

XXXIII

While these various incidents transpired, amour continued to make progress in the hearts it had touched.

On the morning of the day after the Red Fruit Festival, Philippe Martinvast informed his young cousin that he had a keen desire to leave for Paris immediately.

To what was that sudden resolution due? It was because Fanny Listor, to judge by her letter, was getting ready to set out on her travels again. If he wanted to see her before her departure, there was no time to lose. Philippe had been thinking about that all night, and he had got up with the fixed conviction that it was necessary to go right away.

At first, Jacques did not understand that unexpected declaration, and for a few moments he stood there looking at his cousin with a perplexed and inquisitive gaze. "What's the hurry?" he said. "We still have a good deal of information to seek out here. What about our excursion to Valognes? And our meeting with the archivist?"

Philippe was not in the habit of dissimulating, so he replied to these objections by making the true motive for his decision known in a fraternal manner. He confessed that, although he never talked about Madame Listor, he thought about her constantly, and could not restrain himself from going to find her. He added that by going on ahead in the itinerary of the voyage, as a scout, he would be doing his young relative a favor; that it would be interesting for each of them to travel alone for a while...

Jacques did not insist; but his heart lurched and his expression darkened. He had not asked to come to France. If he had crossed the sea, it was in order to accompany Philippe—and now Philippe was leaving him alone. At the same time, the thought of the future made him anxious. Where would this infatuation lead his cherished companion? Were there not grave dangers on their common road?

What if I said to him...? he thought. *But no; he's older than me; he's always gone by the straight route...and, at the end of the day, he's free...*

Rosa Myrtil, informed of Philippe's plan, only saw one thing: that she would find herself alone with Jacques. Jacques interested her, as we already know, and, oddly enough, she felt all the more attracted to him because of his very coolness. His indifference seemed to her to be a sign of superiority over other men, who had so little self-control in the face of feminine action. His blond beard, his delicate nature and his innate grace continued to seduce her by offering her a mirage of the gentlemen of times past. The slightest attentions that Jacques afforded her, at the hotel or in their walks through Saint-Lo, assumed in her eyes the value of the most tender cares.

Here too the seed of love had sprouted; and from day to day it was developing, insinuating itself further and further.

Philippe, therefore, left for Paris on his own, while Jacques took the road to Valognes, accompanied by Rosa Myrtil.

Valognes, it will be remembered, was the place of origin of the female founder of the Martinvasts of Saint-Denis: the ancestress who had emigrated in 1891. Jacques had too strong an attachment to his own mother not to be particularly enthusiastic to look for traces of the family's first maternal stock.

We ought to say right away that, in spite of his good intentions, he found nothing, or almost nothing, in that excursion. The former Château de Val-Saint-Jacques had been transformed into a vulgar cider factory and even the name of its ancient inhabitants seemed to have been forgotten.

To conclude the trip, Jacques and Rosa Myrtil headed for a nearby beach that had just opened for the bathing season.

As they approach the shore they perceived a tall man with a long beard, at the tip of a promontory, silhouetted against the blue back ground of the liquid mass, who was waving his arms and agitating his entire body. Around him, lined up on the edge of the cliff, was a mute, attentive crowd made up of men, women and children.

"What's going on over there?" said Jacques, turning to Madame Myrtil.

"It's a preacher—at least, I assume so. We now have a number of open-air orators, for whom the vaults of churches, theaters or courtrooms are too narrow. They go into the countryside, or public squares, to speak to crowds. No eloquence is more powerful. In a city, these people install themselves on the steps of a monument, o a balcony, or even on top of a carriage. In the country, they stand on top of a mountain, on a rock, or in front of a scene like that one, or even in a boat off the shore.

"Among the adepts of the profession there are some that the people love passionately, following them in a crowd and showering them with gifts. Some are isolated, others are attached to societies of preachers. There are some whose authority extends over a vast region, like the prestige of the African sages whose counsel directs the tribes and whose tombs become places of devotion. The first of them were the great lords and opulent financiers who swore, on the night of the fourth of August 1899 to hasten the realization of the egalitarian ideal, by giving all their superfluous wealth to the nation and who then went all over France, exhorting the rich to abandon their fortunes. Let's go closer—you can make our own judgment on that kind of evangelism."

They could already hear the orator's voice. It was launched freely into infinite space, and was genuinely impressive. The man who was speaking was exerting himself and exhausting himself as if he were prey to an irresistible inspiration.

"Oh, I recognize him!" Rosa Myrtil exclaimed. "It's the famous Dom Barnabé. I've heard him before. He does a tour of the seaside resorts every year."

"Why Dom Barnabé? One would think that he was a monk."

"Not at all. 'Dom' has no particular significance. It's a way of designating that kind of zealot. Some take the title of apostle, others that of prophet or bard."

"But what interest can the man have in spreading his ideas in this manner? What can it matter to him whether people think like him or differently?"

"Oh, you know, my dear Monsieur that there are people with that particular kind of mania everywhere, and always have been. They have a thought that they deem to be good; they want everyone to share it, and until then, they cannot stop or rest. Nothing can be done with them; their brains drive them; they're not their own masters."

"The people, however, given as they are to incredulity, can scarcely believe any longer in any inspiration, I imagine, no matter what it might be."

"Of course not—but what do you expect? They're always gripped by admiration for those whose sonorous tongues develop grandiose thoughts. A benevolent respect grips them when they're confronted by a man of conviction striving to persuade others. This one, however, is only an antireligionist, rather tedious and maladroit."

"What do you mean?"

"I mean that Dom Barnabé is one of those who don't think that the idea of religion has yet been sufficiently erased. He's afraid of seeing it reborn, and he's always on the lookout for its reawakening, ready to denounce it. Oh, he's far from having the tact and ability of those councilors of yesteryear who, in order to provide a diversion for popular credulity, attempted to open Museums of Religion or to display before European eyes, in a universal fair, the practices of the Buddhist religion, He imagines that he's battering a breach in a ruined house, but he's shoring it up; blowing on the embers as if to extinguish them, he's reanimating them. Can you hear him now?"

Rosa and Jacques were now close enough to be able to hear what the orator was saying distinctly; they stopped.

"There are still some among us, Brethren," said the preacher, "who vaguely regret the absence of religion, and want, at certain times, I'm told, to kneel down on the ground and pray. But don't you see that those are the unhealthy remi-

231

niscences of an abnormal state of mind that reason ought to banish forever? This God, after whom you sigh, and to whom you therefore pay attention, is an imaginary being, fashioned in your image. Praying to God, I swear to you, is as puerile as praying to the rumbling storm, the passing wind, the rain, fire or the sun. Religion, Brethren, is the daughter of fear or ignorance. Proud and enlightened people have no need of it. They pause respectfully before the unknown, and do not seek to fill it with their chimeras.

"Love one another; that is the true religion—or, at least, tolerate one another with as much cordiality as possible. And if sadness and regret sometimes grip you, look at the sky. Our consolation is still there: not the Christian heaven, full of little infantile images, but the sky, the empire of light; the beautiful, profound sky that is there before our eyes, with its changing colors, its free birds soaring overhead, its benevolent breezes, its radiance, which pants the land and the sea with such charming appearances. Delight in nature. Nothing is as calming, Brethren, as the serene contemplation of its innumerable aspects."

As he said that, Dom Barnabé, his eyes lost in infinity, seemed to want to launch himself into the ether and draw into his wide-open arms the entirety of creation.

"What is the purpose of religions?" he went on. "To give patience to the unfortunate, to close the shutters on libertinage. The objective is good, but the means are based on error, and accompanied by abuse. We have suppressed crime, vice and despair, by assuring everyone, in all things, the necessary. The assured satisfaction of human needs; that is our fundamental rule.

"Once, Brethren, there were drunks; they were among these who were not always able to slake their thirst. There were thieves; whence were they most frequently recruited? From among those who lacked the indispensable. There were luxurious men, as if rabid, who raped women and children. Why? Because the work of life was never within their reach.

"Today, the administrator of the people cannot rest until everyone within the scope of his administration is furnished with what is essential to existence: an adequate supper, adequate shelter, and all the rest. That is why life is happy and how humanity has contrived to be worthy of the frame in which it moves. That is why we have no need of religion.

"Silence, silence those, if any still remain, who say that God is Jesus of Nazareth; those who dare to affirm the existence of an ulterior and definitive life. Their lips lie."

When he had finished, to orator slowly came down from the cliff. The men took off their hates respectfully and shook his hand. The women, kneeling down, kissed his arms or knees as he passed by. Followed by his audience, he headed toward the sea, and at a certain moment, he came close enough to Jacques and Madame Myrtil for them to be able to see him quite distinctly. Around his head, in the radiance of his soft and piercing eyes, an iridescent aureole stood out, every similar to the impalpable nimbus that Christian painters had depicted above the heads of their saints.

Participating in the general attraction, Rosa Myrtil drew her companion forward into the path of the preacher. When Dom Barnabé passed by, her turned abruptly toward Jacques de Vertpré and stared at him as if he had sensed that he was an adversary. His face, frankly expansive until then, was suddenly covered by a shadow of suspicion.

Jacques observed him with the same fixity. *Alas*, he thought, *here's a victim of hallucination, an unfortunate visionary. O atheism, is this where you lead? When human reason no longer has a revelation from on high to support it, it goes forth to beat the fields for one... Poor man, I pity you. What can there be in that divagation of an evidently troubled mind that is so attractive to the crowd?*

The listeners rushed forward in confusion.

"But where are all those people going who are marching so bravely in his footsteps?" Jacques asked.

"Where are they going? They don't know themselves. Oh, the power of human speech! All those people are now under the empire of suggestion."

As she said that, Rosa Myrtil drew her companion toward her, trying to get him out of the crowd. She liked hanging on Jacques arm in that fashion, while answering his questions.

XXXIV

When they arrived on the beach, they paused briefly to watch the bathers of both sexes. It was high tide, and although the season was only just beginning, there were a great many people in the huts on the water's edge.

The shore was, according to custom, divided into a number of sections entirely separate from one another, one for boys, another for girls, one reserved exclusively for men and one exclusively for women, and finally, the largest of them all, open to both men and women.

Jacques approved on the young people being made to bathe separately. As for the enclosures exclusively consecrated to one or other sex, he did not pay much heed to them. It was, in any case, rather difficult to get a god view of them, for the huts tightly-packed huts, situated as close as possible to the water, constituted veritable defensive walls against external gazes in those sections. In fact, there was hardly anyone in those particular categories but old, sick or infirm individuals who were dressed from head to toe in order to go into the sea. The large common space, by contrast, was well calculated to attract the voyager's serious attention.

There, in order to make space for the beautiful Naiads and Apollos of the waves, a fairly broad strand had been contrived between the huts and the water, which permitted the public, artists and connoisseurs to follow in detail, at close range, the comings and goings of the bathers. The latter, ornamented with a certain care, were much less extensively dressed than the inhabitants of the neighboring sections.

Obviously, these dispositions differed quite sharply from the relatively correct beach etiquette of Bourbon. The classification was, so to speak, inverted. And yet, Jacques did not say a word: no questions, no reflections. For a few moments, he let his astonished and scandalized eyes wander over the saraband that was agitating close at hand in the first undulations of the waves, in the midst of splashing water. Then, turning round, he started thinking about the old times of Greece and Rome, those dances and games depicted in ruined bas-reliefs, that liberty of mores that had been, for a while, the joy of antique cities, and then had precipitated them into an irremediable decadence. Was it really France that he was treading beneath his feet? Was it not rather the shore of Cythera?

He was lost in that reverie when Rose Myrtil, leaning over to catch his eye, said to him: "Well, Jacques, are we going to bathe too?" As she said it, she had the most innocent of smiles on her lips.

"Again..." said Jacques, swiftly. At the same time, his head came up, as if jerked by a spring, and then immediately came down again, as he turned his eyes away. The idea that he might perhaps be in Tahiti, in the waters of Queen Pomare,[24] crossed his mind momentarily.

Then, coldly, and with an affected indifference, he replied: "No, Madame, not today. I don't feel like it."

On that, the both went away over the sands—far away, to where they could no longer see, between the cliff and the sea, anything but the vague forms of a few people hunting or fishing, and in the air, a few large grey birds soaring over the shore.

They had been walking for some time, always getting further and further away from the town, when one of those birds, a curlew, suddenly stopped in mid-flight, fell to the ground not far from where they were. Jack had seen a man raising a rifle some distance away, but he had seen no flash or smoke, and no sound had reached his ears.

The noise of the sea must have prevented me from hearing it, he thought.

Having got considerably closer to the hunter, he saw him make the gesture of taking aim again; he saw a second bird fall, but again he heard nothing.

---

[24] Queen Pomare reigned in Tahiti from 1827-77.

Mechanically, he felt his ears, wondering whether he had gone deaf.

"What's happening now?" he said, intrigued, turning to Rosa Myrtil. "He's fired two rifle shots, but they didn't make any sound."

"No, of course not," the young woman replied. "The projectiles are emitted without any detonation. You didn't know that?"

"No…then what had become of powder, the invention of which people were so proud?"

"Powder, my dear friend? What powder? Explosive powder? We use it on festival days to make a racket."

"But war…"

"What about war? It has been colder, less thunderous in the most recent clashes of peoples, but it no less terrible, I can assure you."

"My God, where are we going?" Jacques cried, turning round. "Where are we bound? How can one imagine a battle without noise? What kind of courage must one have now? What tactics are employed? Oh, I like our old rifles much better, which sound death, and our old cannon, which thunder, sowing terror among the enemy from afar. That's the music that goes to the heart of warriors."

Having said that, Jacques retreated into himself yet again, and for some time the two of them continued waling in silence. Rosa Myrtil respected her friend's meditation—except that, from time to time, she turned to look at him, as if trying to read his thoughts.

The day was approaching its end. Out to sea, the horizon was gradually reddening. The breeze, blowing from the land, carried the perfumed scents of the fields.

For the sake of good will and politeness, Jacques occasionally tried to restart the conversation, but his mind was still elsewhere. The negative result of his trip to Valognes, Philippe's departure and the reversal of things of which he had just seen evidence several times over—all those ideas—were agitating his thought simultaneously, drawing him into melancholy. It would not have taken much, at that moment, for a fever to grip him, as it was already gripping the sea.

Rosa Myrtil, instinctively taking account of what was happening to her companion, tried everything to attract his attention and distract him.

The sun's disk was sliding into the waves in the bosom of a horizon full of spangles when they spotted the hull of a grounded boat, and sat down on it before retracing their steps.

"You're sad, Jacques," said Rosa Myrtil, taking his hand.

"No; I'm just thinking about what I've seen, what I've learned..."

"You're said; I can feel it. Our society doesn't please you."

"You think so?"

"You're rather be back in Bourbon, isn't that so? Don't deny it—it's futile."

At these words, a furtive tear rolled down Jacques' cheek. While he was trying to wipe it away, Rosa Myrtil put her arm around his neck and gently drew his face toward her own.

"Your pain is making me suffer too, Jacques. To cure your heart, I wish I could cast a spell on the new France that would render it beautiful, enviable and lovable for you." Then, after a pause, she added: "Would you like us to love one another, Jacques? For myself, I love you."

At the same time, she let her head fall upon her companion's shoulder and remain there momentarily, her arms slack, her eyes languidly extinct.

Jacques' first impulse was to stand up—but as he did so, he regretted his abruptness, and, sitting down again beside Rosa Myrtil, he took her hands and spoke to her softly.

"That's not possible," he said. "You know that very well, my dear friend. Why are you abandoning yourself like this to tenderness? Oh, generosity and sympathy are urging you, I know; but have I not already told you that my heart is sealed, absolutely sealed, against the attainment of love—love as you conceive it, as you practice it? Let me be, I beg you. I will retain of you, of your obliging sentiments, of your noble heart, a pure and tender memory. Let there be no question of anything else."

She got up first, straightening her hair. "Well, so be it," she said, curtly. "Let there be no further question of anything; let's forget everything."

Evidently, she had made up her mind; her impulse was repressed, her caprice banished.

They headed back to the town in silence. From there to Saint-Lo, the journey never ceased to be constrained and embarrassed. In opposite corners of the railway carriage, they pretended to sleep. In reality, they were in a hurry to get back.

Jacques escorted Madame Myrtil to the door of her room. The next morning, when he went to greet her, there was no reply. She had disappeared. He never saw her again.

Thus was abruptly severed the bond of attraction that chance had forged between the young man and the young woman. There was, to be sure, a certain analogy of temperament between them, but their thinking was so dissimilar! In those circumstances, accord was very difficult. It would have required a conversion. A conversion! Yes, it's true. In the same way that a bolt of lightning can reduce a tree to ashes, whereupon a single scratch of a fingernail can cause a centuries old oak to crumble into dust, one sometimes sees the fire of love cause to human beings to change their nature, personalities disappearing like a puff of smoke to give way to different personalities in the same human beings. But how could such an effect be anticipated here? Jacques and Rosa were both steeped far too indelibly in irreconcilable ideas. Then again, the character of each of them guaranteed them against the torrential impulses that sometimes carry impetuous nature away. Between the two of them there had not, in reality, been anything but the fantasy of an imaginative woman, an 'amour of the head,' as Dr. Priot had put it so well.

Thus, it was without any explosion, without remorse and without tangible dolor, that the amour in question was extinguished.

XXXV

Jacques de Vertpré no longer dallied thereafter in making his preparations to rejoin his cousin in Paris. Two days later, furnished with all the family documents that the archives of Saint-Lo had been able to provide, he set out, this time choosing the aerostatic service as a means of transport.

To say that he experienced no apprehension on seeing himself thus drawn away for the first time into the mass of the air would not be in conformity with the truth. Nevertheless, his emotion did not extend as far as dread. What struck him most of all was the serenity of the journey and the insensibility of the prodigious speed at which he was moving.

His gondola not experiencing the slightest jolt, he took advantage of that immobility after a while to write. On a postcard, doubtless destined for the Île de Bourbon, he traced a few lines that began with the words: *In mid-air, five hundred meters above the soil of Normandy...*

When he had finished the note, he began to look around.

This system of locomotion is really very comfortable, he thought. *No lurching, no pitching, no dust...what a fine discovery for victims of travel sickness! Railways will doubtless only be transporting goods soon.*

The province of Normandy seemed admirable to him, seen on the wing like that. The fields, the rivers and towns went by, gliding beneath his eyes, succeeding one another like the unrolling of a tapestry.

The earth, Jacques said to himself then, *no longer grips us with its immensity. Our eye can measure its dimensions and search its nooks and crannies. The largest nations, condensed as they are today, by their system of communications, are not as extensive as Hellas and Latium were. The Roman empire, with its distant provinces, must have been, with regard to the length of distances, more difficult to govern than the United States of Europe are today, or even the old continent in its entirety. It's not surprising that peoples have formed syndicates, that leagues of States have been formed and that the familial or cooperative spirit has extended throughout all humankind.*

At intervals, he let his eyes wander mechanically over the advertisements that covered the interior of the gondola, the prospectuses, petitions, cards and newspapers that surrounded him, strewn on the floor and the cushions. These appeals to the public were sometimes sufficiently eccentric to catch his attention.

On the ceiling, there was: *Le Havre. Great Butchery of the Pampas. This establishment receives large quantities of first-class meat every three days from America. It supplies all the cities in Normandy and guarantees the freshness of its products all the way to their destination. Unprecedented bargain prices.*

On the back of the bench on which he was sedated, Jacques was able to read: *Thermal springs of Montezuma (Mexico). The administration will pay for the return trip for people wanting to spend the season there. The veritable Fountain of Youth. Prolongs to the most advanced age the usage of all vital faculties. Roulette round the clock.*

The newspaper of small advertisements, left gratuitously at the disposition of travelers with between twenty-five and thirty pages, included the most varied announcements, of festivals, tourist caravans, places in hunting parties, sales, houses to rent, new pharmaceuticals, etc...

No more white hair; no more teeth falling out; no more failing eyesight.

"Good!" Jacques murmured. "Still the same miseries, the same illusions, the same charlatans!"

The next advertisement, designed with great artistry, took up an entire page.

Seraphic Brasero. After a good dinner, what do you need? You need coffee. After coffee, what do you need? Once, there were cigars; now...a lacuna. There is no longer anything to continue the enjoyment, to fill in the time that goes by until the next meal. That enormous lacuna, we have filled. The cigar being finished, gather, men of taste and women of refinement, around the Brasero of the seraphim. It emits a delectable vapor, whose undulant caress delights all the senses. In the bosom of a nirvana mingled with ecstasy, the body renews all its appetites. Chat, dream, read, sleep in its magical atmosphere. It's there that connoisseurs of the art of living find the ideal vessel that leads them from pleasure to pleasure, with no interruption of delight.[25]

"Well! I thought that sobriety and temperance reigned everywhere as a sovereign mistress; it's obvious that a few epicureans still remain among the new puritans. Let's see—what else?"

For hire, the yacht Albatro. *This forty-eight tonner initially belonged to the international club known as the Boors, Place de l'Étoile, Paris, and was then bought by the Lycée de Versailles. The employees of the Bazar de l'Automne bought it in their turn for two years; then the famous dentist Donatelo was its owner. The yacht it presently part of the Luban & Co. flotilla, a society organizing pleasure trips by land and sea. The crew is well-trained, polite and discreet. It would be easy to extend the engagement. The hire may be paid annually, seasonally, per voyage, per month or per week. Recommended for individuals, couples, artists, societies and town halls.*

"That would be quite convenient, particularly in Bourbon, where our coasts are so beautiful," Jacques murmured. "What enchanting trips one could take there. How strong and refreshed one would come back! We don't sail enough out there. We go canoeing in calm water, that's about all. Oh, I'm not insulting oars; the oar is probably the only machine than can strengthen both arms equally; but, all things considered, we don't open out lungs to the salty air sufficiently. I need, if I can, to obtain a larger place for yachting in my country's sports. Oh! Here's something else."

---

[25] A literal translation of *Brasero* would be "brazier" but what is being advertised is presumably what we would call a sauna.

Madame Letitia Benares (A7, third floor, no. 40 Rue Lincoln, Paris-Chaillot) has lost a diamond necklace in a side-path in the Boise de Boulogne. The object has no great value, but Mme. Benares is very fond of it. To the person who returns it she will give as a reward a curious collection of Sadi Carnot earrings, from the last epoch.

"Oh!" said Jacques. "Ear-rings must have become museum-pieces. So much the better. It's truly barbaric to pierce women's ears...but then, perhaps diamonds have fallen to the rank of mere pebbles? People must have found a way to manufacture them some time ago. I'll have to tell my friends and relatives in Bourbon."

Before closing the paper Jacques happened on the section of matrimonial engagements. At the top, in large letters, he read: *Available women.* Then there was a series of advertisements.

Madame C. X***, 35; brunette, seven children; height 1m. 67; weight 75 kilos; waist 60 cm; bust 98; hips 118. Madame C. X*** has lived in community for three years with Lord Carrick, an English commercial representative. Serious character. Ready for a long attachment. Requires a lease of at least three-six-nine. No defects, never ill. Several medals in calisthenics competitions. Address requests to Agence Jonathan.

"Oh, the cynicism! Would you put your name down, Madame, in a market hall or a stud-farm. What debasement! What effrontery!"

Then, a little further on:

Madame Estelle Bonnenfant, Mistress of Civic Philosophy at the Lycée Louise Michel (Paris-Belleville) is free to travel during the next vacation (July and August). See her portrait and noticed at the Cercle Sophie Arnould, also known as the Horizontal Disk.[26]

---

[26] Sophie Arnould (1740-1802) was a famous actress and singer who became a symbol of the decadence of Louis XVI's reign, notorious for the alleged laxity of her morals. Louise

"Ah—at least that one's funny," said Jacques.

Then, tearing up, screwing up and scattering that mess of solicitation around him, he turned to the window and stayed there for a long time, his gaze lost in space.

At Evreux there was a brief stop to let passengers on and off. Jacques was not sorry to get his feet back on the ground, and to mingle with the passers-by on the narrow terrace between the two openings of the elevator.

The station-master had not noticed him at first, or he would have prevented him from leaving the gondola, in view of the short duration of the stop. When he perceived him, bareheaded and wide-eyed, posed as an observer in the midst of the crowd, he hurried over to him and asked him politely to get back aboard.

"Right away, Monsieur," said Jacques. "I didn't know that it was forbidden to get off. I was trying, I confess, to see whether there might be a part of the gondola less cluttered with advertisements than mine. In the one where I was, one sat on advertisements, one had them in front, to the side, overhead—everywhere. It's an obsession."

"We have luxury seats," the station-master replied, "in which one is sheltered from the inconvenience you mention, but I must warn you that they're more expensive. The seat you're in is very cheap—that's because the publicity companies meet all, or almost all, of the expenses."

Jacques reflected momentarily. The station-master was waiting to blow his whistle. He had to hurry. "Well, no," said Jacques. "Another time." And he got back into his compartment.

Michel became notorious when charged with lending support to the Paris Commune and transported, and she became one of the most colorful and troublesome figures of the far left on her return from New Caledonia; she was, however, a qualified schoolteacher and there really is a Lycée Louise Michel now (though not in Belleville).

Not without surprise he found three people there who had just got on: a woman of about thirty-five wearing the high collar indicative of conjugal engagement; a girl not yet certified as nubile, but nevertheless tall and sturdy; and, beside them, a young man of twenty-two or twenty-three, wearing the insignia of puberty.

After a few moments, the four travelers, hitherto unknown to one another, had introduced themselves. Naturally, they asked one another who they were and where they were going. The young man was on his way to take a examination in Paris, with a view to entering one of the State services—the Highways Administration. The lady was an inspector of telegraph personnel who had just made a tour and was returning to headquarters. The girl was at the Pupillat d'Evreux, which she had entered after leaving the lycée; she had, it appeared, shown improvement at the school and a particular talent for painting on glass, and was being sent to an academy in Paris in order to take lessons there from expert teachers.

Jacques, obliged to explain his situation in his turn, said that he was coming from Saint-Lo, that he was originally from Saint-Denis in the Île de Bourbon, and that he was traveling by air for the first time. He remained nonplussed by the ease with which people familiarized themselves with others. He had already seen evidence of it during his railway journey, but that simplicity of manners had not struck him as much as it did on this occasion.

It's extraordinary, he said to himself. *The custom in this country, therefore, is to compromise oneself at random. It's no longer assumed, then, that it's necessary to mistrust and disdain someone that one does not know. For today, that's all right, but I must admit that I'd have difficulty submitting to that indiscreet communication in all circumstances. If a person is introduced to me, in the correct manner, by someone that has already been introduced to me, that's fine; I can let myself go, for I have every guarantee—but to have to reply immediately, like this, to someone I've never seen before; really, that's a trifle improper. One might think that one man, no matter who he might be, is worth as much as another, neither more nor less. Why not, then, let everyone address one another as* tu *right away?*

Inevitably, Jacques was interrogated all the more by his traveling companions because he was a foreigner. No matter what he thought of modern customs, he replied with a good grace to the questions that were addressed to him, and learned in the course of the conversation some things of which it was well worth making a mental note.

Thus, it had appeared rather astonishing, with regard to the new principles of education, that the young girl sitting opposite him had sat down in a gondola left at the disposition of the entire public. It seemed to him that persons of that category, who were generally separated from adults, properly speaking, ought to have reserved compartments. It was explained to him that, indeed, such persons usually did travel separately, in company with their tutors, in order to preserve the liberty of older people; but it was added that at present, the aerostatic service did not yet have reserved compartments, either for passengers of different ages or sexes, and that, in any case, the society of older people held no dangers for children, for contemporary mores were sufficient to prevent any danger of pernicious influence.

"Thus," said the lady inspector, "it is sufficient that the presence of a child or an adolescent of either sex should be identified in a company of fully-grown people for any action contrary to the reverence due to youth to be immediately out of the question, in consequence of a silent command. Penalties are prescribed for those who infringe the rules of that elementary beneficence, as there are for those who cause inappropriate things to be heard or seen in the streets or public places.

"That is not to say that children should be kept in ignorance of what nature herself breathes in everyone's ear when the time comes. No, a state of innocence can no longer be retained in the kind of life we lead now, and the sacrifice has been made. There is no point in deluding oneself with vain appearances any longer, all the more so as one runs the risk, by doing so, of bringing children up in hypocrisy. Nothing is hidden from them any longer, therefore; no false ideas are inculcated in them. Today, the art of the educator consists of leading them tactfully along the path of truth to the threshold of adulthood. Oh, it's difficult, but many things are difficult today; the business was simpler with the belief in the particular fecundity of cabbage-patches and the catechism—but at the same time, the public refrains all the more carefully, in their presence, from any intemperate excitation or misplaced statement."

As for the fact of a young girl traveling alone, Jacques was not overly surprised by it. Not that it would have been permissible in Bourbon, but he knew that the custom had been introduced into the Northern regions, and was not astonished to see that independence affirmed in a republican state. He wondered, though, with a rather keen curiosity, what might become of women themselves in such circumstances. *What is the attitude of men with respect to them?* he asked himself.

The lady inspector also informed him on that subject, thanks to a private moment, carefully contrived, in one of the corners of the gondola.

"We who wear the high collar that you see—much more visible than your matrimonial rings—are generally left tranquil in our journeys by men, as in our solitary walks. If they happen to press us, we point a finger or otherwise bring into evidence the sign of our engagement, and things go no further. It's not the same for free women. One can advance a little further with them—never very far, though, for as a general rule, the free will of women is respected absolutely.

"Man proposes, woman disposes—that's the formula in operation among us, with another aphorism: woman does not resist; man does not insist. That truly gallant manner of treating the pursuits of love is incontrovertibly one of the most fortunate progresses of our civilization. To think that it took such a long time to get here! Finally, on one side and on the other, we have become reasonable. Met with a refusal, a man

247

says: 'No matter! For every woman who says no, several will say yes. A woman is only a woman…'"

At these words, Jacques shifted on his bench and abruptly turned his back on his interlocutor. That was too much! *A woman is only a woman! That's thought to be gallant! Damnation!*

The blood had rushed to his head. The words "animosity" and "horse-trading" rose to his lips. Fortunately, he contained himself—but it required a real miracle of strength on his part.

As for the lady inspector, she bit her lip slightly. What had she said? What should she have said? She reflected momentarily, and thought it be to return discreetly, without saying another word, to the place she had originally occupied.

When Jacques came back, he found the young man beside him. He took advantage of that to resume the conversation with him.

XXXVI

"So, Monsieur," he said to him, "you're doubtless hoping to get into the École Polytechnique?"

In citing that college, Jacques had it in mind to show the young student that, in spite of his foreign origin, he was still familiar with French higher education. Alas, he had been deceived once again by the time and place. The student understood, and initially replied to his question with a smile. Then he added:

"The École Polytechnique! Oh, Monsieur, how far we are away from that! Presumably, you're talking about that scientific barracks founded under Napoléon, which survived him for such a long time, we're told, because of the spirit of camaraderie of its former pupils; the school where young men, educated for the most part at the expense of the nation, were simultaneously excused military service—which did not prevent them from wearing the sword and seeing their years of instruction counted as years of campaign. Yes, I've heard mention of it. I've been told that candidates there presented themselves, for the most part, with a vocation in engineering, but that they mostly emerged with an officer's epaulette as a makeshift. It was, it must be confessed, a system of indirect recruitment for the army. Today, the institution no longer exists; we're astonished that it contrived to last as long as it did."

"Really?" Jacques put in. "But we've transported it wholesale to the Île de Bourbon!"

"Oh, for the Île de Bourbon, perhaps it's not bad. Small population...services of which the frame is drastically reduced. For you, it might still be appropriate. Here, things are different.

"Personally, Monsieur, I simply hope to enter the École Professionnelle de la Voirie, which has announced that it has a number of vacant places. According to my university reports,

I'm qualified to enter that service. It only remains for me to compete with the other candidates."

"I understand," said Jacques, listening with increasing attention. "Doubtless I have the honor of speaking to a holder of the baccalaureate."

"Baccalaureate!" exclaimed the young man, clutching his raised ones in his arms and making his entire body rock. "Baccalaureate!" He was displaying a cherubic smile. "Oh, pardon me, Monsieur! The baccalaureate seems as outmoded to us as the baralipton and the rest of scholasticism. No, though, I ought to bring you up to date right away. This is approximately how things go today.

"To begin with, we have general courses—which is to say, the course of general education that goes from the A-B-C to what you would call, I suppose, secondary education, Then we have special courses, in which each science—or, rather, each group of sciences—becomes the object of an exclusive and profound study. Corresponding to these courses there is a series of professional or applied schools open to receive, when the time comes, the pupils whose education is complete.

"Thus, first there is education narrowly defined, in courses, then an apprenticeship in the practical endeavor, in the schools. Instruction—which is to say, the preparation, preparation for technical life—is composed of those two terms.

"When is the transition made from general courses to specialized courses? When is the transition made from instruction to the applied schools? That depends on the individual.

"Consider a child whose mind is quickly saturated and whose apprehensive faculties soon reach a terminus, without any change of resumption or reawakening. He is taken out of education while still young and introduced into a school like that of working the land or woodworking, or some other manual activity, from which he will soon emerge in order to apply himself to useful tasks proportionate to his strength.

"Now consider a child who demonstrates a specialty, a particular natural gift, for the exploitation of which he requires an extended general education. He's a rhymester or a sculptor. Professional education is vitally necessary for him. He's immediately enabled to learn one or two languages, as well as the international language, in order to study the sources of poetry, in which his imagination can, when necessary, steep itself.

"Another young subject seems to have an aptitude for work of a superior order, for enterprises that assume extended notions and intellectual qualities that are rather rare. He exhausts the series of general courses, passes on to the specialized courses, and only enters at a later stage into the practical school that suits him. You see what I mean, don't you?"

Jacques nodded vaguely—a gesture that seemed to say: *go on*.

The student continued: "The juries responsible for ruling on the transition from one milieu to another are, so to speak, permanent. For the general courses, the program and maintenance of which are the responsibility of the cantons, the jury consists of the mayor, the senior physician and one or more pedagogues.

"For the specialized courses, the program and maintenance of which are the responsibility of the provinces, the mayor is replaced on the jury by the governor.

"I have no need to tell you that the function of the jury is considered as having an exceptional gravity. Thus, it is surrounded by all imaginable guarantees. It is so well regulated that it is possible to repair accidental errors if any occur, by revising past decisions. If, for example, a pupil does not confirm the expectations he has inspired, if he suddenly atrophies, or if, on the contrary, he suddenly emerges from a state of intellectual lethargy, the jury can amend that. That's very important, social troubles having been fomented, for the most part, by people who are suffering from not being in their true place.

"As for the professional schools of apprenticeship, they may belong to the canons, the provinces or the State, according to whether the classes, in order to be sufficiently numer-

ous, are obliged to recruit cantonally, provincially or nationally. As a general rule, the State, in addition to its own services,
controls education at all levels, and furnishes the provinces
with what they can't produce. In the same way, the provinces
provide the cantons with what they cannot procure for themselves.

"In order to leave nothing out, I'll add that above the
State schools there are those of the Latin League, to which the
professions whose adepts are very rare are recruited.

"The majority of these schools, being open to pupils of
unequal intellectual advancement, are themselves divided into
sections. Thus, the schools of land-working received both ap-
prentice laborers and future farm-directors, who are already
past-masters in chemical and natural sciences. Some retain
their scholars for a long time; others for only a matter of days.
For certain professions, professional schools no longer even
exist; they are replaced by a spell in the domicile of a practi-
tioner."

Jacques followed the explanation of his system with sustained attention. *To be sure*, he said to himself, *here's a perfectly methodical organization that would be worthy of a prize
at an exhibition of intellectual conceptions*. In reality, though,
he did not have a very clear grasp of the mechanism.

For his part, the student, carried away by his subject, was
beginning to perceive that he was no longer being fully understood. It was time for him to offer some examples.

"Let's imagine," he said, "a student following the general course. The jury decides that it's time to withdraw him
from instruction. What does it do? It looks at his notes, inter-
rogates his teachers, establishes his physical condition, checks
his readiness by means of interrogations, compositions, and
then gives him a leaving certificate, in which it declares him
good for one profession or another, or some public service or
other. The pupil is then free to choose between the various
applications assigned to him. If, after a certain interval, he has
not found an appropriate place, he'll go back to the jury,
which must then ensure him a definite employment.

"Until then the student is educated at the expense of his canton, under the supervision of the cantonal education committee. Once in apprenticeship in a school, a studio or an office, he belongs, so to speak, to the career he has chosen and is supported thereby."

At that point the student stopped, as if to judge the effect of his latest explanations. Jacques, who had been looking or a pretext to speak in his turn for some time, took advantage of the pause.

"If I've understood you correctly, then, Monsieur," he said, "You've followed the general and specialized courses, and at a certain point you found yourself at the level necessary for a kind of work that pleased you. You felt able to undertake great enterprises of earth-working or construction, have asked for your leaving certificate, have been declared good for some service or other, especially for large-scale engineering, which is a State service, and you're going to present yourself for it."

"That's right."

"There's no longer any question of age limits, then?" Jacques went on.

"No, Monsieur—the narrow limits of old, at least. We can say, in general, that we've prolonged youth for at least five years. Its extent has been doubled.

"Oh, how hard things were in the good old days, in the times of Latin and Greek, dead languages; how hard it was for the young generations! Far more application was demanded of them than of adults. It was a cruel abuse of strength…and what a pity for the race! How, with that system, could we make fine specimens of the human animal? What a danger, at the same time, for mental equilibrium and good public order!

"Today, youth works, but most of all, it plays; it lives in the open air, fortifying the body and being penetrated by good humor. It is submissive to the boarding-school regime, it's true, but the colleges are as large as villages. They display themselves on the outskirts of towns like versant oases. It's no longer your boarding-school. Infancy, in particular, is carefully protected. Thus, in rudimentary courses—what you call, I believe, primary school, or something like that—there are never any classes in the afternoon. On the other hand, at all ages, a certain amount of manual application is required, of variable extent. Pupils of all categories are required to do a certain amount of useful work."

"Competitions and examinations still exist, at least," said Jacques.

"They still exist, in a certain measure. Thus, I myself, as I've told you, am going to take part in a competition, for the number of vacant places at the engineering school is fewer than the number of candidates. From another viewpoint, that kind of ordeal is still necessary, in order to give an indication, at a given moment of the general level of education. But we're careful not to use it badly or excessively. With excessive competition, one might get to the stage of making it necessary for competitors to waste their time learning a great many things outside the profession they're pursuing. Isn't that wrong?

"Examinations still exist too; I think I told you that explicitly—but if you knew how all of that has been modified in a century, with regard to regulation and the thinking behind it! Permit me to say that the examinations of old were lotteries, or, rather, feats of strength. We've heard talk of those encyclopedic interrogations made on a fixed date, of a child of a certain minimum age, by a stranger absolutely ignorant of the candidate's past, his work, his character and his particular aptitude. We've been told how the worry of that examination weighed upon the imagination throughout youth, and how it sometimes haunted the dreams of an entire life. Fortunately, those nightmares have vanished."

"Do you have, by chance, what we honor by the name of the four faculties?"

"Four faculties, you say? Are you sure of possessing so many? If you have remained faithful to the ancient errors of our country, you would only have two: that of science, the foremost and the true; and that of letters, which includes, along with languages, the adventitious products of the human mind. Those are the two branches of the encyclopedia—of philosophy, as it was called in antiquity. As for the faculties of law, medicine and theology, they aren't faculties, they're mere professional schools or apprenticeships. They deliver, it's true, doctoral qualifications—but why not, then, have graduates in architecture and doctors of mechanical construction? Can you tell me?

"So, no, Monsieur, we no longer have faculties in the sense that you mean. There are special courses that take their place, with the difference that the teachers are no longer content, as often happened in times past, to emit their particular theory one some subject of their choice, then pick up their hat, drink their glass of water and leave. There are always discussions between the master and his audience; there are always questions, proofs. It is no longer enough today to throw the seed into the furrow; it is necessary to supervise its germination, get one's hands dirty—to do the job, in short—no matter how knowledgeable one is personally. In a word, it's always for the pupils that educational posts are created, never for the professors.

"There are other differences too. Once, certain faculties produced nothing, or almost nothing. Thus, for every hundred doctors made by the faculty of medicine, there were scarcely five doctors of sciences and three doctors of letters, and even those were almost always destined for intellectual reproductions—which is to say, pedagogy. We no longer have that kind of inequality. Finally, technical qualifications are no longer awarded by the university but by the professional service of apprenticeship, and they are much more numerous than among our ancestors, and doubtless among you. There are qualifications for electricians, journalists, administrators, hydraulic engineers, dentists, men of letters, etc. To think that there was once no truly professional school except for the army, the clergy, medicine and pedagogy! That there was none for public government, or diplomacy, or for officers of justice, or those of the treasury! How, then, could the intelligence that ought to animate them be inspired and maintained in these careers in the bosom of a caste-free democracy? We have as many schools and qualifications as there are professions and functions. You understand better now, I suppose, why we no longer have an École Polytechnique?"

"Yes, I understand," Jacques replied. But in addition to all those establishments of instruction, is there nothing else connected with science?"

"I beg your pardon. There is a whole assemblage of laboratories, research stations, observatories, missions, libraries, conservatories and archives, the purpose of which is to extent human knowledge and record its progress. Those institutions are mostly under the direct supervision of the State..."

"Very good," Jacques put in. "That's sufficient to reassure me of the interest that continues to be taken here in advanced studies."

"Oh, you can be tranquil on that score, Monsieur Voyager. Fundamentally, you know, we esteem as equals the worker who only uses his hands and the one who only uses his brain, but it's no less true that the cooperation of the cerebral worker in the national endeavor is superior to that of the manual worker; his range is often much more considerable; the strength that he expends is a more precious essence. It's certain, for example, that the distance is less considerable, with regard to power, between a sickly infant and a Hercules than between an ignoramus and an inventor like Edison, the greatest man of the second half of the 19th century. Intellectual strength has an incomparable span. So we do everything that we can to liberate, as much as possible, our communal intellectual capital, which is our primary wealth. Nevertheless, thanks to destiny, we achieve that without any sensible hindrance to equality in the matter of salary and fortune, pecuniary gain no longer being the unique spur to effort, as it was in the final period of the Middle Ages."

At this point the conversation was interrupted by the sudden appearance of the conductor, who, with the aid of his rope-ladder, was going from one nacelle to the next collecting tickets.

"What? Are we in Paris already?" exclaimed the student, raising his head abruptly. At the same time he went to the window, followed by the other passengers, who had also not expected to reach the end of their journey so soon.

Jacques de Vertpré had been the first to rush forward. "What am I seeing?" he cried. "How can that be Paris? What are those immense docks that I see down there, those innumerable steamships?"

"But that's Paris Seaport," the young girl replied, delighted to be able to teach the young foreigner something in her turn. "Didn't you know?"

"No, no," Jacques repeated, somewhat dazed. At the same time, another thought crossed his mind, and as he drew away from the window he said: "By the way, has the Pas-de-Calais tunnel been constructed too?"

"Not the tunnel," the girl replied, again, "but the bridge—a bridge thirty meters wide."

"A bridge! A bridge!" Jacques could not say any more, and for a few seconds he retained the strange, helpless expression of people who "can't get over it." *All the utopias of the past have been realized, then*, he thought. *France has done everything of which it dreamed. What will it imagine now?*

The conductor was behind him. Jacques saw him, and hastened to hand over his ticket.

What! The employee palpated the ticket, turned it over, sniffed it, weighed it in his hand; then he put on his spectacles in order to get a better look; finally, he slipped it into a little notebook that he slid carefully into the most secret of his pockets. What was all that about? Jacques wondered for a moment whether his ticket might perhaps be fake.

The conductor passed on to the other passengers then. The lady inspector had a travel pass provided by the State, the girl a travel pass provided by her province and the young man a travel pass provided by his canton. The conductor took all these passes without even casting a glance at them, and then went back to the door, not without darting a final glance at the young Bourbonnais.

Scarcely had he made his exit than Jacques, addressing the others, exclaimed: "Did I seem suspect to the conductor? Did you notice the strange way in which he looked at my ticket?"

"Yes, we saw it," said the lady inspector, laughing, "but don't worry about it." She did not seem displeased to see our Bourbonnais dumbfounded yet again by someone other than her. "What took the employee by surprise," she added, "was the fact of finding a ticket."

Jacques still did not understand.

"Well, yes," she said. "Tickets are very rare—almost phenomenal. The general rule today is that one does not pay for one's seat. The seat is free, or reduced in price; or rather, it's the object of an account, either with the State, a society or a canton. The only people who pay directly for their seats are foreigners and a few unfortunates reduced to the role of mere individuals." As she pronounced the final words the inspector assumed an expression of genuine pity.

"How you regard the mere individual, Madame! Among us, the individual flourishes; he's someone..."

"In Bourbon, perhaps, Monsieur—but here, woe betide the solitary man. He needs to be part of something, to feel someone's elbow. The solitary man is crushed, exploited, consumed by others. Remember that..."

They had arrived in Paris and moored to the Eiffel Tower. Our travelers hastened to pick up their hand-luggage and went their separate ways.

XXXVII

Philippe Martinvast was there, waiting for his cousin. Alas, the poor fellow who had been in such a hurry to leave Saint-Lo had arrived in Paris too late to meet Madame Listor there. The latter had already left, and was only due to return, he had been told, in two or three days' time. He had spent the time that he had been on his own getting bored, so he was delighted to see Jacques de Vertpré disembarking. Having told him briefly about his misadventure, he took him to a nearby hotel, situated on the heights of the Trocadero, which bore the name Hôtel Cosmopolite.

"I hope," he said to Jacques, "that we'll be comfortable here. Since my arrival, I've had for neighbors at table the Vicomte de Lao-Tsin, the correspondent of a Chinese newspaper, and a young Brazilian sculptor, who praised the establishment to the skies. By the way, you've disembarked at a good time. We'll be here, my dear chap, for the finest festival of the season. Tomorrow—Sunday—there are international races; on Thursday, Paris celebrates Beauty.

The location was, in fact, well chosen to permit our explorers to have the spectacle of modern Paris constantly before their eyes. The center of the great city, one might say, extends today from the Eiffel Tower to the Arc de Triomphe. It develops there over an ensemble of admirably tree-lined roads, sticking as close as possible to the Bois de Boulogne, beyond which the dormitory quarters have retreated, occupying the heights of Suresnes and Saint-Cloud.

The next day, from midday on, Jacques and Philippe found themselves at the center of an extraordinary movement headed toward Longchamps racecourse. There were carriages of every sort, from huge berlins with eight horses to donkeycarts, railway trains, boats, trams, aerostats, pedestrians, horsemen and women, mobile armchairs for old people and babies, and also electric bicycles, rapidly snaking through the

259

crowd, stopping to top up on electricity, and then setting off again at top speed.

At first, that vertiginous movement of a great city rushing toward a general meeting-point left our two cousins slightly dazed. For a few moments, their eyes were anxious. It seemed to them that they were about to lose their footing and that a torrent would carry them away somewhere. After a little while, however, they recovered their equilibrium, and the scene they had before them seemed truly admirable. On the wooden pavements the flow of the population scarcely produced a dull murmur like that of the wind or the sea, against the background of which stood out, gaily, the crack of whips, roulades pearled with laughter, joyous shouts and the tinkling bells of dogs galloping amid the wheels.

Philippe was delighted.

"How beautiful it is!" he murmured. "What life! What superb people! What a display of joy! It's France in her most numerous agglomeration that we're passing in review, my dear Jacques. What an admirable sight it is! Don't you think so? Is there a popular flood anywhere under the sun that spreads out so brilliantly, so easy in its movements, so rich with joy, good taste and spirit?"

Jacques could not entirely forbid himself a similar sentiment, and yet, it was Sunday. *Sunday*, he thought, *is for prayer and meditation, not for pleasure and fatigue.* But how could one avoid yielding to a certain momentum? Outside of the Christian Sunday, this one was certainly not without merit.

One of the effects of the gathering that they noticed immediately was that the men, all of them bearded, were almost all dressed with the same elegance. Between the women, differences of costume were more evident, but adornment never went as far as extravagance. No more huge birds or gardens suspended over the head; there was no longer any question of bustles, petticoats or crinolines. Feminine garments, having become more sober, announced on behalf of their wearers a saner, more elevated taste, rid of childishnesss and barbarity.

There were, moreover, no sordid outfits; no intoxication, no indecency.

At one o'clock, they set out for the Bois de Boulogne themselves, in company with the two table companions that Philippe had mentioned. The latter, although they were foreigners, knew the capital very well. The Vicomte de Lao-Tsin had made the choice of his position a long time ago, in order to lose his darts against the beleaguered Mandarinate. As for Monsieur Henriquez, the Brazilian sculptor, he had been frequenting studios, expositions and courses at the national École des Beaux-Arts for six months.

When they arrive at the racecourse, our two cousins stand in amazement before the colossal amphitheater, whose terraces the public have invaded. No, they had not had any idea of such a human gathering, and had not imagined that such a vast assembly could take place without collision and disorder. Their memories of Bourbon come to mind; they recall the wooden stage on the lawn at Saint-Denis, with the king's box, those of the peers, the first-, second- and third-class seats, and make the comparison. Here is a two-kilometer amphitheater, rising toward the skies, and on the steps, an entire people confused without distinctions of any sort, as if they wanted to provide, in those amphictyonic seats, an image of their egalitarian constitution as accurate as possible.

Only the directors of the racecourse are separated, in the central pavilion.

Pay attention, though! Here's the first contest. Our voyagers have not yet had time to find seats in the amphitheater.

"How many horses are there?" asks Philippe, hurrying forward.

"Twenty-five," replies Monsieur Henriquez.

"Twenty-five! But that's enormous."

"There are at least twenty-five of them, I can assure you. Oh, the racehorse industry is flourishing today. Stables are funded by shares. Since the nation no longer squanders its resources on eternal preparations for war and machines have invaded agriculture and the transport industry, the horse has become both an instrument of pleasure or gymnastics and an object of lucrative speculation."

At that moment, the host of horses appear before them, striding out in superb fashion.

"Quickly—let's go to the galleries!" exclaims the Vicomte de Lao-Tsin. And all four break into a run, in order to be able to follow the last phases of the race from higher up. When they reach the terraces, the horses are no longer in view, masked by a corner of the wood. On the contrary, the gigantic character of the semicircular edifice serving as an amphitheater appears to our young cousin's eyes, with its full imposing and gripping effect. They are struck with veritable amazement while taking their places in the monument, surely more colossal than all the circus of antiquity, with eyes upraised.

The race is to be a long one, for it is a test off stamina. Our spectators therefore sit down, and Philippe, addressing the Brazilian seated beside him, says: "Have these terraces existed for a long time?"

"Yes, Monsieur. There was some question of building them in stone in the Roman style, but iron was thought to be more practical. They were, I believe, able to utilize the old materials of some exhibition or other."

"And to whom does the building belong?"

"To the State. The State lends it, according to circumstances, to the city of Paris or to associations. When it holds solemnities on its own behalf, the central pavilion is occupied by the authority and the stages of honor."

"On that subject, tell me, who are the present authorities?"

"The authorities?"

"Yes—to begin with, the President of the Republic."

"The President of the Republic? But the Republic has no President. It can't have. How do you think that a people with the pretention of governing itself could have a President, a leader? Did the Greek and Roman Republics have a president? The American Republics had one for a long time, but they gave it up, for in politics, it's necessary to be wary words that are simply inappropriate.

"A president, you see, only has a role in a deliberating assembly. In France, there is a President of the Parliament, who is the foremost of all the dignitaries. Parliament, for its part, appoints—and removes, if necessary—the Central Director of Administrative Services, who is also the President of the Council of Ministers."

"You say Parliament. Presumably there's only a single Chamber now, a single administrative council. There's no longer either a Senate or a Chamber of Peers?"

"Certainly not; you've understood immediately that it couldn't be otherwise in an egalitarian democracy. Here, the peers are the electors."

"Very good—but the ministers, who are they? And the Governor of Paris, the Grand Master of the University, the Garde des Sceaux, the Grand Chancellor of the Légion d'honneur, the Generalissimo...in brief, the principal functionaries?"

"Oh, you're asking too much, Monsieur Martinvast. I don't know... For one thing, there's no longer any question of the pompous titles you list. Then again, governments operate by themselves now; they are, in a manner of speaking, impersonal. The advantages conferred on the members of the Central Administration being less than in the past, they're less envied; people scarcely bother about them. Thus, I'd have great difficulty in naming any of the ministers for you. And yet, they're always the same. When a good minster is found, he's employed until his dying day..."

"You must know some of them, though. The First President of the Cour des Comptes..."[27]

---

[27] There is no precise British or American equivalent to the old French *Cour des Comptes* [Court of Accounts], but the United Kingdom's Audit Commission or the American's General Accounting Office do a similar job, albeit in a manner that is

"The Cour des Comptes!" Monsieur Henriquez echoed, raising his arms and jumping on his bench. Then he turned to the Vicomte. "Lao-Tsin!" he exclaimed. "These people still have a Cour des Comptes."

"Impossible."

"It's true. Monsieur Martinvast just told me. We ought to go and see that, oughtn't we?" Turning back to Philippe, he said: "The Île de Bourbon must be a museum: a collection of curious fossils, a retrospective gallery."

"I beg your pardon—not at all. We consider, on the contrary, that the Cour des Comptes is the indispensable guarantee of good financial management. And that venerable institution continues among us, powerful and uncontested, under the aegis of two fine words calculated to inspire respect: magistracy and permanency."

An immense gale of laughter, emerging simultaneously from the lips of the Chinese and the Brazilian, drowned out Philippe's voice again.

"Oh, I'd like to see that," Monsieur Henriquez went on. "I'd like to see those canons of finance putting on their red robes to verify schedules and memoirs, holding their audiences gravely before an invisible public, judging dead or absent book-keepers in effigy, then declaring their verdict solemnly, in the midst of recriminations regarding the harshness of service and emotional panegyrics addressed to defunct colleagues who never mislaid a centime in the balance of their old forgotten accounts... By the way, after how long does their verification take place in your country?"

"Once it was after eight or ten years. Now it's after five, four, three years…but what efforts it requires! If you knew..."

"Well, in France now, the State budget is verified in less than a year.

"By whom?"

---

less cumbersome by virtue of not being formulated as a kind of legal tribunal.

"By special employees—visiting accountants, as they're known. There are a certain number of them attached to each ministry. Oh, they're not hindered by judicial apparatus in carrying out their work, and they no longer form what was once called 'a Great Body of State.' Their work is speedy, though, and produces useful effects; and, as it operates under the supervision and direction of Parliament, it combines all the desirable guarantees of exactitude and probity."

As this conversation finished, the race ended, suddenly throwing the crowd into great turbulence. Cries of every sort went up. Numbers were repeated, and a quantity of special expressions that Philippe and Jacques did not understand. They looked on and listened silently. It seemed that people around them were making electrical contacts in order to correspond...with whom? They had no idea. They also saw telephones functioning. Tickets and cards were being exchanged, and numbers were displayed to either side whose appearance produced sudden sensations in the crowd.

Our young Bourbonnais realized that it was a matter of wagers being settled, but the mechanism of the wagers escaped them. In any case, it hardly mattered. What was truly extraordinary was the immeasurable development of gambling deployed before them.

To begin with, Philippe and Jacques thought it abominable. Such license made them afraid; it spoiled the entire spectacle in their eyes, and they wondered how God could allow one of the most diabolical vices of Hell to triumph so resoundingly in such a vast theater, without hurling down thunderbolts. They kept these impressions to themselves, however, suspecting that they would not be understood by their companions.

Philippe Martinvast became feverish; his heart beat faster and his gaze became intense; the slightest impulse, a mere breath, would have been sufficient then to drag him into the mêlée. He did not budge, though; nor did he get carried away; a thread, feeble as it was, restrained him.

After a few seconds, turning toward Lao-Tsin interrogatively, he said: "All the same," he said, "this might be called speculation."

The Vicomte's only response was to nod his head and produce a few indecisive vibrations in his pharynx.

"If he saw this," Philippe continued, "would Confucius be content?"

At these words the Oriental turned round sharply. "How can we know? Firstly, I ought to tell you that we in the Young China party have abandoned Confucius somewhat. Did he prohibit gambling? It's possible, but I doubt it. Your Christ didn't condemn it. Oh, to be sure, when one has lost a great deal, gambling seems a horrible thing, but when one wins, eh? When one wins, Monsieur Martinvast..."

Here the Vicomte paused momentarily, his little almond eyes fixed on Philippe, full of fire.

"Gambling," he continued, "is a pleasure for many. Is that sufficient reason to forbid it? Yes, say certain professional moralists. No, we now say, for the most part. If it's a pleasure, let's enjoy it. And in order to enjoy it for a long time, let's not indulge in it to excess."

"Very well," Philippe retorted, "but isn't it excess that we have before our eyes?" And he pointed at the turbulence of the crowd.

"How can we know?" said Lao-Tsin once again. "Can we weigh up the situation of all these thousands of gamblers? Everyone is acting according to their own interest and on their own responsibility. It's not for us to judge what other people do."

"Agreed; put if all the money passes into the hands of monopolists..."

"Oh, then it's no longer gambling; it's fraud. It's up to the police to intervene. But so long as gambling really is gambling, what reproach do you want to offer? What means of making money is more praiseworthy than others? Is there a less dolorous means of losing one's own? What hazard takes from us, hazard will doubtless return. Can one imagine anything more amusing? Besides, is the difference so very great and clear between what is called gambling and what is called work? There are forms of so-called labor that are merely games, and everyone knows that gambling presents real difficulties. Ask your industrialists, agriculturalists and bankers to what they devote their efforts. They'll reply: 'to get chance on our side.' Gain most often results from what? From exceptional strength or superior intelligence, from good or bad weather—which is to say, from an accident. Why can it not come from good luck, combined with flair? The instinct of divination is not to be disdained. Mere foresight is often praised..."

The young Celestial continued, after a moment's pause: "Well, yes; gambling has the keys to the city nowadays; it's well-received in society; along with sport, it's the principal occupation of the young. We practice it in all its forms, and it's a blessing for States, provinces and cities, which obtain the most reliable of their revenues from it. Monaco has become a school. Gold and silver, we say, are made to circulate. They may be in one pocket today, another tomorrow, but the communal capita is the same, and everyone therefore profits from it in turn, without strife, effort or hatred, according to the dictates of luck. Come on, let the circuit complete itself...and you, precious metals, melt, liquefy, in order to go everywhere, bringing the reward of superfluous enjoyment."

The Vicomte was becoming enthusiastic, but Philippe, who was privately conflicted, wanted to put on a show of continuing the struggle.

"Oh," he said, that would be all right if gambling didn't often compromise individual needs..."

"Needs!" exclaimed Lao-Tsin, interrupting him. "Never. The necessary can't be seized. The necessary is guaranteed. Money only serves whimsy."

"Oh!" said Philippe, as if he had no further objection. "In that case..." And he turned to Jacques and Monsieur Henriquez who were listening.

"Which is to say," the latter supplied in support of the Vicomte, "that gambling is the first order of the day, for it's the chance, the unknown, the destiny that is God. Gambling is the last word in civilization, which suppresses pain and replaces it with pleasure. Temples have been consecrated to gambling. You'll see, Messieurs, the former church of the Madeleine; it's now the Lottery Bourse. It's there that the entire world places its bets; it's there that the results from all the race-tracks, regattas and all other imaginable wagers flow…and on what can't one bet?"

During this time, the sequence of races continued. Our four companions decided to leave before the end, because they did not want to miss any of the returning procession. In order to watch it they positioned themselves in the Place de l'Étoile, on the famous corner of the Bankrupts' Club—and indeed, the entire audience passed before them, more rapidly than it had arrived.

Before going back to their hotel, they went down the Champs-Élysées on foot. The Vicomte de Lao-Tsin and the Brazilian sculptor pointed out the principal establishments on the celebrated thoroughfare to our young cousins. There were hotels, vast caravanserais, immense bazaars into which the old docks of the Louvre and the Bon-Marché would have fitted ten times over. Further down, the buildings as large as ministries were the head offices of newspapers—and our Bourbonnais could not fail to be impressed by the importance and wealth of which the latter constructions gave evidence.

"These press palaces are, indeed, as grand as ministries," Philippe observed.

"As grand," repeated the Vicomte de Lao-Tsin, "and even more considerable in terms of influence and authority. They're the ministries of opinion. Would you like to know where the movement of Europe and the entire world originates? It's from there." With a wave of his hand he designated three or four large printing-works of the principal newspapers. "Do you know," he added, "how long it takes nowadays to put together an issue of a newspaper? A few minutes. With slightly-transformed writing-machines, we detach the typographic characters and thus form our proofs."

"Impossible! But what about the real ministries—where are they?"

"Almost all the State buildings are massed at the Louvre, in the Île de la Cité and on the banks of the Seine, along a fortified zone that the national domain has reserved for itself, and which extends as far as the exit from Paris. Remember, though, that when one talks about a ministry today, one simply means an administrative workshop, not a sumptuous palace capable of exciting the envy of politicians, not a tow house organized with a view to hosting high society balls and banquets at the nation's expense."

"And the embassies?"

"Oh, the embassies are no longer anything but simple offices for the ambassadors, courtiers and businessmen. Diplomats have no great status since they ceased, for the most part, to represent kings, and their exterritorial privileges have fallen into disuse."

"Look, here are the clubs," said Monsieur Henriquez, drawing the attention of the two cousins in another direction, "the clubs where all the clubs in all the big cities in the world rally..."

At that moment, however, all four of them are surrounded, swallowed up and dragged away by an immense disorderly crowd that surges behind them like a frightful avalanche.

It is Rigthon, the famous jockey, the winner of the big race, who, according to tradition, is descending the avenue in triumph, escorted by an enthusiastic crowd, while an infinity of cheers, flowers and ribbons descends from windows and balconies. The triumphant rider has passed along the Avenue des Acacias mounted on the superb Campéador, still streaming with his noble sweat; he has followed the Avenue de la Grande-Armée and paused momentarily beneath the Arc de Triomphe to receive the official palm, in the midst of vast applause. His triumph is to continue as far as the Place de la Concorde. He is getting closer, and the passion of the increasingly-excited crowd rises to the point of delirium.

Our voyagers have had great difficulty resisting the pull of that human tide. Huddling behind the trees, they cling on to the trunks as best they can.

Now that the eagre has passed, they seek one another out like shipwreck victims, and, while they adjust their clothing, they exchange their reflections. "What do you think of that?" exclaims Lao-Tsin. "Beats the processions of antiquity. Even we don't have anything like it, in Peking."

"Did you feel the motive force of that living mass?" said Monsieur Henriquez. "It's a pity that industry can't utilize it."

"That the glory of today, is it?" murmured Jacques de Vertpré, in a low voice, smoothing his shirt-front, stained green by contact with a plane-tree.

"What a horse!" exclaimed Philippe, beside him.

When they had recovered somewhat from their emotion and saw that the crowd had moved some distance away, they resumed their stroll slowly, while chatting. They took nearly half an hour to reach the Place de la Concorde.

When they got there, Philippe suddenly stopped. "But I don't see the obelisk!" he exclaimed. "Where's the classic obelisk? Ah! There's a statue, which has doubtless replaced it. How large and superb it is. What does it represent?"

"The obelisk," Monsieur Henriquez replied, "is now on the threshold of Parliament, serving as a thousand-year-old boundary-marker for the entire nation. As for the group you see there between the fountains, that's an allegorical statue of Life, with her different attributes around her."

"Life...always life..." muttered Jacques, dully. "Where have they come to, with that deification of life?"

A few minutes later they were in front of the Madeleine.

"It's true, then," Jacques went on, still addressing Monsieur Henriquez. "This temple of pagan architecture has returned to paganism. You said, didn't you, that it's a Lottery Bourse?"

"Yes, my dear Monsieur. You only have to go in to confirm it."

Our two cousins climbed the steps of the majestic stairway, followed by their companions. Jacques went in first, but scarcely had he set foot inside than he threw himself backwards, as if shocked.

"No, never, never—I can't stay in that furnace!" he cried. "It's Hell. How can men not perish in the midst of such a barbecue?"

"Come on," Philippe observed, mildly. "Impossible—you're exaggerating. Let's try…come with me..."

And they went in together.

They had before their eyes a spectacle with which we are all familiar, to which we have grown accustomed, but which, it must be confessed, is liable to startle foreigners. Our young Bourbonnais considered it with alarmed expressions. The seething racket astounded them. And in the midst of that cacophony, the statue of Mary Magdalen drew their attention. She was there, as before, the amorous saint, her disheveled figure rising above the crowd, with her beautiful marble bosom and her bare arms, but she was no longer the image of humble and suppliant love; she was like a personification of the thirst for gain; she was Fortune herself, with her fascinations and intoxications.

After pausing for a few seconds, our voyagers retraced their steps, and went back to their hotel by railway.

XXXVIII

The next day, our two cousins made a grand tour of the city, solely accompanied by the Vicomte de Lao-Tsin. First of all, as they had said, they wanted to obtain a view of the capital in its entirety.

On visiting the Parliament, they learned that France as governed by an administrative council with less than a hundred members. That seemed quite extraordinary to them, for in Bourbon there were two Chambers, both much more numerous. A first they were tempted to infer that the country had become poor in Statesmen, but other novelties awaited them.

"Parliament," the Vicomte told them, "functions all the year round. It gives orders and supervises their execution. There are no pompous speeches here; they discuss business like businessmen. Members of the public can come to listen, but the members of the assembly don't see them; their presence could only serve to excite boasting."

"That's a Parliament on a small scale," Jacques observed. "No more theatrical setting, no more intrigues in the wings, no more vacations!"

"No, Monsieur, no free trips or exquisite cigars, nor any special immunity. One is obliged to be punctual, and one cannot devote oneself to any other profession concurrently."

"The position of Parliamentarian lacks all charm, then. It's truly no longer worth the trouble of launching oneself into the fatigues, humiliations and expenses of an electoral campaign."

"You're right—so today, it's the elector who goes in search of the candidate; the latter waits—and an election costs nothing."

Jacques shook his head. He seemed to be saying: *That's another profession spoiled.*

"By the way," Philippe asked, "can the députés also be Ministers?"

He seemed, in saying that, to attach considerable importance to the question, as if it were a decisive point in his view.

"No, Monsieur," said Lao-Tsin. "What do you expect? The Republic, at its third attempt, remained almost completely bogged down in consequence of that fatal accumulation."

At the Hôtel de Ville, the Vicomte brought them up to date with the principal modifications introduced into the administrative organization of Paris.

"You've heard mention," he said to them, "of headless bodies. Well, Paris was once a bodiless head. Imprisoned in the smallest département in France, its legal influence scarcely extended as far as Sceaux. Thus maintained on the edge, Paris roared with impatience, and in its moments of fever it talked about launching forth to conquer the whole of France. Today, as well as being a city or an agglomeration of cities, and a capital, Parris is the hub of a province. It has a field of influence proportionate to its importance, and Paris is calm; it no longer frightens the rural areas, and no longer talks about seizing the reins of national government. The governor of the Île-de-France lives on good terms with the Prévôt who is at the head of the syndicate of Parisian cantons."

Philippe and Jacques seemed delighted with the surprise of what they had just learned, and looked at their interlocutor with astonished eyes. The latter then explained to them the rule that had presided over the formation of the new provinces.

"A province," he said, "extends exactly as far as the influence of its urban hub. There, where that influence encounters the attraction of another large city, the limit is established. Paris, which is the French city best served by communications, is at the head of the largest province. One could say that it contains all the localities whose inhabitants could easily come to Paris to spend a considerable part of the day between dawn and dusk. In one direction, it extends all the way to the sea, at the mouth of the Seine. In other directions it borders the provinces of Laval, Bourges, Dijon, Nancy and Lille. Thus, Paris has a major part of the action, being the seat of the Central

Administration and the largest Provincial Administration in France."

Next they went to the Palais de Justice,

There, what struck the young Bourbonnais was that there were no robes to be seen, black or red. *How can one conduct trials with neither toque nor toga?* they wondered.

There were still enough distinctive signs, though. Thus, they suspected strongly that the little blue collars worn by some, and the yellow and red collars worn by others, corresponded to different functions.

"The blue collars," said Philippe Martinvast, "are doubtless the judges, aren't they Vicomte?"

"Yes, the ordinary judges who arbitrate disputes arising between two or more individuals—otherwise known as arbiters."

"And the red collars?"

"The red collars are the magistrates who rule on claims of repression, whether made by the administration or individuals. They're commonly known as jurists."

"Ah! And the yellow collars? Those, I imagine, are ushers, attorneys or advocates?"

"No, the yellow collars are the procurators—which is to say, representatives or parties, their patrons and defenders. One says 'procurator' because the word 'prosecutor' has fallen into discredit. The distinction between attorneys and advocates has disappeared. As for ushers, they no longer play any part in hearings. It was thought that there was absolutely no need for a public officer to shout "Shh!" and announce the cases.

They walked together through the various rooms that opened before them. First, the Vicomte showed them the halls off cantonal justice.

"Each canton," he said, "is obliged to ensure a judiciary service capable of handling all the cases that arise within its circumscription, of whatever nature. Those giving rise to civil sentences aren't very numerous, for all contracts are obliged to contain a clause designating a private arbiter. As for penal cases, they offer the character of not only being judge by heard in public, and that preventive detention, to which they sometimes lead, remains absolutely separate from repressive measures."

"And what happens," asked Jacques, "when, in a personal conflict, the contending parties belong to different cantons?"

"They address themselves to mixed tribunals organized by the Province—and if they're from different provinces, they go before State tribunals."

"Very good—but what happens in case of appeal?"

"In case of appeal? What appeal? Do you mean the appeals of old, which, after long months, put back in question a gain, a right or a responsibility? That no longer exists. Does someone condemned to death have a right to appeal in your homeland? He is, however, judged by inexperienced juries. Why, then, allow it to a man who has failed in a litigation settled by a jurist or has been condemned by a magistrate to a small fine? Is it to procure fiscal resources, entertain unnecessary professions or multiply public functions?

"The French of today envisage every judgment as a definitive transaction and think that in judiciary matters, there's no less contingency in the second instance than the first. They want, above all, not to eternalize the process, to the point that it's better in their eyes to lose a case that win it after interminable anxieties.

"There does remain another kind of appeal, though, Monsieur de Vertpré: an appeal against the arbiters or jurists on the grounds of error of fact or law. That is deferred to tribunals of revision, which occasionally grant an indemnity to unjustly-convicted parties.

"At the expense of the judges, no doubt?"

"No, at the expense of the administration."

"And who appoints the members of the tribunals of revision?"

"The canton, for cases concerning errors of fact or judiciary errors relating to cantonal legislation; the province if provincial legislation is involved; the nation if it's communal legislation that has been injured."

"All that's very good," Philippe exclaimed. Then, after a moment's reflection, he said: "You said that there are no longer many civil proceedings—but are they still as long-drawn-out? Are they still as expensive?"

"Fortunately not, Monsieur. One might say that lawsuits are now cost-free."

"Impossible!" cried the two Bourbonnais, in unison.

"And justice is also swift."

"No, truly," the two cousins went on, laughing. "Admit that you're joking. Since the world has existed, and in all countries, Themis has always been slow; it's necessary to believe that it's in her nature. Come on, quite frankly: a double reform after which generations have sighed in vain? You can't make us believe that it has already been solved in the new social organization."

"But yes," Lao-Tsin affirmed. "And you'll understand that it's very simple. A part of the budget has been allocated to the court. Because a man has the misfortune to have a lawsuit, that's no reason to skin him alive. If one wants to reduce the number of conflicts, there's a simpler means: suppress the judges. A citizen once needed a sheet of paper to formulate a complaint or to spell out a defense; it was sold to him for its weight in gold, although the paper used to print newspapers and novels costs almost nothing. Is that just? On the other hand, the procurators have become public functionaries. If an individual has a case to bring, he has it inscribed by a clerk assigned to him by one of the procurators. The latter receives neither sweeteners nor honoraria. He's in the same situation as the judge and the clerk."

"Then there are no longer any but official advocates?" Philippe observed.

"That's right. And in addition, take note, the judge never decides without having summoned the parties to appear before him."

As they were chatting in this manner, they arrived at the large offices, whose windows were surrounded by rather large groups. Above the windows the words *Judicial Office* were legible.

"Why," said Jacques, "here we are, at the clerks."

All three drew closer, our two young people drawing their companion with them.

There was, in fact, one detail that had attracted the keen attention of Philippe and Jacques. In the hands of the employees and the clients they not see anything but portrait photographs. *What are those portraits for?* they wondered.

"One might thing one were in a photographic studio," Philippe remarked, aloud.

"Oh, I was about to tell you," said the Vicomte. "The office is like the registry office of the population; it's the great book of identity. With the prevailing similarity in positions, and the frequency and extent of movement, it's become an essential service. One finds here not only the civil, electoral, judicial and sanitary status of every individual of both sexes, but also an anthropometric description, a signature and a portrait. The latter is renewable every ten years and must correspond with the one that each individual has integrated into their passport. That explains the comings and goings you have before your eyes. The majority of the people you see have come to provide a new print for their identity card."

"What order! My God, what order!" retorted Philippe, with feigned gravity. "Well," he added, "It's not yet perfect, Monsieur de Lao-Tsin; the last word has not yet been said."

"What more do you want?"

"The label, my dear Vicomte. I want the universal and obligatory label, a pretty tattoo, each to check—placed here on the hand, for example, at birth—which could, if you wish, only be entirely decipherable with the aid of a magnifying-glass, and which wouldn't be disfiguring. Everyone in the world stamped!"

Lao-Tsin started laughing. "Who knows," he said. "Perhaps it will come." And with these words, he led our two young cousins out of the Palais.

After a certain time, they arrived in a large square analogous to the ancient Esplanade des Invalides, The square was packed, and above the crowd were banners of every kind, floating in the wind.

"This," said the Vicomte, "is the Forum, or meeting-place. It's the location consecrated to large public gatherings in the open air. Here, all demonstrations can take place freely, whereas organizing them elsewhere requires the permission of the Administration."

All three of them walked through the cried for a few moments, taking note of the rallying cries, listened to the orators hoisted on to high podia and reading the large placards held up above heads.

Just as they were about to leave, two new processions arrived, one from the left, preceded by a white flag, the other from the right, dominated by an immense red standard.

Jacques de Vertpré was looking to the left. "Oh, look, Philippe!" he cried. "It's the flag of the Île de Bourbon."

"Possibly," said Philippe, who was looking to the left. "But over there, I can see the red flag."

Jacques turned round and they both looked momentarily, not without a vague emotion, at what they considered, according to their traditions, to be the flag of insurrection. Such tolerance on the part of the police in the matter of exhibitions left them quite confused.

"What!" said Jacques, addressing the Vicomte. "The French of today permit the simultaneous raising of our forefathers' standard, which signifies good order, and the baleful red rag that has always served as the emblem of demagogy! How can that be?"

"It simply means, my dear Monsieur, that the French have added to their freedoms—the freedom of the press, the freedom of assembly, freedom in love—one more freedom: the freedom of the banner. No color is proscribed nowadays, not even the noble red color that once seemed so beautiful in a judge's or cardinal's robes, or a soldier's uniform, which was so useful as a signal, and—no one knows why—so terrible when it was on a pole at the end of a street.

"Make no mistake though—the hues don't have the significance you think. Red is the color of the Unitarians; white has been adopted by the Cantonalists. Do you know what Unitarians are? No? Well, I'll tell you."

With these words, Lao-Tsin drew his two interlocutors to one side, and continued:

"There are a certain number of parties in the country, between which the inhabitants are distributed according to their character, their education and their acquaintances. Alongside the mass of those who are indifferent or impotent there are, at the present moment, two principal groups that draw opinion in opposite directions. Some want more centralization, and hence more uniformity. They're the Unitarians. The others think that the canton doesn't have enough autonomy, that it's not sufficiently independent. They're the Cantonalists. The entire history of the Republic, here as in many other countries, has been summarized for many years in an incessant alternation of oscillations in one direction and the other. Tick tock, tick tock…such is the chromic movement of general politics. Tick tock…that's the shuttle passing through the weft; then the weft crosses over, waiting for the shuttle to come back. Tick tock. So flows national life, just as that of the Earth flows, alternating from winter to summer, and from summer to winter.

"The movement occasionally drifts in its coming and going, increasingly toward centralization. The individualism of localities that has superseded the individuality of persons fades away gradually, day by day. It's an honorable cause that courageously denies itself, in a retreat worthy of praise. When one examines, after a certain time, the path that the country has traveled, one is obliged to observe that similarity is extending its progress and taking back legislatively that which, in certain epochs, it seized by force. It regularizes itself, classifies itself and identifies itself with the national temperament, while ethnic variety gradually but inexorably decreases.

"Thus, you see, Messieurs Bourbonnais, everything has changed in the matter of flags and political groupings, but oppositions of tendency have persisted; they are imperishable. What do the Unitarians represent? It's the left, reaching for novelty. And the Cantonalists? It's the right, trying to hold on to the *status quo*. On the left, what does on see? Innovators, fanatical for improvement, the anxious, the discontented, the envious and the inspired; generally relatively uneducated personalities, not very sympathetic, but whose ideas—some of them, at last—are in conformity with justice and called to success. Who is in the ranks of the right? The satisfied, the tranquil, the disciplinarians, the lovers of routine, the orderly; perfectly sociable for the most part, although slightly haughty; little inclined to violence, practicing the law of respect and supporting themselves on a certain authority, but nevertheless doomed to eventual failure by reason of the interested nature of their claims, and because of the mania, doubtless very human but detestable nevertheless, which instinctively holds them back with a view to preventing the elevation of those who will come after them. The left, today as in the past, represents for the country action, effort, the offensive. The right is rest, sometimes repair; it's defensive, resistance if not retreat. And progress—I don't say improvement this time, no, simply the forward march—progress remains regulated by the combined and alternative effect of those two factors, each of which is the moderator of the other."

Philippe and Jacques listened very attentively to what Lao-Tsin was saying. Nevertheless, to tell the truth, they could not take clear account of that disposition of political forces. Like the majority of humans, they scarcely understood any but the state of affairs prevailing in their own country. Now, in Bourbon there was only one party: the party of honest people; which is to say, theirs, that of good royalists. The rest did not count.

While the Vicomte was speaking, the Unitarians and Cantonalists had gathered, and each company was increasing in size with new adherents. The meetings were called to order; information was communicated, and money was poured into the hands of collectors. Not coins, but paper—bills of all denominations, coupons, pieces of cardboard, lottery tickets, etc.

Philippe Martinvast remarked on that, thus providing Lao-Tsin with the opportunity to explain, while they went back to the Hotel Cosmopolite, the considerable role that fiduciary money fulfils nowadays.

"But where does all that paper come from?" Philippe asked.

"It comes from the State, Monsieur Martinvast, for the provinces, the cities, societies, even simple capitalists." And the Vicomte cited some famous bankers who could have successfully thrown bonds into the public market designed with their names, which would have had as much value as metal money.

"Then anyone can issue money?" Philippe persisted.

"And why not? What can prevent me from putting into circulation, in the form of a schedule, warrant or mandate, a delegation of right that I might have on a business or a bank, on crops, merchandise or whatever? It's so convenient, useful and simple."

"And people don't fear seeing the signatories go bankrupt?"

"Not at all. The documents are put in circulation in circumstances that render that impossible. But times are no longer the same. Today, to tell the truth, for transactions carried out within the Latin league, paper is very nearly sufficient. Perhaps it will be in future throughout the ancient continent— which is to say, Europe and Asia."

Which is to say, my dear Vicomte, that in your opinion, metal money could eventually find itself out of use."

"Perhaps, Monsieur Martinvast, it will be replaced by merit points."

All three laughed.

281

"That would be all very well," said Jacques, intervening in his turn, "if paper money weren't so easy to simulate."

"How can your mind conceive such a dread?" exclaimed Lao-Tsin, gravely. And, making a noble gesture, he added: "The prescribed penalty for forgery is in proportion to the peril run and the social interest threatened."

"What is that penalty, then?"

"Death—death with no possibility of pardon."

As he pronounced these frightful words, our three companions found themselves at the door of their hotel. Monsieur Henriquez was sitting on the steps, waiting for them, while thumbing through the *Almanach de Gotha*.[28] The Vicomte de Lao-Tsin confided the young Bourbonnais to his care, and then took his leave for a while, Before supper, he had to go to the Rue de Grand-Mogul to speak to the chief bonze.

---

[28] It is not obvious why M. Henriquez would be consulting a guide to European royal families; perhaps the famous *Almanach* has changed its purpose?

XXXIX

It was with Monsieur Henriquez that Philippe and Jacques made their second excursion into Paris.

The young sculptor's preference directed their attention to the artistic side of the city; and to begin with, sculpture was the particular object of his indications.

It seems that the degree of civilization of a country can be measured by the importance and perfection of the sculptural products exposed to the view of passers-by in the streets, in squares and along porticos. Now, our young Bourbonnais had no idea of the unprecedented development that lapidary ornamentation, especially in statuary, had undergone in the last century. They knew Paris slightly as it had been in 1880, thanks to photographic views of that era taken with them by the founders of the Kingdom of Bourbon, but they knew nothing about the Second Renaissance, a hundred times more fecund and imbued with genius than the first, by which the definitive liberation of the human spirit had been signaled.

The luxuriant creation of marble and metal, which, since their arrival, had been displayed to their eyes, had made a deep impression on their minds. There was no square or crossroads that did not present to them a statue, a group or a bust. At intervals, the sky outlined against its blue background the fugitive lines of endless colonnades. On the frontons of monuments and the façades of houses they saw veritable virtuosities of the chisel gleaming everywhere.

What struck them particularly was the character of universality of the works of art. It was not only France, no longer exclusively political and military merit, that these compositions evoked. What they had before their eyes addressed the entire world, and all the human virtues were celebrated there. The spectacle by which they were surrounded gave the sensation of an immense Panthéon open to the sky, dedicated to the glorification of everything in the universe that had been beautiful, useful and memorable.

As your young men seemed surprised by the eclectic and cosmopolitan character of that admirable figuration, Monsieur Henriquez said to them:

"As you can see for yourselves, my dear Messieurs, Paris is no longer the Parisians' own city. It has been a long time since ancient Lutèce has been invaded by the surrounding provinces. Today, Paris is not only the capital of Europe, it's the uncontested metropolis of the world—in a word, the city of all "urbs." Humankind, continuing its Westward march, has fixed its sights thereon for centuries. We Brazilians are as much at home here as in Rio; we have our quarter here, like the North Americans, the Australians, the Japanese and the South Africans, with our meeting laces and even our temples, although the Parisians have repudiated any religious cult for themselves. That's why I can show you the splendors of all nations.

"By this means, as you can see, all ideas, even the most contradictory, all efforts and all devotions, even the most opposed, have been symbolized. That reflects the fact that the French have become, I won't say skeptics, but broader believers; just as they don't deny any epoch of their history, they don't reject any sincere aspiration, and endeavor whose motives and objectives were good, even those that ended in failure and were actually based on error. These people, who have been iconoclastic in certain eras, have fallen by virtue of reaction into the superstition of carved stone. They extend their respect a long way; you'll perceive certain mediocrities that have found a place next to works that are generally worthy of high esteem, but it is sufficient today that human endeavor has touched a stone for that stone to be sacred."

Among the sculptural curiosities of the ecumenical quarter, Monsieur Henriquez first took them to see the amphitheater where the benefactors of humankind are gathered. He was glad to be able to show them, in that place of honor, Dom Pedro, the last emperor of Brazil, the destroyer of slavery, of whom he remained very proud. Beside him was Washington.

"Here," said Monsieur Henriquez, "is the founder of the Republic, the eternal model of the leaders of great democracies. It is to him that the Federation of the United States owes its grandeur and its prosperity; it was the Congress over which he presided that formulated the admirable synthesis on which the French of 1789 based their declaration of the rights of man. The French, so proud of their Revolution, eventually came to comprehend that that Revolution, a distant repercussion of the Reform, came to them from the other side of the Atlantic, and have testified their gratitude by means of this statue.

As they headed toward the Place de l'Étoile, they passed under a portico dedicated to the friends of France. All those were there who, since ancient times, had manifested sympathy for our nation from beyond its frontiers: those who loved the sons of Gaul. One of the most recent was Emilio Castelar, the great sower of ideas.[29] Monsieur Henriquez pointed him out proudly, considering him as a sort of compatriot.

When they walked through the Russian quarter, the bust of a poor, thin old man at a street corner attracted the gazes of Philippe and Jacques. They approached it and read: *Prince Kropotkin*.[30] At the same time, surprised, they turned to Monsieur Henriquez with expressions that seemed to say: *Come on, isn't that pushing the cult of sincerity and a tendency to statuomania a bit too far?*

Monsieur Henriquez understood what they were thinking and replied: "Well, yes, Kropotkin. You've heard mention of

---

[29] The Spanish political writer Emilio Castelar y Ripoli (1832-1899).

[30] The geographer and anarchist Pyotr Kropotkin was arrested in France in 1882 and imprisoned for his membership of the International Workingmen's Association; after assiduous campaigning by his supporters he was released in 1886 and went to England.

the statue of Marshal Ney that was erected in the place where he was executed by firing squad. That bust you're looking at it's a kind of counterpart. The laws of the time when the prince lived had to be severe for that intransigent innovator, but posterity has rendered homage to his good faith and his spirit of sacrifice. In the same way, among the ancients, people sought to appease the manes of unfortunate heroes and misunderstood pioneers."

When they reached the Arc de Triomphe, all three paused to admire the incomparable view offered by that location. Then, as they were going under the arch, Philippe Martinvast suddenly stopped. One might have thought that he had been gripped by fear.

"What, a bourgeois here!" he exclaimed. And he pointed to the statue of a man in a frock-coat that was beneath the arch, overlooking the admirable streets coming from all directions to terminate at the grandiose crossroads. "And what has been done with Napoléon?" he added.

Monsieur Henriquez drew closer in order to reply. "When the smoke of his personal glory had cleared," he said, "Napoléon no longer reminded the French of anything but an invasion preceded by countless massacres. His monuments were retained, but the man was relegated to the second rank, and even the extraordinary mission that he had accomplished as a general in the service of the Republic was largely forgotten. The gentleman you see there is simply an engineer. He was the man who created those large avenues decorated with admirable foliage; he was the one who brought Paris to the rank that human evolution had assigned to it. He was a rival of the great city founders a modern Amphion. Bow down: that's Alphand, everyone's host."[31]

---

[31] Jean-Charles Alphand (1817-1891) worked closely with Baron Haussmann on the renovation of Paris, and was given the position of Director of Public Works by Haussmann's successor, Léon Say. The remodeling of the Bois de Boulogne

Philippe and Jacques took off their hats mechanically.

Since their arrival in Paris, it seemed to them that their brains had been squeezed, while the orbits of their eyes had expanded. They were incessantly gazing and seeing, storing countless images in their memories, but their minds were enervated, their reason seemed to want to fade away into oblivion. They remained in that state until the end of their exploration. When would they emerge from that accumulation of impressions, so strange to them? What would its effect be on the already-differing tendencies of their thought?

After a few moments, they found themselves on the site of the Great Exhibition of 1889, a place already covered, as everyone knows, with large gardens. They were able to pass in review, in the form of marble statues, the illustrious individuals who represented the genius of France in the epoch of the first centenary of the Revolution. It is a good idea of our aediles to have thus summarized the recent epochs of our history, in various locations in the city, bringing together the epoch-making personalities one lustrum at a time. The sight of the notable individuals connected with the eighteenth lustrum of the century before last—1885-1890—had a particular interest for our two companions, because for them it was the final period of what they knew of our history, and they were curious to know which of the contemporaries of the Exodus posterity had illuminated.

First, Monsieur Henriquez led them to the monument representing the politicians of the time, seated around a large carpet in collective deliberation. "At the center," he said, is Sadi Carnot, the fourth of the bourgeois kings who reigned on the throne of the Élysée before France became entirely Republican.[32] Beside him is Lockroy. The latter might have been the

---

was one of his projects, and he also did a good deal of work in preparation for the 1889 Exposition.

[32] Sadi Carnot, the descendant of a prominent dynasty of scientists and statesmen (he was an engineer himself) was the President of the Republic when *La Cité future* was written and

foremost of his epoch. He had an early intuition of the new political route to follow, and there was nothing standing in the way of his becoming the leader of the French Whigs—no attachment to any old party, nor the memories of his early education, nor the opposition of his family, unpopularity, physical or intellectual insufficiency or poverty. The fairies had given him all their gifts—plus, alas, a grain of nervousness. Perhaps he wanted to move too quickly. Now, in matters of social evolution, slowness—extreme slowness—is indispensable, especially at turning-points. What one must have is a good sense of direction. Lockroy also had a little too much wit, it seems, and the man in the street of that era did not like masterful men, adventurers or rabble-rousers; he was of the opinion that witty men are not serious enough to govern. At any rate, his glory consists of having authorized, in spite of the opposition of the artistic gentry, the erection of the Eiffel Tower, which you can see outlined beside him.[33]

"Then Freycinet, playing with a little white mouse. You're familiar with his name. Conversely to the first of the Carnots, he organized defeat and then, by means of a superbly-engineered plan, he enthroned the deficit—but he put such talent into it, such a persuasive seduction, such perfect good faith, that he remained for all his life 'the indispensable man'; people always hoped that bad luck would let him alone.

"After him is Jules Ferry, bent beneath of a monstrous article seven. Over his convulsively swollen face remorse has spread its somber expression. From what is he suffering? Ah,

---

published. A prominent member of the group known as the Opportunist Republicans, had previously been Minister of Finance while Jules Ferry and Charles de Freycinet (also an engineer) had served as prime minister.

[33] Édouard Lockroy, who acquired that pseudonym while he was an actor, was a radical Republican who was briefly included in Opportunist ministries in the late 1880s as a sop to his popularity, but went on to greater success in the 1890s when he became the leader of the Radical faction.

there it is! He called himself a Republican, and misunderstood the Rights of Man. He thought he was a liberal, and was led to become an inquisitor. As a jurist, he set out vilely to besmirch the old codes with a view to oppressing the weak. As an administrator, instead of enabling peace to reign, he unleashed civil discord, bringing the Republic itself to within an inch of its ruin. Behind him, in a sinister attitude, are the two hirelings of whom France made use in its hours of madness to do its dirty work. The first, who is holding an ax and a big bunch of keys, is Constans, the violator of domiciles. The second, who is wearing the costume of the President of the Supreme Court like a carnival disguise, is named Cazot. On the band of his toque, as you see, one can read: 'The judiciary guarantee is me...'[34]

"Further away is Monsieur Floquet. The artist has represented him with puffed-out cheeks, which make him resemble Aeolus the king of the winds. Do you see the volume he's leafing through? It's an anthology of sensational phrases. A good fellow, he let people believe, a pastiche of Gambetta... His neighbor is none other than Clemenceau. He was not a minister, but at least he overturned a great many ministries. He is wearing mourning for his victims, and his accoutrements seem to be imprinted with the livery of funeral pomp, as if to recall the nickname of 'the gravedigger,' by which he is remembered. And in last place, Tirard, one of the foremost utilities of the time. Very commendable capability, a noble and honest man."[35]

---

[34] While prime minister, Ferry took robust action against the troublesome General Boulanger, assisted in his repression by the Minister of the Interior, Ernest Constans, and the Garde des Sceaux, Théodore-Jules Cazot.
[35] Charles Floquet was President of the Council in 1888-89. Georges Clemenceau was only at the beginning of his career in the late 1880s, but he was the prime architect of the fall of Ferry's 1885 cabinet and played a leading role in bringing Jules Grévy's Presidency to an end and installing Carnot in his

"What, that's the lot, already?" observed Jacques de Vertpré.

"Yes, that's all; that's the fine ministerial or patrician flower of the day. Would you like to see the journalists now? Oh, the sculptors have given themselves much freer expression with them. Look, that paladin waving his huge sword in both hands is Cassagnac *fils*. The other one, with his pen tucked behind his ear, placing himself *en garde* with a naked foil is Aurélien Scholl. On the lintel that connects them you can read the words that were like the first commandment of the gentlemen of the press of that era: 'If you want to be respected, and to have the right to say anything, be a good swordsman.'"[36]

"Ha ha!" Jacques observed. "It appears that the writers of the day were prudent men."

"Indeed," replied Monsieur Henriquez. "In attack as in defense." Then he returned to his subject. "Between those two warriors, do you see that series of busts? That cunning and muffled face in the *éminence grise*, the counselor Ranc. Beside him is Vacquerie, another high priest of journalism. The next one is Arène, a very fine pen and a very fine tongue too, certainly the wittiest of the Opportunists. And yet, how much cleverness and malignity there was in that sovereign association!"[37]

---

stead. Pierre Tirard was finance minister under Ferry and prime minister under Carnot for two relatively brief spells.

[36] Paul Cassagnac was still a député in the late 1880s, as well as being the editor of the right wing *L'Autorité*, but his once-busy dueling days were behind him by then. Aurélien Scholl was the editor of the *Echo de Paris*.

[37] Arthur Ranc was a former Communard who was one of Cassagnac's dueling opponents and seconded Clemenceau is some of his duels, succeeding the latter as editor of *L'Aurore*. Auguste Vacquerie had been famous in his day, joining Victor Hugo during his exile, but he was a spent force by the late 1880s. Paul Arène was best known as a Provençal writer.

"Yes, we know."

"Alongside them, the third, emerging from a nest of vipers...I doubtless have no need to tell you his name. You know that characteristic, Mephistophelean face, one which the remains a sinister reflection of the labor camp and the prison. Look, in any case, at the two words engraved on the pedestal according to modern orthography: "*Je conspu.*"[38] It's the Marquis de Rochefort-Luçay."

"We knew that," said our two cousins, swiftly.

They noticed in the same category a handsome musketeer by the name of Cornély, an amiable two-faced Janus, Nestor on one side and Columbine on the other; and beside him, John Lemoine, the political writer, a fine dilettante known as Wolf.[39]

Then, from journalists they passed on to actors. "Don't be astonished," Monsieur Henriquez said to them on this occasion, to see statues representing men and women of the theater in our public squares. They're considered today with the same eye as other artists.

There, our visitors had before their eyes Coquelin regretting his homeland—the Rue Richelieu—Sarah Bernhardt lying on a lion-skin in the attitude of a sphinx, and Paulus, singing while jogging on the spot.

It was then the turn of the painters and sculptors.

"Here is Puvis de Chavannes, sketching in broad strokes the human odyssey across the world. Meissonnier is holding

---

[38] An untranslatable pun, which implies—with a stretch excused by the reference to "modern orthography"—both the past tense of the verb conspirer [to conspire] and the present tense of the verb conspuer [to boo or shout down]. Rochefort-Luçay was the founder of *L'Intransigeant*, most notorious in the late 1880s for its support of General Boulanger, with whom he was imprisoned and went into exile.

[39] Jules Cornély was on the staff of the royalist paper *Le Gaulois* in the late 1880s. John Lemoine worked for the *Journal des Débats* but was long past his heyday by 1885.

an invisible brush in his hand and is in the process of creating his marvelous little masterpieces to delight the future. Between the two, the impeccable, Raphaelesque and more than perfect Bouguereau, then Dagnan and Breton, the former painting what rocks, woods, clouds and other unconscious entities are thinking, the second transfiguring the fields and all of rustic life. There are others, too: here are Bonnat, Hener, Delaunay, J.-P. Laurens, Carolus Duran.[40]

"Among those who worked for the distant future, symbolizing the thoughts of their contemporaries in stone and bronze, here are Dalou, Falguière, Rodin, Dubois, Chapu and Barrias.

"And that's not all of them, the artists. There were a great many of them in those days; they were the jewels of France as it then was. They consoled the motherland for its afflictions and distracted it from its anxieties."

In a shady walkway it was the useful men—the inventors—that they encountered: Pasteur, Berthelot and Chevreul, each with his attributes and his discoveries.

Who is the man on the mound with the luminous forehead and the attentive ear? His being seems to resonate with an interior symphony, and one might think that he were collecting the harmonies that glide through space overhead. Our voyagers pause momentarily; they have read the name of Gounod.

"What about the men of letters?" the two young men ask. "Where are they?"

"Ah! Come this way."

And beneath an arbor shaped like an academic cupola, Monsieur Henriquez introduces them successively to Dumas fils, Sardou, Feuillet, Guy de Maupassant, Anatole France and Pierre Loti.

---

[40] As noted in the introduction, the most striking thing about this unusually long list is the omission of anyone we would now think of as outstanding contributors to the art of the period: Cézanne, Seurat, Degas etc., etc.

Philippe and Jacques are astonished that a period so fecund in books had produced of few literary glories. "Aren't there any others?" they ask.

"No," replies Monsieur Henriquez. "That's all, or almost all, of them." But he continues immediately: "Oh, yes, I forgot. You see that individual over there, in that discreet corner, on top of that public toilet, holding his nose for all eternity. That's Zola, a Chevalier de la Légion d'honneur."

In the center of the gardens there is, as everyone knows, a kind of large circular lawn, in the middle of which appear in their white form the various celebrities outside the classified categories. There one sees, pell-mell, Monsignor Lavigerie launching a crusade against slavery, and Félix Pyat declaiming, in the bosom of a rural landscape, an ode to the bullet; the armorer de Mun preaching Christian socialism; Basly in a tavern pitying the coal-miners toiling underground; Lord Léon Say and Sir Waldeck-Rousseau, ready to take direction of the Tory party, waiting for the political terrain to be completely rid of old moribund parties; Montjau, the Pontiff, claiming with imperturbable eloquence, in the name of ever-imperiled freethought, the inalienable and superior right to rout those who get in his way; Taine, the investigator dissected with blinking eyes a man, a century or a nation, ready to reform history according to the methods of microscopy; etc., etc.[41]

---

[41] Given that these statues are commemorating a five-year period before the supposed emigration, it is not entirely surprising to find some individuals who would surely have joined it, including Cardinal Charles Lavigerie and Adrien de Mun. The Communard journalist Félix Pyat and the trade-unionist Émile Basly would definitely have not been among them, though. It is not obvious why Léon Say and Pierre Waldeck-Rousseau are not to be found in the politicians' section. There was a member of the Madier de Montjau dynasty in Parliament in the 1880s, but he failed to distinguish himself for anything except having famous ancestors, so his presence here is a

293

This bizarre assemblage cannot help attracting a few smiles to the lips of our young Bourbonnais. Fantasy has indeed, been given free rein. The contrasts and juxtapositions they see there are sometimes singular.

"Look," Monsieur Henriquez continues, "here's Renan chatting with Père Hyacinthe. He's explaining to him, in a friendly fashion, that there are at least two ways of defrocking oneself, one of which leads to honors wealth and the enjoyment of life, while the other leaves you by the roadside, frustrated and confused. The two former priests are, as you can see, holding figurines of a woman in their hands; Renan's resembles an abbess, Père Hyacinthe's a new Héloïse.[42]

"In the center, that superb hero mounted on a large black-veined horse is General Boulanger, whose plume resembles a meteor; the tall groom in an overcoat holding the horse's bridle is the patriot Déroulède."[43]

Our young men are really beginning to enjoy themselves, and Monsieur Henriquez is enjoying their pleasure.

---

trifle surprising. The social scientist Hippolyte Taine had been around for a long time but was still active.

[42] Ernest Renan abandoned his vocation for skepticism and scholarship without ever taking holy orders, and his wife was from a family of Dutch painters; although Hyacinthe Loyson married an American heiress some time after his excommunication in 1870, the two events were unconnected, so the author's snide remarks are even more unjustified than usual; yet again, both were long past their prime by 1885.

[43] The placing of the General Boulanger among the outsiders, in spite of his having been the dominant figure in French politics in the relevant period—briefly integrated into the government because the Republicans feared that he might launch a right wing coup—is a harsh judgment, though not unreasonable. Paul Déroulède was the co-founder of the Ligue de Patriotes, which supported Boulanger's loud calls for France to take revenge on Germany for the Franco-Prussian War

Now it is the Naquet group that attracts them. A certain number of liberated wives are doing a hectic dance around the apostle of divorce. It is almost a reproduction of Carpeaux's dancing group. Naquet seems quite touched by the manifestation, but he is trying hard—without success—to get out of the circle surrounding him. The women continue their inflamed frolic: *Evohé! Evohé!*[44]

To the left, supported by a snowy peak, Elysée Reclus is contemplating universal matter at long range and getting ready to narrate the glory of the Earth.[45]

"That man," says Monsieur Henriquez, "had the misfortune to arrive too soon in a world too young. A misunderstood fugitive, he only found shelter in the mountains.

"To the right is another exile, the Duc d'Amaule. From the far side of the frontier he is extending an imploring hand, in which a miniature of Chantilly can be seen. A streamer emerges from it, on which is written: 'Is it my fault that I'm a prince?' Fortunately, he was allowed back in."[46]

---

[44] Alfred Naquet was also a politician, initially on the extreme Left, although he had become a Boulangist by the late 1880s. His one great political triumph was his campaign to re-legalize divorce, finally achieved in 1886. "Evohé" is the Dionysiac cry of the Bacchae in Euripides' tragedy.

[45] Elisée Reclus (I assume that the author's misspelling is deliberate) was a strident anarchist who was exiled from France after the fall of the Commune, and used his exile in Switzerland to become a noted geographer, like his friend and ally Pyotr Kropotkin. He continue to stir up controversy with his founding of the Anti-Marriage Movement

[46] The Duc d'Amaule was one of Louis-Philippe's sons, who had a distinguished military career during the Second Empire and never caused any difficulty for the Third Republic, but fell foul of the anti-Royalist Act of Exception in 1883 and had to bequeath his Chantilly estate to the Institut in order to persuade the government to allow him to return from exile in

"Oh—there's a fine beard!" cries Philippe Martinvast, all of a sudden. "Anatole de La Forge. Who's that?"

"A second-magnitude star that shone quite brightly in his time. Anatole was an honest man, who acquired popularity by good fortune in the second half of his life. He was the arbiter of questions of honor in an era in which dueling was very fashionable."[47]

"What about that pretty statue with no inscription—the distinguished fellow, a veritable type specimen of artistic elegance, who seems to be doing the honors in this marble salon?"

"Yes, that's the Parisian of Paris, the man of the world of the period. He's here as the representative of exceedingly Parisian men. As a characteristic symbol, he's wearing a monocle. No monocle, no chic. The lady he's escorting is the Parisienne of the Exposition, still swollen with pride by virtue of the tributes laid at her feet by the entire world.

"Behind them, closing the parade, you can see a newsvendor, an important personage of the era, the great elector, the king of the sidewalk...the voice of the people."

The Brazilian continued, amiably: "But you know, Messieurs, it's not only statues that we have to see. You might be resentful that I've lingered more than is reasonable on these products of my own art. It's time we cast an eye over some paintings. Don't you agree?"

"Yes, indeed," the two cousins replied.

"Well then, let's head for the museums."

1889. He would surely have emigrated in this alternative history.

[47] The "good fortune" to which the author refers is the fact that La Forge, a Republican journalist, was drafted into the national defense during the Franco-Prussian War and was in command of the French troops that scored the only French victory in that war, when the Germans (whose intelligence was faulty) sent too few troops to take a town where large number of conscripts had been stationed.

XL

For several hours they examined painted canvases, engravings and drawings.

For Philippe and Jacques, that first glance could only serve as a general glimpse, and they both resolved to return to the milieu of those treasures of art in order to study its various aspects one step at a time. What preoccupied them that day was seeking the keynote of the present era.

They observed with real satisfaction that our artists had not fallen into the peril of certain so-called naturalist experiments carried out in an earlier epoch. Pictorial art seemed to them to be sincere, true, always in love with beauty and sentiment. Perhaps, to their insular eyes, the love of nudity and the nudity of love occupied too large a place there, but that tendency did not astonish them, given the knowledge they had of the general tone of modern literature. They took account of the fact that there was no vicious inspiration in that kind of painting, and for them, that was a relatively benign symptom that was worthy of note.

Oh, there are no more Madonnas and images of Crucifixion, of course; evangelists, martyrs and poor saints in a state of ecstasy are over and done with. It is always men, women and children, and various human sentiments, whose images are on offer; but the general theme is that of human verity. Science and observation guide the painter in the choice of subject as in the details of the work.

What our Bourbonnais notice, above all—what leaps to their eyes—is the technical skill that reigns in all the frames, large and small. Oh, talent has made great strides. If dominating geniuses are rare, as they have been told, the overall return has been multiplied a hundred times by these thousands of creators, all well endowed and estimable, who are furnishing France with one of its principal treasures. How can genius be distinguished now in the midst of the numerous consummate talents that surround it? The man of genius is no longer anything more than the first among equals. Who is the man whose virtuosity is the most highly elevated? Who is the one who is richest in imagination? It would be hard to say.

Imagination! That word returns repeatedly to the lips of our two cousins at the sight of the thousand forms of human thought staked on top of one another. "What imagination!" they repeat as they walk. "What fecundity of inspiration!"

And Monsieur Henriquez, easily enthused by the artistic atmosphere, following their expressions from the side, said to them:

"Yes, all that is the crop of the imagination, the foremost of human faculties. When the mind perceives, it's the intellect that acts; when it retains it's the memory; when it works thereafter with the acquired materials, it's the imagination that operates. With it, humans create in their own manner—which is to say that they dispose in a certain order discovered by them the elements they have borrowed from without. The imagination that has inspired a painter in the disposition of his picture has already inspired the idealist in his personification of the types reproduced there—for many of the faces that you find there are, as you've noticed, fictitious individuals. It's imagination that furnishes the architect with new projects, the administrator with rules, the orator with rhetoric, the apostle with faith, the genera with plans of campaign, the inventor with patents. It is to the imagination that we owe pleasure, for it is made of sensitivity, and the heart only moves in its wake. It's thanks to imagination that hope and desire make us taste in advance the joys of anticipated happiness. To think that it was one called the madwoman in the house!" As he expressed himself thus, the young artist shrugged his shoulders all the way to his ears. "But the fire in the hearth, too, is domestic madness, for if one isn't careful, it might burn the house down. And yet…"

He said no more. He judged by the attitude of Philippe and Jacques that he was preaching to the converted.

The latter were, nonetheless, beginning to feel their attention becoming fatigued. They made that known to their companion, who hastened to take them into a square in order to rest.

While they were there, seated on a bench, watching the pedestrians come and go, mechanically following with their gaze the sparrows and pigeons playing on the edge of the fountain, suddenly disappearing into the trees and then returning to perch on the hand or the head of a statue, various sounds, rising above the murmur of the city, struck their ears agreeably. There was, in the distance, a bell with brazen sonorities ringing at full tilt. Closer at hand, through a set of windows open over a garden, an organs sent its chords, mingled with singing.

"Can you hear that?" Jacques aid to his cousin. "One might think that it were a church bell."

"Indeed," Philippe replied. Turning to Monsieur Henriquez, he added: "Are they ringing it because of a fire?"

"Oh no, my dear Monsieur; the alarm bell is only used in small towns. In Paris and big cities, people refrain from sounding alarms too loudly in instances of misfortune. Besides which, it's rare for fire to take hold on a large scale. In all buildings precautions are taken in a permanent fashion in order to be able to put out any flame that manifests itself. These precautions are rigorously imposed and inspected. The distribution of extinguishing liquids, combined with the distribution of water, guarantees these measures considerable efficacy.

"Companies insuring against fire no longer have anything to do, then?" Philippe suggested.

"No, Monsieur Martinvast. "For a long time in fact, insurance companies of all kinds have been founded in the cantonal administration."

"And what about firefighters?"

"The firefighters of Paris intervene in cases of major conflagrations caused by explosions or lightning. They're still there, in case of any serious accident or public danger whatever—floods, collapses, earthquakes of storms. I've no need to

299

tell you that they're elected and paid by the city. You'll presume, of course, that we no longer employ for that purpose soldiers obtained by forced recruitment. For one thing, there's no longer any conscription of that sort, and for another, the city of Paris no longer has any pretention to privileges that other big cities don't have."

"Personally," said Jacques de Vertpré in his turn, "I'd assumed that there were no more bells at all. I was quite astonished when I found some in Saint-Lo."

"Why?" replied. Monsieur Henriquez. "Why did you think there wouldn't be any more bells? Bells are indispensable; you know full well that they can say anything you wish. Yes, bells still exist, cheerful or sad, according to circumstance. Here in Paris they don't play a large role, but they serve to regulate some cantonal exercises; they announce meetings, inspections and civil festivals. In smaller cities and towns, however, they've retained their old importance. In addition to deaths, births, meetings and fêtes, they're rung at dawn and sunset, as well as noon, in order to regulate the work of the population. It's still the common summons, evoking the idea of the directorial thought that watches over everyone's interests.

While they were talking, the choir that had been singing overhead had fallen silent. For a few moments, the organ alone had been continuing its melody. Then the voices resumed. They were undoubtedly male voices.

Monsieur Henriquez pointed at the windows from which the music was coming. "Can you guess what that is?" he asked.

"Doubtless a choral society," Philippe replied.

"A company of amateurs," Jacques opined.

"No, it's simply a circle of friends."

"Oh," said the two young men.

"Yes, working men."

"Impossible!" Philippe exclaimed.

Jacques, even more surprised, had already opened his mouth to ask whether it was, perhaps, a Catholic group, but he contained himself when he suddenly realized that he was about to commit an anachronism.

Monsieur Henriquez could not quite understand his companions' astonishment. *How is it,* he wondered, *that these young people seem bewildered by the idea that workers—or, as we call them nowadays, manual practitioners—might found an independent group of their own accord to meet and relax? It has happened since time immemorial in many countries in Europe and America...*

"And do the gentlemen in question play the organ?" Jacques asked, timidly.

"Certainly—why not? What's extraordinary about that?" Monsieur Henriquez as increasingly intrigued.

"Nothing," said Jacques de Vertpré. "I would have thought the piano more likely..."

"Ah!" exclaimed the young artist, finally beginning to understand his interlocutors' attitude. "The piano, you say—but that's a very meager keyboard instrument. People are content with it is the country, in the desert, where there's no electricity supply, but in Paris, only the organ is in use—the electric organ in particular. One sees it everywhere, in clubs hotels, theaters; it's installed as a standard fixture in comfortable apartments, replacing the ancient fireplaces that have become unnecessary since heat became an object of urban distribution."

"But that's another revolution!" Jacques exclaimed, standing up as if to leave.

"Oh, a very peaceful one, you must admit."

"That depends," said Philippe, following his cousin's example. Suppose someone activates a powerful Barbary organ not far away from you, and leaves it on indefinitely..."

"Oh, yes, in that case," Monsieur Henriquez replied, laughing, as he stood up in his turn, "people might have a right to intervene."

The remainder of the afternoon was employed in visiting ancient monuments, old churches transformed into communal buildings, former palaces that had become seats of administration, conservatories or workshops. At Les Invalides, our three companions were glad to find the old military trophies of which their ancestors had talked. At the Panthéon, now fitted out as a "columbarium," they were able to pass in review the recent pages of the history of France, written in the form of epitaphs on the funerary urns. In the Basilica of Sacré-Coeur, today a temple to Glory, they found all the noblest actions in the annals of our country represented in the bosom of a paradise of marble and gold.

The ancient cathedral of Notre-Dame, employed as a museum of Catholicism, retained them longer than the rest. There, Philippe and Jacques found themselves in a familiar environment.

Jacques especially, felt profoundly moved in looking at all the souvenirs of the faith of his fathers. He went back and forth, leafing through, so to speak, that reliquary of French Christianity, stopping repeatedly, retracing his steps, recognizing all the great orators, the scholars, the champions of charity, the orders of monks and nuns, the seals of popes, cardinals and abbés.

"Everything has been preserved with perfect care," he murmured. "It seems that all these elements of religious history have been arranged by a loving hand. Why does this edifying synthesis only have a posthumous exhibition?"

From time to time, he felt griped by anguish, and his eyelids reddened.

When did it die, then, my dear religion? he asked himself. *For I can't attach any great importance to the degenerate vestige that was presented to us in Marseilles. When did the veil fall?*

Here's a series of portraits that might settle the matter. They're the images of the Archbishops of Paris. Jacques counts them and examines the dates... *Nineteenth century... Here's the series of archbishop martyrs... after the, how many were there? About ten. Ah! Here's the last cardinal... Simon, Jules Simon...*

"What's that?" he said, aloud. "That's impossible!"

302

And, going to fetch Monsieur Henriquez, who was examining a bas-relief a few paces further on, he drew him back by the arm, showed him the portrait and said: "Do you see that cardinal? Those are his Christian names, aren't they, underneath?"

"No, no," the Brazilian replied, turning round. "That's the surname under which the individual has always been known, under which he wrote, although he was then only a simple spiritualist, books like *L'Ouvrière, La Religion naturelle*, and others. The author, my dear Monsieur, rose in rank and, in the latter part of his life, became a very zealous prelate, sometimes preaching three sermons a day. He was known as 'His Unction, Monsignor Simon.'"[48]

Toward dusk, feeling peckish, our friends stopped for a short time in a bar. All the drinks and hors-d'oeuvres in the world were assembled there, mingled with the latest inventions in the art of patisserie, in a superb hall, kept cool by glacier-water, beautiful water from the lakes of Switzerland, which streamed and jetted everywhere. Monsieur Henriquez ordered beer and champagne.

---

[48] This highly unlikely promotion does not explain why Jules Simon, one of the most prominent politicians and journalists of his day—the effective leader of the Opportunist Republicans and a writer for both *Le Matin* and the *Journal des Débats* in the late 1880s—was not featured in the sculpture park, even though he never held office during the relevant period. *La Religion naturelle* had been published in 1856 and *L'Ouvrière* [The Working Woman] in 1861. The author's citation of the second—not one of Simon's better known works— might be significant, in the light of his feminist opinions; not long after the publication of *La Cité future* Simon and his son Gustave published *La Femme du XXème siècle* [Twentieth-Century Woman] (1892), a speculative work that went through thirteen editions before the end of the year.

"You'll be somewhat healthier in this environment than that of a smoky tobacco-den. You're going drink beer, my young Gauls, and tell me what you think of it."

The beer was blond, fresh and delicious.

"It's truly worthy of comparison with French wine," Philippe observed, putting down his glass. "Is it at least French?"

"Yes, of course."

"So much the better," said Philippe, preparing to unseal a minuscule bottle with a gold top. "Our compatriots have finally been able to acquire a high rank in that traditional industry."

At that moment the cork leapt out of the bottle. All three gazed silently sand admiringly, as if with respect, at the sparkling foam that overflowed the glasses, and, at the same time, at the little bubbles rising through the rosy liquid to burst at the surface.

"There!" exclaimed the Brazilian. "That's the triumph of France. We certainly think so, we foreigners. Why is Paris Paris? Because it's beside Epernay and Aÿ. Come on, Brothers; today there are many sparkling wines in the world, but there's only ever been one, unique Champagne. Fortunate land!

Then they had the idea of going to the theater. The Odéon was close at hand. They went in.

The performance, begun at six o'clock, was supposed to last for the approximate time that a spectator could remain seated without budging from the seat. The entr'actes were filled with pieces of choral music or special exhibitions. At supper-time—which is to say, about half-past eight—everything was supposed to finish.

Unfortunately, the play on the program belonged to the old repertoire. We say "unfortunately" because our young colonials would naturally have preferred to do for the dramatic art what they had done for painting: take its pulse and check the level of Parisian production. It was a classic piece taken from the 19th century repertoire. Philippe and Jacques thought nevertheless that it was worth seeing, the actors being better in

Paris than in Saint-Denis. The superiority of the interpretation alone ought to be sufficient to add charm to a familiar piece.

It was not the same for Monsieur Henriquez. Thoroughly imbued with modern taste in scenic matters, yawned as if to dislocate his jaw and had no ideas how to make his excuses to his friends.

"What do you expect?" he said to them. "Everything I hear rings hollow in my ears—hollow absolutely hollow. I've tried, but there's no possible illusion for me. That poor woman we see on the stage—what is she complaining about? She's suffering from being married to a brutal husband. Well, get a divorce! There, on the other hand, is a betrayed husband; he's torn between the regret of an exclusive possession and the fear of fingers being pointed at him. What interest can I have in him? How can his honor be further diminished by the involvement of society? Nor can I treat it as a joke to be the victim of a felony. In my eyes, though, his egotism is puerile. Don't men and women have equal rights in connubial matters, in the variety and multiplicity of attachments? How many men are there who've only been acquainted with a single woman? Why don't women enjoy the same latitude? On condition, of course, that there's no self-delusion, that people don't lie to one another, that one is, in brief, honest in intimacy, as one is in banal relationships. No, you see, these actors are speaking French, but I don't understand them.

"That young virgin is troubled; her bosom is seething and her mind is opening up to new horizons. She's left to agitate in the void, and you're amused by her ignorance? Why not tell her that it's maternity that's calling out to her? Good! Now she's crying, hiding away, ashamed and confused. What's the matter? Oh, it's because she's conceived, without preliminary administrative formalities. Can anyone imagine such an enormity: a woman blushing with shame at the thought of becoming a mother? That's not all: have pity on yourselves, sensitive spectators, now they're preparing the scaffold. The ingénue has become a criminal; she's killed her newborn. Abomination! Isn't it monstrous, the prejudice that

305

makes a mother an executioner? You know, I'd rather watch Manchu or Arab plays, with Manitous, fetishes and witchcraft as means of intrigue, than waste any more time on these soft springs of adultery, marriage, bastardy, monogamy and monandry.

"Oh, we're no longer in the times, either in Brazil or France, when the first half of life was spent learning conventional falsehoods of which it required the second half of life to rid oneself. Our existence is better employed, thanks to destiny. The experience of those finishing their careers is immediately put in the service of those beginning them, and that's how humankind can improve itself.

"On the other hand, we no longer have two educations, one for men and the other for women—a singular duality that contributed in large measure to falsify the ancient institution of marriage. Look at that strong-minded fellow in the third act. He pleads the ignorance of his other half—and he's the one who maintained her in that ignorance. Why? In order to be sure of the faithful compliance of his companion and simultaneously maintain his own independence. He's found nothing better, the worthy fellow, than depriving his spouse of intellectual enlightenment. Oh—it reminds me of bird-trappers who blind finches in order to make them sing better."

Monsieur Henriquez ended up laughing, but it was a dry and sardonic laughter. Philippe and Jacques watched and listened without saying anything. They had no antidote to such great annoyance. They curtailed their session in his favor, however, and offered to leave before the end.

When they got outside, the electric beacons were scintillating like stars descending over Paris as darkness fell. The lighting of the streets and houses had changed. The latter, less warm than that of the sun, brighter than that of the moon, gave the city a calming and serene light as it prepared to go to sleep. It was like an Elysian dusk, which invited strolling. Our three friends profited from it to go back to their lodgings on foot.

XLI

The next day, Monsieur Henriquez had to go to his teacher's studio. The Vicomte de Lao-Tsin had been summoned to a meeting by the Celestial Empire's chargé d'affaires. Our two Bourbonnais were, therefore, left to their own devices.

Philippe took advantage of that circumstance to go out in the morning to obtain news of Madame Listor, two whom his private thoughts reverted incessantly. She was still not at home, but at least he learned from the young black maid who opened the door to him that she was back in Paris and that her apartment was fully installed.

"You'll see her tomorrow," the maid added, mysteriously.

"Tomorrow?" Philippe repeated, rather intrigued.

"Yes, tomorrow." And gently, with a polite smile, she closed the door in his face.

"Tomorrow, tomorrow," Philippe muttered, as he went away. "Does that mean that she'll come to see us at her our hotel, or that I ought to come back?"

He had not yet found the answer to that question when he rejoined his cousin. "Well, what are we going to do today?" he said.

"Whatever you wish."

They wasted rather a long time deliberating. Should they go further afield? Should they go to a concert in order to observe the orchestra and get to know certain new instruments about which they had been told good things? Should they devote the afternoon to rest?

To cut a long story short, after much prevarication, they find nothing better to do than march straight ahead at hazard. That takes them via the quais along the winding course of the Seine.

As they pass in front of the Institut Charcot they pause to consider the distant profile of its frontons and colonnades, whose whiteness stands out on the hillside.[49]

"What can that Parthenon be?" they ask one another.

They approach the gate that opens on to the quai and look at the bas-reliefs ornamenting its arch. There's a cripple throwing away his crutches, beside someone rising from his sick-bed; above them is a soldier, risking a thousand deaths, going to plant his standard in a collapsed breach. There's a believer marching to martyrdom. Lower down, Jeanne d'Arc is listening to her voices, and Mohammed and Christ, in retreat in the solitude of the desert, are preparing their preaching.

The porters, recognizing foreigners, invites them to come in.

"This house," he tells them, is a place of meditation where the sick are treated by personal influence. We cure physical ills; we reform vicious habits; and we prepare men for heroic, sublime and impossible deeds."

"Oh—we're in the temple of suggestion and hypnotism," Jacques whispers to his friend.

And they go in.

Immediately, an intern comes to meet them and to place himself at their disposal.

"What, then?" Jacques said to him, "are the maladies in whose treatment you specialize."

"We treat them all," the intern replied, "for in all of them, or almost all, there is room for the action of the imagination, and it's that action that our system brings into play. We even combat infirmities contracted long ago. How many paralytics there are who, when the imperious voice of our celebrated healers shout 'Walk!' have walked! How many blind peo-

---

[49] There never was a Charcot Institut, although it would not have seemed implausible, shortly after the founding of the Institut Pasteur, that the neurologist Jean-Martin Charcot might be similarly honored.

ple have seen, deaf people heard! This is the true land of miracles, the only one now, for all the ancient pilgrimages have been abandoned. We had the idea of making a collection of all the crutches and other orthopedic instruments; you can see them in our long galleries of offerings—there are too many to count."

These initial explanations were, as one might suspect, not calculated to please Jacques de Vertpré. He was did not feel inclined to go meekly in the direction that the intern had taken as soon as he started, so he tried to return to the tack he had initially taken.

"We understand," he said, "but there are doubtless some maladies that lend themselves better than others to your treatment."

"Obviously," said the intern, without any hesitation. "The diseases with which we are moist familiar, I may sway, are those of the brain. We obtain astonishing results in that area. When the subject is insufficiently docile to the action of the suggestive physician, we subject him to a preparatory treatment that leads him to the desires degree of suggestibility. If he has been under the mental domination of someone he knows who influences and guides him, we appeal for the collaboration of that recognized influence and regulate its effect.

"Perhaps you've already heard that we prepare men for heroic deeds. Would you link an example? When Alsace returned to French jurisdiction no one could be found in Strasbourg to go to the top of the cathedral bell-tower to hang the tricolor flag. The thing seemed unrealizable. Well, our predecessors selected a tiler who was both very suggestible and very skillful, and said to him: 'In three days, at such an such an hour, you'll go up to the top of the steeple and you'll hoist this flag.' Three days later, at the appointed hour, our colors were floating in the wind at the pinnacle of the famous edifice."

"You're wielding a very dangerous weapon there, Doctor," Jacques observed. "A blade with two edges, as powerful for evil as for good."

"That's true," the intern replied, "but for ourselves, we're bound by solemn engagements. We promise, on entering into responsibility, never to attempt anything contrary to social interests, and we renew that promise periodically, not as a vain formula but in conscience and with mature reflection. On the other hand, the penal law represses the abuses of hypnotic power at the same time as it establishes the innocence of its involuntary victims."

Everything that our two cousins saw in the establishment seemed strange to them. They had no notion of a therapy of that kind. The part that seemed most extraordinary was the rehabilitation section. There were children of both sexes there, and even adults, some of them naughty, others thieves, some gourmands and other lustful; it was a matter of reforming them. They were told that the reform was obtained quite easily, without taking much time and without any danger of relapse.

"Is that possible?" Philippe murmured.

Jacques shook his head, and wondered whether the Devil might not be playing a large role in the business.

They went into the gallery of offerings hereafter. It was interminable, and absolutely monotonous. Such and such a person, afflicted by such and such horrible disease...cured in such a year...an honor to the science... Eternal devotion declared to the doctors of the Institut Charcot. Long live hypnotism! Etc., etc. In short, a very tedious list.

That gallery led to an enormous room in which an encyclopedic history of seemingly-supernatural facts, scattered through the ostentation of humankind, were presented to the eyes in various forms—painting sculpture, tapestry—in a thoroughly didactic manner. Above the fronton, in golden letters, was inscribed: *Museum of Miracles*. From Aaron's rod to the high achievements of the Madonna of Lourdes, the entire legend of the marvelous unfolded, passing via the pythonesses, magicians and astrologers, pausing at the demoniacs and ecstatics of the Middle Ages, parading the stigmatized, fasting and barking women of all countries, offering specimens of tombs, wells and mountains fertile in phenomena, ultimately adding everything concerning the spirit-rappers and table-turners of more recent times. It was like a great practical lesson, emanating from a collection that might have been interesting in itself but was, we have to say, not to the taste of our visitors. Let us, therefore, pass over it rapidly.

As they returned to the exit, the conversation turned in a general manner to the novelties of modern medicine.

"We don't only have curative suggestion," the intern old them. "We also have metallic or dynamic treatments. According to the temperament of each patient and the malady to be treated, our colleagues responsible for induction determine by the application such and such a metal contacts and currents that are extremely effective.

"Furthermore, few maladies remain that are absolutely incurable, even among diseases of recent appearance. I must say, though, that we prevent much more than we cure. Hygiene is our great preoccupation. By means of good practices, we have contrived not only to make the body healthy but to embellish it. Thus, in particular, we have succeeded in avoiding obesity, that reef of maturity. How, otherwise, would women of a certain age be able to profit from the advantages that their new costume offers them? It's the same for premature baldness. It's not just diseases that we attack, it's their source, their cause..."

At that moment, Philippe interrupted: "But where does all this progress come from?" he asked. "What is its origin?"

"It flows simultaneously from physical and chemical discoveries, certain new products acquired from distant countries, and most especially from advancements in phrenological science. Today we know almost everything about the brain and its annexes; it's the high point of anthropology, for the brain, the pith, is the whole man, the whole of life. We know how the brain is formed, what it contains, the influences that act upon it, how it develops, how it deteriorates, and how it is cured.

311

"When we see a man, the first thought that comes to the mind of specialists like us is: *How is his brain made? What is its volume, its weight, its delicacy, its energy? Are its circumvolutions prominent? Are the folds of its sinuses, its ridges and its stria developing—O marvel!—in perfect regularity, all the way down to the imperceptible and the infinitely small?* That's what we say to ourselves. Oh, why can't we replace the bony vault of the skull with a crystal plate? We could then follow all the movements of life like a chronometer behind its watch-glass!

"A physician can tell you today how thoughts, tendencies and innate or required habits react on the form of the body, notably the physiognomy. Would you like me, Messieurs, to define you by means of your facial features, the dimensions of your head, the color and thickness of your hair, the nature of your epidermis? I can tell you your origin, your character, your vital force, your aptitudes and your defects, and accurately weigh your value. Would you like that?"

"No thank you," said Jacques. "Much obliged."

They were very close to the gate when Philippe, pausing and taking the arm of the young physician, leaned toward his ear and said, half in jest and half seriously: "There's one problem. Doctor, that you haven't yet resolved, I'm sure, and never will."

"What's that?"

"That of predicting the sex of a child."

"Oh, that, no!" exclaimed the intern, stepping backwards. "That hasn't yet been discovered. Anyway, is it really necessary to occupy oneself with such questions? Doesn't nature anticipate our wishes, by distributing better than we could the two elements of human nature?" He changed his mind, however, and added: "Even so, we'll have to see. Let's not prejudge the future. There's a society, I know, that was founded some time ago precisely to discover what it calls 'the law of sex' and the part of the influence that is due either to the father or the mother. It has begun a statistical investigation in order to establish a preliminary prognosis. The questions it asks in that regard are very numerous and very detailed. It hopes to arrive subsequently at an important social result: to increase population growth or slow it down, according to circumstances, by increasing or decreasing the number of daughters."

"Well, Monsieur," said Jacques, abruptly, cutting in, "when you know all that and other things, do you know what will happen?"

The intern opened his eyes wide. Philippe seemed anxious.

"What will happen is that God will unchain the sea and cause the volcanoes to vomit fire. The mountains will crumble on humans infatuated with their knowledge, and you will go into the caverns, to constitute prehistoric cadavers in your turn for those who, in the new worlds, will want once again to climb the tree of knowledge. Beware: those who nourish science will perish by science. God is jealous of his domain. If you try to penetrate it, he will annihilate you."

Philippe did not know what to think about his cousin's untimely outburst. He did not give him time to continue. By means of a rapid and dexterous movement, he placed himself between him and the intern, spoke momentarily about something else, and finally dragged Jacques out of the Institut.

On seeing them depart, the intern considered them with a regretful expression. He had just scented a interesting pathological case, and had not had time to analyze it.

As they drew away, Jacques said to his cousin: "No, you see, it was just too much in the end. The spirit of evil has conquered our land of France. It's Hell that reigns here, I repeat, the Inferno minus the flames: an organized, civilized, regulated Hell. Oh, I'm dying in this atmosphere…if you only knew how desperate I am to leave!"

Philippe calmed him down with kind words, encouraging him to be patient. "Voyages have bad days," he told him, "but they're still the best way of learning. Be brave. In a little while, if you're determined, we can think about leaving."

XLII

The Festival of Beauty is certainly the most popular solemnity of the year. It is celebrated, as everyone knows, in every commune in the land, on the day of the ancient feast of Corpus Christi.

For it is beauty that people adore today: human beauty. It is for that alone that there is a cult.

It must be thus in a nation that has established the continuous improvement of the race as an ideal—which is to say, the production of ever-stronger and ever-healthier generations. Beauty, in fact, consists of strength, health and grace. The beauty the French honor is the human model whose mature form reveals a perfect constitution; it is the irreproachable type specimen that the species ought to generalize.

The festival in question has replaced that of Reason. It has been understood that intellect, always so limited and decrepit, is not worthy of being honored. Beauty, on the contrary—or, to put it better, that which we consider as beauty—has already acquired, among us, appearances well worthy of praise. Furthermore, it is in beauty that each of our senses finds its most complete satisfaction. What spectacle will ever be worth as much for the eyes as that of a certain smile, a certain gaze? Is there any sound more agreeable to the ear than that of a beautiful voice?

Philippe and Jacques set out early on Thursday in order not to miss any detail of that important day.

In the morning there was a procession is each quarter; and in the afternoon, all the processions met up in a triumphal cavalcade that went from the Opéra to the summit of the Butte Montmartre. It was that march, indescribable in its effect, that impressed them most profoundly. For reasons that the readers will discover momentarily, the memory of it was to remain forever engraved in Philippe's memory as well as Jacques'.

The procession was composed of large floats drawn by teams of horses led by hand. All around were heralds on foot and on horseback, in theatrical costumes. Here and there between the floats there were bands and choirs. From top to bottom of their façades, the flag-laden houses overflowed with avid heads and hands ready to applaud. Above the roads, great red veils were extended, which gave the atmosphere a rosy tint. Silk standards undulated softly in the caress of the breeze. Joyful cries and musical chords could be heard resounding everywhere. The flowers that fell like rain on to the cortege surrounded it with a delightful scent.

All the men and women we shall see, successively, in that quasi-sacred chain have been selected by special juries, by reason of their corporeal merit.

At its head appear the representatives of early childhood. Oh, what a charming collection of curly heads and pretty smiling faces! Hail, beautiful flowers of life, charming harvest of amour. Go, may happiness remain with you.

After them, the adolescents; the girls first, then the boys. What treasures of grace and strength! Look at them; is it not truly beauty that is passing by, the beauty of youth, which provokes the sentiment of pure admiration? In the midst of the crowd massed on the route, masculine youth quivers; virgin hearts flutter and cause sudden rushes of blood to many faces.

Then the adults—which is to say, beauty in its full bloom; that which gives love its nobility and generates new life.

At the age when humans begin to descend the downslope of their existence, there still remain many elite bodies, whose vigor is far from extinct, and whose form henceforth reveals either a life of labor or the long toil of thought, the generosity that one has diffused profusely or the energy with one has supported the struggles of existence. It is at that moment that reason has its greatest amplitude. Look at them, those men and women who are now passing by, who represent the French race in its maturity. They have acquired experience and they still have strength. What imposing and significant faces! To them command, to them authority.

Behind them, the old arrive. O venerability! O mansuetude! Beneath those fleeces of white hair, the gaze of life still shines with an intense flame. All those ancients, all those beautiful ancestors rejoice in being part of the fête. To those who cheer them their paternal smiles seem to say: *Live like us; be sober, active and plaid, and beauty will keep you company until your final days.*

But the whole of that long series of floats is only, in reality, an advance guard. Only now does the centerpiece of the cortege appear. One might think that an enchanted mountain were advancing. It is a pyramid of foliage and flowers, at the summit of which there seems to be an alabaster statue.

Make way, make way for the goddess's quadriga. It is beauty itself, personified and incarnate, that is about to pass by. That human form at the top of the pyramid is the elected Queen, the annual Deity.

Cavaliers and Amazons make up her escort: a multicolored myriad in which one sees, on all the quadrupeds that serve human beings as mounts, horses of various races, zebras, donkeys, mules, reindeer and camels, the types and costumes of all the countries in the world. The float itself, whose platform rises to the level of the second stories, is drawn by elephants. In front, on tall dromedaries, march drummers and musicians, whose long trumpets, ornamented with banners, sound a rallying call.

There she is, coming closer. Around her, the air resounds with hurrahs and frenetic cries. In the midst of the crowd great waves swell and current form, as in the bosom of a tempest. Here, people become excited and surge forward; there, fanatics gripped by a religious respect seem ready to drop to their knees and prostrate themselves. Serene and motionless, she passes like a vision.

The two cousins are there, side by side, both watching with all the might of their eyes.

Suddenly, a strange, hoarse, inhuman cry pierces the noise of the fête and attracts the attention of the crowd. It is Philippe who has uttered it. Then, confusedly, he utters a few scarcely-articulated words: "Oh! It's her—look!"

And, running away from Jacques, he hurls himself full tilt through the crowd. He cuts through it sideways, straight ahead, at a slant, zigzagging. At the sight of his surge, and the sound of his stammered words, the most tightly-packed groups separate to give him passage. After a few seconds, there he is beside the float at the top of which he has recognized Fanny Listor. He has scaled the first foundations, and is suddenly seen to stop. His gaze has met that of the goddess. Transfixed and illuminated, he remains momentarily posed in an attitude of invocation. She raises her hand to her lips and bows him a kiss...

The crowd, hesitant for a moment, swells again and swirls like a whirlpool. Cries of every sort rise from the midst of the tumult. Philippe, torn from the pyramid by unknown hands, finds himself thrown into the middle of the cortege. He is dazed and bewildered. Where is he? What is he doing? Is it a dream?

Without taking a single step, he remains there in the middle of the procession, like a reef dividing the course of a river. He sees nothing more, he hears nothing more. Here come banners, trophies, rallying signals; there are societies of every sort—esthetic, philanthropic, economic, philosophical, scientific—then fanfares, and then singers. All of that flows by without him taking account of it. For the moment, his consciousness is eclipsed.

Fortunately, Jacques de Vertpré has also stayed behind, rooted to the spot where Philippe abandoned him. He has followed the tail of the procession—everything that came after the triumphal float—with his gaze, and now the procession has passed, he searches with his eyes for his companion.

It does not take long for them to come together again. What can they say after such a scene? In what state of mind will they find one another?

It is Philippe, still stunned, who speaks first.

"Oh, Jacques, my dear Jacques, don't say anything, I beg you. I'm no longer myself. Wait...who am I? No, it's no longer Philippe Martinvast who is talking to you; it's no longer Philippe, your cousin, of Saint-Denis on the Île de Bourbon..."

Jacques squeezes his hand, moved to pity, and, at the same time, puts an amicable hand on his shoulder.

Philippe raises his head anxiously, and continues: "How has my entire being been transformed in an instant? Is it the fire of Heaven that has fallen on my head? Tell me, Jacques, how have I been changed? Oh, my poor friend, I feel that I have been knocked off my feet, turned upside-down, converted."

Jacques felt his heart lurch. Philippe wiped his forehead and his eyes began to shine again with their ordinary light. A shiver of relief passed through his breast.

"It's to her," he said, "to her that I'm henceforth...yes, to her...entirely... Farewell, liberty! I no longer belong to myself; subjugated...I'm subjugated...I must go where the force takes me..."

He said all that in short bursts, both his hands on his heart, his eyes raised to the Heavens. Finally, a sob escaped his lips. The two cousins fell into one another's arms...

When they started walking again, Jacques spoke in his turn. It was his task now to pour the calming words into his cousin's ear that bring peace to an agitated individual. He did his best, seemingly not overly astonished by the revolution that had overtaken his elder, but advising him to wait, not to allow himself to be immediately carried away.

His voice, which he tried to render soft, was grave. It had a poignant expression. To what kind of emotion was he prey himself, then? And to what resolutions would it lead him?

"Listen, Philippe," he said, after a pause, "I too have been struck; my mind has received a violent shock. Before leaving the Île de Bourbon, as you'll remember, I went to see the reverend father who was the master of our final years of study. That saintly man, who combines consummate experience with the most ingenious devotion, and who is also well-versed in pagan iconography, gave me some paternal advice. 'I don't know in what state you'll find our dear France,' he said to me, "and perhaps you'll have some difficulty in taking exact account of her state of mind, her thoughts and her tendencies, especially in religious matters. Does Christianity still have roots there? Has it, on the contrary, succumbed completely to the prolonged effect of neutrality in popular education? That will doubtless be the great preoccupation of your voyage. Now, if God, in his impenetrable designs, has permitted that the religion revealed by him is temporarily extinct there, you will recognize it by one characteristic, decisive, infallible sign. Every time that, in some people of times gone by, paganism has reigned as an exclusive master, that sign has appeared. It is like the bacillus of naturalism.'

"Well, Philippe, that sign I have already remarked several times since our arrival in France, in the decoration of monuments, in the furnishing of houses, in the illustration of books, even in feminine jewelry—and yet, I didn't attach any great importance to it; it didn't yet appear to me as an admitted, classified, officially-endorsed symbol. But just now, behind the cart on which I have just seen indecency glorified, at the moment when you abandoned me, it reappeared in the place of honor, borne in triumph in the midst of banners, trophies and patriotic emblems. *It is indeed the case*, I said to myself, *that the religion of our fathers is extinct. France is no more*. I shall return to Bourbon with shame and pity on my face, and to my friends I shall say: 'Don't go there; it's no longer your country.'"

Philippe had had time to recover his senses, and his attention had been reawakened under the effect of his young cousin's low and solemn diction.

"What is that sign, then?" he asked, stopping abruptly.

Jacques looked at him for a moment. Then, in a whisper, he said: "It's the Phallus."

Philippe did not reply. He had expected a graver revelation. He too had encountered before his eyes that ancient emblem of vital force, but he had not paid any heed to it. Whether that sculptural motif was part of a statue or isolated as a fragment, mattered little to him. He saw nothing esthetic therein, but nothing frightful either.

As for Jacques, resuming after a pause in the same tone he added: "It must, in fact, appear at the end of atheism, that revolting sign of the Greek and Roman decadence. Horror! The Bible itself is forgotten. The civilization that now breathes here comes from I don't know what barbaric, brazen and obscene region; it remains incomprehensible to our old race. No, I would never have believed that the decadence of Christianity could have dragged our unfortunate country so low. Why, in the epoch when a course was deliberately set toward irreligion, was no voice found to cry to France: 'Look, behold the terminus, the ignominious terminus, at which you will end!'

"Oh holy Christian candor! White dove of Jesus; mystic flower of snow, from which ethereal love, truly pure, exhales in a sublime perfume of innocence; pearl divine, whose spark uplifts our wretched humanity…this is what Progress has put in your place!

"Alas, what are we going to do? You Philippe, gripped by an impossible love; and me, saturated to the depths of my being by nauseating disgust.

At that moment, the procession appeared on the heights of Montmartre. The air was diaphanous, as impalpable a beneath the beautiful sun of the Midi in those delightful hours that preceded the fall of darkness, when the sun, no longer sending forth heat, still streams with light. Slowly, after unrolling in a spiral along the slopes, the cortege was consolidated on the plateau, at the highest point overlooking the great city. Thanks to the transparency of the atmosphere, our two cousins, from the place where they were standing, could easily grasp every detail.

When Beauty's float came to a halt in the front row, a general silence fell along the crest. The songs and fanfares became quiet at the same time, and the entire human mass gathered there stood still.

Then the goddess, taking handfuls of rose-petals from a basket that a child held out to her, threw them with a noble gesture over the city suspended at her feet, thus blessing Paris and France.

Immediately afterwards, the music struck up again. Songs rose up again in the streets: songs of triumph and glory, mingled with the cheers and bravos of all the assembled people.

At the same moment, a fountain of fire sprang up behind the float. It was the signal awaited down below. All the bells of the city started to ring together: grave booms, silvery tinkles, clear carillons. Inside the houses, all the musical instruments were animated, organs resonating noisily; and at the windows, in the streets, in the carriages and in the boats that were circulating, nothing could be heard but trumpets, flutes, violins and cymbals. It was like a tribute to the great city and the divinity of the day.

Until sunset, that immense racket continued without interruption. It seemed that the city of Paris, for which that apotheosis constitutes an exclusive privilege, wanted to extend the echoes to the extremities of the land, in order that everyone, even in the remotest cantons, might be touched by it.

In the midst of those vibrations and clamors, the procession dispersed. When night fell, a magical illumination succeeded the daylight. And it was in the midst of fires of joy and jets of multicolored water that the dances and games continued all over the city until morning.

XLIII

We will not astonish our readers by telling them that Philippe Martinvast had nothing more urgent to do the next day than visit Madame Listor.

As soon as they saw one another, a double cry resounded, and they were in one another's arms. For a long time, in the midst of a silence interrupted solely by the sound of kisses, they remained there, holding one another tightly. From time to time, they detached themselves from the embrace and looked one another in the eyes. Tears of emotion pearled beneath their eyelids. Then they recommenced the embrace, their heart beating as if to burst in their oppressed breasts.

When that initial fever had passed, Madame Listor drew Philippe with her to a divan and said to him:

"I expected you, my beloved; I sensed that you would come. Oh, how often I've thought about you since our separation! The love that has just burst forth, to my joy and yours, was already brooding within me when I left you. But since then, you see, I've felt it growing immeasurably from day to day. How has it invaded me completely in such a short time, to the point of no longer having but a single thought—of seeing you again? Oh, how I've cursed the obstacles that have keep me from your presence for so long! If you hadn't been in Paris I'd have summoned you for the occasion of the festival—but I knew that I'd find you there, and then, I wanted to wait a little in order to give you a surprise...and a test. Yesterday, throughout the procession, I had but one idea. Is he there? Will I see him? Will he see me? What will he say when he sees me appear? Yes, you were there. You ran toward me, and my heart filled with joy. I told you, by means of yesterday's gesture, that I love you; I repeat it today for your ears. I love you...I love you, Philippe; I will be yours when you wish."

Philippe was assailed by a sentiment so powerful and so new to him that he hesitated to speak. It was not only the fire of life and youth that was ignited in his bosom. All the way to the profoundest depths of his being, he felt a general renovation taking place, an intellectual upheaval, the effects of which resonated in all his senses, his conceptions, his desires, his judgment, his will and his affections.

He tried, however, to say a few words in reply.

"You're good, Fanny," he said, "as good as you're beautiful. How happy I am! With what pride I'm replete! How has the celestial beauty that France adored deigned to lower her gaze upon the young Bourbonnais scarcely disembarked from his island? But I shall be worthy of you, believe me. While my being was attracted by yours, I felt my spirit spreading its wings, changing region and coming to place itself by your side, on the heights where you soar, and where humankind, nature and destiny appear in their positive reality. In attaching myself to you, I shall unite myself with the new France."

He got to his feet at that moment, becoming animated.

"Yes France is my country, and I am coming home. When you are my wife, Fanny, France will become my homeland again. France and Fanny will henceforth be my two loves. From today on, I have the same faith as you, my beloved; it's you who are right, you who see life clearly, while I was in the wrong, molded by lies. But now I've awoken in the torchlight of your gaze; my eyes see; my ears hear; my hands touch; it's you who have enlightened me. How beautiful this new world is, on whose threshold you appear to me, ornamented by all the graces, tenderized by the most indulgent of amours."

While speaking thus, Philippe had knelt down.

"Then it's true," said Madame Listor. "You'll stay here; you'll adopt our mores; you'll be one of us."

"Yes, it's true."

"What joy! And what I fine proselyte I would have made! I too am proud, be assured, to have contributed to freeing a man like you from his swaddling-clothes. You're beautiful, my Philippe; we shall have a superb child."

"Yes, a daughter as beautiful as her mother."

"No, Philippe, a son as gentle on the eye as his father."

They both resumed their embrace. Then Madame Listor offered to show her friend her apartment. It was overflowing with flowers and works of art.

"All this," she said, "is yesterday's triumph. The number of bouquets, presents, letters and telegrams I've had is incalculable. Well, all these tributes are nothing compared with the success I've had over you. Today my glory is extinct; I've become a mere mortal again—but my love remains; that's better than divinity."

Her bedroom was preceded, according to custom, by a marble bath full of warm perfumed water, incessantly renewed.

"Here, my beloved friend, is the lustral water in which, if you wish, we shall bathe our bodies this evening..."

At the same time, they crossed the threshold of the room, a true tabernacle of amour. Philippe linked arms with Madame Listor.

"This evening, you said?"

"Yes, this evening." And, suspecting that Philippe had perhaps not expected that brief adjournment, the young woman added in a caressing and jovial tone: "Daylight, my friend, is not suitable for a sacrament of love. Oh, romances no longer reach their denouement abruptly, as in the good old times, like a simple physical malaise, devoid of décor. We put some form, some beneficence into it...out of self-respect, and respect for love itself...for the love whose laws we always obey, but of which we now make of ourselves, blindly, the victim or the slave... Yes, we'll wait; it's for lovers, is it not, that night extends her veils and spreads her silence. This evening, you'll come back, and you'll see the Queen of Beauty again."

While speaking, she led her visitor to the door. Again, before separating, they covered one another with kisses.

"Yes, this evening," Madame Listor said, for a second time, as a gesture of farewell. "This evening, you'll be mine and I'll be yours. Until this evening, my beloved..."

Dazed and drunk with happiness, Philippe had not yet recovered possession of himself when he found himself back in the street. All of his blood was seething in his veins and his cheeks were burning.

Gradually, walking calmed him down. His stride gradually took on a certain ease, and even bravado. After a few hundred meters he was strutting, looking straight ahead, twirling his cane and humming a tune.

From time to time he stamped his foot. *This*, he seemed to be saying, *is my true native soil. It's here that I ought to live. I've found my element. France is the country where I can breathe easily. It has changed, but it's still the same. I'm French, like my early ancestors, like my great uncles, like all the Martinvasts, with a few exceptions. To be French, to have love in one's heart, the love of the most beautiful of French-women—what joy!*

As he went back into the hotel he saw Jacques de Vertpré, who was moving back and forth, bare-headed, between the office and the correspondence-room, seemingly busy. His first impulse was to run toward him, to make him party to his contentment, but his cousin's glacial, irritated expression held him back.

"Oh, there you are!" said Jacques, speaking first. "Well, I can tell you that I'm leaving. I've just written to my mother. In sum, my voyage has brought me nothing but disappointments. Leaving aside a few artistic manifestations and certain industrial applications by which my curiosity was piqued in passing, I've found nothing that could keep me here any longer. I've already seen too much; I've made up my mind. I'm choking, burning…quickly, quickly, give me the air of my island, the affection of my family, the presence of my God…"

"And what about me?" Philippe exclaimed, interrupting him.

He had certainly foreseen that Jacques would return once again to the idea of the anticipated departure, but he had not supposed that he would have fixed the day and the hour without conferring with him.

"You?" said Jacques, not without a certain embarrassment. "You'll come back a little later..." His voice slowed down as he stared at his cousin. "Unless you decide to leave immediately, with me..."

It was not without intention that Jacques opened that latter prospect to Philippe. Internally, he feared great dangers for his elder, a fatal resolution, and he wanted to try, while there might still be time, to tear him away from the penchant that was about to carry him away.

But it was too late. Philippe had already made his plans, definitively. The opportunity having been offered for him to explain himself, he hastened to take advantage of it.

"No, my dear Jacques," he said, in a definite tone, "I won't be leaving with you, and I won't be leaving later. I'm staying permanently. I'm French."

Jacques shivered. For a second time he stared at Philippe's face, which seemed transfigured. It no longer had the same expression. His physiognomy, in its entirety, had changed. He understood that there was nothing to be done against such dispositions and, lowering his eyes, he turned round, saying: "Well, then, I'll go and finish packing."

XLIV

Twenty-four hours have gone by. Philippe is more determined than ever to stay. As for Jacques de Vertpré, he is about to leave.

The two cousins have met in order to spend the last moments that will elapse before their separation together. The prospect of the severance that is about to occur is making the emotional. Their sentiments of longstanding friendship are returning to the surface of their hearts and gripping them. They are both wondering what people will say out there, on seeing Jacques return so soon, and alone.

Let's listen to them. It's Jacques who is speaking.

"If you decided not stay behind, my dear Philippe, I'd experience an unalloyed satisfaction and experience a sentiment of deliverance. How, in fact, can one live in such a society? No more religion, no more hierarchy, no more property, no more family, no more anything…between humans and animals, an almost absolute resemblance. The sons of God now take inspiration from the beast to regulate their conduct. They ignore the Providence that guides them, and beyond this brief life they neither hope for anything nor dread anything. Forgive me for speaking ill of an organization of which you now approve and to which you subscribe, alas, but my heart is too full; it's necessary that you allow it to overflow momentarily.

"This equality that one sees reigning everywhere, which governs the world and reduces individuality to nothing; this equality that makes the Earth the planet of Monotony; this equality, for the establishment of which a quantity of vexatious and yet impotent laws has been made; this equality, I curse. It is intolerable to me."

He struck his breast. "I feel superiorities within myself, and I want them to be affirmed. It does not matter to me whether I have beings above me more powerful, more noble and more perfect, but at the same time, I need to feel that I am

327

above others whom I surpass in value, whom I master, and in whose company I feel like a leader. To what did all our ancestral lines devote themselves, how did they employ their existence, if not to raise themselves ever higher above others? Ought I to throw away all those accumulated efforts, and abdicate my preeminence, so dearly acquired? Never. To my privileges, my advancement over others, I shall cling as to my life. I would rather die than fall. Better, in my eyes, not to be than to be equal to everyone else."

Philippe refrained from interrupting his young cousin. From time to time however, he raised his head as if he had an objection or an observation to make. He even seemed, at times, to manifest the commencement of impatience. One might have thought that he had already been wounded in the new faith of which he was a neophyte.

"How can you admit," Jacques continued, "that the heart can find its affective nutrition outside of family ties? Friendship, fellow feeling, humanitarian sympathy are sufficient, it's said, to replace them. O chimera! How can such affirmations be sustained? The French of today don't have the slightest idea of what the life of the heart ought to be—and yet, that's all of life.

"And then what? Am I to be deprived of superfluity, confined within the necessary? But for centuries, my entire family has had no anxieties with regard to the necessities of life. The necessary, for us, is that which shines, which charms, which glorifies. An existence limited to the satisfaction of natural functions, assimilative or excretory, is for others. It's for the mind that we live, we who have a taste for luxury and aspire to the enjoyments of the soul.

"But the real reason, you see, why I wish death—yes, death—upon this abominable world, that that it has abolished modesty, and simultaneously degraded womankind."

"Degraded womankind!" Philippe exclaimed.

"Yes," Jacques replied, raising his voice, "yes, she has been robbed of her most beautiful charm. Oh, woe! Thrice woe! Love has been depoeticized. Civilizations, Philippe, are judged according to the flower—which is to say, according to the womankind—that they produce. You can have admirable lovers, ornamented with all the qualities that a perfected intellectual culture bestows—but never, understand me well, never will you find Christian womanhood, a sublime alloy of innocence, devotion and tenderness. Oh, the ineffable smile of the pious virgin who abandons herself, beneath the wing of God, to our first and only love, sharing thereafter our entire life, embellishing it with her grace, embalming it with her perfume. That is a happiness you will never know, Philippe. For myself, I want to know it; that's why I'm returning to my island."

At that moment, Jacques' voice began to tremble. Philippe thought that the time had come to speak in his turn.

"Go, my dear Jacques," he said. "Go to where affection draws you and be happy there, as I shall be happy here. Let's not waste our time in futile comparisons. When you get back, believe me, don't speak too harshly of France. It's no longer propitious, it's true, to those privileged existences that once, it's said, had a reason to be, but which have one no longer—but it has improved the lot of millions of people and has remedied involuntary poverty. That's a fine result, as you know very well. Momentum has been restored to population; war has been suppressed; human life has been augmented. All that is something.

"People no longer believe in God, it's true—at least, not our God—but don't you think that, in Bourbon, they believe in him a little too much? People there know everything that he has done, everything that he thinks, everything he wants. They know his history and his family life, since the relatively recent day when he created the world. Don't you think, truly, that they believe in him to excess?

"Then again, there's no more future life. No…come on, descend a little way into yourself. Do you really have any serious reason for counting on it? And whether there is one or isn't one, isn't there agreement now, almost everywhere, in saying that it's necessary to lead the present life as best one can?

329

"Modesty too has disappeared, and in its place, according to you, is the great abyss that will separate us henceforth. That's unfortunate, I agree...and yet, was it, in truth, an essential virtue? Some might consider it to be merely one of the thousand forms of coquetry. According to others, it flows from the sentiment of a sin already committed or yet to be committed...and that's how it appears in the legend of Eden. Today, the idea of sin has been effaced from love; it's understood that there is, strictly speaking, no more modesty. And yet, under the name of modesty, or that of decency, I'm certain that a little remains.

"No, you see, my dear Jacques, it's almost always necessary to make a choice in planning one's life: to make the more-or-less voluntary choice between truth and illusion, according to whether one invests one's happiness in knowledge of the truth, limited as it is, or the simple wellbeing of conscience, which has no other basis than artificial faith. The truth is often harsh, arid and narrow, but it is the truth. Illusion is charming and infinite, lends itself to all fantasies and responds to all desires, but it's error. What is truth to you? You only seek peace in a comfortable arrangement of life. While as for me, what I prefer, I now realize, is reality; and outside of that, the unknown no longer frightens me.

"But I don't want to argue. It's not appropriate for me to criticize beliefs that were still mine yesterday, and I don't have the right, as yet, to speak in the name of the theories to which I've rallied. And to tell the truth, it's not, in any case, in themselves, outside of the love that has served as their vehicle, that they enthuse me. No, I'm even obliged to make a effort to adopt them, for they take more from me than they give, and I don't have the good fortune to have been subjected, like the others, to their slow and gradual progress, day by day. I have to hoist myself up to their level in a single bound. But what can you expect? As I say, they're true. Yes, above all, alas, they're true, in their pitiless negations; and furthermore, they're inevitable henceforth—inevitable, you understand? At least, I consider them as such today. Oh well, I don't want to go to them with death in my soul; that's not in my character; I shall go valiantly, like a Frenchman.

"Listen. I don't know what the future has in store for you. Perhaps these ideas, which you consider to be new, will take root one day, without your suspecting it, even in the soil of Bourbon. Like seeds fortuitously brought by a distant wind. It's difficult, at the present time, to erect barriers against what the crowd acclaims as truth and progress. If that happens, remember that your cousin, your brother Philippe has made those ideas his own, and be indulgent to their new recruits.

"Don't speak too harshly of me either. Explain to our friends and relatives that I was suddenly gripped by a grand passion, and, at the same stroke, by an ancient ferment of patriotism that has risen within me and holds me here enchained. Tell all our islanders that, if they come to France, I shall welcome them, guide them, and protect them, if I can...

"As for me, I shall never go back; I feel that my attitude would be constrained there. People would no longer understand me. Having changed my views, I must change my country. That renunciation is hard, but it's imposed upon me."

At that moment, Philippe took Jacques hands in his.

"It's over, then," said the latter. "You won't come back."

"No,"

"You'll let me depart alone."

"Alas! What do you want? Oh, this is the sad inverse of the seductions that delight me." As he said that, Philippe let a sob escape.

"Well," Jacques went on, in a resigned tone, "since I must, I'll carry that fatal message home with me. Many eyes will weep, you know, and sadness will reign for a long time in our houses. If any of the women of our age, at whom you might have smiled, comes to talk to me about you, what shall I have to say? That you preferred a pagan to her..."

"No, Jacques," Philippe said, snatching away his hands, "no. I swear to you that I have not acted out of preference. It was without knowing it that I found myself bound. Now that bond is my joy, my consolation and my glory. It is sufficiently dear to me that I am leaving everything for it. That's what I can say. But you, why are you in so much haste to leave me? Aren't you taking an extreme resolution very quickly, on the basis of a few unfortunate impressions? There still remain many things for you to see, which might have made you revise your judgments. Who knows? Perhaps you'll regret having yielded to your first impulse. Before separating forever, we who have always lived together, can we not spend a few more days together?"

"No, no, don't deceive yourself any further, my dear Philippe. For myself, I have nothing more to learn about this new world, of which I've made a tour. What good would it do to linger over a spectacle that appalls and offends me at every step? Then again, love is invasive. To yours...oh, don't worry, I shan't criticize it; I respect your independence and I shan't forget that you're my elder...to yours, I say, it would not be appropriate for me to be a witness. Our mothers and sisters might find that objectionable."

He paused momentarily, as if to await the effect of his last words. Then, as Philippe maintained the same attitude, he added: "So, you see, there's nothing for me to do but go back."

"You're right," said Philippe.

And the two cousins threw themselves into one another's arms.

They stayed there for a few seconds, united in that fraternal embrace.

When they pulled apart, their eyes were moist with tears. Simultaneously recovering their energy and facing up to one another nobly, however, they exchanged their last thoughts in steady voices.

"Adieu, Philippe Martinvast. Abandon yourself to the moving waves of the unchained sea, and may your lucky star preserve you from shipwreck. For myself, I shall resume my life on the basis on which our ancestors placed it."

"Adieu, Jacques de Vertpré. Go, resume the path of our recent ancestors; remain faithful, by opposing its extinction or transformation, to the traditions in which our childhood was cradled. For myself, I shall go forward and remake the missed phases. The Earth turns; I shall allow myself to turn with it. Adieu, let us both be happy. Fortune smiles in all regimes upon men of good will, firmly decided to grasp life by the horns."

A few hours later, our two cousins separated forever.

SF & FANTASY

Henri Allorge. *The Great Cataclysm*
Guy d'Armen. *Doc Ardan: The City of Gold and Lepers*
G.-J. Arnaud. *The Ice Company*
Charles Asselineau. *The Double Life*
Cyprien Bérard. *The Vampire Lord Ruthwen*
Aloysius Bertrand. *Gaspard de la Nuit*
Richard Bessière. *The Gardens of the Apocalypse*
Albert Bleunard. *Ever Smaller*
Félix Bodin. *The Novel of the Future*
Alphonse Brown. *City of Glass*
André Caroff. *The Terror of Madame Atomos; Miss Atomos; The Return of Madame Atomos; The Mistake of Madame Atomos; The Monsters of Madame Atomos*
Félicien Champsaur. *The Human Arrow; Ouha*
Didier de Chousy. *Ignis*
Captain Danrit. *Undersea Odyssey*
C. I. Defontenay. *Star (Psi Cassiopeia)*
Charles Derennes. *The People of the Pole*
Georges Dodds (anthologist). *The Missing Link*
Harry Dickson. *The Heir of Dracula*
Jules Dornay. *Lord Ruthven Begins*
Alfred Driou. *The Adventures of a Parisian Aeronaut*
Sâr Dubnotal *vs. Jack the Ripper*
Alexandre Dumas. *The Return of Lord Ruthven*
Renée Dunan. *Baal*
J.-C. Dunyach. *The Night Orchid; The Thieves of Silence*
Henri Duvernois. *The Man Who Found Himself*
Achille Eyraud. *Voyage to Venus*
Henri Falk. *The Age of Lead*
Paul Féval. *Anne of the Isles; Knightshade; Revenants; Vampire City; The Vampire Countess; The Wandering Jew's Daughter*
Paul Féval, *fils. Felifax, the Tiger-Man*
Charles de Fieux. *Lamékis*
Arnould Galopin. *Doctor Omega*; *Doctor Omega & The Shadowmen*
G.L. Gick. *Harry Dickson and the Werewolf of Rutherford Grange*
Edmond Haraucourt. *Illusions of Immortality*
Nathalie Henneberg. *The Green Gods*
V. Hugo, P. Foucher & P. Meurice. *The Hunchback of Notre-Dame*
Michel Jeury. *Chronolysis*

Gustave Kahn. *The Tale of Gold and Silence*
Gérard Klein. *The Mote in Time's Eye*
Jean de La Hire. *Enter the Nyctalope; The Nyctalope on Mars; The Nyctalope vs. Lucifer; The Nyctalope Steps In; Night of the Nyctalope*
Etienne-Léon de Lamothe-Langon. *The Virgin Vampire*
André Laurie. *Spiridon*
Gabriel de Lautrec. *The Vengeance of the Oval Portrait*
Alain le Drimeur. *The Future City*
Georges Le Faure & Henri de Graffigny. *The Extraordinary Adventures of a Russian Scientist Across the Solar System* (2 vols.)
Gustave Le Rouge. *The Vampires of Mars The Dominion of the World* (w/Gustave Guitton) (4 vols.)
Jules Lermina. *Mysteryville; Panic in Paris; To-Ho and the Gold Destroyers; The Secret of Zippelius*
Jean-Marc & Randy Lofficier. *Edgar Allan Poe on Mars; The Katrina Protocol; Pacifica; Robonocchio; Tales of the Shadowmen 1-8*
Xavier Mauméjean. *The League of Heroes*
Joseph Méry. *The Tower of Destiny*
Hippolyte Mettais. *The Year 5865*
José Moselli. *Illa's End*
John-Antoine Nau. *Enemy Force*
Marie Nizet. *Captain Vampire*
C. Nodier, A. Beraud & Toussaint-Merle. *Frankenstein*
Henri de Parville. *An Inhabitant of the Planet Mars*
Gaston de Pawlowski. *Journey to the Land of the 4th Dimension*
Georges Pellerin. *The World in 2000 Years*
Pierre Pelot. *The Child Who Walked on the Sky*
J. Polidori, C. Nodier, E. Scribe. *Lord Ruthven the Vampire*
P.-A. Ponson du Terrail. *The Vampire and the Devil's Son*
Henri de Régnier. *A Surfeit of Mirrors*
Maurice Renard. *The Blue Peril; Doctor Lerne; The Doctored Man; A Man Among the Microbes; The Master of Light*
Jean Richepin. *The Wing*
Albert Robida. *The Adventures of Saturnin Farandoul; The Clock of the Centuries; Chalet in the Sky*
J.-H. Rosny Aîné. *Helgvor of the Blue River; The Givreuse Enigma; The Mysterious Force; The Navigators of Space; Vamireh; The World of the Variants; The Young Vampire*
Marcel Rouff. *Journey to the Inverted World*
Han Ryner. *The Superhumans*

Brian Stableford. *The New Faust at the Tragicomique;The Empire of the Necromancers (The Shadow of Frankenstein; Frankenstein and the Vampire Countess; Frankenstein in London); Sherlock Holmes & The Vampires of Eternity; The Stones of Camelot; The Wayward Muse.* (anthologist) *The Germans on Venus; News from the Moon; The Supreme Progress; The World Above the World; Nemoville; Investigations of the Future*
Jacques Spitz. *The Eye of Purgatory*
Kurt Steiner. *Ortog*
Eugène Thébault. *Radio-Terror*
C.-F. Tiphaigne de La Roche. *Amilec*
Théo Varlet. *The Xenobiotic Invasion; Timeslip Troopers* (w/André Blandin); *The Martian Epic* (w/Octave Joncquel)
Paul Vibert. *The Mysterious Fluid*
Villiers de l'Isle-Adam. *The Scaffold; The Vampire Soul*
Philippe Ward. *Artahe*
Philippe Ward & Sylvie Miller. *The Song of Montségur*

MYSTERIES & THRILLERS

M. Allain & P. Souvestre. *The Daughter of Fantômas*
A. Anicet-Bourgeois, Lucien Dabril. *Rocambole*
A. Bernède. *Belphegor; Judex* (w/Louis Feuillade)
A. Bisson & G. Livet. *Nick Carter vs. Fantômas*
V. Darlay & H. de Gorsse. *Lupin vs. Holmes: The Stage Play*
Paul Féval. *Gentlemen of the Night; John Devil; The Black Coats ('Salem Street; The Invisible Weapon; The Parisian Jungle; The Companions of the Treasure; Heart of Steel; The Cadet Gang; The Sword-Swallower)*
Emile Gaboriau. *Monsieur Lecoq*
Steve Leadley. *Sherlock Holmes: The Circle of Blood*
Maurice Leblanc. *Arsène Lupin vs. Countess Cagliostro; Lupin vs. Holmes (The Blonde Phantom; The Hollow Needle); The Many Faces of Arsène Lupin*
Gaston Leroux. *Chéri-Bibi; The Phantom of the Opera; Rouletabille & the Mystery of the Yellow Room*
Richard Marsh. *The Complete Adventures of Judith Lee*
William Patrick Maynard. *The Terror of Fu Manchu; The Destiny of Fu Manchu*
Frank J. Morlock. *Sherlock Holmes: The Grand Horizontals; Sherlock Holmes vs Jack the Ripper*

Antonin Reschal. *The Adventures of Miss Boston*
P. de Wattyne & Y. Walter. *Sherlock Holmes vs. Fantômas*
David White. *Fantômas in America*

SCREENPLAYS

Mike Baron. *The Iron Triangle*
Emma Bull & Will Shetterly. *Nightspeeder; War for the Oaks*
Gerry Conway & Roy Thomas. *Doc Dynamo*
Steve Englehart. *Majorca*
James Hudnall. *The Devastator*
Jean-Marc & Randy Lofficier. *Royal Flush*
J.-M. & R. Lofficier & Marc Agapit. *Despair*
J.-M. & R. Lofficier & Joël Houssin. *City*
Andrew Paquette. *Peripheral Vision*
R. Thomas, J. Hendler & L. Sprague de Camp. *Rivers of Time*

NON-FICTION

Stephen R. Bissette. *Blur 1-5. Green Mountain Cinema 1; Teen Angels*
Win Scott Eckert. *Crossovers* (2 vols.)
Jean-Marc & Randy Lofficier. *Shadowmen* (2 vols.)
Randy Lofficier. *Over Here*

HEXAGON COMICS

Franco Frescura & Luciano Bernasconi. *Wampus*
Franco Frescura & Giorgio Trevisan. *CLASH*
L. Bernasconi, J.-M. Lofficier & Juan Roncagliolo Berger. *Phenix*
Claude Legrand, J.-M. Lofficier & L. Bernasconi. *Kabur*
Franco Oneta. *Zembla*
L. Buffolente, Lofficier & J.-J. Dzialowski. *Strangers: Homicron*
Danilo Grossi. *Strangers: Jaydee*
Claude Legrand & Luciano Bernasconi. *Strangers: Starlock*

ART BOOKS

Jean-Pierre Normand. *Science Fiction Illustrations*
Raven Okeefe. *Raven's L'il Critters*
Randy Lofficier & Raven OKeefe. *If Your Possum Go Daylight...*
Daniele Serra. *Illusions*